His Dark
VENDETTA

BONDED IN BLOOD BOOK TWO

His Dark VENDETTA

KATELYN BREHM

*To immigrants everywhere.
May your courage and resilience be met with respect and opportunity.*

Author's Note

I chose not to italicize the Italian words and phrases throughout this book. I wanted the characters' speech to flow seamlessly between American English and Italian given they are first-generation Italian Americans. In addition to Italian, I used Italian-American slang to lend authenticity to the regional Italian American experience. Any mistakes in the application of Italian or Italian-American slang are entirely my own, but the sins were committed despite my best intentions.

To hell, allegiance! vows, to the blackest devil!
Conscience and grace, to the profoundest pit!
I dare damnation:—to this point I stand,—
That both the worlds I give to negligence,
Let come what comes; only I'll be reveng'd
Most thoroughly for my father.

— Hamlet, 4.5.149-154

Chapter One

Luca

48 Hours Later

The tip of my cane struck a ridge in the uneven cobblestones and threw me off balance. With a pop and a grind, my right knee buckled, and I stumbled forward. I caught myself on the staircase handrail but landed awkwardly on the unforgiving concrete.

Stabbing pain shot up my legs. The dull ache in my head morphed into a steady throb that pulsed in time with the beat of my racing heart.

I squeezed the handrail. The cold, familiar iron steadied me and reminded me where I was—home.

My body was weak despite having drained two Sources; weeks of torture without food or water or blood will do that. Dreading the climb ahead, I pressed into the cane and forced myself upright.

The stairs led to a mahogany door. It looked the same as it had any of the countless times I'd stood at the bottom of those steps throughout my life. Back when the DeVitas and Morettis were one big happy family.

So much had changed, but not that door.

The stairs inflicted fresh punishment one excruciating step at a time, each movement a sharp reminder of the torture I'd endured. And deserved. But that hell was nothing compared to the pain of a life stolen, a child abandoned, and a crime left unavenged. My suffering was nothing compared to the pain I'd inflict on the family who murdered my father.

Panting from exertion, I needed a moment to catch my breath. I pressed my hand into a long crack I'd put in the door when I was a teenager and had gotten into it with Marco for the first time. He never patched the aged wood, and the crack stared back at me with unmasked reproach. It was wider now than when I'd slammed the door in a fit of rage and split the wood. Twenty-five years and weather and neglect had deepened the untreated wound. Was it possible to fix such a rift now?

I moved my fingers from the crack to the doorbell, and the silence after the ring twisted my empty insides. The deadbolt clicked, and the door swung open.

Mamma Gina's hand flew to her mouth. The other gripped the doorknob like she needed an anchor. "Luca," she whispered and reached for my cheek with shaking fingers. "Il mio dolce ragazzo." Her bottom lip trembled, and tears spilled down her cheeks.

"Mamma Gina."

She stepped back, and I hobbled into my childhood home. I bent to hug her, desperate for her safety and comfort. She took my face between her hands, kissed my cheeks and forehead, and wrapped her arms around me, holding me close. She rocked us back and forth like she used to when I was little, muttering, "Il mio Luca," and "Il mio ragazzo," between more frantic kisses. I squeezed her tight.

She clasped my shoulders and held me at arm's length, examining my face. "Il mio povero, dolce ragazzo. Cosa ti hanno fatto?" She ran her fingers over two-and-a-half-weeks' worth of unkempt stubble and the edge of the bandage covering my right eye.

"Nothing I didn't deserve." My voice cracked over the truth.

The grandfather clock standing guard over the living room announced the first toll in its midday warning. It cut through the silence, and with each chime, the relief and worry in Gina's face transformed into hurt and anger.

"Dannazione!" The curse resounded over the final bell of the old clock, and she slapped me across the face hard enough to let me know she meant it. Her lips pinched, and her breath heaved in her chest. Red specks appeared in her deep brown irises.

Tears welled in my eyes—from the sting of her hand across my face or the sting of the pain I saw in hers, I couldn't be sure.

The red glow of her eyes dimmed, and her breathing slowed. She took me back into her arms and kissed my cheeks. "Andrà tutto bene. Sei a casa, adesso. Everything will be okay," she murmured.

Was she trying to convince me or herself?

She pulled back and gripped my biceps. "You're so thin."

I nodded.

When Vinnie'd asked where I wanted his driver to take me, I hadn't hesitated. "Gina." But standing there, I didn't know what to say. I'd hurt her. I'd hurt Marco. Nothing I said would change those simple facts, and nothing she said would change the reasons I'd done it.

"Va bene," she said and patted my arms. She helped me out of my jacket and hung it by the door. She came to the side opposite my cane, slung my arm across her shoulders, and held my hand. "Andiamo."

At six-four, I towered over her, but I'd lost so much weight, when I leaned on her for support, she held me up.

"Easy," she said and wrapped her arm around my waist.

She led me into the kitchen, and with a grunt and a wince, I lowered myself onto a chair and set my cane down.

"Did you feed?" she asked.

"Yesterday. Twice."

"And before that?"

I gritted my teeth. She didn't need to know that I'd been blood-starved for weeks. Without a Source to replenish my blood's power, my body turned on itself for nourishment. Each round of Vinnie's torture took longer to heal from than the last. Only to have him destroy my body again. She didn't need to know he'd taken me to the brink of immortal death before ending my ordeal.

"When was the last time you ate?" she asked.

"Not since they took me."

The refrigerator door opened and closed. Dishes rattled. A cork popped followed by the splash of wine against crystal. I shifted my weight, and the old chair creaked. The sounds of home. They transported me back in time, and the tightness in my chest eclipsed the ache in my head and knees. The onslaught of memories hit like a battering ram, and I flattened my palms against the polished wood of the kitchen table for stability.

"Antonio, get the phonebook for Luca."

"Nooo, Nonna!" I whined. I tapped Papà's arm. "Papà! Tell her! Tell her I don't need it anymore. I'm six!"

"You heard him, Mamma." Papà looked at me and winked. "He's too grown-up to sit on the phonebook now."

Zio Marco stood behind me and started messing up my face, smooshing it under his hands.

"Stop it, Zio!" I squirmed in my chair and swatted his

arms. *I didn't really mind; he always did that just to mess with me. Zio Marco was the best.*

He grabbed my shoulders and squeezed. "Our boy is all grown-up, Mamma. He can sit at the table like the rest of us. Right on his chair."

Zio Marco stared down at me, a proud smile on his face.

I rubbed my sternum. The emptiness in my heart was as deep and profound as the emptiness in my stomach. All that was left was pain.

Gina handed me a glass of red wine and sat down at the head of the table, her mouth stern.

The strong red immediately went to work. Warmth spread across my chest and down my limbs, and for a moment, I thought it might be possible to breathe again.

She leaned forward and folded her hands on the table in front of her. "The weight will come back in time. You'll stay here in your old room until you're healed."

I watched her over the rim of the glass, skeptical and wary.

"Marco leaves for Italy tomorrow," she said. "He and Anna stopped by this morning to say goodbye."

I opened my mouth to protest.

"It's not open for discussion." When Mamma Gina used that tone, when she gave you that look, you didn't argue.

Truth was, I didn't want to go back to my house in Saugus. Not yet. My eye hadn't fully regenerated, and its absence gave me blinding headaches. My knees hadn't completely healed either, even after being set by Vinnie's doctor. I could barely get in and out of a car, much less drive stick.

Her eyes bored into me, and I knew what was coming—an earful. I stared at my hands resting on the base of the wine glass.

"I'm not going to lecture you about how you betrayed my

brother," she said. "I don't need to. You know how badly you hurt him."

As angry as I was with Marco, as much as I resented him for not taking action, the pain I saw in his eyes the night he disowned me haunted me every day.

"Despite what you did, you're as much a DeVita as you are a Moretti. Always have been. Just like your father. I'm not going to lecture you about how you betrayed our family, because you already know how badly you hurt me."

I raised my eyes to meet hers, guilt overpowering my need to escape her reproach.

"But if you think for one second I'm not going to lecture you about how badly you hurt yourself—how you *keep* hurting yourself with this vendetta bullshit..." She shook her head. "You forget who raised you."

Anger clashed against regret, but I couldn't hold it back. "I didn't come here for a lecture."

"Too bad. My house, my rules."

"You'll never understand."

"I understand plenty," she snapped. "Do you have a death wish, Luca?"

I looked out the kitchen window and ground my teeth so hard, my jaw started to throb as badly as my head.

"Do you? Because that's the only reason you'd do something as stupid and reckless as you did.

"Marco gave you a choice when you turned eighteen. I know, because as your foster parents, we had long discussions about giving you that choice. You chose to get involved. You chose to get made. And that means you play by the rules." She held up her hands as if forcing herself to slow down. "What the hell were you thinking?"

My pulse roared, the pounding in my ears as loud as my labored breath. I clenched my fists, trying to contain the torrent of emotion.

Mamma Gina placed her hand atop mine. "Look at me," she said softly and wriggled her fingers into my fist to hold my hand. "Guardami, Luca."

My breathing slowed, and my shoulders relaxed.

"You've spent too much time in Italy obsessing over this vendetta. You've lost sight of what matters—your family, your community, the people who love you. We'll help you through this. And if we can't? If we can't help you heal?" Her lips trembled, and she swallowed. "Then I've failed as a mother," she finished, her voice shaking through a declaration that only deepened my guilt.

Tears made the crimson specks in her dark brown eyes sparkle. They pleaded with me as strongly as the strain in her voice.

But she didn't understand. She could never understand what the Shaughnessys took from me. My father. My childhood. My sense of belonging. Nothing could fill the hole they left behind. Nothing but revenge.

The oven beeped.

Gina rose from the table and busied herself with my meal.

The promise of revenge had sustained me through the weeks I'd spent in that Valenzano hellhole. It had consumed every waking thought. I'd held on, knowing that if I made it to the other side, I'd make the Shaughnessys pay for the life they'd stolen and find some semblance of peace.

Gina set a plate steaming with baked ziti in front of me. My stomach rumbled. I picked up my fork and shoveled a huge bite into my mouth.

"Slow down! You'll make yourself sick."

But I couldn't slow down. The aroma and flavor and texture of food after starving for so long...

"Allora. What's your plan?"

I washed the bite down with the rest of my wine. "I work for Vinnie now." I stabbed the salsiccia with my fork and tore a chunk off with my teeth. My body ripped through the food almost as eagerly as it had devoured the blood of the two Sources I'd drained.

"And the rest of your life?"

I shrugged and licked the thick sauce from my bottom lip. "Ancora vino, per favore?"

Gina pressed her brows together, as unhappy with my non-answer as she was with my attitude. But she was as close to a mamma as I had, so she got up, grabbed the bottle off the counter, and filled my glass.

The Moretti family blood debt demanded payment. The stain had to be removed from my hands, not to mention the DeVitas' and the Valenzanos'. An eye for an eye. Blood for blood. I was owed my sliver of peace even if it was a fraction of what I deserved. But I'd learned my lesson; I would play by the rules this time.

Mamma Gina tidied up the kitchen, and I finished my meal. Plate and glass empty, I leaned back and ran my hands over my full stomach.

"There are a few things in your room from when you renovated your house. I'll go to Saugus tomorrow and pick up anything else you need."

"Grazie."

"Figurati. But now you need rest. Andiamo."

She wasn't wrong. I could barely keep my eyes open now that I'd eaten, especially after all the wine. I grabbed my cane, and Gina helped me to my feet.

My knees shook with each step through the living room. I stopped short before the hallway, my eyes fixed on a portrait that might as well have been a bullet through the head.

We'd piled into Nonno's station wagon to drive to the studio. Nonna'd said we needed a family picture before Marco and Gina left for Italy. It had been time for them to relocate, assume the identities of their children for a few decades before returning to the States. Nonna'd explained that because we were special, because we were blood demons, we all would experience that adventure someday.

I sat on my father's lap. His arms wrapped around me. I held his thick thumb in one of my little hands. The other held onto Gina standing to my right. I had a big gap-toothed grin on my face; I'd lost my first front tooth days before. Papà told me that if I smiled nice for our family picture, he'd take me to Mike's Pastry for cannoli. Marco stood behind and to the left of my father, resting his hand on my father's shoulder. Nonno e Nonna stood behind them.

The DeVitas. Complete with two Morettis. Our family.

My throat constricted, and rage clawed its way up from my chest to blaze through my eyes. I gritted my teeth, trying to cage my emotion, but the loss was too profound.

Mamma Gina squeezed my arm. "Come on, Luca. Let's get you to bed."

Marco's hand on my father's shoulder filled my vision and swelled my anger. It was bad enough I'd lost my father to Pádraig Shaughnessy, but to lose my foster father to a rat?

Siobhán Connelly—Siobhán *Shaughnessy*—had destroyed my relationship with Marco. She'd broken our bond with her scheming.

I'd known she was a liar, leading me on with that fake fucking accent. Irish, my ass. But a fottuto Shaughnessy? A maledetto rat? She'd lied to me and my family for the last time.

My vendetta wouldn't be complete until both crimes were avenged. Lucky for me, there was one Shaughnessy whose life would pay full price.

Chapter Two

Siobhán

Boston, Massachusetts, April 2024

The scene played out like a meet-cute from one of those feel-good made-for-TV movies. You know the ones. The ones your mam used to watch on Sunday afternoons. The ones that made you roll your eyes while you secretly dreamed it would happen to you. The ones with the happy endings.

Eyes catch across the room. Time stops. Everything in the shot fades to background. Everything except the leading couple. Their stunned faces remain crystal clear while the rest of the world goes about its out-of-focus business, oblivious to the two souls destined to find love at the end of ninety minutes.

March 20, 2022. The first day of spring. Pretty messed up I remembered the exact date we first laid eyes on each other. We exchanged one look, stolen across the Terme di Boston lobby, but that one look changed everything. The proof? Two years later and Luca Moretti still held me captive every time he smiled at me, his sleepy eyes and pouty lips a Technicolor version of Marlon Brando in *A Streetcar Named Desire*. But now I'll never see his handsome face again or get the chance to change our movie's finale.

Our relationship unfolded per the script at the beginning. But we never recovered from our "dark moment," and the rest of the tale played out the opposite of happy. A Moretti and Shaughnessy? Might as well have been a Montague and Capulet. I'm not sure I'd go so far as to call our story tragic, but some days my heart ached like the ending had been that cruel.

I cleared the lump in my throat and put on my game face. I didn't need to drag Anna into my melancholy, especially given the news I planned to drop. But brooding had been par for the course over the past month; nostalgia claimed my mood with the simplest, most innocuous trigger.

Today's bout hit as soon as I walked through the copper-clad doors of the spa. It had been my refuge for the past two years since moving back to the States and working at Terme di Boston. I'd hoped the soothing atmosphere would make the conversation with Anna easier to stomach. Instead, I got a trip down memory lane.

My first few months back in Boston had brimmed with promise, not just for my career but for the budding, screen-worthy romance. I should've known better; fate was never that kind.

"Are you glad to be back?" Not the question I wanted to ask, but the one that came out of my mouth. I wanted to ask about Luca. I needed to know he'd met with a quick and pain-less end.

Anna soaked in the mineral bath next to mine and rolled her head along its stone lip to face me. "I am." Her shy smile was a soothing balm to my preoccupied mind. I'd missed the little goose and her nervous glances and fidgety hands. "We hadn't planned on staying that long, but after everything…"

"Tell me about it. I took a few days off myself." It hadn't

been enough. Not by a long shot. My defective stomach ached with the stress of it all. More than usual. In the two weeks after Vesuvio, I barely ate.

"Marco had to deal with Terme di Roma and Terme di Sicilia." Her eyes followed her hands swirling through the mineral water. "Angelo is going to manage the Italian properties for now." She tentatively lifted her gaze to meet mine. The poor thing looked as sick as I felt.

I sipped my martini. The vodka took the edge off my nerves and abdominal pain, but I couldn't exactly waltz through life drinking martinis to settle my stomach. I needed more than a few days of vacation. I needed to get away from Terme di Boston and the DeVitas. Permanently.

But I had responsibilities, and I wasn't about to leave Marco high and dry while he did damage control in Italy. I was the strong one. Always. Even if it made me sick. Even if I couldn't remember the last time I smiled. Probably sometime before the night at Vesuvio when Luca fucked things up beyond repair by trying to start a war between our families and nearly killing Anna in the process. So I forced a fake smile onto my face and powered through.

"It's okay, Anna. You don't have to pretend like he never existed. I'm a big girl. I can handle that he's gone. Besides, it's not like we were together. It's not like we were ever going to be. We hated each other, remember?" I leveled her with a knowing look. "Not to mention, I don't get involved with those types of men."

She narrowed her eyes, an unspoken challenge.

I waved a hand through the air, brushing away her knowledge of my unwanted feelings. "You got lucky with Marco. He adores you. That man wouldn't look at another woman even with a gun to his head." I shook my head. "They're not all like that, girl. Marco's a unicorn."

Lately, I had to remind myself that it hadn't always been

sunshine and roses between me and Luca. Far from it. He'd been a complete asshole for an entire year, ever since The Incident. Then again, I hadn't been very nice either. He'd hurt me, and I'd lashed out with snide comments and death stares at every opportunity.

I was pissed at myself for ever trusting him. You don't grow up in a mob family and not know better than to trust men like Luca. They were all cut from the same lying, cheating cloth. But I'd let my guard down, suckered by his charm and the way he smiled just for me. And I paid for that lapse in judgment with a broken heart and a friend turned bitter enemy.

Even after The Incident, even after that night at Vesuvio, a part of me that I hated remained fixed on all the wrong things, holding onto a hope that someday we'd get a second chance. It was a sickness, really. It was time I took off my rose-colored glasses and focused on the truth—Luca Moretti and Siobhán Connelly had never been destined for a happy ending. Not that it mattered; the Mafia didn't leave loose ends. Luca was gone, dead, and we'd never get another chance.

"I'm sorry. I didn't mean to bring up—" Anna's shoulders deflated, and she stared at me blank-faced, the way she did when she couldn't find her words.

"You don't need to be sorry. The past couple of months have been a lot."

I could barely cope with what happened—nerves on edge, stomach on the offensive—and I spent the first eighteen years of my life around that type of bullshit. Granted, I'd removed myself from Boston and any association with the Shaughnessys for nearly twenty-five years, but that didn't mean life in a mob family wasn't familiar.

"Anyway..." I said, eager to change the subject. I raised my eyebrows and sipped my drink.

"Anyway," Anna continued, "a month was a long time to be away. I hope Sophie behaved herself."

"She's a lover. I'm going to miss having her around. Even if she woke me up every morning screaming for food."

Anna smiled the exasperated smile of a cat-mom.

"It was fine," I said. "Made me want to get one."

"You should!"

I huffed. "Girl, I can barely take care of myself."

She chuckled. "You're the General Manager of Boston's most exclusive resort. I'd say you're doing just fine."

I frowned. "About that..."

I set my martini down, folded my arms atop the stone floor between the two mineral baths, and rested my chin on the backs of my hands. Anna sat up and faced me, leaning against the edge of her bath.

"What happened at Vesuvio..." I started.

She looked away and reached for a necklace that wasn't there. She was still struggling. I didn't blame her.

The illegal, after-hours gambling hall on the second floor of Marco's nightclub Vesuvio had been raided, and in our mad dash to escape, Anna was hit by a car and almost died. To make matters worse, the entire charade had been orchestrated by Luca to frame my family and get Marco to move against the Irish.

My cousin Ciarán had been furious, ready to retaliate. He called the Italians a menace, one his father should have put to rest decades ago. He told me if I was smart, I'd help him, refusing to acknowledge the glaring truth—the Shaughnessys were as much of a menace as the Valenzanos or DeVitas. I walked him back, assuring him that Marco knew he hadn't sanctioned the raid.

I'd never betray Marco or let Ciarán hurt any of the DeVitas if it was in my power to prevent it. They'd been more of a family to me than any of the Shaughnessys.

"When Marco brought me on, he didn't just hire me, he treated me like one of his own. And after everything you and I have been through, you're more than a friend, Anna. You're family, and I don't use that word lightly."

I reached out and squeezed her hand, knowing what I was about to say would probably send her into a fit of sweaty palms and stuttering.

"You asked me once how I knew so much about this world. I'm sure Marco filled you in. I'm a Shaughnessy. On my mother's side. I trust you not to share that information with anyone." She swallowed and gave me a slight nod. "I left Boston when I was eighteen to get away from them. I only came back two years ago to take care of my parents. I don't want to be a part of this world, and I've spent my entire adult life making sure I'm never in a situation where I have to live like that again."

I swallowed the thickness creeping up my throat. It rose any time I was reminded of what growing up in the Irish mob had done to me, the damage that could never be repaired.

"I didn't figure out Marco was connected for more than a year after I started at Terme. When I finally put it together, Terme seemed so separate from all that, like Marco couldn't possibly be involved."

Looking back now, I think I knew. The signs had been there, but I'd willfully ignored the evidence right under my nose. My parents needed me. What else could I do but rationalize away the truth?

"He did so much for me, giving me a chance in such a prominent position, accommodating my needs. So I chose to believe he was less involved than he was. But then Vesuvio happened. And Luca..."

Anna lowered her eyes.

"I've worked too hard building a life that isn't tied to the Shaughnessys. I clawed my way into this position, and I won't let my career be destroyed by my family. I need to find a new job away from all of this. I'm leaving Terme di Boston."

"What? No!" Her eyes widened, and her lips parted as if she wanted to say more but couldn't find the words.

"I'm taking the next two weeks off for interviews. I filed the vacation request while you were in Italy. But no one knows why, not even Marco."

She swallowed, and I gave her the moment she needed to collect her thoughts. She'd argue that Marco would shield me from my family and his, that he would never allow Mafia matters to impact me. But they already had. I'd lucked out that night at Vesuvio, walking away unscathed. Next time, I might not be so lucky.

"He's not going to like this. He—he—" She held up her hand and took a settling breath. "I'm not saying this to make you feel guilty. I'm saying this because it's true. He thinks of you as part of our family. Like a—like a niece. He'd do anything for you."

"I know. But I already have a family, and they did an absolute shit job of keeping me safe. One thing my life has proven to me is that I'm the only person I can trust. And that's especially true when it comes to family. I have to stay away."

She deflated on an exhale and wrung her hands. "He's going to be angry, but you know—you know it's because this is going to hurt him. Losing you after losing—" She stopped short, and I swallowed the fresh lump in my throat.

I drained the rest of my martini and slipped back into the bath. I let my head fall back to rest on the edge and stared at the ivy-covered ceiling.

The click of heels on the porous stone floor. The cool, humid air lightly scented with eucalyptus and toasted almond. The warmth of the mineral bath cradling my body. I loved this space. I came here any time stress got the better of me and made my stomach burn. I had more than colleagues and friends at Terme di Boston, I had a sense of family, of home.

My insides twisted in a mess of sadness and frustration, of anger and resentment, but it couldn't be helped. I had to protect myself. I had to leave.

"I know," I whispered. "And if there was any other way, I'd take it just to spare him the pain. But I can't live like this. I won't."

I cleared my mind of the impending conversation with Marco and the sadness in Anna's expression only to see a charming smile built for cameras. Eyes as dark as a stormy night. A still captured from a lunch at Vittoria a little over a year ago when things were simpler, when a future with Luca Moretti hadn't seemed impossible.

"Sorry I'm late." He squeezed my shoulder and rounded the table.

My heart leaped at the sound of Luca's voice.

He tucked a length of chocolate-brown hair behind his ear, revealing a jawline that would make a runway model jealous. It was covered in a day's worth of scruff, and the added roughness made my stomach flutter. His full mouth turned up in a smile so genuine it reached his eyes. He didn't smile like that often. Most of the time he hid behind a paparazzi-worthy catalog of staged looks. But he smiled like that for me, and every time he did, I crushed on him a little harder.

"Marco's a slave driver," he said with a wink. He unbuttoned his suit jacket and folded his tall, muscular frame into the chair across from me.

"He gets like that when he's focused. You get like that when you're focused."

He chuckled.

"I hope you don't mind. I went ahead and ordered." I gestured to the soup in front of me. "I have a one o'clock. Can't be late for my own meeting."

"Not at all." He leaned back and lifted a hand. "Scusi."

A waiter came over and took his order.

Luca returned his attention to me. "By all means, go ahead."

"How long are you in town?" I asked and took a bite of minestrone. The tomato in the broth was mild and the vegetables were cooked enough to be safe for my stomach. I relished its warmth on the cold December day. And his company.

"Just the week. I need to get back to Roma before Natale. It's our busiest time."

Every now and then Luca would say something in Italian like Roma or scusi or Natale, and if I didn't know it was impossible, I would swear cartoon hearts floated above my head.

"We're always so busy when I'm in town," he continued with an edge of frustration.

"At least we get to have lunch." The words sounded as empty as my feigned smile.

Marco introduced us about eight months ago, finally breaking the ice. Instead of furtive glances and hidden stares across the lobby, we chatted whenever he was in town. Chatted and flirted. Neither of us stopped smiling any time we were together. One lucky day, we ran into each other at noon. Since then, we never missed an opportunity to share lunch when he was in Boston, but it never felt like enough time.

His eyebrows drew together. "No. These lunches are too rushed." He pursed his pouty lips and ran a hand through his hair. "I'll be back in early February for the quarterly. I'd like to take you out for dinner. Somewhere we won't be interrupted. I want to know you, Siobhán."

A tear escaped from beneath my closed eyelids. Pretending to scratch my cheek, I swiped it away; I didn't want to cause Anna more stress. The ache in my heart had nothing to do with her, Marco, leaving Terme di Boston, or even the troubles with my family. The ache in my heart had everything to do with what might have been, for the happy ending to the made-for-TV movie I'd secretly hoped I would find with Luca but was lost forever.

Chapter Three

Luca

The parking lot of the Sleep and Stay on the outskirts of Foxborough was a spectacle of contradiction to anyone who didn't know better. To the right behind the Employees Only sign, a half dozen generic beaters formed a row of rust and dents. They matched the dingy, weathered exterior of the building, the cracks in the pavement, and the overgrown bushes that blocked the view of the street. To the left of the main entrance, Vinnie's Rolls-Royce stuck out like a sore thumb, especially with the Mercedes-Benz SUV with Rhode Island plates parked next to it. Two Beamers continued the luxury-car lineup on the other side of the Benz. No sign of Marco's Range Rover, but my contribution wasn't going to make the display any less conspicuous.

My Ferrari purred like a big cat, roaring up the driveway and across the lot. I parked my baby diagonally across two spaces; I didn't need some asshole dinging the paint. I climbed out and buttoned my suit jacket just as a white Mercedes pulled into the space beside mine.

Gio Agosti—short, stout, and dressed like it was 1965—

emerged from the passenger seat. His driver leaned against the hood, lit a cigarette, and pulled out his phone.

"Ciao, Luca," Gio said and held out a hand. "Come va?"

"Ciao, Gio. Bene, bene." I grabbed his hand, and he slapped my shoulder and kissed my cheeks.

The Valenzano family consigliere was old school like Marco and Vinnie and had been around for almost as long. Big Frankie brought him over from Italy after Marco split ways with the Valenzanos and took Vito with him. If Gio had his way, I didn't think he'd ever speak English.

"You settling in over at The Dollhouse?" He started for the entrance, and I followed. "Tieni gli occhi aperti," he tossed over his shoulder. His driver nodded and went back to scrolling his phone.

"So far so good."

Vinnie'd put me in charge of The Dollhouse—his largest strip club and a front for his Source racket—as soon as I was well enough to work. The Dollhouse and its seedy older sister The Playground were Vinnie's big money makers. Profits were down across the board, and I had experience running two multi-million-dollar properties for Marco. Vinnie was too shrewd a businessman to pass up an opportunity to turn things around.

"Bene. You spent too much time holed up in Italy doing hotel management," Gio said derisively. "Time for you to start earning."

Didn't I know it. I'd been ready to start earning since I was eighteen. Now that I was out from under Marco's thumb, I finally had a chance. And what better way than the Source racket.

Richie Amato was the capo in charge of Vinnie's blood demon outfit. He'd done an okay job, but the Source racket had grown too big for one person, especially when that person had the financial acumen of a toothpick. Vinnie split the work between us, a good thing considering he wanted to expand. I managed the fronts—the books, the day-to-day operations at the clubs—and Richie managed the Sources themselves—recruiting, oversight, and payments.

"You're a Moretti," Gio continued and leveled me with a weighted look. "It's in your blood."

I chuffed out a snort and pulled open the door.

The hotel lobby reeked of burnt coffee and cheap air freshener. The generic dust-covered prints on the walls and the worn, stain-marked carpet were as unappealing as the smell. I understood the need for a neutral location; a sit-down of this magnitude couldn't take place on anyone's territory. I also understood the need for obscurity and a low-key front, but this was ridiculous.

Vinnie waited for us on a stiff pleather couch. Richie and Johnny "Lam" Lamendola—the other two Valenzano captains joining the sit-down—hovered over the complimentary coffee.

There were rules for sit-downs, especially ones this big. Each family was allowed the same number and rank—the dons, of course, their consiglieri, and three capi. Five crew members. Had to keep up the appearance of equality.

"Luca. Gio." Vinnie pushed his ample frame off the plastic couch, and it creaked.

Gio joined Richie and Johnny at the coffee. He poured a cup for himself, then ushered the two men down the hall to a set of double doors.

"You ready?" Vinnie asked.

"Yeah." I passed a hand through my hair. "Yeah, I'm ready."

He patted my cheek and raised an eyebrow. "Now you'll see what happens when you play by the rules."

Like I needed the reminder. I gave him a tight nod.

If you asked any of the dons, there wasn't a power imbalance among the New England families. But anyone walking into the shoddy conference room at the Sleep and Stay Foxborough would have been hard-pressed to believe that bullshit.

Roman Patrizi sat at the head of three tables organized in a *U* across from the entrance like a king waiting for his audience. The Don of Providence's silver-streaked hair was slicked back like a crown, and the three-piece suit told everyone he meant business.

The men seated on either side of him eyed us as we filed into the room. Vinnie took the center seat on the right side of the *U*. I sat next to Gio closest to the door.

The families who ran the Boston territories had always taken a backseat to Providence. The rivalry between the Italians and Irish dated back earlier than even Big Frankie Valenzano's arrival in the States, and the constant struggle for territory in a city a tenth the size of NYC had forced a handful of the big players south. To make matters worse, the FBI's crackdown on Italian organized crime in the '80s had done more damage in Boston than any other major city. They'd attacked the Valenzanos from both ends by using the Irish mob—Pádraig Shaughnessy in particular—to weaken Italian control.

The Patrizis, on the other hand, had grown in strength and influence over the decades. Uncontested in their control of Providence, their reach extended south into Connecticut and bordered the Five Families of New York. Providence had a lot of clout, and Roman Patrizi knew it. But Vinnie was no slouch, and over the past twenty-five years he'd rebuilt the Italian power base in Boston, creating a crew that rivaled even Don Patrizi's.

There was a long pause after everyone sat, long enough to let the Patrizi and Valenzano crews know they were waiting.

The double doors swung open, and the DeVitas filed in, a not-so-subtle reminder that there had always been a silent third party, a dethroned king who'd returned to take his rightful place. Never outdone, least of all by Vinnie, my foster father strode into the conference room wearing importance and indifference like a suit of armor. As if we should have expected to wait for him. As if nothing could commence without his presence. As if the DeVitas were the family in charge.

Carmine and Angelo led the way with Vito and Matteo bringing up the rear. They stood behind their chairs until Marco removed his hat, unbuttoned his suit jacket, and took his seat opposite Vinnie. Only then did the rest of the crew sit.

I masked a snort with a cough and looked down so no one would see my smirk. Marco knew what he was doing. So did Vinnie and Roman Patrizi.

Cocky prick.

Marco placed his palms flat on the table. "Don Patrizi. Don Valenzano." His smooth, commanding voice dominated the room as easily as his presence. He met their eyes, securing a nod from each, then landed his penetrating gaze on me.

He raised me to play life like a game of poker, a mantra he'd drilled into me since I was a kid. So I held his eyes without moving a muscle—no tells—until he released me from his ironclad grip. I exhaled and allowed myself to blink again before examining the rest of the playing field.

Angelo and Carmine stared me down. Their expressions revealed nothing, but the intensity of their focus spoke volumes. The only people who knew that I'd skimmed the profits of DeVita Enterprises International's European branch and orchestrated the raid on Vesuvio occupied the inner circle of the Boston dons. Marco and Vinnie, of course. Angelo, Carmine, and Vito. Gio, Vinnie's blood-demon enforcer, and the single soldato demone del sangue who'd helped him torture me. That was it. Marco and Vinnie were determined to keep the affair under wraps. Knowing their don had been swindled would undermine the crew's confidence just as he ascended to his throne. Even if my punishment had been more brutal than death. Better to use the expanding Source racket to cover up my fall from Marco's grace.

Don Patrizi cleared his throat. "We're here to discuss Don DeVita's formal reentry into Cosa Nostra and the New England families. To acknowledge, among our ranks, a second family in control of Boston and to reestablish the division of territory in New England." He gave Marco a knowing smirk. "Bentornato, Marco."

Roman Patrizi was human but in the know. In his late fifties, he'd been in the game long enough to see that Marco and Vinnie hadn't aged. But like them, he was old school. Omertà meant something. He'd never divulge our secret. He'd take knowledge of blood demons to the grave. He also made it clear he'd never get involved in our affairs; too much risk for a people that weren't his.

Marco tipped his head. "Roman."

"In terms of territory, not much will change," Vinnie said. "Don DeVita has always maintained a presence in the city, however unofficial. His fronts in the North End and the Commons remain undisputed. I also have fronts in the North End, but for different businesses, and our families have shared that territory for over fifty years without dispute. I'll maintain control of the northern suburbs starting with Revere."

Vinnie turned to Marco; Marco nodded his agreement.

"I recently expanded my holdings to include a property in the financial district," Marco added. "Untouched territory within the city. I'll be running the same businesses there that I run in the North End."

Don Patrizi cocked an eyebrow.

"A strategic move that benefits both families. The financial district is key to maintaining a power balance with the Irish.

They can't move in without creating a turf war, and they know it."

Marco caught Vinnie's eye, and Vinnie held up both hands. "No contest."

Don Patrizi looked between the two men. "It's settled—the financial district is under DeVita control. What about points west and the suburbs?"

For the next two hours, the New England dons cycled through a litany of territories, rackets, and concessions, their consiglieri furiously taking notes. If there was ever a dispute between the DeVitas and the Valenzanos, Don Patrizi would arbitrate, and no one wanted the details of this agreement left open to interpretation.

The only thing we couldn't talk about was the Source racket. Ironic given that the growing demand for Sources and Vinnie's plans to expand the racket had driven Marco to finally take his rightful place. But Roman was the only member of the Patrizi contingent who knew blood demons existed, and even Johnny Lam—Vinnie's top human capo—wasn't in the know. Given the urgency, Vinnie and Marco along with Gio and Vito worked out the details of the arrangement before Marco left for Italy.

Marco made Matteo a captain and gave him responsibility for the portion of the Source racket that ran through Terme di Boston. He'd been a trusted soldier for years and more suited to desk work than bouncing. Now he managed long-term stays for high-end Sources at Terme, appointments and payouts, and coordinating with me and Richie on availability and taxes. We'd only run a couple trial appointments, but the preliminary profits proved just how lucrative the joint venture could be. It also took pressure off containment; the more venues for booking Sources, the less likely our secret would get exposed.

"Before we break," Vinnie announced, "we have one more matter that needs to be settled. Luca?"

I stood, buttoned my suit jacket, and scanned the room. I made eye contact with every man there, making sure they knew I meant business. Angelo and Carmine resumed their knife-edged regard, and when I reached Marco, his lips twisted as if restraining the parental urge to tell me to sit down. Fuck that.

The DeVita family made me, but the Valenzanos appointed me captain of an active crew. Under Vinnie, I had every right to make my case. My time had arrived.

"November 12, 1988. Antonio Michael Moretti was murdered without cause by Pádraig Shaughnessy in the Charlestown shipyard. The Irish mob took my father's life. They spilled Moretti family blood. A made man's life was cut short, and thirty-five years later, the crime is left unanswered." I stared at Marco in silent condemnation. "Thirty-five years later, the Shaughnessys still haven't paid the price."

I refused to break eye contact even as his jaw ticked in pain or frustration or anger—I didn't care. He needed a reminder that it had been his responsibility to make the Irish pay, that as his best friend, as his brother in everything but blood, Marco had failed my father. He had failed me.

I clenched my fists and drove my knuckles into the table. "As Antonio Moretti's son and the last member of the Moretti family, it is my right to seek vengeance for this crime. I want restitution."

"I knew your father," Don Patrizi said, respect thick in his words and the severity of his expression. "He was a good man, one of the best in the Northeast." He turned his attention to Vinnie. "Why was this crime left unanswered? A made guy. A capo." He reclined in his chair, steepled his fingers, and raised a judgmental brow. "Thirty-five years?"

"It was 1988," Vinnie snapped as if the year was all the explanation he needed. "Maybe you don't remember what it was like back then in Boston, but I sure as hell do. The feds were up our asses, taking down businesses left and right. The Shaughnessys were on the take, and we couldn't afford the heat."

I ground my teeth on his excuses; I'd heard them for decades.

Don Patrizi's accusatory gaze shifted to Marco, and a deathly quiet descended over the sit-down. My blood ran hot with rage, but the temperature of the room seemed to drop. The chill of Marco's icy glare slid across every man in attendance, freezing them in place.

"Antonio was my brother." Marco's dark declaration filled the room. His eyes locked with mine and tunneled into me as deeply and harshly as they had the night he disowned me. "Had I thought for one moment that seeking revenge for Tony's death wouldn't have put my family at risk, that seeking revenge wouldn't have put *all* our families at risk"—Marco's words were glacial, and flecks of red dotted his irises—"I would have burned the entire fucking city until every last Shaughnessy was dead."

I swallowed, my mouth dry from the steel in his voice and the stunned silence of its aftermath.

Vinnie cleared his throat, turning his wary gaze away from Marco and back to Don Patrizi. "Any move against the Irish would have started a war," he continued in a conversational tone. "Which was what the feds wanted. They stretched us thin, arresting our soldati and capi left and right. We took out a small crew in Charlestown. Two, three men tops, but we didn't go after Paddy. He was baiting us, and we couldn't afford to take the bait. But now?" Vinnie turned to me.

"It's time," I said. "Voglio vendetta. Blood for blood. I demand no more, and I'll take no less."

"As is your right, Luca Moretti," Don Patrizi said, levelling his gaze on Vinnie and Marco. "È un suo diritto." He finished in a tone that brokered no debate. "But," he added, turning his attention back to me, "even now, we can't afford a war. Ciarán Shaughnessy is off limits."

I nodded. Vinnie'd warned me Roman was likely to stipulate the condition, and if he didn't, Vinnie would. With the feds poking around and the tip-off from Mayor Kelson that they'd been talking with the Irish, the last thing we needed was an all-out war. And taking out Ciarán Shaughnessy would end in an all-out war.

"An eye for an eye and this blood feud is over, Luca." Don Patrizi raised his brow. "Capisce?"

"Capisce," I said and took my seat.

Marco's eyes bored into me from across the room. They tugged on my attention with all the horsepower of my Ferrari. I licked my lips, knowing the lecture I was about to get through a single look. A muscle in his jaw twitched—the only sign Marco ever gave that he was pissed off. His eyes grabbed mine and suspicion colored his expression as if I'd been too reasonable, as if he expected I already had a plan.

But I held his stare without flinching. He'd sat on my father's death my entire life. He'd lorded over every decision I made. He'd disowned me. Fuck him. Me and my plan were none of his goddamned business.

Roman Patrizi stood and broke our silent standoff. "Gentlemen," he said.

Marco and Vinnie rose and walked around the tables to meet him. The three men exchanged handshakes and kisses, a performative display for everyone else in the room. The alliance was sealed, and the sit-down between the New England families was over.

The rest of us stood, shook hands, slapped backs, caught up. Boston and Providence didn't come together often, and we took the opportunity to remind each other that New

England was bigger than either city. Putting faces to names helped everyone remember not to fuck with the wrong person.

We filed out of the conference room, ready to go back to our cities, back to our rackets, back to earning, and for me, back to my vendetta, sanctioned after all these years.

I pushed through the glass doors of the shitty hotel. The sun blazed overhead. I reached into my suit jacket for my sunglasses, and a hand clamped onto my shoulder.

"Didn't see you at the gym this morning." Vito's gruff voice held as much question as admonishment.

I'd hit Vito's gym every day since Vinnie dropped me at Gina's. After what I'd been through, my strength wouldn't return from just eating and feeding. And despite his allegiance to Marco, Vito didn't treat me like a pariah.

"We all make mistakes," he'd said. "Sometimes they're big. I've done my share of fucking up. You paid your dues, kid. This is your second chance. You only get one. Don't fuck it up." That had been the sum total of his lecture, and after those pointed words, he didn't bring it up again.

The days I didn't lift, he trained me in the ring, but he wasn't doing it for me. Gina felt better knowing he'd taken me under his wing, and he wanted to ease her worry. No doubt she held onto the hope that the connection between me and Vito might heal the rift between me and Marco. Not fucking likely.

Gio's driver stepped in front of us, blocking our way, and jerked his head toward the street. "We got eyes."

A gray sedan with tinted windows was parked across the street from the hotel. A man wearing sunglasses and a serious expression watched us from the driver-side window.

"Goddammit," Vito grumbled.

I stepped around Gio and flipped the asshole off. "Vaffanculo!"

The guy lifted a long-lens camera, and I lifted my middle finger, obscuring my face. "Got that? Fucking *cagacazzo!*"

Vito put a hand on my shoulder. I showed the camera my back and lifted my chin at the men walking out of the hotel. "Watch it," I warned, and me and Vito started down the path toward our cars.

The unkempt hedges blocked the fed's line of sight after only a few strides. "Must've tailed us all the way from Boston," I said.

We couldn't stop them. The street was public property, and we didn't own the hotel. Not to mention, they'd be hard-pressed to pin me with any RICO charges. Still, I didn't need permanent records that could be used against me after a couple decades of not aging.

"They're a nuisance." Vito growled and glanced at me sideways. "More than usual."

That said a lot coming from Vito. Agent Johnson had been snooping around Terme for a while, but if Vito was concerned...

I stopped on the driver's side of my Ferrari. Vito pulled a soft pack of Marlboro Reds from the inside pocket of his suit jacket, tapped one out, and stuck it between his lips.

"The gym?" He raised an eyebrow over the *flick* and flame of a black Bic.

I shrugged. "The morning got away from me."

"You mean Marco's back, and you don't want to run into him," he said around the cigarette.

I glared at him, but he wasn't wrong. I couldn't stand the disappointment and judgment on Marco's cocky face.

Vito's eyebrows drew together behind a plume of smoke. "Marco comes in after work. Stick to the mornings. Keep that rage in check. Got it?"

"Yeah," I said and ran a hand through my hair.

"When's the last time you saw Gina?"

Vito knew the answer, otherwise he wouldn't have asked.

"Not since Marco's been back."

"We've been working on your guard, right?"

"Yeah."

"You can't avoid him forever. Learn to put up a guard."

He held my eyes and burned the rest of his cigarette in one long, slow drag. "And don't do that to Gina." He dropped the butt on the ground, stepped on it, and closed the distance between us. He squeezed my shoulder, his expression severe and uncompromising. "She doesn't deserve it. She loves you like a son, and she's suffered enough loss in that department."

"I'll visit her Friday after the gym."

"Bene. See you in the morning." He pulled out a set of keys and unlocked the Range Rover.

I took off my suit jacket and climbed into my Ferrari. The engine roared to life, but neither the vibrations nor the cool touch of the steering wheel brought me back to the present. Friday waited on the horizon, a bright, shining beacon into a future free from my torment.

I revved the engine, and anticipation revved my heart as if its furious beat might accelerate my endgame. I peeled out of the parking lot, raced up the street, and punched the gas onto the freeway, speeding back to Boston. Speeding toward Friday.

It was going to be a big day. The biggest day of my life. First, the gym. Then, Gina's. And finally, my revenge.

Chapter Four

Siobhán

My parents' house was southwest of downtown just north of Dorchester, but with traffic, even after laying on the horn and cutting off one hot-tempered cabbie, I didn't start my parking search until twilight darkened their narrow, packed street. Friday was my night to help with supper. To be fair, most nights were my nights to help my parents. God forbid my idiot brother step up and take more than one night a week. No, he was content reinforcing my long-held belief that if I didn't do something, it wouldn't get done. Which was the reason I was late in the first place. It was the Friday before my two-week vacation, and I needed to make sure my department heads had their marching orders. My team was solid, but I never left anything open to interpretation.

I slowed to a stop ahead of a space only inches longer than my BMW and shook my head at the irony of parallel parking between a Volvo and a brand-new Rivian. The neighborhood had become a trendy hot spot for young professionals, a far cry from the '80s and early '90s when it was one of the most dangerous in the country. I'd spent my entire life trying to get out of Southie, and now people were trying to move in.

Over the past twenty years, most Irish Americans had moved to West Roxbury or Dorchester. Southie was more diverse now, but a good quarter of the residents were still Irish, holdouts like my parents. Until a few years ago, Da still worked at his shop. He didn't chop for the Shaughnessys anymore—hadn't in years—but even before he quit, I doubted he'd made any real money. But working on cars made him happy. It gave him purpose, and he refused to leave his shop behind and move with the rest of Mam's family.

And now? I slammed the door, slung my purse over my shoulder, and darted across the street. Now it was too late. Da's dementia worsened with each visit, and Mam was convinced that leaving the only home he'd known since moving to America would turn his world upside down. They had a routine, and as long as they stuck to the routine—in their house in their neighborhood—everything would be fine. I was too tired to argue.

How this would all work with a new job was beyond me. I already ran myself ragged between managing Terme and my parents' household. Not to mention keeping my own life afloat. Add in a longer commute to wherever—if I found a job that wasn't a step backward in my career—and I had serious doubts I'd ever sleep again.

The old chain-link gate shrieked open, then clattered shut. I hurried up the narrow path between century-old detached row houses to the back porch. Mam kept the front door dead bolted. It made her feel safe, even if that safety was an illusion.

I held the screen door open with my hip and unlocked the back door. It opened into the kitchen where I was immediately accosted by the smell of... garbage.

What. The fuck.

"Ma!"

"We're in the TV room, Siobhán," she yelled back, as much as my mother had ever yelled in her life. Soft-spoken was an understatement.

"What is that smell?" I asked, my face twisted in disgust. The rancid stench was no less prominent in the living room than in the kitchen. I dropped my purse next to the potted plant and hung my coat on the back of one of the dining chairs. "And why is the heat on? It's April!"

I was just there Tuesday. How were things already falling apart?

Da sat in his chair, a dirty old thing upholstered in that drab olive color so popular in the '80s. He refused to get it restuffed or reupholstered, swearing it would ruin his sitting experience. He was completely focused on the TV and didn't spare me a glance. Mam sat on the sofa crocheting oven mitts. She set her work in her lap and turned her wrinkled face up to give me a smile that landed somewhere between disappointed and resigned.

"It's the garbage, dear," she said. "We had corned beef and cabbage a few nights ago for supper. Maureen O'Sullivan brought it over. You know Maureen—from St. Mary's? I haven't taken it out yet."

"Why not?" I snapped, horrified that my parents were living with rotting garbage.

"My hip's been acting up." She looked down and lifted her crocheting. "I didn't want to fall," she said, barely above a whisper. Mam had gotten her hip replaced after a tumble on an icy patch on the back porch two winters ago. The surgery had been successful, but she hadn't been the same since.

"Why didn't Rory take it out last night?"

"Rory didn't come over last night. He was busy."

"Jesus Christ," I mumbled.

"Watch yer tongue," Da barked from his chair, but his eyes

never left the television. "'Tis an Irish-Catholic house. We dinna use the Lard's name in vain."

As dementia claimed his mind, history reclaimed Da's accent. He'd lost the thick Irish brogue after decades of living in Boston, but over the past year it had returned with a vengeance, as though his mind was rewinding to a simpler time.

"Sorry, Da," I grumbled and went back into the kitchen.

My parents' declining health dragged me back to Southie two years ago. Dragged me back kicking and screaming all the way across the Atlantic to where my family—the Shaughnessys—ruled over Irish organized crime. However much I resented coming back, the overflowing garbage and a sink filled with dirty dishes were proof enough that I'd made the right decision. It had been the *only* decision.

I propped my hands on my hips, closed my eyes, and let my head fall back. I could've strangled Rory. Our parents needed us, and I couldn't trust my own brother to make sure they weren't living with rotting garbage.

Mam kept the heat on because the cold made her hip ache, but it was cooking the trash and making the smell worse. I turned off the heat and threw open the windows. She could use one of her eight million crocheted blankets if she was cold. I gathered up the bag, took it out back, and got to work on the dishes.

Rory and I had an arrangement. He had one night, and I had the rest. I didn't give a flying fuck about his bullshit excuses. I couldn't do this alone. A new job would likely take me out of Boston. What then? There weren't many high-end hotels and resorts in the area, and I refused to sacrifice a career I'd busted my ass to build because Rory couldn't get his shit together.

Not only did Mam refuse to move closer to family or into an assisted living facility, she also refused hired help. My only recourse? Threats. I had to threaten Rory with Ciarán just to take care of his own parents. But to be completely fair, I didn't trust Ciarán any more than I trusted any other man. The whole situation was a flaming dumpster fire.

I set the last of the dishes in the drying rack, and the back door swung open. A man who could have been my twin walked into the kitchen.

"Speak of the devil." I gave my cousin an irritated glare before opening the fridge.

Ciarán Shaughnessy was six feet and two inches of pure Celtic genetics. He had more gray in his blond hair than I did, but you wouldn't know it since he buzzed his head. An explosion of freckles covered his arms, but only a sprinkle was visible across the bridge of his nose and cheekbones. Just like me. His eyes were the same pale blue as mine, but his laugh lines etched deeper troughs in his face. Made sense given the rough life he'd led while I was in Ireland. Those differences aside, the resemblance really was uncanny.

"What did I do?" he asked, brow furrowed.

"Do you smell that?"

"Unfortunately."

"Guess who didn't show up yesterday?" I pulled salad ingredients out of the fridge and set them on the counter.

"How is that my fault?"

"Rory works for you. I'm assuming his excuse—once he decides to grace us with his presence—will be that you had him driving somewhere or doing something more important than making sure his parents are safe, fed, and not living with rotting garbage."

I slammed the salad dressing on the counter. My cheeks were hot, and their color no doubt matched the pitch of my voice. The Southie had come out too. The polished accent I worked so hard to curate always fell away in heated moments. Especially when those moments involved my family.

"Everything okay in there?" Mam called in her little voice.

"We're fine, Aunt Maggie," Ciarán called back. "Just getting supper ready."

"What are you doing here anyway?" I asked, my words clipped as I prepped my parents' late meal. A meal I couldn't even eat. After working an eleven-hour day.

Ciarán leaned against the counter and shoved his hands into his jeans' pockets. The old leather jacket he'd had since high school fell open revealing a Henley covered in grease. He must have come from Da's shop. "I wanted to talk to you," he said.

I chopped the half cucumber I'd found in the fridge. "About what?"

"About your boss."

I shook my head. "You're *bahking* up the wrong tree, Ciarán," I said, my accent in full force after that comment.

He raised an eyebrow. "I haven't asked you a question yet."

"Doesn't matter." An innocent red pepper now received the brunt of my frustration. "I refuse to say anything about Marco to you just like I'd refuse to say anything about you to Marco." I paused and shot him a heated glare, my irritation with my family pressing against my chest. "At least he has the decency not to ask." I resumed chopping.

"What the hell, Vahnie?" Ciarán snapped back, using the nickname he gave me when we were kids. He straightened off the counter and pulled his shoulders back. "You're a Shaughnessy, or have you forgotten?"

I set the knife down and looked him in the eye, exerting as much control as I could so I wouldn't explode. "No. I haven't forgotten. My scars remind me of that unfortunate fact every day."

Ciarán's lips twisted, fighting a grimace or a frown—I wasn't sure which and didn't care. I didn't care if talking about my scars made him uncomfortable. At least he didn't have to live with them.

"You know better than to ask, Ciarán. Don't involve me."

His shoulders deflated. He rested his forehead in his hand and rubbed his temples.

I drizzled dressing over the salad in each bowl and, happy with my prep, ventured into the living room. I moved the remote off Da's armrest and notched the volume down to a decibel level appropriate for humans. "Time for supper, Da."

He tore his eyes away from the TV long enough to give me a blank stare, his eyebrows knotted in confusion. "Who are you?" he asked in an accusatory tone.

Loss and regret punched me in the chest. "It's Siobhán, Da."

His condition had worsened over the past six months, and things weren't going to get any better. But I didn't have time to mourn. Someone had to keep this ship from sinking. So I pulled out the TV trays and set one in front of each of my parents.

"Thank you, dear," Mam said and tucked her crocheting into the basket at her feet. "Are you staying for supper, Ciarán?"

Ciarán leaned against the doorjamb between the kitchen and the living room and patted his stomach. "Nah. Thanks, Aunt Maggie, but I already ate."

I passed him on my way back into the kitchen to retrieve the salads, and he leaned back, looked over his shoulder, and lowered his voice. "You've been involved. You've been working for the DeVitas for two years. Don't forget, you called me when that shit went down at Vesuvio."

I stopped in front of him with the salads, forks, and napkins. "For the eight millionth time, I didn't know who he was when I took the job. It was an amazing career opportunity. And, thanks to you and my idiot brother, I couldn't walk away just because of his rumored connections. Someone needs to make sure my parents aren't living with *rotting garbage*. And for the record, the reason I called you that night was to prevent the two people I love most in the world from killing each other. *That's. It.*"

I marched past him and put the salads in front of my parents.

"Thank you, dear." Mam made the sign of the cross and folded her hands in her lap. .

"I want to know who tried to frame me," Ciarán demanded.

I held up my hands. "I'm not getting involved." He stepped into the living room like he was about to launch into an argument, but I cut him off. "And why does it matter? Seriously. Marco knows it wasn't you. I made sure of that. There won't be any retaliation. Let it go."

"You know I can't let something like that go. If this happened because of Italian in-fighting, some sort of turf war within the Mafia, I need to know."

"Why?"

"Let's not talk about such matters in front of your da," Mam said. She wrung her hands in her lap. "It upsets him."

It didn't upset Da; it upset her. It never used to. She'd always had a backbone when it came to mob stuff. Hell, her brother's death and what happened to me hadn't fazed her. Just part and parcel of being a Shaughnessy. But Da's steady decline and her decreased mobility had shaken her foundation and turned her into a nervous wreck.

"Why?" I lowered my voice and closed the distance between myself and Ciarán. "So you can take advantage of it?" I hissed.

He shoved a finger in my face. "Don't question my motivations or my authority when it comes to the family business, Siobhán."

I swatted his finger out of my face. "I'll question whatever the hell I want, *Ciarán*. You may be the boss of this family, but you are *not* the boss of me."

He pressed his lips together.

I grunted in disgust. "Let's say, for the sake of argument, there's in-fighting. You going to join the party? Put yourself and your crew at risk? Start an all-out war with the Italians?"

"This city would be safer without the Mafia in it." He bit the words out. "My father should have finished the job he started. I'm not going to make the same mistake."

Panic rose. The instinct to escape, to get away from my family and this entire mess with Vesuvio made my muscles twitch to bolt out the door, head straight for Logan International Airport, and get on the next plane to Ireland. I'd never be safe if I was caught in the middle of a turf war between my family and the DeVitas.

I glanced over my shoulder. Mam daintily ate her salad, feigning indifference, but the slight shake of her fork told a different story. And Da... Poor Da. Once so strong, he poked at his salad like he wasn't sure what to do with it. The acid burn of worry for my parents and the frantic need to leave Terme di Boston stabbed at my stomach and made me nauseous. I closed my eyes and released a long, frustrated sigh.

"Look, Vahnie. I know you don't believe me, but you're safe. I'll protect you. I've got things in the works—" He clamped his mouth shut and examined me. "There are things in the works I can't tell you about, deals I've put in place to protect our family. You gotta trust me."

"Cosa Nostra..." Da's rough voice carried over the TV. Ciarán looked past me, and I glanced over my shoulder. Da stared at his salad. "That's what they call themselves. There's somethin' wrong with those Italians," he grumbled. "The devil in 'em."

Mam crossed herself.

"Paddy seen it. Conor and Liam too. Red eyes. Shot one of 'em point blank. Right in the chest. He kept on comin'. Eyes blazin' red. That's why ye need the head shot." He tapped his forehead with his index finger. "Right here, Paddy said. That's how he got that devil Moretti. Gotta get 'em with a head shot." He trailed off, and my stomach burned hearing Luca's name in Da's paranoid rant.

I took a deep breath. That's the way it was with Da now. No recognition. No participation in conversation. Then out of the blue, as if suddenly transported into the past, he'd ramble on about one thing or another before going back to staring at the TV and ignoring the present. It was painful to watch.

To make matters worse, this wasn't the first time I'd heard those ridiculous stories about the Italian Mafia in Boston. It had been a recurring theme growing up. Mam's family was devout Catholic and superstitious as hell. I don't know if Uncle Paddy believed the shit he was spouting, or if he was trying to make his rivals seem evil so his crew could be the righteous saviors of Boston while lining their pockets. Either way, he'd never let up with the stories of red-eyed monsters who couldn't be killed. They became a joke once Ciarán took over, but there were still a handful of superstitious Irish mobsters who thought Italian mafiosos were possessed by the devil.

I shook my head and pushed past Ciarán into the kitchen. "The only person I trust is myself," I said, returning to our conversation before Da's interruption. I opened the fridge and took out the leftover meatloaf and mayonnaise. "I don't want to be involved." I retrieved the bread from the pantry and two plates from the cabinet and rested my palms on the counter. "But I'm going to give you a piece of advice, because I do love you, and I don't want this to blow up in your face."

I looked into my cousin's eyes, intense wild-blue fire.

"Don't make the same mistakes as your da." Ciarán hadn't said outright that he'd made a deal with federal law enforcement, but his vague statements reeked like the rotting garbage. "Don't get in bed with people you shouldn't be sleeping with."

He pressed his lips together and gave me a short nod.

The back door opened, and my brother walked in. A couple inches shorter than Ciarán, Rory looked more Connelly than Shaughnessy with dark curly hair, a stout build, and a face covered in freckles.

"Look who decided to grace this house with his presence," I snapped and spread mayonnaise on the bread for my parents' cold meatloaf sandwiches.

"What's that smell?" he asked and wrinkled his pug nose. He reached for a piece of meatloaf, and I slammed the mayonnaise-laden knife down on the counter.

"That would be garbage. And it was a hell of a lot worse when I first got here. Do you know why?"

He grimaced, backed up empty-handed, and stood next to Ciarán.

"Because someone didn't show up yesterday. Because someone decided they had better things to do than take care of their parents. Because someone doesn't give a rat's ass that their sister has a full-time job and a life of her own!"

"Ahhh, fuck, Vahnie." He scrubbed a hand back and forth through his floppy curls. "I was working." He looked to Ciarán for support. Ciarán's eyes widened, and he shook his head. "I lost track of time. I'm sorry."

"Don't apologize to me." I picked up the knife and pointed it at the living room. "Apologize to them. They're the ones who had to live with rotting garbage for two days." I cut the sandwiches in half and placed them on the plates. "You need to get your priorities straight."

"Hey, now. I got my priorities straight. When Ciarán asks

me to do something, I do it. And he had me on a job last night."

My temper had been simmering since I'd arrived, but my brother's dismissal turned it up to a rolling boil. "Not if it interferes with your responsibilities to our family!"

I turned my death glare from Rory to Ciarán. He lifted his hands in an I'm-staying-out-of-this gesture.

"You kids get along in there," Mam called.

I let my head fall back and expelled an exasperated sigh. "I need to know I can rely on you to take care of them when I'm not around," I said to the ceiling before lifting my head back up. "This is a lot on all of us, and I can't do it alone. Not this."

"Christ, Vahnie. I just forgot."

"No," I said and walked to the pantry to get the potato chips. "No more excuses. There's always an excuse, and then I have to clean up the mess. But that's not going to fly for the next two weeks while I'm on vacation."

Rory and Ciarán exchanged guilty glances.

"Jesus, Mary, and Joseph, help me." I put a handful of chips onto each plate. "You forgot, didn't you?"

Ciarán looked at his feet, and Rory eyed the meatloaf on the counter.

I picked up the plates and looked between my cousin and my brother. "As I mentioned—multiple times—I am on vacation for the next two weeks. And as we've discussed—multiple times—your schedules, the chores, grocery lists, everything is on the fridge." I widened my eyes and craned my neck. "Got it?"

"We're on it, Vahnie," Ciarán said and stood straighter. "You don't have to worry about a thing. Just enjoy your vacation."

I shook my head and turned toward the living room. Not worry about a thing. Right. It'd be a goddamn miracle if this place was still standing after two weeks without me.

But I needed to remove myself from the volatile situation between my family and the DeVitas, which meant I needed two weeks off for interviews. I just hoped a new job outside of Boston would be enough; I didn't want to think about leaving my parents' fate in the hands of my idiot brother if I had to move back to Ireland.

MY HEELS CLICKED against the wooden steps up to the second floor of my duplex in Somerville. It wasn't the flashiest of places, and I could afford more, but it suited me. It was about as far away from Southie as I could get without being inconvenient. I shared the duplex with a lovely Irish couple who'd lived on the first floor for thirty years. The bakery next door was an added bonus. The owners came in super early each morning to bake donuts and cakes fresh for the day. It made the entire house smell like the inside of pastry bag.

The side door at the top of the steps opened into my living room. I hung my purse and jacket on the hook next to the door and kicked off my shoes, wiggling toes that had been cramped inside heels for sixteen hours.

My days were long when I visited my parents. Da's dementia was getting worse, and Mam's physical ability seemed to mirror his mental decline. And tonight, Da's outburst had Mam crossing herself and wringing her hands more than usual. I hated to see them like that, but I hated the thought of them alone and struggling even more. So I'd stayed later than usual after dinner to clean and sit with Mam until her nerves calmed and she went to bed.

I untucked my blouse and pulled it over my head as I walked down the hall to my bedroom.

Ciarán coming over hadn't helped either. He was as much a brother to me as Rory, but the last thing I needed, or wanted, were his opinions on the Italians or his vague hints about "deals." I loved my family, but I also loved my found family. I owed as much loyalty to Marco as I did the Shaughnessy name. Ciarán fishing for information and implying he had plans made my stomach clench with anxiety. It also pissed me off, and the confluence of emotions added to the bone-deep weariness that no amount of sleep ever seemed to cure.

I tugged on the chain of the art deco lamp that stood in the corner of my bedroom. A muted orange glow lit up my cozy retreat. I tossed my blouse on the bed, unzipped my skirt, and let it fall to the floor. I'd deal with it later, eager for the soft comfort of leggings, an oversized sweater, and fuzzy socks.

Something rustled in the living room. I paused, one foot into my leggings.

Nothing.

I pulled them on the rest of the way, unclasped the back of my bra, and threw it on the bed. I rifled through the bottom drawer of the dresser for my favorite sweater, pulled it over my head, and pushed up the sleeves. Heaven. I yanked pins out of my hair and dropped them onto my nightstand. I rubbed my scalp, finally free of its bindings, and tied my hair back in a short ponytail.

I spun around, thirsty for a martini to take the day's edge off, and slammed into a hard body.

I yelped. So much adrenaline poured into my system, my vision went dark. A thick hand clamped over my mouth and muffled my scream. I thrashed and swung my fists. Blood rushed in my ears.

My vision cleared as survival instincts kicked in, and my eyes went wide with disbelief. I stopped flailing mid-swing, and my arms fell to his biceps even as breath came short and frantic through my nostrils.

Luca Moretti wrapped an arm around my waist and held my body flush against his. I stared into the depths of his smoldering eyes and breathed in the unmistakable scent of his cologne.

Luca was alive. He was holding me in my bedroom.

Tears burned my eyes. I searched his face for an answer to my silent question—*is it really you?*

His hand covering my mouth relaxed, and he dragged his index finger across my parted lips, along the curve of my cheek, and down my neck. He lowered his lips to my ear.

"Did you miss me, Shamrock?"

Chapter Five

Siobhán

"Luca," I whispered and placed my palms flat against his chest, needing the resistance to prove he was there. I nudged him back enough to see his face, doubting reality. Dark eyes under long lashes looked down a straight nose. Plump lips pressed into a tight line. Unfamiliar facial hair covered the sharp angles of a familiar face, but it was him. It was Luca.

I hiccupped a sob, and my hand flew to my mouth before any more of my relief and confusion escaped. With shaking fingers, I brushed aside the hair falling across his cheek, afraid that if I touched him in earnest, reality would dissolve into imagination.

"I can't believe you're here. I thought you were—"

"You can't get rid of me that easily." His words held a bitter edge.

I blinked rapidly and frowned. "What? What are you talking about?"

His lips twisted into an angry sneer.

"Luca." I fisted my fingers in his shirt. "What happened? Where have you been?"

"It doesn't matter. I'm here now. And don't pretend like you don't know what happened. It's time for a reckoning, Shamrock." His low, gravelly voice was thick with menace. It made me dizzy with questions. You didn't do what Luca had done and live to tell the tale. Not in this world.

And that nickname...

All at once, the rose-colored glasses came off, and harsh reality replaced the dream I'd conjured of our star-crossed love story. Luca Moretti hated me, and there were no secret warm feelings behind his hatred.

His arms tightened around my waist, and I pushed at his chest. "What's wrong with you?" I looked past his shoulder into my living room. "And how the hell did you get in here?"

"Not important." He glanced at my fingers still gripping his shirt. He released me and peeled them apart, tossed my hands aside, and stepped back. I didn't know if I wanted to push him farther away or crawl back into his arms. "Put some shoes on," he ordered. "We're going for a ride." Luca's abrupt demand was as surreal as his unexpected arrival.

I followed him into the living room and crossed my arms. "Luca Moretti, back from the dead. You know, I haven't even had the time to process the fact you're alive much less standing in my living room, and you're ordering me around?" I scoffed. "I'm not going anywhere until you tell me what the hell happened and why you're here."

The vintage lamps cast shadows across his face. They highlighted the salt in his beard and gave his mahogany eyes an almost reddish glow. Trepidation added itself to the storm of my emotions, but then he donned one of his signature flashy smiles, and damn if my heart didn't beat faster even knowing it was fake. Luca was alive and so was our second chance.

"Fine." I grabbed my sneakers from the entryway and sat at the dining room table to put them on. "Where are we going?"

He looked at his watch. "I want to show you something."

I glanced over my shoulder at the microwave in the kitchen. "At one in the morning?"

"You sure have a lot of questions," he snapped.

"Can't imagine why."

"Come on," he barked, voice devoid of teasing or taunting and filled with impatience. He opened the door and stared at me from the landing. "Let's go."

I grabbed my purse. "There better be coffee wherever we're going."

I closed and locked the door behind me and dropped the keys in my purse. Luca's hand clamped around my biceps.

"Ow!" I winced and pulled away. At least, I tried to pull away. His grip tightened, and he dragged me down the stairs. "What the hell, Luca? You don't have to squeeze so hard. Jesus."

He spared me a fleeting glance but kept his punishing hold and pace all the way to the sidewalk.

"In fact..." I yanked my arm back. "What's with the manhandling? I can walk on my own."

He stopped and glared at me, examining my face as if looking for a lie, then resumed marching up the street.

I hurried after him, my curiosity getting the best of me. This behavior was odd even for him. He'd been an asshole ever since The Incident, but this was next level. I wanted a chance to talk to him, find out how on earth he was still alive. And if the opportunity presented itself, chew him out for what he'd done to Marco and Anna.

We turned into a cul-de-sac. A bright red Ferrari was parked in the shadows.

"Holy shit." I snorted. "You drive a 308 GTS Quattrovalv-ole?" His head snapped up, disbelief evident in his frown, but you don't spend as much time as I did in a chop shop as a kid without knowing a thing or two about Ferraris. "Why am I not surprised?"

He opened the passenger-side door. "Get in."

I glared at him as he climbed in on the driver's side. He ignored me and started the engine. It rumbled to life, loud and fierce, and he finally spared me a glance.

"What's wrong with you?" I snapped. "Here I am, all happy you're alive, and you're being an even bigger asshole than usual."

"What's wrong with *me*?"

He peeled out of the cul-de-sac onto the empty residential street, and the disgust in his voice reverberated over the scream of the tires. The force threw me back against my seat. I felt around for the seat belt, my trepidation growing with each rev of the engine.

"Happy I'm okay..." He scoffed and slapped me with another angry glare. His eyes flashed, wild and erratic beneath each passing streetlight. "Like you give a shit about me or the DeVitas."

"What the hell is that supposed to mean?"

"You lied to me." He slammed on the accelerator and took the next turn like we were on an F1 course, flinging me into the door. "Not once, but twice."

"We've been over this—taking speech lessons to get rid of my Southie accent is not lying."

"You told me you're Irish."

"I am Irish!"

"No... You're *South Boston* Irish." He said South Boston like it sickened him to have the words touch his tongue.

"Are we really doing this again?"

He ignored me.

I huffed at his dismissal. "I would love to hear how I lied to you a second time. I can only imagine the story you've concocted."

He sped onto US-1 heading north out of Boston, and I watched the empty stretch of highway emerge through the windshield.

"You didn't just lie to me. You lied to Marco. And I'll never forgive you for that. I'll never forgive you for being a Shaughnessy."

My stomach dropped through the seat and onto the concrete where the back tires of the Ferrari sped over it like roadkill. Luca knew? How? The only person I'd told was Marco, and he knew better than to tell anyone. Right?

My mind raced.

Being a Shaughnessy was the only thing worse to Luca than being South Boston Irish. He probably thought I'd kept it from Marco. Why would I keep something that huge from Marco unless...

Trepidation morphed into dread. I shifted in my seat to face him. "Luca," I said as calmly as I could even though adrenaline was tangling my insides into a knotted mess. "Listen to me. I never broke Marco's trust. Not once. I could never do that to him. He's family."

Luca shot me a hard look even as he eased off the accelerator, stomped on the clutch, and downshifted. The orange lights beneath the top deck of the Tobin Bridge reflected off his eyes and made them look like they burned inside his angry face.

Red eyes. Da's unhinged rambling shot into my mind. The old superstitions latched onto my stomach and squeezed.

"Don't talk to me about family. A Shaughnessy stole my father from me." His jaw shifted under the strain of his emotion. "And a Shaughnessy is going to pay the price."

The acid burning my stomach surged. An eye for an eye. The Cosa Nostra way.

Oh my God. Luca is going to kill me.

I pitched forward and threw up on the plastic floor mat.

"Cazzo!" He shouted over the growl of the engine. "Are you fucking kidding me?"

He downshifted again and pulled over onto the shoulder of the bridge. The car jerked to a stop, and I heaved again, splattering watery puke atop its vintage interior.

I wiped my mouth with the back of my sleeve. "What did you expect?" Tears poured down my face as reality sank in. "That I'd be okay with this? That I wouldn't freak out that you're going to kill me?"

"You should have thought about that before becoming a rat." He unbuckled his seat belt and sneered. "Your people may be trash and have no code, but they don't tolerate rats any more than Cosa Nostra."

"I'm not a rat," I shrieked through wild sobs.

"Right, and I'm not Italian." He opened his door, climbed out, and slammed it behind him.

My vision blurred behind an ocean of tears, but my mind became sharp as a knife, cutting through the shock and fear to save my life. I couldn't run from him. No way. He'd catch me. There was nowhere to hide on the bridge. I couldn't hurt him. Luca was huge, and I had no weapon. But I did have my cell phone. I rifled through my purse.

Luca flung the passenger door open, tore my purse from my hands, and tossed it onto the driver's seat.

Only one option left—beg.

"Luca." His name came out soft and wavered under the intensity of my terror. "You need to listen to me."

He unfastened my seat belt, clamped his hand around my arm, and hauled me out of the car, nearly pulling my shoulder out of its socket.

The bottom deck of the bridge was dark, and he'd stopped us between overhead lamps. The only other light came from the docks on the far side of the river. The cold night wind off the mouth of the Charles whipped through his hair, making it dance around the harsh lines of his shadowed face.

I grabbed the front of his shirt. "Listen to me, Luca. I'm not a rat. I never lied to you. Marco knows everything. I told him myself."

His jaw twitched, and his eyes flashed. But a glimmer of uncertainty broke through the rage there, and hope sparked in my chest.

"I moved to Ireland when I was eighteen. I want nothing to do with my family. The only reason I came back was to take care of my parents." My shoulders and voice shook with emotion. "I didn't know who Marco was when I started at Terme. I swear I didn't know!"

Luca's chest heaved; his hot, fast breath flared his nostrils.

I clung to his shirt and tugged him closer. "You have to believe me!"

"Nice story, Shamrock," he ground out. "And I'm supposed to believe you now? When all this time you conveniently left out certain details?" He grabbed me by my throat and lowered his face to mine. "Like the fact you're a Shaughnessy?" He squeezed. I released his shirt and clawed at his fingers, desperate for air. *"That your fucking uncle killed my father?"*

Luca's heated words mingled with the tears searing my cold cheeks. I didn't want to die, but the only weapon I had was the truth, a dull blade against the steel armor of Luca's hatred.

"I am so sorry, Luca," I wheezed from beneath his unrelenting grip, my vision darkening. "I have nothing to do with them. I promise."

He released my throat. I gasped for air, coughing and sputtering, dizzy from the influx of oxygen. He hauled me up onto the ledge behind the chain-link fence, the only barrier between us and the open night. "You know the punishment for being a rat," he shouted over the rushing wind.

We hadn't stopped because of the floor mat.

My knees buckled. He held me up with one hand wrapped around my biceps.

"Please! You have to believe me!" My voice and shoulders shook. "I would never betray Marco. He's more family to me than mine ever was!"

"Lies!" He screamed the word in my face. "All! Lies! You live a life of lies and expect me to believe this horseshit?"

He reached past me and yanked on the metal fence, sliding the section on its track. The locks holding the gate had been cut, and the severed and twisted metal clanked against the chain links. "You're just trying to save your ass," he growled.

My heart pounded against my ribs. All sound was drowned out by the blood rushing in my ears. I looked over my shoulder and searched the highway for a passing savior, but the bridge was empty except for a semi. It sped past us and out of view. No other headlights dotted the northbound deck of the Tobin Bridge.

Panic launched me from the ledge back onto the shoulder. I jerked and twisted my arm, trying to break free, but Luca's grip held fast. He pulled me into him, spun me around, and pressed my back against his front. He wrapped his arms around me, pinning them to my sides, and lifted me off the ground without so much as a grunt despite my squirming and kicking.

He stepped back up onto the ledge, and I stilled. The wind buffeted us from every direction. The dock lights glinted off the choppy water near the shore, but beneath us, there was nothing but a black abyss.

The wind gusted, an icy breath against my wet cheeks. I dug my fingers into Luca's thighs, desperate for purchase. If he opened his arms and pushed, I'd tumble into oblivion.

Fear consumed the last moments of my life. Fear and grief over the loss of my future to the great unknown. My head fell back and rested against Luca's shoulder. My eyes fluttered closed. I waited for my end, for the moment he threw me over the edge, and I fell into my watery grave.

Chapter Six

Luca

The wind had bite coming off the water, and at this height, it struck with force. It cooled the fiery rage burning my cheeks and whipped the loose strands of Siobhán's hair into a frenzied halo. Her pointed fingernails dug into the skin beneath my jeans. She clung to as much of the fabric as she could, pinching it between her bony fingers. She pressed her back into my front, trying to get as far away from the edge as possible, and rested her head on my shoulder.

The gaping maw of the Charles River was pitch compared to the bright lights of the docks. I stared into the void, and a gust of wind delivered the sweet scent of Siobhán's hair.

I sat on the bench behind the stripper pole at Vesuvio. Siobhán ground her ass into my lap. She leaned back and rested her head on my shoulder. I nosed her neck beneath her ear and drank in her luscious scent.

She shivered. I tightened my grip around her waist.

"Please, Luca," she whispered. "Please believe me."

A flicker of reflection off the docks pierced the blackness beneath us, and her pleas, barely audible above the wind, pierced the blackness of my heart. After everything the

Shaughnessys had taken from me, after all Siobhán's lies, part of me wanted to believe her.

I lowered my lips to her ear. "If it wasn't for your family, I'd still have a father."

She's a Shaughnessy, Luca.

"If it wasn't for you, I wouldn't have been tortured."

She lied to you. She lied to Marco.

"If it wasn't for you, Marco wouldn't have disowned me."

That's all that matters.

My pounding pulse and the wind whipping across the bridge muted her soft sobs. She shook in my arms.

I'd killed before. Without remorse. I'd kill again. Especially now that I was part of Vinnie's crew.

But doubt gnawed at my resolve, and sentiment stung my chest.

Another gust slammed into us. Her body jerked as if falling, and she wrapped her hands around the backs of my thighs, clinging to me—her captor, her killer—as if I'd save her from pitching over the edge.

Siobhán falling...

Her body disappearing into the void...

My arms tightened around her, shocking the hell out of me and making me furious.

I moved to release her, to avenge my father, but my body wouldn't obey. Instead, I lowered my nose to her hair. Peaches and cream and Siobhán. The sting in my chest transformed into a deep ache that reached my deadened heart.

I inched forward, closer to her end and my revenge.

Bright lights flashed in my periphery. Over my shoulder, two pairs of headlights sped toward us.

"Cazzo," I mumbled under my breath. I hadn't expected the bridge to be completely empty, but I also hadn't expected my plan would take this long.

I looked down. Siobhán's pale face was wet with tears, her eyes and lips squeezed shut.

My gaze snapped back to the bridge. One of the cars slowed as it passed. I blinked hard and another set of headlights appeared in the distance.

"Goddammit," I spat.

The headlights crept closer.

No good. Too many eyes.

"Cazzo!"

I lifted Siobhán by the waist and backed off the ledge and onto the shoulder. I set her down and moved to open the passenger-side door, but she fell to her hands and knees, collapsing under her own weight.

"Fucking hell." I hoisted her to her feet. She sagged, limp and shaking, and sobbed in my arms. I maneuvered her into the car and her feet away from the splattered vomit. What a fucking mess.

I slammed the door and got in on the driver's side. I reached across to fasten her seat belt. "You're really going to make this as difficult as possible, aren't you?"

She buried her face in her hands, and her shoulders shook through each pained sob.

For one unhinged moment, instinct grabbed me by the thread of empathy left in my heart and dragged me forward, urging me to wrap my arms around her and kiss her tears. Tell her I'd make everything okay.

No fucking way.

I forced myself back, pulled on my seat belt, and turned the key. The Ferrari roared to life. I revved the engine, threw it in gear, and peeled out onto the bridge. The tires shrieked with fury.

My foot pressed the accelerator. My hands strangled the wheel. What the *fuck* was I going to do now? I hadn't considered a Plan B. My torment was supposed to end with Siobhán

Connelly plummeting to her death from the bottom deck of the Tobin Bridge. Yet there we sat—me no closer to ending my vendetta, and her glassy-eyed and sniffling in my passenger seat.

We exited the bridge onto an empty stretch of toll road and headed north toward Saugus—Vinnie's territory and my house—even though I had no fucking clue what I was going to do when we got there.

I needed to calm the fuck down. Getting pulled over by some crooked cop would make the night infinitely worse. I eased off the gas.

She crossed her legs away from me, wrapped her arms around her middle, and rested her forehead against the window. We passed beneath a streetlight, and her reflection in the glass showed a face glistening with tears and smudged makeup. Only a fraction of her hair remained bound in her short ponytail. The rest fell to her shoulders or stuck behind her ear. A rumpled, distraught version of a woman always so put together.

I should have pushed her over the edge and been done with it.

But those fucking cars.

And the way she clung to me. The sweet smell of her hair. *Cazzo!*

Memories sped toward me, a bullet train with its horn blaring, and there was nothing I could do to get out of the way.

VESUVIO WAS busy for a Wednesday night. It was early enough that the downstairs bar was full. I figured I'd grab a drink and people watch before heading upstairs. Good decision on my part. I would've missed her had I come in the back.

Would've missed our one night together before everything went to shit.

I spotted her as soon as I walked through the door. But I would've spotted her a mile away in a sea of people. That's how it was with us. Like magnets.

Siobhán's hair was pulled back into a tiny ponytail. She didn't usually wear it that way. It exposed the full length of her creamy neck and made her stunning features even more arresting. She had an angular face, heart-shaped with a pointed chin and high cheekbones. A porcelain canvas for pale blue eyes, a button nose, and ruby lips. Not too plump and not too thin, she always painted them red, and when she tossed her head back in laughter, they parted to reveal a bright white smile with a front tooth just crooked enough to add character. Her eyes sparkled when she smiled, and the bar lights danced across the field of blue like moonlight over crystal water.

Her style was singular. I'd never seen her outside of Terme di Boston, and apparently her flair for retro fashion didn't stop at the resort's doors. She wore a pair of '50s-era high-waisted jeans above vintage kittens and a cropped long-sleeved sweater that accentuated her lithe frame. Christ, she was gorgeous. A modern-day Grace Kelly but with a devilish side that belied her angelic features. And with her tight little body and the exposed skin of her collarbone and neck, my fangs ached and my dick twitched, desperate to sink into every inch of Siobhán Connelly.

We were finally going on a date. The main event was scheduled for Saturday night. After a year of flirting and lunches, I was ready to make my move, and as luck would have it, I might not have to wait until Saturday.

She walked toward me, chatting with two other women I wouldn't be able to pick out of a lineup if I tried. Siobhán consumed every ounce of my attention, and as if drawn to me by the uncanny connection tying us together, her focus shifted from her friends to me.

Our eyes met. Hers grew wide and sparkled with delight. I smiled, so broad and genuine it hurt my cheeks. She stuck the tip of her tongue between her teeth and scrunched her nose. God, I was one lucky fucker.

She grabbed her friend's arm and mumbled something into her ear. Her friends glanced at me furtively, said their goodbyes, and walked past me to the door.

I met her where she waited with one hip cocked and a smirk on her red lips. "It must be my lucky day," I said. "Buonasera, Siobhán."

"Hello, Luca. Did you just get in?"

"This morning. I need a couple drinks if I'm going to power through the jet lag. Care to join me?"

She laughed, and the sound sparkled as brightly as her eyes. "The bartender just announced last call. Good luck finding a place that's open on a weekday in this town."

I placed my arm around her shoulders and spun her in the opposite direction. "This place doesn't close as early as you think." I whispered into her ear and ushered her toward the back of the club.

Her brows pinched in confusion, and I winked.

Matteo stood in front of the roped-off spiral staircase. The upstairs patrons knew to come in the back, but Marco kept a man inside to make sure no one wandered where they shouldn't.

"Ciao, Luca! Come va?"

"Ciao, Matteo. Bene, bene." I clasped his hand and kissed his cheeks. "Just here for a couple drinks."

He eyed Siobhán.

"It's okay. She works for Marco, and she's with me."

He flashed a smile and gave me a nod. "È bello vederti,

fratello." He unclasped the rope and stepped to the side. "Prendiamo qualcosa da bere mentre sei in città? Okay?"

"Assolutamente," I said and slapped him on the shoulder. I glanced at Siobhán. "After you."

She eyed me warily but started up the metal stairs, giving me a view I did not mind.

She stopped when she reached the top and took in Vesuvio's second floor with a mixture of surprise and apprehension. "What is this place?"

I stepped up the remaining stairs and stood next to her. Despite the action on the first floor, Marco's illegal gaming club was unusually slow. Only one card table worked in earnest, and a couple of guys watched sports highlights at the bar. None of the girls were on the pole.

"It's..." I rocked my head from side to side. "An after-hours club. Members only."

She arched one of her perfectly sculpted eyebrows.

I shrugged a shoulder. "You're the GM of my zio's flagship resort." I leveled her with a serious look. "He trusts you. I trust you."

"Gotcha." She made a zipping gesture across her lips. "The NDA I signed when I started working at Terme was epic."

I laughed. "No doubt."

"Don't worry. I won't say anything." Her lips twitched around her declaration, and the wariness reached her eyes. They darted around the room as if she'd walked into a lion's den and was looking for an escape. "Besides, Marco has been nothing but good to me."

"Come on," I said and pressed her forward. "Let's get a drink."

We sat at the bar, and her tension eased as we talked about Marco, Terme, and the resorts I operated in Italy. We drank. We laughed. Conversation came natural and easy, and after a year of thirty-minute lunches, coffee breaks, and quick how-are-yous, we didn't stop until we'd drained two cocktails a piece and were the only ones left in the club. I was wide awake with jet lag, and Siobhán didn't appear to be flagging at all.

"You want another one?" I asked.

"Absolutely," she said with a sultry turn to her voice.

I gave her a once over. "I don't know where you put it."

She laughed and swatted my arm. "I'm Irish. I have a reputation to uphold." She stuck the tip of her tongue between her front teeth, and fuck if I didn't want to kiss that mischievous expression right off her face.

"Enzo."

"Yeah, boss?"

"Grab us another round and then you can go for the night. I'll lock up."

His eyes darted to Siobhán and back to me. "You sure?"

"I've got it."

"All right," he said. He pulled the bar rag off his shoulder and pointed it at me. "Don't fuck up my bar."

I chuckled and held up my hands. "We're going to play some pool, then we're outta here." I looked at Siobhán and raised an eyebrow.

"Yes!" She hopped off the barstool, made a beeline for the pool table, and started racking the balls. I stared after her in awe.

She's perfect.

Enzo poured a dirty martini and raised an eyebrow, the slow movement full of judgment.

"Relax," I said and sipped my scotch.

He washed out the shaker, put it in the drying rack, and grabbed his keys off the back counter. "Later, Luca." He walked around the end of the bar toward the break room.

Siobhán started chalking a cue. I handed her the martini, and we clinked glasses. "Salute."

"Sláinte," she replied with a wicked grin and sipped her drink, never breaking eye contact.

I set my scotch on one of the high tops. "You want to break?" I rolled up my shirtsleeves.

She shrugged. "I'll do my best."

She placed the cue ball on the felt, lined up her shot, and without releasing me from her mischievous stare, broke.

The balls scattered across the table in a perfect break. Siobhán walked around the end of the table and lined up her next shot. "Stripes," she declared and sank the number fourteen in the far corner pocket.

I laughed. Hard. "All right, all right. Consider me schooled!"

"Oh, the schooling's just begun."

Absolutely perfect.

She lined up her second shot, and with a lift of her hip to get the right angle, sank the number nine in the near-side corner pocket. She spun her head to look at me, tongue between her teeth and nose scrunched in that adorable expression of hers that drove me wild.

I shook my head and chuckled. "There has to be a story here."

"Not a very thrilling one," she said dryly. "I worked my way through college at a pub in Cork." She stood across the table from me on a diagonal, holding the cue upright in front of her, and examined the felt playing field. "Number ten. Side pocket." With swift efficiency, she sank the ball.

She walked over to where she'd left her martini waiting on the high top next to my scotch, leaned against one of the stools, and sipped it delicately. "Depending on the shift, I had a lot of time on my hands." She shrugged. "Started playing with some of the regulars. They gave me tips." She placed her drink back on the table. "I got better"—her wicked smile returned—"and then I was the one giving tips."

I snorted. "I have no doubt."

She stepped up to the pool table and frowned. "Hmm." She shifted her weight and tilted her head. "Thirteen. Near corner."

She bent over the table, and my body reacted on impulse. I stepped behind her on the opposite side of her cue, placed a hand on the side rail, and leaned in.

She sucked in a quick breath and looked over her shoulder. "What are you doing?"

"Trying to learn from a master. I want to see how you line up a shot."

"You wouldn't be trying to distract me, would you?"

I wiped the smile from my face and covered my heart with my free hand. "Never. That would be cheating."

The corner of her mouth lifted in a wry smirk, and she turned back to her shot. I lowered my hand from my heart to her hip and gave it a gentle squeeze. The ball ricocheted off the far rail and rolled toward the near-corner pocket. It tapped the edge and bounced slightly to the left before coming to a stop along the rail on the short end of the table.

She spun around and glared at me even as her lips twisted, fighting a smile.

"My turn," I said.

She threw her head back, and her throaty laugh filled the club.

I scoped out my shot and tried to focus on sinking the ball. Not easy with a semi-hard from standing behind Siobhán with her ass in the air.

"Why don't we make this interesting," she said and brought the martini glass to her lips. Her eyes glinted over the rim.

"Yeah?" I refocused my attention and sank the number two. I walked around to the far side of the table and lined up my next shot.

"Loser has to give the winner a lap dance."

I scratched; the cue slipped out from between my fingers and brushed the side of the cue ball.

She chuckled, and a wicked smile danced across her sinfully red lips. She looked past me. "I felt inspired."

I followed her gaze to the stripper pole on the far side of the room. I turned back to face her, grinning at the challenge. "Oh, you're on."

"I've never seen a man your size give a lap dance. You sure you want to take this bet?"

I strode back to her side of the table, and she eyed me like a rival predator tracking an alpha it knows it can't defeat. I'd seen the way she looked at me over the past year. The heat in her blue eyes when I smiled. The hope that sparked in them when I finally asked her to dinner. The way her lips parted whenever we touched. We'd teetered on the precipice of inevitable since the moment our eyes first locked across the Terme di Boston lobby. Anticipation had built into a frenzy, and with only a couple days until our date, any motion was bound to send us tumbling over the edge.

I closed the distance, not stopping until I hovered over her. A few strands of hair fell out of place and caught in her lashes. I swept them away, more slowly than necessary, and her lips parted at the brush of my fingertips across her forehead. "I'm feeling lucky tonight," I said and lowered my head enough for her to feel every degree my blood heated from our closeness. "I have my little shamrock, don't I?"

She sucked in a breath. Pink tinted her porcelain cheeks, and her heart sped up, its beat thumping over the sudden rush of her blood. Her chest rose and fell more swiftly. So did mine.

"Want another drink?" I asked and backed away, needing to douse the flames with another round of scotch.

"Please," she croaked and cleared her throat. "Yes, please."

"It won't be as good as Enzo's."

I mixed a quick dirty martini while Siobhán examined the table, then made my way back to our felt-topped battlefield.

The game slowed, each of us taking our time to consider options, line up shots, and stand too close to the other. Or right in their line of sight.

Siobhán sank the thirteen; only the eight ball remained. An easy shot for someone with her skill. She'd have to bank it off the rail, but after what I'd seen, there was no way she'd miss.

"You better pick out some music," she teased. "It's hard giving a lap dance without a good beat."

I groaned and downed the rest of my scotch, swallowing my pride in preparation for... Fuck, I didn't even want to think about how ridiculous I'd feel, much less look.

She pulled back her cue and took the shot. The ball kissed the rail, rolled to a stop just short of the pocket, and hovered at the lip. Time froze waiting for the ball to drop over the edge but slammed back to full speed when it didn't.

"Nooo!" Siobhán squealed.

"No fucking way," I whispered.

"Goddammit!"

"Ha ha! Yes!"

She slammed her pool cue into the rack. "Winning on an eight-ball scratch isn't something to be proud of."

"A win is a win, baby." I waggled my eyebrows above my best smarmy smile.

She rolled her eyes.

"And a bet is a bet." I crossed the club to the bar and turned on the satellite radio, selecting the station the girls used on slow gambling nights. "There." The sultry beat of a deep bassline filled the club. "Oh!" I dimmed the lights. "Perfetto."

She glared at me.

I laid the self-satisfaction on thick with an easy stride to the leather bench behind the raised platform with the stripper pole. I eased myself onto the plush seat, leaned back, and threw an ankle over my knee. I reached into my left breast pocket and pulled out my cigar case.

Siobhán walked across the club, lips pressed together, martini glass dangling from red-tipped fingers. I cut, lit, and puffed a cigar to life. She stopped next to one of the booths to the right of the platform and cocked a hip.

"Whenever you're ready." I sipped my scotch and raised my eyebrows over the rim.

She plucked the olive out of the glass, shot back the rest of her drink, and set the empty glass on the table. As if easing into a hot bath, she took slow, steady steps in time with the music until she stood on the platform in front of me. She leaned back against the pole and brought the toothpick to her parted lips, wrapping them around the olive. Her eyes danced with mischief as she eased it off the toothpick and into her mouth.

My dick throbbed with a sudden influx of blood. I pulled hard on my cigar, hoping the sting would temper my raging desire. I refused to let myself get hard from being teased with a fucking olive.

She tossed the toothpick and swayed her hips like a pendulum, each movement a mesmerizing arc of seduction. She dragged her hands up her body to her hair and pulled out her ponytail. Her short blonde tresses fell around her face in a golden halo. She gripped the pole behind her and slid down its length, never stopping the hypnotic rhythm of her hips.

I wanted to claim Siobhán like a goddamn animal—grab her by the hair, thrust my dick between those swaying hips, and sink my fangs into her neck. Unsettled, I shot back the rest of my scotch and hoped it would stop my fangs from descending.

She slinked back up the pole and moved toward me, lips

parted beneath hooded eyes. I removed my ankle from my knee and spread my legs. She stepped between them.

I brought the cigar to my lips, an anchor in the storm of Siobhán. Smoke swirled between us. It danced in the low light of the club and did nothing to calm my desire and everything to make the scene more sexy.

She shoved her fingers into her hair, tilted her face to the side, and bit her bottom lip while performing the same move she'd performed against the pole—swinging her hips and slowly sinking between my legs before rising back up to standing.

"Lap dance rules apply, Mr. Moretti," she said, low and husky. "Hands to yourself."

I lifted both hands in surrender, cigar between my teeth.

She smirked and placed her hands at the top of her hips, circling them. She turned with each little arc until her ass was in front of my face.

I braced myself, palms flat on either side of me, wishing I had something to hold onto.

She glanced over her shoulder. Her red lips parted, and her hands twisted in her hair as though in the throes of ecstasy.

My dick strained against my slacks, fully erect and aching for release. Temptation plagued me, the urge to impale her with every rock-hard inch of my desire testing my restraint. But I held on, determined to let her continue her game of seduction, let her know who was in control.

The beat picked up, and the mood shifted with it. The air crackled with urgency like we'd transitioned from foreplay to the main event. Siobhán moved faster, and her hands slid down her legs to rest on her thighs. She braced herself there and, with a flip of her hair, thrust her ass back and down until it hovered above my lap.

With each circle of her hips, her ass brushed my erection. And just when I thought I couldn't take anymore, she braced herself on my thighs, dug her fingertips into my quads, and lowered herself down.

I grunted, a stilted sound from trying to cage the animalistic growl percolating in my lungs.

Her head snapped around, eyes wide and smile knowing, and ground her ass into my hard-on. The friction was everything I needed and nowhere near enough.

"Fucking tease," I growled.

My fingers twitched around the cigar. I brought it to my lips, not wanting her to know how close I was to losing control.

She laughed and pressed herself into me, wiggling her ass as she did it. "A bet is a bet," she purred and leaned back until her head rested on my shoulder. She tilted her face enough to see me, putting her lips dangerously close to mine. "Just holding up my end of the bargain."

Siobhán filled my senses. The weight of her body. The movement of her hips. Her smell. I buried my face in her hair and nuzzled her neck beneath her ear. The sweet, fruity scent of her shampoo cut through the cigar smoke and enveloped my world.

"You missed on purpose, didn't you?" The question came out hoarse, barely above a whisper.

She replied with a husky chuckle that reverberated through her back and into my chest. "You did call me your little shamrock." She slid down my front until her biceps rested on my thighs, then twisted around and knelt between my knees. "Looks like your good luck charm worked."

Holy fuck.

She unbuckled my belt with slow, methodical movements.

I sucked down my cigar, needing to do something with my hands and calm the heat racing through my blood.

She unbuttoned my slacks.

I set the cigar in the ashtray and pressed my palms into the bench on either side of my thighs.

She pulled on the zipper, achingly slow, and raised her eyes. They burned with seduction and desire. With a final tug, the minx lifted the corner of her mouth in a devious smile.

She reached into my boxers and pulled out my dick. It jerked at her touch and became impossibly harder. She wrapped her delicate fingers around its base and took in my size. Her pupils dilated with genuine surprise, and she licked her lips. She met my eyes and held them—held me—and ran her tongue up my hard length from its base to where pre-cum leaked from the tip.

My hands fisted in a desperate attempt to maintain control, but when she wrapped those ruby red lips around the head of my dick, I groaned, deep and guttural. My body tensed and relaxed with the sweet release of having Siobhán Connelly worshiping my body as surely as I worshipped her.

I CRACKED THE WINDOW, blinked my eyes, and rolled my shoulders, pissed at myself for letting the image of that Shaughnessy rat get the better of me. That happened a lifetime ago before I knew the truth—before I knew about her lies.

I exited the highway and stopped at the light at the end of the off-ramp. Siobhán sniffled and wiped her nose with the back of her sleeve. She sat up straight, but her puffy eyes and smudged mascara destroyed the perfect picture she painted for the world.

My anger resurfaced at what might have been had she not turned out to be a two-faced rat. I strangled the steering wheel, not sure what was pissing me off more—Siobhán's bullshit or the memories that had tormented me for over a year.

The light turned green. I stepped on the gas.

Wide lawns, white picket fences, Cape Cod houses—the suburban sprawl north of Boston all looked the same. The only differences between neighborhoods were the upkeep of the lots, the size of the houses, and the kinds of cars parked in the driveways. Most of Saugus housed working-class families —a lot of Italians—who'd escaped the city to find safe, affordable housing. But there were pockets of affluence, and that's where we were headed.

I knew better than to speed on Walnut at that time of night, but it made the short drive off the highway slower than I wanted. I turned onto the narrow, wooded road on the outskirts of the Lynn Woods just south of Walden, and the ache of nostalgia crept up my throat. The familiar pang of loss that hit every time my mind wandered to my father reared its unwelcome head between the highway and my house. *His* house.

The two-story colonial at the end of a cul-de-sac overlooked Birch Pond. It was set back from the others, providing an unobstructed view of the water from every south-facing bedroom. I'd grown up in that house, at least for the first six years of my life. My father purchased it for my mother after he found out she was pregnant. He'd wanted to make it our family home. "Your mother always wanted a quiet house on the water," he used to say, his eyes distant and expression pained.

Fate had other plans for us Morettis.

I eased the Ferrari up the driveway and into my garage, the door open and waiting for what was supposed to have been my victorious homecoming. Instead, I turned off the car and stared out the windshield in silence, an unwelcome silence interrupted by the pops and clicks of a settling engine and Siobhán's fingernail tapping against her teeth.

What the fuck was I going to do now?

Chapter Seven

Siobhán

Lights sped by in streaks through my tears. I probably should have paid attention to where we were going, but all I could think about was the wind whipping off the Charles River, the sensation of falling, and how my worst nightmare had come true. I was going to die from the exact thing I'd spent my life trying to escape—my mobbed-up South Boston Irish family. And to twist the knife, I'd once seen myself in a future with the man who was going to kill me.

We pulled up a driveway into a garage. Luca turned off the Ferrari, and we sat in strained silence. I stared out the passenger window at everything and nothing and clicked my fingernail against my teeth in time with my heartbeat, a nervous habit I'd developed in the hospital as a teen. My heart rate climbed with each second he didn't move, each drawn-out breath bringing me closer to my end.

"Stop that," he barked.

I dropped my hand from my mouth and faced him. He pressed his lips into an angry line. Tears welled in my eyes at the hatred in his, and that seemed to piss him off even more.

My stomach cramped. The acid made me nauseous and

ate at my remaining composure. I wrapped my arms around my middle and folded forward, trying to ease the burn.

Within moments, Luca was out of the car and outside my door. "Out." He grabbed me by the arm and pulled. "Don't step in that shit."

I unbuckled my seat belt and climbed out, careful to avoid the puke-splattered mat.

My legs wobbled, but he held me upright. He moved me to the side and leaned forward, inspecting the damage my stomach had done to his interior.

"Goddammit!" He put his face within an inch of mine. "Don't. Move," he ordered through clenched teeth and released me.

My poor arm had taken a lot of abuse. I rubbed the soreness, certain he'd left bruises. I glanced over my shoulder at the open garage door, ready to bolt, but my legs shook so badly, I was sure my knees would give out before I made it to the driveway.

Luca extracted the floor mat like it was covered in hazardous waste. He looked around the garage and finally lifted his chin to the big city trash can. "Open that for me."

"Don't be so dramatic." The quiet words were derisive despite my terror and stomach pain. "It's rubber. Just hose it off."

"I'd rather buy a new one that isn't tainted."

"Those mats are original." My voice rose with irritation. "Where are you going to find a floor mat for a 308 GTS from 1985?"

"Fucking open it!"

"Fine!" I opened the stupid trash can. "What a waste."

He tossed the mat in and wiped his hands on his pants. He grabbed me—luckily by the other arm this time—and yanked me toward the door at the back of the garage.

"Jesus!" I stumbled to keep up, and anger pierced the all-encompassing shroud of terror. "I get it. You hate me. You're going to kill me. Message received. Is the manhandling really necessary?"

He shoved me through the door. "Take your shoes off," he ordered above the rumble of the automatic garage door. He flicked the lights on, shut the door behind him, and brushed past me. In his socks.

The entryway opened into a spacious kitchen sparkling with bright white tiles, pale blue accents, and stainless steel. It looked like something out of a magazine or a showroom, not someone's actual house. He tossed his keys on the stone countertop of the island and his jacket over the back of a black leather barstool.

To the left of the island, an eight-seat dining table with a polished natural finish stood before a wall of French doors obscured by vertical blinds. On the right, an archway led into the living room. It was dark, but the outlines of a sectional, a coffee table, and a big-screen TV were unmistakable. A hallway and a set of stairs between the kitchen and the living room led upward into darkness.

Luca went to the refrigerator and pulled out a beer.

"Now what?" I asked, irritated but shaky. "You take me into the woods and chop me into pieces?"

He pulled a lighter from his pocket and used it to pop the cap off the bottle. "Shoes." He swigged the beer and raised his eyebrows. "Off."

I stepped on the heels of my sneakers and pried my shoes off one by one. "You didn't answer my question," I grumbled and stepped into the kitchen.

He pursed his lips and examined me.

I examined him right back. I hadn't noticed how different he looked. Not through all the shock—him being in my house, him being alive, him trying to throw me off the Tobin Bridge. But now, under the bright kitchen lights, Luca looked different than I remembered. Harsher. With thicker muscles and a close-cropped beard. He'd always been clean-shaven. And when he walked toward me, there was a hitch in his step, a slight limp I'd never noticed before.

He set his beer on the island. "You'll stay here and help settle my vendetta."

"What?" I shrieked. "Stay here?" I made a hysterical noise somewhere between a sob and a laugh. "Are you fucking kidding me?"

He shrugged, an easy, callous gesture, and drank his beer.

I stared at him in horror, unable to believe he would be so cruel as to prolong this torture. And be so nonchalant about it. This had to be some kind of sick joke.

"Good night, Siobhán," I said, laying on a thick British accent. "Sleep well. I'll most likely kill you in the morning." I shook my head, dislodging fresh tears. "This is beyond fucked up."

My stomach boiled with acid. If Luca didn't end me soon, my stomach would do the job for him. I wrapped my arms around myself. "What the hell did I do to you, Luca? Huh? Exist? Is that my crime?"

"Don't play around, Siobhán." He pointed his finger and his beer at my face. "You're a liar and a rat. Don't act like you don't know what happens to rats."

"I'm not a fucking rat!" I swatted at his finger, and he pulled his beer back, the angry sneer on his face blurred through fresh tears. "And I never lied to you. Ever."

"You're lying right now," he growled, low and hot.

"What are you talking about?"

"That fake fucking accent. One big lie."

"It's not a lie! I left Southie when I was eighteen. I got the hell out of there and *never* looked back. I worked my ass off to build a new life, one without any ties to my family—not even my accent." I stepped closer, reaching for him, wanting to recreate the connection we once had, wanting him to feel the truth of my words. He didn't pull away even as I clutched his forearm. "It's me, Luca. It's Siobhán. The same woman you've always known. The one you met for lunches. The one who flirted with you across the lobby. The one you wanted to date—"

He slammed the bottle on the island, and I jerked my hand away. Beer frothed and spilled over the edge as explosive and violent as the fury that teemed behind the flecks of red shining in his dark eyes.

My adrenaline spiked, and I stumbled back. I slammed my eyes shut and tried to slow my frantic breath. Fear was driving my imagination wild. When I reopened them, my vision cleared. Luca's eyes were their normal coffee brown.

He stepped forward, closing the space I'd opened. "You led me on," he said, accusatory but pained as though he'd dragged the words from a festering wound. But I had wounds of my own, wounds he'd created. Ones that spewed hot lava any time he picked at the scabs.

"Wait a minute." I held up my hands and gave my head a slight shake. "Let me get this straight—*I* led *you* on?"

"You told me you were from Ireland. The first time we had lunch. 'I'm from Cork,'" he said with an affected accent. "Trying to pass yourself off as some refined Irish woman when you're just a fucking Shaughnessy from Southie."

My blood boiled. Anger overtook fear, and I couldn't contain the explosion. "You are such an asshole, Luca Moretti! *You*"—I stabbed a nail into the brick wall of his chest—"*You* were the one who asked me out. *You* were the one who was all too happy to get a *fucking blowjob* and then suck face with some bimbo the night before our date. *You* did that. Not me. So you tell me who led who on." My voice rose with every word, my breath coming in short, heated bursts.

He clenched his teeth. "I told you. That wasn't what it looked like."

"Bullshit. It was exactly what it looked like."

"Believe what you want, but it doesn't matter. It doesn't change the fact you're a liar." He swigged his beer.

"Argh!" I shrieked and punched him in the chest. "I am *not* a liar, and even if I was, that sure as hell isn't a reason to kill me!"

"Isn't it?" He cocked his head. "Why not tell me you were from Southie? Why not use your real accent?" He set his beer down and inched forward until I had to look up to meet his eyes. "Unless you were trying to hide something. Because you're a rat." He overenunciated the *T*, and his eyes narrowed. "Fact is, you didn't want us to know you were a Shaughnessy, did you? Couldn't keep feeding information to your cousin if Marco got rid of you." He leaned closer. I leaned back, but he grabbed the back of my neck and yanked me into him. "I've seen Agent Johnson hanging around Terme. Ciarán's in bed with the feds, isn't he?"

I shook my head. "What?"

"Just like his father. Trying to take us down."

"You're insane," I whispered.

"Am I?" He tightened his grip, and I winced. "I had a lot of time to think in Vinnie's warehouse. A lot of time to reflect on how I ended up there, how Marco found out." He pressed his lips together, and his nostrils flared.

Whatever happened in that warehouse, it wasn't good. Terror claimed the front seat of the emotional rollercoaster I'd been riding all night.

"If you aren't involved with your family, if you aren't a rat, how did you know it wasn't a Shaughnessy raid? How did you know your family wasn't involved?"

"I already explained that to Marco. I—"

"Marco can't see what's in front of his own face. Not

when he doesn't want to believe it and not when it might drag him into a war. You knew that. You used that."

"No. That's not true. None of that's true. And not to put too fine a point on it, but that's exactly what you did. To your own family. Hypocrite." I spewed the venomous truth, and the muscle in Luca's clenched jaw twitched. "But unlike you, I don't want a war. I don't want to see the people I love hurt. I tried to protect Marco. I told him it wasn't a Shaughnessy raid so he wouldn't retaliate."

Luca seethed, and his fingertips dug into my neck, cutting off my air. "Nice story, Shamrock." He spit the nickname, tossed me away, and backed up to retrieve his beer. He drained half of it.

"I remember when you called me that and it wasn't a slur," I mumbled, rubbing my neck, and the bitterness in my heart spread to engulf my entire body. "You really do hate me, don't you?"

He pointed at me with his beer. "You stole Marco from me. You destroyed my chance at vengeance. You sentenced me to that—that hellhole."

"No! You did that all to yourself, Luca! Don't try and blame me for your mistakes. *Again*."

He walked back to where I stood, clamped a hand around the front of my neck, and squeezed hard enough to make me scratch at his fingers. "I want blood. Shaughnessy blood. And because of your lies and because you're a rat, I want that Shaughnessy blood to be yours."

My mouth fell open, but nothing came out. There was nothing left to say. He'd channeled all his hatred and resentment into a single focal point—me. And in the face of abject terror, in the face of knowing I was going to die, the shock of losing Luca—the hurt, the confusion, the anger—swept through me for the third time in my life. If I hadn't known better, I'd have thought that was how he intended to kill me.

THE PALM-LEAF CEILING fan spun in slow circles. It flickered the shadows cast by the moonlight. I stared wide-eyed at the spinning blades from beneath the bedsheets, emotionally and physically exhausted, but unable to sleep.

Luca hadn't said another word to me after declaring that he wanted to take payment for his father's blood with mine. Just finished his beer without so much as a glance in my direction.

He locked my purse in the cabinet beneath the TV in the living room, then dragged me upstairs by my abused arm, shoved me in a room, and locked the door.

I immediately checked the window. It slid open with ease, but there was no way to climb down. Just sheer brick all the way to the ground. I screamed at the top of my lungs—"Help! He's going to kill me! He's a fucking psycho! Help! Please!"— hoping a neighbor might hear and call the cops. Instead, Luca stormed into the room, yanked me back with so much force I thought he dislocated my shoulder, and slammed the window.

His eyes had burned with fiery menace. "One more time and we're going out on Birch Pond tonight and ending this. Drowning with chains around your ankles is just as effective as breaking your neck from hitting the Charles."

The threat shocked me into silence.

He tossed me onto the bed. "I'm a light sleeper. Don't try anything." He walked out, leaving the door ajar.

I followed the fan's rhythmic whir with my breath, trying to slow my heart rate. All I could do was close my eyes and attempt sleep and hope an escape opportunity presented itself in the morning. Maybe with a clear head and calm body, I'd find a way out.

But closing my eyes introduced a fresh source of torture— images of a packed Vesuvio. I rolled away from the door, squeezed my eyes shut, and shoved my face into the pillow, trying to dislodge the memory of when everything fell apart.

I'd wanted a quiet night out with the girls—one free drink after dinner enjoyed in a corner booth instead of slammed against the bar before heading home. I had a date the next night and didn't want to be hungover, tired, or both. Luca was finally taking me out, and after our unexpected late-night tryst Wednesday, I was more than ready for whatever came next.

We headed toward the back of the club, navigating past Friday night corporate partiers, sweaty clubbers, and college coeds. It was darker in the back, but there were fewer people, and I spotted a single empty booth along the wall. Score.

I met my friends' eyes and lifted my drink. One of them tipped her chin at the corner booth where a couple was partaking in PDA best left in private.

I twisted my face in disgust. "Gross," I shouted over the music.

She nodded and rolled her eyes. But there was only one empty booth left, so we'd have to deal with inappropriate neighbors.

We made a beeline for our unlikely prize when my attention snagged on the corner booth, pulled back to the scene by some unknown force. I stared at the shadowed couple. In particular, the silhouette of the man's head and shoulders. His hair blocked his profile, but something about the way it fell just past his chin...

He came up for air, dislodging himself from the woman's neck. He tucked his hair behind his ear, revealing a devastatingly handsome jawline, a perfectly straight nose, and full, pouty lips I'd recognize from a mile away.

Luca.

My stomach lurched, and my hands started to shake. I squeezed the stem of my martini glass like it was his neck. My feet propelled me forward, controlled by heartbreak-fueled ire.

"You fucking asshole," I said, loud enough to hear over the

music, but calmly enough that anyone within earshot knew I was deathly serious.

His head snapped up, and his eyes went wide. "Siobhán," he said, and his throat bobbed through a swallow.

The woman next to him smiled and straightened a few loose strands of hair.

I lost it. "You fucking asshole!" I screamed and tossed the martini in his face.

The woman squealed and scooted away.

He wiped the drink out of his eyes and examined his martini-soaked shirt. "What the fuck?" He climbed out of the booth and shook vodka and olive juice from his hands.

A spiderweb of cracks formed at the center of my heart. My temper rose as the fissures spread and shattered the bruised muscle into pieces. I strangled the empty glass, holding onto the stem like it was a club and wanting to hit him with it and hurt him as badly as he'd hurt me.

He held up his hands, and his face softened with concern and regret. He stepped forward and lowered his voice. "Listen, Siobhán, this is not what it looks like."

"Not what it looks like? Ah you fahcking kidding me?" My cheeks burned. I was embarrassed, enraged, and utterly devastated, and my remaining control evaporated with his lame excuse. "You were attached to her neck like a leech. The night before ah date. Two days after—"

I hiccupped a sob, my throat hot with emotion at the thought of what I'd done. What I thought we'd shared. I clamped my lips shut and bit the inside of my cheek. I'd be damned if I let him see me cry.

He narrowed his eyes and studied me like he'd never seen me before. He closed the gap between us, and his eyes burned with an anger that seemed to spark in the low light of the club. "What happened to your accent?"

"What?" I snapped.

He loomed over me, dark and menacing. "What happened to your accent, Siobhán?" The question was clipped and heated, and his face twisted with anger and hurt as palpable as mine. "You lied to me."

I rolled onto my back, cheeks wet from reliving that horrible night for the millionth time. How had it all gone so wrong? How had I believed that he was any different from every other macho, womanizing man in my life? How had I forgotten what that night had done to him? How his pain—as deep and as real as mine—had transformed something more than affection into disdain and distrust? And how had I forgotten what that night had done to me?

I closed my eyes. Silent tears fell onto the pillow, and I wept myself to sleep.

Chapter Eight

Siobhán

My body jerked off the bed and I gasped. I pushed my hair out of my face and rested my hand on my heart, waiting for the adrenaline to dissipate and my breath to calm. Plummeting from the Tobin Bridge into the icy mouth of the Charles River wasn't exactly how I wanted to wake up.

I climbed out of bed and pulled back the drapes. It was dark outside, but the pale light of dawn had started to brighten the sky above the tops of the trees and the calm water beyond.

We must be near Walden, I thought, the only area like this for miles in any direction.

There was no way I was going down without a fight. I'd fought this long to separate myself from organized crime, I sure as shit wasn't going to stop now.

I peeked out the door. There were three other rooms on the second floor, and the door to the master suite was open.

It was so quiet, you could have heard a pin drop on the carpet. I crept down the hallway to the stairs. The house was old, even if it had been recently remodeled. One creak and I was done for.

At the bottom of the steps, my red-painted toes wiggled atop the cherry wood floor. The front door was directly ahead, but my shoes were on the other side of the kitchen in front of the door to the garage. Should I take the time to put them on? I wouldn't get very far without them, especially if I had to run.

My heartbeat reverberated at the pulse in my neck and against my temples, but I had no choice. I had no phone, no money, and only a passing sense of direction. All I had was my two feet and determination.

I tiptoed across the kitchen and lowered myself to the floor next to my shoes, moving like I was underwater, slow and smooth. But with my heightened awareness and Luca's warning that he was a light sleeper, each pull of my laces echoed like boulders tumbling down a craggy mountain, each tap of my rubber soles a jackhammer against the hardwood.

There wasn't an alarm system attached to the front door, at least not one I could see. Not that I'd know how to disarm it even if there was. I wrapped my fingers around the cold copper of the deadbolt and twisted, slowly adding force until it started to turn. The first *click* made me jump. My eyes darted to the stairs. Not a sound but the incessant beat of my pounding heart. I resumed turning the lock as gently as I could.

Click.

CLICK!

The *swoosh* when I flung the door open resounded like a crashing wave, and my feet on the pavement like hammers striking an anvil as I sprinted out the door, across the walkway, and down the long, sloping driveway.

A terrible athlete and an even worse runner, I barely reached the end of the property before my lungs burst into flames. But my life was on the line, so I pushed through the burn in my legs and in my lungs, pumped my arms, and followed the curve of the road. If I could reach the bend, if I could escape the line of sight from his house...

Footfalls slapped the pavement behind me, closing fast. My heart rate spiked, fueling my pathetic excuse for speed. Within half a block, Luca's thick arm wrapped around my waist and hauled me off the ground as easily as a rag doll.

"Nooo!" I wailed and thrashed.

He clamped a hand over my mouth, and my chest heaved as I tried to breathe through my nose. I kicked and squirmed, but he ignored my feeble attempt at fighting back as if it was no more nuisance than a fly.

He started back toward the house, one arm holding me aloft, the other hand covering my mouth. I stopped flailing; I needed to catch my breath if I was going to try and break free.

"For someone with legs as long as yours, you really suck at running," he snarked in that smug, taunting voice he used any time he wanted to get a rise out of me.

It worked. Winded or not, I balled my fist and aimed for where it would hurt him the most. He swiveled his hips just in time and lifted me further off the ground, and my punch connected with the rock-hard plane of his lower abs instead.

"Stop squirming," he hissed in my ear, "or I'll tie you up. And not in a fun way."

My body went slack. What was the use? He hadn't even been trying. He wasn't even wearing shoes. And I believed him when he said he'd tie me up. He was completely unhinged.

He plopped me down inside the front door and slammed it shut. "Take your shoes off," he barked and pushed past me.

I'd never seen Luca in anything but shirtsleeves, suits, and formalwear. Now he strode into the kitchen in a wifebeater and basketball shorts. The wide span of his shoulders tapered to a trim waist, his round, muscular ass accentuated by the cling of basketball shorts. He yanked the refrigerator door open and pulled out a bottle of water. Not to be outdone by his back, his bare arms, thick with corded muscle, bulged when he twisted the cap off. His pecs flexed indecently beneath the thin material of his shirt. Especially with that gold chain and the pendant that landed at the scoop of the neckline. It drew my attention to a sprinkling of dark, trim chest hair.

My brain short-circuited under the assault of all that stereotypical Italian masculinity, and I caught myself gawping. What the hell was wrong with me? The man kidnapped me and sentenced me to death, and my body still reacted like a horny teenager. Worse was the reminder of how I'd fallen for him. How I'd trusted him. How I'd grieved for him when I'd thought he was dead instead of remembering him for what he was—an arrogant asshole.

"I hate you," I said.

"Ditto. Why the fuck did you run out?"

"Oh, I don't know. Maybe because you're going to kill me, and I don't want to die?"

He scowled and took down half the bottle of water. His gaze dropped to my feet. "Shoes."

"Ugh!" I groaned and rolled my eyes. I toed off my shoes and folded my arms across my chest. "There. Happy?"

He arched an eyebrow and shrugged.

Sunrise poked its head above the tree line beyond the wall of sliding glass doors between the kitchen and the deck. People were probably getting ready for work, taking their morning runs, walking their dogs. Not a great time to commit murder.

"What's the plan, anyway? I suppose you have to wait until it gets dark before you can toss me off..." I swallowed the lump in my throat and waved a hand through the air. "Something."

He looked out the French doors and shoved his fingers into his hair. He fisted them at the ends. "I don't know yet."

"What do you mean you don't know yet?"

"I mean, I don't know yet."

"You can't just keep me here."

"Why not?"

"Well, for starters, kidnapping is illegal."

He snorted and dropped his arm.

"Eventually people will notice I'm missing." I'd taken the next two weeks off work. Marco, Anna, and my family knew, but Luca didn't.

He licked his lips.

I sneered, self-satisfied. "Didn't think of that, did ya?"

"Oh, I thought about it," he snarled, "but you're supposed to be floating in the Charles River right now, not standing in my kitchen." He set the water bottle down on the island. "With your connections, anyone with a Shaughnessy bone to pick could've kidnapped you." He craned his neck. "And a lot of people have a bone to pick with your family."

I ground my teeth and averted my gaze. He wasn't wrong. But neither Ciarán nor Marco would rest until they found out who'd taken me.

I may not have trusted either of them to protect me and keep me out of mob and Mafia affairs, but I did trust them to lose their shit after the fact. These men were all the same. As much as they professed wanting to keep you safe, they'd never leave their criminal lives behind, content to clean up the messes they created instead of preventing them in the first place. I'd learned that lesson the hard way, and after what I'd been through as a teen, I didn't need to learn it again.

"What about Marco?" I asked.

"What about him?"

"I was there when he realized you—"

Luca surged forward and pointed a finger in my face. "Because you're a fucking rat."

I flinched and held up my hands. They shook, but I ignored his bait. "I saw what it did to him. How angry he was. How hurt. How do you think he'll react when he finds out about this?"

"He already disowned me, thanks to you. Handed me over to Vinnie. There's nothing more he can take from me." He canted his head, a vicious sneer on his plump lips. "Not even this vendetta. It's my blood right. As long as the blood I spill isn't Ciarán's, I have the support of the New England families."

My stomach pumped out a fresh supply of acid, and I winced. "Marco would never..." I whispered, unable to finish. No matter what words I added to end that sentence, they wouldn't be true.

"That's where you're wrong, Shamrock. Marco did. A Shaughnessy for a Moretti. Justice served."

Dread coiled its barbed arms around me, squeezing until my chest constricted under its thorny pressure. Stars danced in my vision, darkness clouding its edges. My acid stomach continued its relentless attack.

My mind went blank. No thoughts. No emotions. My consciousness detached itself from a reality it didn't want to experience, one it couldn't handle, and I watched myself like an avatar making its way through a fucked-up movie.

I walked across the kitchen, stiff and robotic, stopped in front of the fridge, and yanked open the door. Beer, water, condiments. A couple leftover takeout containers with *Porta Via* printed on their sides in swirling red letters. Stange to have such a big fridge with so few items. I grabbed a bottle of water and shut the door.

"By all means..." Luca's voice echoed in the cavern of my disassociated mind.

The cold water coated my mouth and throat. It quenched my thirst but landed in an empty bath of acid. My stomach needed attention. I opened and closed kitchen cabinets.

"What are you doing?" That voice again. A question this time.

"Hm?"

"What are you looking for?"

"Tums."

"I don't have any Tums."

"Oh." I closed the cabinet and walked into the living room.

I picked up a throw pillow, wrapped an arm around it, and climbed into the corner of the couch. I crossed my legs, hugged the pillow to my chest, and sipped my water.

Silence.

I'm in shock. The logical conclusion of my external observer. It didn't matter. Nothing mattered. I was going to die, and there was nothing I could do about it.

The black TV screen reflected a small blob in the corner of the sectional. A second blob entered the reflection, this one upright. It stopped in front of me.

Thick forearms dusted with dark hair crossed over a white undershirt. I lifted my gaze and met eyes as black as the TV. They examined me from behind a fall of chocolate brown hair. It framed familiar features like curtains. Lips pressed into a line, eyebrows drawn together—if I hadn't known better, I'd have thought the expression was one of concern. But I did know better.

I stared into the shadows cast by the early morning light peeking through the split in the curtains.

"What are you doing?" he asked.

"Waiting."

"Waiting for what?"

"Waiting to die."

He stiffened, and his energy changed as if he was on the verge of saying something.

I rested my head on the back of the couch. If only I could go back to sleep, shut my brain down until he took me back to the bridge. Or into the woods. Or out onto the pond with chains tied around my ankles. There was no way I could sleep though. The different ways I might die jumped in my imagination, demanding attention.

The light behind the curtains brightened. I sipped my water.

At some point, the upright silhouette vanished from the reflection in the TV screen.

Drawers opened and closed in the kitchen.

"Hey. Yeah. I need you here by eight thirty." His voice was blunt and even. "All day. I'll fill you in when you get here. Uh-huh. Yeah."

More kitchen rustlings. The whir of an espresso machine. The smell of coffee.

"Do you want caffè?" He was talking to me this time.

I rolled my head along the back of the couch until I faced the kitchen. Coffee the same color as Luca's eyes dribbled into two shot glasses. He poured milk into a stainless-steel jug, and the hiss of steam replaced the loud rumble of the espresso machine. He looked at me with an odd combination of frustration and concern that deepened the lines in his face.

The smell of coffee wafted into the living room, and my mouth watered. My stomach couldn't handle the milk, but without something to cut the acid in the espresso, the pain in my gut would worsen. Everything with my digestive system was a trade, and this morning I chose the lesser of two evils, especially considering I might be dead by the time the lactose reaction kicked in.

"Sure."

He constructed the drink with meticulous attention, carefully pouring the espresso and the milk into a wide-mouth mug. He spooned foam onto the top. "Sugar?" He set the mug on top of a saucer.

"No. Thank you."

He studied me and the couch and scowled. He set the

steaming cappuccino on the island. "You have to drink it in here," he said and got to work discarding the used espresso.

I let go of my safety pillow, climbed off the couch, and walked into the kitchen. I sat on one of the island barstools, cupped the mug in both hands, and sipped. A perfect balance of espresso, milk, and foam. Future Siobhán was going to hate me, but I desperately needed the cappuccino's comforting flavors and warmth.

"This is delicious."

"I'd be a terrible Italian if I couldn't make proper caffè."

The milk steamer hissed and burbled.

"Who taught you?"

"Gina DeVita."

"Marco's sister."

"Yes. She raised me. Well, her and Marco, but Marco wasn't around much until we moved to Italy."

The casual conversation was surreal but better than ominous silence. I didn't know much about Luca's early years. We'd never really talked about our upbringings before.

"When was that?" I asked.

"When I moved to Italy?" He glanced over his shoulder, and I nodded. "I was ten, so... '92?"

He retrieved another mug and saucer from the cabinet and assembled his drink.

"How long did you live there?"

"Till I was eighteen. I came back for college."

"Where?"

"Harvard, believe it or not."

"I believe it. We spent almost a year talking business over lunches and coffee, remember?" One thing Luca was not was stupid.

He sipped his coffee, set it down, and started cleaning. I watched with fascination as he wiped down the entire machine, washed and dried the jug and shot glasses, and sprayed the entire counter with cleaning solution, polishing it like he'd prepared a Thanksgiving meal. A little excessive for two cappuccinos but given his fixation on my shoes, maybe I shouldn't have been surprised.

He leaned against the counter and crossed one ankle over the other. "I remember," he said, a gravelly admission. "It wasn't my choice. I wanted to stay in Italy, but Marco was determined. Control freak," he finished derisively.

I huffed. "Understatement."

"Try living with him."

I honestly couldn't imagine. Anna was a saint.

Luca looked out the French doors. "He and my father had nothing growing up. They never went to college." He snorted. "Hell, I'm not even sure they finished high school." He faced me. "I think he was trying to live vicariously through me."

"Can you blame him?" I shrugged. "He also could've just wanted you to have the opportunities he didn't."

"That's certainly the way he'd spin it."

I focused on my cappuccino. Time to end the small talk before we crossed into territory that would start another fight. I didn't have the energy to argue about Marco. My fight was gone.

The milk in the cappuccino balanced out some of the acid in my stomach. I'd pay for it later, but I needed a reprieve before the cramps became too intense to sit up straight. I walked my dishes to the sink and rinsed them, not wanting to stoke Luca's ire. I retrieved my water bottle and went back to the living room. I opened the drapes, letting in the bright morning light, and resumed waiting on the couch.

Luca puttered around the kitchen. I stared out the window and wondered how my parents would get by without me.

Maybe Rory would finally step up. Would Ciarán? I hoped so. The rotten garbage smell shoved its way into my nostrils and with it, unwanted images of my parents. Mam wringing her hands, unable to take out the garbage because she was scared of falling. Da's vacant eyes staring through the TV. Him muttering something incoherent, causing Mam to make the sign of the cross.

"I'm leaving soon." Luca's blunt declaration snapped me back into the moment. I wiped my eyes with the back of my sleeve and faced him. He leaned against the archway between the living room and the kitchen. "One of my guys is coming over to watch you. Don't try anything stupid."

I stared at him, not sure what to say.

"I'll be back tonight."

"In time for a trip to the bridge?" My voice shook despite my attempt at sarcasm.

His eyebrows drew together, and he licked his lips. "We'll see. More likely the pond," he said and went upstairs.

The thin plastic water bottle crinkled beneath my fingers. It was empty. Nothing left. Tears dripped onto my safety pillow. I allowed myself a moment to cry, to mourn my parents, and then I was as empty as the bottle. Nothing left but the cold reality of being born into the Irish mob. A reality where, at any moment, your life could be snatched away. No matter how fast you ran.

Chapter Nine

Luca

My arms shook, and my pecs burned. I grunted and gritted my teeth and pressed the bar up.

"Come on, Luca!" Vito demanded, voice gruff.

The strained sounds of my effort grew louder, and with a final roar, my elbows locked. Shallow, staccato panting replaced my grunts and growls.

"Bene." Vito spotted me from behind the bench and guided the bar loaded with four hundred pounds back to the rack. I dropped the bar, and it hit the iron with a *clank*.

My chest heaved and sweat poured down the sides of my face. I sat up and rested my forearms on my knees.

"Bene," Vito said again. He handed me a towel. "First time you benched that much."

I'd known Vito my entire life. My foster father's consigliere was as much a fixture of my childhood as Marco, so I didn't miss the undercurrent of question beneath the pride in his voice.

He had every reason to be surprised. Only a month had passed since Vinnie let me out of his warehouse of horrors. I'd never bothered with the gym in the past; I always relied on my superhuman strength and speed. But the gains of regular lifting and boxing took my abilities to the next level. I'd never been this big and cut, never been this fast.

Although, in this case, it wasn't just the training that had me doing three sets of eight at four hundred.

"Persistence pays off," I said with a shrug and wiped the sweat from my face.

Vito walked around the long end of the bench and stood in front of me, arms crossed and eyebrow cocked.

I picked up my water bottle and squirted it into my mouth.

"What's eatin' you, kid?" he asked.

Talk about a loaded question. I puffed out my cheeks and exhaled long and slow. I hadn't been right all morning, not since I dragged Siobhán back into the house and told her I planned to use her to even the score between the Morettis and the Shaughnessys. Her reaction unsettled me to my bones.

Siobhán had moxie. She commanded any room she blessed with her long legs, impeccable style, and Hollywood-starlet looks. But that morning, her light had dimmed, her indomitable spirit shattered. No sly grins. No sharp replies. No tip of her tongue between her teeth. The spark I'd admired for so long had been snuffed out. By me.

I grabbed the back of my neck and rolled my head, trying to ease the tension there. But Siobhán's vacant stare and the downturn of her playful lips gripped my insides and wouldn't let go.

I'd dated a lot of women, fucked even more, but never once considered pursuing anything more than a casual lay or feeding. Not until I met Siobhán. The weeks between asking her on a date and the night she caught me feeding had been the longest dry spell of my life. I'd fed, of course, and enjoyed it, but I couldn't bring myself to have sex. She did something to me, to my insides. Something that made me want to be far more than casual. I didn't like it. It made me uncomfortable.

Only to find out she wasn't Irish. That she was from Southie. I went straight from uncomfortable to pissed off.

"Just a lot on my mind," I said and met Vito's eyes, holding mine steady. I didn't need him calling me out on account of a tell. "Lunch and meetings this afternoon with Matteo and Richie. Source traffic is picking up at Terme."

He eyed me as if gauging for bullshit. "Helluva time to expand the Source racket," he grumbled and turned for the ring.

A couple of civilians sparred. Another blood demon new to Marco's crew—been around maybe five, six months tops—worked the speed bag.

I pushed off the bench and followed. "Why's that?"

"Agent Johnson and his goons been showing up more than I like," he said. "Especially after following us to Foxborough."

"I don't think that's related to Sources. No way the feds are keyed into that yet. It's barely off the ground. The first appointments at Terme were just last week." I shook my head. "If I had to guess? It's the new property in the financial district. It's Pompeii."

Vito narrowed his eyes. "They never stuck their noses in Vesuvio business. What makes you think it's Pompeii?"

"The Shaughnessys were poking around city hall, right?" I grabbed a roll of tape and started wrapping my knuckles. "Asking questions about the financial district and that property? Wouldn't be the first time those Irish fucks were in bed with the feds."

"The Shaughnessys aren't the source of all our problems, Luca. No matter how much you want them to be."

"Maybe. Maybe not." I shrugged. "But it's more plausible than the Source racket."

"Doesn't matter why that asshole's hanging around. He's got eyes on Terme. If Matteo isn't careful..."

Level-headed as always, Vito was right. It didn't matter. The feds were onto something and looking to cause trouble.

"I'll tell Matteo and Richie," I said. "We need to service demand, but the last thing we need is more federal heat."

"Especially without Ms. Connelly around to chase 'em off."

My head snapped up. "What did you say?"

"Ms. Connelly. She's been a one-woman army keeping the feds off that property. Shame she won't be around much longer."

My stomach bottomed out. How could Vito know?

I blinked a few times and shook my head. "I'm sorry, what?"

"Siobhán Connelly. Marco's GM. The hot blonde you're always sparring with?"

"I'm familiar."

"She's on vacation the next two weeks. You didn't hear it from me, but she's looking for a new job. Has a bunch of interviews lined up."

Vito's words landed like an uppercut, and my head rocked back. Siobhán was quitting?

I finished the wrap, bit the edge of the tape, and ripped it off. "Who'd you hear that from?"

"Gina. From Anna. Ms. Connelly told Marco she was going on vacation but didn't tell him why. Told Anna though." Vito's expression said he wanted to be far away from Marco when he found out.

He stepped up to the ring, hung on the ropes, and shouted at the two men in Italian. I mindlessly wrapped my other hand, preoccupied by this new information. He glanced over his shoulder. "Apparently, the thing at Vesuvio really messed her up."

A new source of guilt hit me like Vito's right hook, and everything Siobhán had said over the past twenty-four hours stormed my head in a mad rush. She'd sworn up and down she wasn't a rat. I chalked it up to her trying to save her skin. But if what Vito said was true, and I tended to believe it was—Anna couldn't lie to save her life—maybe Siobhán *had* kept her work and family lives separate. Maybe she hadn't known who Marco was when she started at Terme. Maybe Siobhán wasn't a rat.

I rocked my head from side to side, cracking my neck, the idea so jarring, I needed to shake it loose. My belief that Siobhán was a rat had fueled me in that shithole with Vinnie, kept me alive. I'd had a target. A focal point for my rage. A real chance at revenge. But if it was all bullshit? An insane story I concocted?

Siobhán was the perfect plant. If Marco bought her story, which he did, there was no reason for her to walk away. Especially with her salary.

Not to mention, if she'd been trying to save her skin, why wouldn't she have told me she was quitting? Use it as proof of innocence?

Because she hadn't thought of that. Because she wasn't a rat.

The explanation was so simple, so uncontrived, it couldn't be anything but the truth.

I bit the tape and ripped. I clenched and unclenched my fists, working the stiffness out of the tape, all too eager to punch something. Hard.

This changed everything. Rats deserved to be whacked, and I had no problem letting one drown. But throwing an innocent woman off the Tobin Bridge for being a Shaughnessy? True restitution required honor, and my vendetta wouldn't be satisfied with a pointless death.

I met Vito at the ropes and tried to pay attention to the

two civilians finishing their round, but all I could see was Siobhán curled up on the corner of my couch, small, scared, and defeated. I hated seeing her like that. I grabbed the back of my neck and squeezed.

The round ended.

"Come on." Vito clapped me on the shoulder. "Better get moving if you're gonna meet Matteo and Richie for lunch."

Better get moving was right. I climbed between the ropes and danced on the balls of my feet. The faster I finished, the faster I could get back to the house and back to Siobhán.

Chapter Ten

Siobhán

My morning pity party ended with the doorbell and a man on the porch announcing, "Pizza!" The aromas of freshly baked dough and zesty sauce wafted across the kitchen and into the living room.

My stomach rumbled. Hunger had grown with each passing hour, as aggressive and persistent as my irritation. "You could have asked if I wanted something," I snapped.

Dominic glanced in my direction, his thick eyebrows drawn together and lips bent in an exasperated version of his roguish smile. My mafioso babysitter was around my age, but you'd never have know it from his impish dimples. "I asked if you wanted a slice."

"I don't like pizza." Not true, but I wasn't about to explain why I couldn't eat pizza.

He shook his head. "Everyone likes pizza."

Typical. I was officially over this hostage business. *So* done with waiting. I launched off the couch, marched into the kitchen, and opened cabinets one by one, searching for something—anything—I could eat.

Dominic got up, walked around the island, and pulled open a drawer. "What are you looking for?" he asked.

"Something to eat. How does Luca have a kitchen this big and no food?"

"He doesn't like clutter."

I narrowed my eyes. "How is food clutter?"

Dominic shrugged, placed the remaining pizza into a reusable container, and walked to the fridge. He exchanged the pizza for a bottle of water.

I shook my head and resumed my search. The only food in the kitchen was in the pantry. The options? Pathetic. A few canned goods, a box of penne, spices, coffee, and a glass container of olive oil. Not to be outdone by the rest of his immaculately organized cupboards, each item was lined up in perfectly spaced rows with their labels facing out. I knew Luca had issues, but good grief. I grabbed the box of pasta and the olive oil.

Dominic eyed me over his water bottle.

"What?" I asked.

He drained the bottle and picked up the empty pizza box. "You better clean up after yourself."

I stuck out a hip and raised an eyebrow. "Or what? He's going to kidnap me? Hold me hostage? Kill me?"

He snorted. "Just sayin' *I* wouldn't poke that bear."

I scoffed. "I'll take my chances." In fact, I'd do better than that. If I was going down, I'd make Luca as miserable as possible in the process.

Dominic held up his empty water bottle and the pizza box and backed up. "I'm going out for a smoke. Behave."

I saluted him. "Roger Dodger!"

He chuckled, shaking his head, and walked out through the door to the garage.

The rumble of the automatic garage door jarred something loose. Like Pavlov's dog, my eyes snapped to the French doors that led out to the deck. Dominic would be at least ten minutes. Plenty of time.

I dashed to the front door, pulled on my sneakers, and tried not to clomp my rubber soles against the wood floors on the way to the glass doors. I glanced over my shoulder toward the garage and stepped out onto the deck.

On my left, a massive grill with a black vinyl cover. On my right, an empty ashtray on top of a round glass table surrounded by four chairs. Beyond that, two lounge chairs covered in clear plastic. Straight ahead, a breathtaking view of Lynn Woods sloping down to Birch Pond. The sky was bright with no sign of rain, unusual for mid-April, and the calm water glinted beyond the tall pines. The clean, crisp air refreshed me and galvanized my resolve.

I placed my hands atop the wooden rail, peeked over the edge, and frowned. The deck didn't lead to the manicured backyard you'd imagine in suburbia. The slope of the woods must have started at the house's edge, because the deck was on stilts, and the drop between the balustrade and the ground was at least eight feet.

If walking in heels was an Olympic sport, I'd hold a record number of gold medals. Unfortunately, strutting my stuff in stilettos on a flat surface was as close to athletic as I came. That drop was probably no big for someone like Anna. She'd vault it and hit the ground running. For me, it was as daunting as stepping off the top floor of the Prudential building. But this deck was my only chance. I had to try.

I bent over the rail, and vertigo swept over me like a tsunami. The ledge of the Tobin Bridge rushed into focus and sent my world spinning. I closed my eyes and took two deep breaths. "Come on, Siobhán. You can do this. Stop being such a wuss. Just don't look down."

I twisted myself sideways and hugged my arms around the rail. I lifted my right leg and tried to get my foot onto the ledge. No dice. Add inflexible to scrawny and out of shape. The only thing I had working for me were my long legs.

I stood on my toes and managed to get my knee up. My breath came fast. I hugged the rail tighter, wiggled my right foot onto the rail, and dropped it over the side.

My stomach and chest pressed against the flat surface, my legs straddling the wood while my arms wrapped around it. I rested my cheek on the cool surface, needing a moment to catch my breath... and scowled.

Dominic leaned against the doorway to the deck, his arms crossed and shoulders shaking. He covered his mouth with his fist.

I lay there like a cat sunning herself, more annoyed than disappointed. "Enjoying the show?"

He dropped his fist and the amusement in his toothy grin reached his eyes. "Sorry, but that was way too entertaining to interrupt. I really wanted to see your next move."

I glared at him. "Can you at least help me down?"

He chuckled. "Sure."

He crossed the deck and offered his hand. I hung onto him like a life preserver, fighting a fresh wave of vertigo. I lifted my right leg back over the rail but couldn't reach the deck with my left foot.

"Here," Dominic said. Two strong hands clamped around my waist, lifted me off the rail, and set me on my feet.

I brushed the hair out of my face and straightened my spine, trying to maintain a semblance of dignity despite my pitiful attempt at escape. "Thank you."

Dominic stepped to the side and held out an arm. "After you."

I lifted my chin and marched back into the kitchen. With my shoes on. Fuck Luca.

Dominic closed the French doors, went into the living room, and turned on the TV.

I opened and closed cabinets, searching for what I needed to boil noodles and make my sad excuse for a lunch.

I was out of options. The deck had been my last hope, but if I couldn't make it over a rail and down an eight-foot drop, there was no way in hell I'd make it out a window.

Escape wasn't in the cards. I'd have to make do pissing Luca off. At least until I thought of another way out of this mess.

I found a pot and colander and set them on the stove. Where were the bowls? I opened the top cupboard next to the fridge.

"Hello, lover," I said to the bottle of vodka staring back at me. At least I could take the edge off while I waited for my demise.

Chapter Eleven

Luca

"What the hell is that?" I strode up the path between my driveway and the front porch.

Dominic sat in the Adirondack chair thumbing through the *Boston Globe*. The door was closed and so were the windows, yet guitar riffs echoed through the walls as loudly as if speakers were mounted on the awning.

He dropped his arms, and the newspaper crinkled into his lap. He glared at me, eyebrows drawn together. "That," he said, "is the third time she's played that song." He folded the newspaper, pushed himself out of the chair, and shoved the crumpled pages at my chest.

My jaw tightened, confusion, irritation, and no small amount of curiosity battling it out for my attention.

"Just wait till she starts singing." He clapped my shoulder and squeezed like he was sending me into battle, then walked down the path to where his truck waited, pulling out his keys as he went.

My fingers closed into a tight fist around the newspaper, and I flung open the front door.

Detritus covered the island and stovetop like war had been

waged against my kitchen. The mess squeezed the air from my lungs as surely as the wall of sound reverberating through my chest. A half-empty bottle of vodka sat next to an open jar of green olives, its lid and toothpicks strewn around its base. Two dirty pint glasses swam in a puddle of liquid. One held half-melted ice cubes. The other remnants of some cloudy liquid. Condensation trailed down both glasses into the shallow pool. A stainless steel pot waited on the stove, probably for someone to empty it, and a colander taunted me from atop the counter, gleefully announcing its escape from its rightful place in the sink.

Opposite the warzone, Siobhán stood on my sectional wearing a pair of my sunglasses, feet separated in a wide stance. She hoisted a martini glass and held the TV remote in front of her mouth.

"Toniiight!" She sang into her makeshift microphone, although calling it singing was generous. The sound was more akin to a stray cat in heat. "I'm a rock 'n' roll star!"

I winced. The ear-splitting, off-key wail was as offensive as the state of my kitchen and made my already tense chest tighten. I marched over to the stereo and killed the power. "What the *fuck* is going on in here?"

"Heyyy!" She propped my sunglasses on her head like a headband. "I was listening to that!"

"Get down!"

She stepped off the couch and landed with a thud, wobbling as she regained balance. "What's your problem?" But it didn't come out like that. It came out, "Wuzz'yer probbem?" like she was talking through a mouthful of cotton and had lost control of her tongue. At least she wasn't wearing shoes.

She teetered forward, craned her neck, and squinted. "You have a really prominent vein on your temple." She aimed a red fingernail at my face. I jerked my head out of the way. "It's pulsating. Maybe you should get that checked out."

My breath came hot and fast, and I crunched the newspaper into a tight wad. "Cazzo!" I stormed into the kitchen, tossed the newspaper in the trash, and rolled up my sleeves. "Che fottuto disastro. There's shit everywhere."

My heart fluttered, making me dizzy. I closed my eyes and breathed deeply, trying to calm my racing heart so I wouldn't pass out. Clean. I needed to clean. I reached under the sink for a spray bottle of disinfectant and fresh rags.

Siobhán climbed onto the barstool and reached for the bottle of vodka. "Dramatic much? There's literally one bottle, a jar, and two glasses."

"And the pot on the stove and"—I craned my neck— "Fuck! Dirty dishes in the sink? There's water and olive juice and toothpicks..." I grabbed the jar of olives and the lid.

"Hey! I'm not done with those!"

"Oh, you are *so* done with those."

"What is it, Luca?" she asked innocently and batted her eyelashes. "Don't like messes?"

I scowled, my hand flexing then fisting. I wanted to strangle her. "And what the hell are you doing anyway? Getting drunk?"

She shrugged and slid the two pint glasses toward her. "Yup." She dumped vodka into one of the pint glasses. It splashed when it hit the melted ice.

"Great. More shit on my counter."

She twisted her face. "Great. More shit on my counter," she mocked in a less-than-flattering Italian accent.

To my horror, she made things infinitely worse by pouring the concoction back and forth between the two pint glasses, spilling more vodka on the counter with each transfer. Then she placed her fingers over the top of the glass with the ice and strained the "martini" into her glass.

I gaped at the mess—not just splashed across my island, but Siobhán herself.

She raised her eyebrows and took a big gulp of vodka. "What? You think I was going to wait quietly on the couch for you to come home and kill me?" She hiccupped, and an amused grin broke through her scowl.

I came around to her side of the island. "So you decided to get shit hammered?"

"I'm not shit hammered," she snapped and spun on the barstool to face me. "I'm pleasantly buzzed," she finished demurely and lifted her chin.

I scoffed.

"You should try it sometime. Might make you less of a dick."

All my worry and dread that I'd irreparably broken Siobhán's spirit vanished in a heartbeat. She was back. Albeit fucking tossed, but she was back.

"You are unbelievable," I said, infuriated and relieved.

"I know," she said, smug and smiling.

I rolled my eyes, and she stuck the tip of her tongue between her teeth.

My stomach flipped. *What the fuck.*

I reached around her, grabbed the two pint glasses, and headed for the sink.

"What did you expect?" she shouted.

I glanced over my shoulder as I rinsed out the pint glasses. Her face was flushed, but not just from the vodka. Her glassy eyes flashed with anger.

"You leave me here all day like a—like a caged animal preparing for slaughter. Of course, I'm going to fucking drink. What the hell else should I be doing? And I would've kept on drinking until I passed out if you hadn't so rudely interrupted music time. Being unconscious is a hell of a lot better than waiting for the man you've dreamed about for two years to come home and kill you."

I froze, stunned silent.

Siobhán seethed, red splotches darkening her pale face. "Oh, don't look so shocked." She relaxed against the back of her barstool, martini glass dangling from red-tipped fingers.

I turned off the water, dried my hands, and leaned against the counter facing her.

"You knew I had feelings for you, and for some demented reason, I thought you had feelings for me too." She averted her eyes, looking out the glass doors, and drained half her martini with a wince. "Whatever," she mumbled. "It doesn't matter."

My jaw ached from the strain of grinding my teeth. It did matter. It mattered more than I wanted it to matter. It mattered so much, not only had I failed to push her off the bridge but seeing her broken that morning felt like a knife to my insides.

Fuck.

I ran a hand through my hair, stared at my feet, and squeezed. "I had feelings for you," I mumbled, unable to deny the truth. The signs had been there. I just hadn't wanted to acknowledge their source.

No response. I let go of my hair and lifted my gaze. Her lips parted, her eyes wide and rimmed with unshed tears.

"But it doesn't change anything. It doesn't change the fact your family killed my father. It doesn't change the fact you lied to me. And it sure as hell doesn't change the fact you led me to believe you were someone you're not." My voice grew louder with each layer of her betrayal.

She pursed her lips and moved her head through a slow nod. She shot back the rest of her drink, slid off the barstool, and walked around the island until she stood in front of me.

"You know what?" She poked my chest with her manicured finger, and the impact caused her to sway like she was on the deck of a ship. "I'm drunk enough and traumatized enough that I'm fresh outta fucks. I. Call. Bullshit. You wanna know what happened? Lemme break it down for you."

I crossed my arms and raised an eyebrow.

"We got too close, and it freaked you out. That's right. I said it. We hooked up that night at Vesuvio, and it was fucking spectacular, and it scared the shit out of you. You couldn't handle having something real, something special, something that wasn't built on your bullshit flashy lifestyle and fake smiles. So you broke it." Her voice wavered and caught. Tears spilled down her cheeks, and her bottom lip trembled. "You ruined it. You went out the next day—the *next fucking day*, Luca—and hooked up with someone else." She punched me in the chest, not hard, but it carried enough of her pain that it struck like a hammer. "You broke my heart, and when I thought it couldn't hurt any more, you tried to blame it on me!"

Her voice rose to a fevered pitch. She pounded the side of her fist against my chest, and I let her. I had no right to stop her.

"You made up this grand tale about how I lied to you, how I was hiding some deep Southie secret, just so you'd have an excuse to hate me, so you could walk away from something most people only dream about. All because you were scared." She hiccupped through a sob and struck my chest again. "And I hated you for it. I still hate you for it as much as you hate me." She struck my chest over and over, tears and sobs shaking her body. "Because even after all that, I still wanted you. Those feelings never went away, and I have to live with them every" —*strike*—"single"—*strike*—"day." *Strike.*

I grabbed her wrist on the last punch, and she broke down crying.

Overcome, I placed my hand on the back of her head and

pulled her to my chest. She rested there for the briefest moment, then pushed off me and wriggled free.

"No," she said and stumbled back, shaking her head. "Don't." She reclaimed her stool, grabbed the vodka bottle by its neck, and took a hefty swig before plunking it back down. She swayed, clutching the bottle on the counter.

"So"—she sniffed and wiped her nose with the back of her sleeve—"excuse me for getting drunk and trying to deal. Excuse me for trying to numb myself while I waited for you to come back and break my body like you broke my heart." She swayed again, released the bottle, and rested her arms on the island and her forehead on the backs of her hands.

I stood dumbfounded, unable to speak or think or move. She sniffled and shifted, and all I could do was stare, because her drunken outburst wasn't contrived. Alcohol was the world's oldest truth serum, and Siobhán had drunk enough that she didn't have any filters left.

The seed of doubt planted during my visit to Vito's gym sprouted. Its roots tangled around my stomach, thickening and squeezing and forcing me to acknowledge that my assumptions about Siobhán had been wrong. Very wrong.

Was she a Shaughnessy? Yes. Did she lie to me? Kinda? Was she a rat? Doubtful. Had she purposefully led me on? No.

I rubbed my forehead, squeezed my eyes shut, and dragged my fingers down to pinch the bridge of my nose. I was exhausted from the brutal, frustration-fueled workout, a stressful afternoon with Matteo and Richie, and now this. I blew out a long, slow breath.

A snort from the island.

Siobhán rested the side of her face on the backs of her hands. Her eyes were closed, her breathing slow and steady, and every so often a snore escaped.

Passed out. All the vodka and carrying-on and she passed out sitting at my kitchen island.

I rolled up my sleeves and rested my hands on my hips, examining the mess. The mess Siobhán created—vodka, olive juice, toothpicks, melted ice—and the mess I created—Siobhán, heartbroken and passed out from a combination of vodka and panic.

I crouched next to the stool and hooked one arm beneath her knees and one arm around her waist. "Come on," I said and shifted her body toward mine.

She sat up and wrapped her arms around my neck. I lifted her into my arms with almost no effort. Despite her height—five-eight?—she was shockingly light. She buried her face in my shoulder and wrapped her arms tighter around my neck.

"Are you taking me to the bridge now?" Her small words stabbed my heart.

"No. I'm putting you to bed."

"Oh."

I turned for the stairs.

"You smell like Luca," she mumbled, her voice muffled by my shirt.

"That's 'cause I am Luca," I said, exasperated. My chest ached at the vulnerability in her voice, but I was equally pained by the wrench she'd thrown in my plans to avenge my father.

"No," she whispered. "My Luca smiled. Every time he saw me, he smiled. A real smile. Just for me." She slid her hand down my chest until it stopped over my heart. "From here." And with those two words, she twisted the knife.

Lunches at Vittoria. Sipping coffee in the lobby. Stolen smiles across a conference room. I reached the top of the stairs eager to get Siobhán out of my arms and remind myself of who she was—a Shaughnessy. My enemy.

I turned sideways through the door to the guest bedroom

and laid her atop the comforter. Her face was puffy from crying, her eyes vibrant blue from the tears.

"It was never going to work between us, Siobhán. You're a Shaughnessy. I'm a Moretti."

She nodded. "So..." She rested one hand on her heart and the other on her stomach. "You'll most likely kill me in the morning?" she asked, her voice soft and quaking with fear.

I grabbed the edge of the comforter and tugged. She wiggled until it came free, and I covered her with it. "Go to sleep, Siobhán."

She closed her eyes, and fresh tears spilled down her face onto the pillow.

I ground my teeth and clenched my fists, hardening myself against her pain and mine and the urge to comfort us both. She rolled onto her side, clutched the comforter to her chin, and curled into a tight ball. I walked out of the room and closed the door behind me.

In the kitchen, I poured myself a finger of scotch and surveyed the other mess. The chaos on my counters was as distressing as the chaos in my mind. I needed order. I needed rightness. I needed to clean.

But even after the clutter was gone and the soothing smell of lemon disinfectant filled the air, the rapid assault of images and words merely slowed. The discordant offensive waged by my emotions continued to hold me hostage.

I splashed more scotch into my glass and retrieved the cigar case and lighter from my suit jacket. I went outside onto my deck, leaving the door ajar. Siobhán was thoroughly passed out, but I wasn't taking chances. Not that I knew what the hell I was going to do with her anymore.

I pulled half a cigar out of the case. I'd cut a fresh one a couple days ago. Unlike Marco and Vinnie, a smoke wasn't permanently wedged between my lips. It wasn't a habit for me, but it came in handy at times when cleaning didn't cut it and I needed something more to calm my nerves and focus my attention.

The wood deck was cold under my bare feet and the damp spring air clean in my lungs. Refreshing after the heat of the past hour. I leaned against the rail and dragged cigar smoke into my mouth, holding it there and letting it ground me.

The woods created a sea of rustling darkness. The light of the streetlamps reflected off the new leaves. They waved with each kiss of the slight breeze.

We'd never kissed, Siobhán and I. After all the pining and yearning, after all the flirting and baiting, after the lap dance and the best blowjob of my life, no kiss. Like we'd struck some telepathic agreement to wait for the perfect moment before taking the plunge into something meaningful. Something we'd both thought had a chance. Something that never happened. And tonight, Siobhán turned the tables and laid the blame squarely at my bare feet.

Smoke swirled in front of me, backlit by the light leaking onto the porch from the kitchen. The only images I had of my mother were from one photo album my father put together when I was a kid. That and the stories he told me about her beauty and kind heart. The way he reverently traced her picture behind the plastic as if he could reach through time and touch her face.

Humans were fragile creatures—an unfortunate lesson my father learned the hard way and one I never wanted to repeat. I kept women at arm's length, especially humans. I always told myself if I ever got into a relationship, it would be with a blood demon. There was no way in hell I'd risk what happened to my mother happening to someone I cared about. Not that I'd ever cared about anyone. Not until Siobhán.

Somewhere along the way, she pierced my armor and squeezed her way through the crack. And I let her. Right up until that night at Vesuvio when the house of cards came tumbling down. She lied to me, and I hated her for that.

The wind gusted and fanned hair across my face. I threaded my fingers through it and pushed it away. Had I wanted her to catch me feeding that night? I took more risks than Marco or Vito, but feeding in the middle of Vesuvio? For anyone to see? I squeezed the thick strands and tugged, trying to pull myself back to what mattered.

In the pit of Vinnie's warehouse, hatred had avalanched into something deeper, something crueler. I wanted to turn her into the instrument with which I took my revenge and eased my tormented mind. She stole that plan from me, a plan I'd held onto as if it were my soul's last chance for survival. I hated her for that.

Uncomfortable feelings swirled like eddies in the river of my emotions—guilt, empathy, worry—but they couldn't eclipse the powerful current of hate. Old memories of us surfaced, painful ones of happier times best left buried. They forced me to question my truths. I hated her for that too.

I pulled on my cigar long and slow. Its earthy flavor settled on my tongue and bit the back of my throat raw and harsh. As much as I hated Siobhán, a part of me wanted to climb up those stairs and into her bed, wrap my arms around her, and tell her everything would be okay. And for that, I hated myself.

Chapter Twelve

Siobhán

Steam filled the bathroom and fogged the mirror. I wiped away the condensation, clearing a patch to see my reflection. I felt like a new woman after the hot shower—out of the clothing I'd worn since Friday and rinsed clean of the previous night's vodka-induced sweats—but I needed to see evidence of life firsthand.

My eyes were bloodshot, my makeup-free face a mess of wrinkles and freckles. I combed my hair with my fingers. Fine and stick straight, it would fall limp when it dried without the help of products and pins and my blow-dryer. I sighed. He was bound to see me like this at some point—Siobhán unplugged.

I dried my hair as best I could with the towel I found in the hallway closet. Luca's bedroom door was ajar, but if he'd heard me, he didn't bother to stop my snooping. I wrapped the big, fluffy towel around me.

My mouth had the taste and texture of an old rug, like it required a scrubbing worthy of one of those carpet-cleaning videos on social media. I rifled through cabinets until I found toothpaste and cleaned my cotton mouth, not once but twice, with my finger.

The shower helped the headache pulsing behind my eyes, but my stomach was tied in a big, ugly knot. The cramps were almost unbearable, and the acid burned its way up my esophagus. I needed food. Actually, I needed my Tums, but they were locked in the entertainment center with my purse. But something more than a bowl of noodles and olives surrounded by a cubic meter of vodka would be a step in the right direction. I'd never been a paragon of nutrition—not my choice—but yesterday was bad even by my standards.

Clouds of steam billowed into the hallway, and the mellow notes of classical music floated up the stairs. I paused outside the bathroom, straining to hear. It was soft. A single violin. I'd never taken Luca for a classical music guy.

His bedroom was empty, bed made. Not that anything different would have stopped me. I wasn't about to wear my stale, dirty sweatshirt or leggings. If he was going to keep me holed up in his house, I needed fresh clothes, and the only fresh clothes were in his bedroom.

Pressed dress shirts paired with suits hung evenly spaced in his closet. His shoes formed neat rows beneath the orderly sets. He had one of those tie racks, and his silks were arranged by color. I selected a thick white cotton button-down, the best option to battle obscenity. Luca was six-foot-four by my estimation, and the shirt would fit like a dress. Good enough until he either tossed me off the Tobin Bridge or decided I needed my own clothes. I buttoned the shirt, rolled up the sleeves, and padded down the stairs.

My head throbbed, and my stomach gurgled in time, cramping violently and threatening to double me over.

The music grew louder with each step, but when I reached the bottom of the stairs and turned for the living room, it was empty, the sound system silent. Confused, I shifted my attention to the kitchen and did a double take. The music wasn't coming from a television or a stereo or a record player but the most unlikely source imaginable.

Beyond the island and the dining table, the blinds were pushed to the side and the French doors that led to the deck were open. They revealed a scene I wouldn't have believed had I not seen it with my own eyes.

Luca stood on the deck in nothing more than track pants. His bare feet peeked out from beneath the light gray fabric pooled at the bottom from being slung so low on his trim hips. His hair, always so neatly combed back and tucked behind his ears, was pulled up, half of it tied in a messy bun. A few loose strands fell around the sculpted lines of his chiseled face. Over the past forty-eight hours, that face had been twisted in anger, all hard scowls and intense eyes, but now his jaw and brow were soft and relaxed. At peace. Eyes closed, his chin rested reverently on a violin, tucked into the crook of his neck like a cherished lover.

His fingers moved deftly up and down the instrument's neck, and he swayed in time with the music. The thick muscles of his arms flexed with each movement of the bow, with each peak and valley of the melody.

I stepped delicately toward the entrancing scene, not wanting to interrupt the beauty emanating from Luca's talented hands. I leaned a hip against the dining table and watched.

The most intensely beautiful man I'd ever seen, Luca was even more breathtaking when he played the violin. He transformed into an angel, however fallen, who laid his heart bare through his instrument. My bruised and broken heart beat for him once more, a metronome he controlled no matter how hard I tried to break free.

I didn't want to die, and I didn't want Luca to kill me. I didn't want Luca to *want* to kill me. How could someone create such beauty, pour so much emotion into their music, and kill an innocent woman?

But he hadn't killed me. Not yet. He hadn't pushed me off the bridge that first night. He hadn't dragged me into the woods with a knife. He hadn't taken advantage of me in my drunken state. Who knew what went through his mind, but forty-eight hours after being kidnapped, I was still alive. And as scared as I was, I knew one thing for certain, one thing I believed deep in my gut—Luca Moretti wasn't going to kill me. He couldn't.

The somber notes slowed and quieted, and the piece ended. He lowered his bow and lifted his chin. I swiped at my eyes to hide the evidence of tears. He must have noticed the motion in his periphery, because he dropped his arm, letting the violin hang at his side, and faced me.

We stood on opposite sides of the glass, separated by the invisible barrier. His calm, relaxed features assessed me without surprise, anger, or delight. But I drank Luca in like I was seeing him again for the first time. His sculpted torso and powerful arms. The breadth of his chest dusted with dark, trim hair. The gold chain and pendant ending between his pecs. To its right above his heart, words etched in black ink.

The sun peeked out from behind a cloud and illuminated his skin's golden hue, the olive undertones a rich base for a tan marred only by a handful of birthmarks on his shoulders and the ridges of his stomach. He appeared mythical in the morning light, as bright as Apollo, the god's lyre replaced by a violin.

He shifted the bow into his other hand and walked inside. A cool spring breeze wafted into the kitchen and pebbled my skin. He set the bow on the table and, with surprising care, placed the violin into its case.

"That was beautiful," I said.

He folded black velvet atop the strings.

"You must have started playing when you were very young."

He closed the case, clasped it shut, and rested his hand on the back of the chair. He glanced over his shoulder and held my gaze for no more than a heartbeat before his eyes dropped to my body. His eyebrows drew together, and he canted his head. He reached across the corner of the table and took the collar of my shirt between his fingers.

"I needed a shower." My whispered words broke, and I cleared my throat. "And something to wear."

His fingers traveled from my collar to a piece of hair stuck to my cheek. He tucked it behind my ear, and I shivered. "I didn't know you had freckles," he said.

"I didn't know you played the violin."

The corner of his mouth tipped up, a cocky bend to his pouty lips—Luca's signature smirk. The one that made women around the world drop their panties and follow him like puppy dogs. The same sexy smile that caught my eye across the lobby of Terme di Boston two years ago.

But there was a sadness in his eyes that belied his flashy charm and the tempting turn of his mouth. The real Luca, trapped behind the face he showed to the world. The Luca I'd seen in brief moments when we shared lunch. The Luca I'd seen talking to Marco when no one else was around. The Luca I'd played pool with at Vesuvio, free of pretense and inhibitions if only for a night.

"How often do you play?" I asked.

"Often enough."

I arched an eyebrow. "If you don't want a conversation, fine. I'll find some breakfast and go back to my prison cell. But lose the fake front. We've known each other too long and been through too much at this point to be anything but real."

The muscles in his jaw twitched, reminding me of Marco, and his near-black eyes held mine, sincere and unwavering.

"Whenever the mood suits me. Whenever I need to clear my head."

"Doesn't a clear head come for free with your pretty face?"

His lips turned into a wry grin, genuinely amused, and his body relaxed as though my snarky comment came as a comfort. "You weren't the only one who had a rough night."

I huffed. "Excuse me if I'm unsympathetic. No one's threatened to throw you off a bridge or is holding you hostage without clean clothes or a toothbrush."

He scowled. "There's a spare toothbrush in one of the cabinets, and I'll get you some clothes. Today."

"Or"—I held up a hand—"here's a crazy idea—you could let me go."

He shook his head. "I can't do that."

Disappointment hit hard. I bit the inside of my cheek and looked past him to the violin case on the table. "Well," I said and shrugged, "I don't know much about music. At least, not classical." I glanced at him sideways.

He folded his arms, and it drew my attention to his chest. His pecs and biceps bulged. My lips parted on an intake. Why did he have to be so unbelievably hot on top of everything else?

I ripped my gaze away from his body, and that cocky smirk of his resurfaced. I rolled my eyes. "Anyway, you play beautifully. With real feeling."

"My father put me in lessons as soon as I was old enough to hold a bow. I could barely wrap my fingers around the neck." The lines around his eyes and mouth softened, steeped in nostalgia.

I grabbed onto the tenuous lifeline. "Most kids are allergic to discipline, and I can't imagine you were a quiet, well-behaved child."

He snorted. "I was a hellion. But I was determined to learn how to play that violin." He nodded in the direction of the violin case. He shifted his weight and licked his lips. "It was my mother's."

The declaration hung in the space between us. It weighed on the silence, loaded with baggage. Despite my surprise, I held his eyes, kept mine steady, let him know I was listening. Because the heartache attached to that simple statement was nearly palpable in its severity. Antonio Moretti was Boston legend, his ending known to anyone who grew up in our world. But his mother? I knew she wasn't in the picture—Marco and Gina raised Luca—but beyond that...

"She was first chair in the Boston Symphony Orchestra." His spine straightened with pride. "My father gave it to me on my sixth birthday, just a few months before he was murdered." He glanced at the case, and his gaze grew distant, his voice strained and hushed. "He wanted me to have something of hers. Something she loved. Something he loved about her." He slowly turned back to face me, as though traveling forward through time. His eyes were glassy, and his nostrils flared.

I swallowed, bracing myself for the answer to the next inevitable question. He spared me the discomfort of asking.

"She died," he said, matter-of-fact and devoid of feeling.

"How?" I whispered. Something about the loving way he handled the violin and the honesty that poured out through the notes forced the question from my lungs.

"In childbirth," he croaked, the rawness in his voice as terrible as the truth.

The space around my heart constricted. "I'm sorry."

Never knowing his mother. Losing his father when he was six years old. The bitterness that ruled Luca's life no longer seemed so strange, and my heart ached for him. Words never escaped me, but I couldn't find any that wouldn't sound trite. No words could ease that kind of loss or provide comfort to a man whose childhood had been weighed down with such heaviness.

"Why didn't you tell me you were on vacation?" he asked.

I blinked rapidly, the question giving me whiplash. "What —what are you talking about?"

"You're on vacation for the next two weeks. Why didn't you tell me?"

"Oh, I don't know. Maybe because I was preoccupied with you being alive. Or because you broke into my house, kidnapped me, and threatened to throw me off the Tobin Bridge?" I shook my head. "My vacation plans didn't exactly seem relevant."

"Even if the reason you're taking the vacation is to find a new job?" He raised an eyebrow.

My head jerked back. "How do you know that?"

"Maybe this pretty face is smarter than you think." He cocked a shit-eating grin and winked.

I huffed. "Anna's got a big mouth."

He shrugged. "Maybe, but I'm not going to toss you off the Tobin Bridge anymore if that helps."

"Decided on chains and the pond?"

He snorted. "I'm not going to kill you, Siobhán."

Relief-induced adrenaline shot into my bloodstream. It made my knees weak, and my vision blurred. I placed my palm flat on the table to steady myself and let out a shuddering breath. My eyelids moved through a slow blink, and my lips parted to let out the hysterical noise percolating in my chest, but instead, I just stood there and gawped.

"Don't look so surprised, *Shamrock*," he said dryly. "I know you think I'm an asshole, and you're probably right, but I'd never kill an innocent person. You're a smart woman, and if it never occurred to you to tell me you're leaving Terme..." He shook his head. "You're not a rat. You may be a Shaughnessy, and you did lie to me about that, but you're not a rat."

My ears started ringing. Heat traveled from my belly into

my head, a rush of fury that burned away the dizziness and boiled over almost as soon as it started.

"You asshole!" I punched him in the shoulder. It was like hitting a brick wall. He dropped his arms and raised an eyebrow. "You were going to push me off that bridge!" I hit him again, harder. "I told you I wasn't a rat!" I swung at him with both fists, right then left, back and forth, pounding on his pecs.

He grabbed my wrists, and I flailed beneath his grip, my breath coming in short, angry bursts.

"Hey. Shamrock. Relax."

"Argh! Don't tell me to relax! You almost fucking killed me! And now you're all, *oops, my bad*. Fuck you, Luca!" I kicked him. "Ow!"

"Stop." He snickered. "You're going to hurt yourself."

I stopped writhing and glared at him, panting fire. My damp hair hung in front of my eyes, and I puffed a breath to get it out of my face.

Luca's gaze travelled to my chest. I followed his eyes. The top button of my shirt had come undone, revealing the tops of my breasts. With his height, he probably had a pretty good view.

"Let go," I snapped and yanked my arms back.

He tightened his grip and dragged his gaze back up to my face. The dark depths of his eyes deepened with sinful promise. He inched closer. "I know how I can make it up to you."

I averted my eyes, unable to withstand the intensity of his indecent attention, but they landed on his chest. His firm, smooth chest. Thick with muscle and covered in trim hair. His gold chain and pendant accentuated the cleft between his pecs. I wanted to run my palms over all that hard muscle and hair and the black ink that artfully scrawled *Antonio & Lucia* above his heart. My mouth went dry, and heat pooled between my legs.

"You're deluded," I said.

He rounded the corner of the dining table and crowded me against it. "Am I?"

I drew back, but the backs of my thighs hit the edge of the table and blocked my retreat. His big body loomed over mine, heating me from the inside, the air between us infused with his masculine scent. Clean, but musky. A hint of yesterday's cologne. All Luca.

My breath quickened, but its shortness had nothing to do with disgust and everything to do with lust.

He released my wrist, and his hand hovered above my nipple, hard and poking against the shirt, straining for him to take the next step. He brushed the backs of his fingers across the sensitive peak, and I stifled a groan, the throb between my legs almost too much to master.

But I was angry—angry with him for putting me through hell and angry with myself for turning into putty at a single touch. I swatted his hand away. "Don't."

He didn't bat an eye, his countenance unfazed, his focus fixed on my chest. He used his thumb to draw lazy circles around my areola, teasing me, making me want to beg.

"I said don't." A harsh order in my head, the words came out quiet and husky. I swatted at his hand again and twisted my body away from him.

He grabbed my wrist and leaned closer, not allowing me to turn away. He lowered his face to my neck and nuzzled the space below my ear the way he'd done in the past just to fuck with me. Now the move felt ripe with sensuality.

I wished I was one of those badass women with enough strength and coordination to headbutt a man right in his smug face. But I wasn't. Worse, my body betrayed me—my knees weakened at the caress of his breath against my skin and the brush of his nose beneath my ear—and I tilted my head to give him better access.

He rubbed slow circles on my wrist with his thumb. "Do you remember what you said to me, Shamrock?" His hot breath tickled, and his lips brushed against the ridge of my ear, sending a zing of desire straight to my core. "That night at Vesuvio? The night you took me with your mouth?"

My eyes fluttered closed and memories of my lips wrapped around his cock flooded my senses. The smell of him. His taste. "Hm?"

"You told me I could return the favor." He nudged my earlobe with his nose—"Seems like the perfect occasion"—and teased it with the tip of his tongue.

I melted. His heat, his smell, his tongue. Years of wanting him so badly it hurt. They all conspired to box out my indignation with ruthless defiance. I sighed, a breathy, wanton noise that announced my desperate answer to his wicked suggestion.

He released my other wrist, and my hand hovered midair, my body frozen in wait for what came next.

I opened my eyes. His burned with desire, the deep brown pools speckled with rich amber flecks that almost appeared... red. The undercurrent of danger raised the temperature, and a shock of desire zipped between my legs. I rested my hands on his chest, hot and hard beneath my palms and begging to be licked, and the sparks in his eyes brightened with feral intent.

He lowered his gaze and lifted his hands to the top button of my shirt. His eyes darted to mine as it came undone, then returned to where his thick fingers worked the next button out of its hole.

I watched him, enthralled, my nipples hard, core on fire, until the shirt parted, an open invitation for Luca to explore.

He pushed the fabric aside, exposing my right breast. My nipple was plump and ready. I was ready. Ready for him to take whatever he wanted. And I wasn't sure who I hated more —Luca or myself.

Chapter Thirteen

Luca

Siobhán's nipple was taut, a dusky rose nub thick with excitement. It stood out from her pale breast, the pert swell small enough I could cup it in one hand while pinching its swollen peak. I licked my lips, ready to see more.

"Is your pussy as ready for me as your nipple?" Her cheeks flushed, and her eyes hooded. "Are you wet for me, Shamrock?"

Her lips parted, the start of an answer, but I pushed the left side of her shirt open, and the backs of my fingers dragged across her other nipple. She sucked in a breath, and gooseflesh pebbled her skin. The tips of her nails pinched my shoulders and sent a rush of blood straight to my dick.

I was already half-hard from her wearing my shirt. The smudged and smeared makeup and mascara were gone, her pale skin fresh and clean. She had wrinkles across her forehead, at the corners of her eyes, and bracketing her lips. And those fucking freckles... They dusted her nose and spilled onto her cheekbones.

Something about her in my house wearing my clothes without any makeup... I wanted to bend her over the table and fuck her until she submitted. Until she admitted she belonged to me. Until I claimed her as mine.

"Mmm." My chest rumbled with satisfaction. "I think you're more than ready." I wrapped my fingers around her ribs and pressed the pad of my thumb into her nipple, rolling it and making myself harder with each circle. I leaned in, so close my lips brushed her ear. "Yeah," I breathed. "You're ready for me to tongue-fuck you, aren't you? And you hate it."

She groaned, soft and restrained, but dug her fingernails into my skin. I chuckled and pulled back to watch her expression. Her eyes flashed with challenge, but her cheeks remained flushed, a rosy glow that matched the pale pink of her lips. Her fury was fighting a losing battle against her desire, and it made me want to dominate her even more.

Anticipation swelled between us, thick and intense. I wrapped my fingers around her breast and squeezed, serving her nipple up like a feast. I sucked it into my mouth, and she moaned, deeper this time and throaty with need. My dick jerked at the sound. Pre-cum smeared the inside of my pants. My erection begged for friction. I pressed my hips into hers, and the wetness was cold and slick against my hip. She rubbed herself against me, straining for contact, and fuck if I didn't want to end this game, drop my pants, and fuck the fight right out of her.

Instead, I nipped and sucked, determined to give her the same mind-blowing orgasm she'd given me over a year ago at Vesuvio. I flicked her plump nub with my tongue until she writhed beneath me. She deserved that pleasure and so much more.

I released her from my mouth and blew on the wet peak. Her nipple pebbled, and her tiny blonde hairs stood on end. I grinned, so fucking satisfied, and looked up, wanting her to see the victory painted on my face.

The kitchen lights backlit her hair, creating a golden halo

around her flushed face. Her blue eyes sparkled, open and yearning. Trusting. If I'd thought her beautiful before, nothing had prepared me for what she looked like in that moment—flushed, needy, and ready for my mouth. It punched me in the chest, and my smug grin disappeared. I brushed the wisps of hair from her forehead and ran my thumb along her brow. For a heartbeat, I allowed myself to stare into her eyes, to share her breath and forget everything but the charge that pulled us together.

Ready for worship, I lowered myself to my knees, never breaking our magnetic eye contact, and slid my hands down the length of her torso. I planted a kiss above her navel then dragged my gaze down the pale expanse of her skin.

Shock froze time. My heart stopped beating. Reality crashed around me as I stared in horror at Siobhán's ravaged stomach.

The next beat of my heart slammed into my chest. Time rushed forward, and I sucked in a startled breath. My hands locked around her hips, and I surveyed the scene, trying to make sense of the carnage.

A couple inches to the right of her navel, the first gunshot scar punched a deep, circular divot into her creamy flesh. Silvery white tissue radiated out from the entry wound before fading to pink. The second was closer to her center but below her navel, the indentation almost completely obscured by a thick crosswise incision scar that spanned her midsection. A third bullet had entered on the left, another inch down, the scar deeper and more puckered. Two additional surgical incisions slashed her abdomen on diagonals, white dots and lines with dark pink outlines adding to the panoply of destruction marring her body's otherwise flawless skin.

My breath quickened, and my eyes started to turn.

She squirmed under my attention, no doubt recognizing

why I stopped, and tugged at the sides of her shirt, pulling them together around her body.

My eyes leaped to hers, and I couldn't mask the horror and anger in them. She looked away, lips twisting with embarrassment and panic.

A frantic possessiveness roared through my blood and threatened to fully turn me. I fought it, gritting my teeth even as the tips of my fangs pinched the inside of my bottom lip. "Who did this to you?" I growled.

She squirmed, eyes focused anywhere but where I stared up at her, her dread visible in jerky motions and her struggle to cover her body.

I pinched her hips harder and fought the power in my blood. "Who did this to you, Siobhán?" I asked again, slow and demanding, every instinct in my body desperate to protect. "Who hurt you?" It didn't matter she was a Shaughnessy. She was mine, and I would kill whoever did this to my little shamrock. Slowly and without mercy.

"It's nothing," she answered, robotic and dismissive. "I don't want to talk about it."

"No." I released her hips, and she wrapped the shirt around her midsection, hugging herself to secure it closed. I rose to my feet and took her chin between my thumb and forefinger.

Siobhán, one of the most feisty, strong-willed women I'd ever met, wouldn't meet my eyes. They darted everywhere but my face, revealing a side of her I'd never seen before, vulnerable and deeply shaken. I didn't like it. I didn't like it any more than the quiet, defeated Siobhán from the couch.

I breathed through my nose, trying to calm the power in my blood, trying to calm her. I took her face between my hands, forcing her to look me in the eyes, and gentled my voice. "Who hurt you, Siobhán?"

Her eyes searched mine as if trying to weigh her next

words based on what she found there. I kept my gaze steady, letting her know we'd entered a truce.

"You're not the only one who's been hurt by my family." Her words and lips trembled, and the sincerity in her pained expression squeezed my heart even as my blood boiled at the significance of her answer.

I smoothed the hair off her face and tucked it behind her ears. I brushed my thumbs across her freckled cheekbones, needing to soothe myself as much as I needed to soothe her. "Tell me what happened."

She closed her eyes and drew in a shuddering breath. "My father was a mechanic in Ireland," she said, quiet and slow, and opened her eyes. "And here, before he met my mother. They met at a pub. Love at first sight. They married three months later. Uncle Paddy told him he could do better for his new family if he started a chop shop."

The delicate muscles of her throat moved through a swallow. "He had nothing. He was an immigrant. I was on the way —we're Irish Catholic, after all." She quirked a sardonic grin. "It was a chance to make something of himself. Opportunity. That's why you and I are here, isn't it? Opportunity? Our parents thought they'd find it here in America."

She looked out the French doors, and I let her, dropping my hands to her neck and running circles over her pulse with my thumbs. Her gaze grew distant, haunted.

"I used to go to the shop after school to spend time with him. Da taught me all about cars. I think he thought I could be a mechanic, too. 'Gel, in America, you can be anything.'" She mimicked a thick Irish accent and huffed. "Maybe that's true for normal people, but it's not true for people like us."

The set of her jaw hardened. "I was sixteen. I went to the shop to bring Da his lunch. I made him a lemonade and a tuna sandwich. It was hot that day." She swallowed, and her eyes became misty. "The garage door was open. A car pulled up the street." Her voice broke, and her lips twisted, working to hold back tears or anger or both.

The story was headed to a dark place, one that would likely enrage me and break her. I cupped her face again, forcing her back to me. Her eyes stayed downcast, and tears slid down her pale cheeks. I fought the overwhelming urge to kiss her forehead, to pull her into my arms and protect her from reliving whatever came next. But it wasn't my place, and I wasn't that guy. Even if a part of me wanted to be.

"It was some new gang. They just arrived from Ireland and didn't know any better, didn't know who ran Southie. They thought taking out a rival shop would give them an upper hand." She lifted her eyes. "Da took one in the leg. It just grazed him." She blinked hard, and another tear rolled down her face. "I wasn't so lucky."

Her mouth bent in a sad, ironic smile. "You were right about one thing last night—we never would have worked out. I've spent my whole life trying to get away from this world, and you keep running to it."

My jaw tightened, my teeth clenching so hard, I thought they might crack. "Siobhán, I—"

She held up a hand. "Let me finish."

I shut my mouth and nodded even though I wasn't sure I could hear the rest. I wasn't sure I wanted to make her relive the horrors that followed.

"You called me your little shamrock once, before everything."

"My good luck charm," I said with a wan smile.

"One of the bullets hit an artery. There was so much blood. But Uncle Paddy and Ciarán arrived at the shop the same time the shooting started. A squad car was there in minutes—one of the Southie cops on the Shaughnessy take. They rushed me to Mass General. Ciarán held my stomach the entire time." She closed her eyes and sucked in a breath. "So yeah. Lucky. By all accounts, I shouldn't be here right now."

My thumb moved back and forth, slow, methodical strokes along her cheekbone. My mind raced through time and conversations, connecting questions with answers. "That's why you moved to Ireland," I whispered.

"I spent the summer before my junior year of high school in and out of the hospital. The doctors stopped the bleeding the day of the shooting, stabilized me, but that was just the beginning. While all my friends were learning to drive, I was having my digestive system rewired." Her words took a bitter turn. "I couldn't eat, couldn't sleep. I woke up screaming every night, jumped at every loud noise. And the worst part?" Her lips twisted into a resentful sneer. "They all told me how lucky I was. Started calling me *Lucky Vahnie*." She scoffed. "Real fucking lucky." She looked away and shook her head. "'You're a real Shaughnessy now.' That's what Uncle Paddy told me. That I'd gotten my scars. That I'd earned my name." Her head snapped back to face me, and her eyes flashed like blue fire. "I was *sixteen*."

If I had the power, I'd have resurrected Pádraig Shaughnessy and killed him all over again. Painfully.

"So when I say I want nothing to do with my family," she said, her righteous anger focused on me, "when I say I did everything I could to get away from them, it's not bullshit. And now you know why. Now you've *seen* why." She gripped my forearms. "We both have scars from this life, Luca. Mine are just on the outside."

I ground my teeth, my emotions pulling me in opposite directions—protectiveness, outrage, confusion. Regret. After seeing her stomach, after hearing the pain and bitterness in her voice, I believed her. I believed everything she'd told me. Where that left us? I had no idea.

"I want names, Siobhán. I want the names of every person who hurt you."

"They're long gone, Luca." She waved a hand through the air. "Uncle Paddy took out the entire crew. You know how it works. He wasn't about to let that insult go."

I ground my teeth. Another sin for which the Shaughnessys needed to atone, this time enacted against one of their own. I'd personally make sure everyone involved—rival gang and Shaughnessys alike—paid their penance in blood.

The doorbell rang.

The neon time on the microwave above the oven read nine forty-five.

"Cazzo. That's Dominic," I said, but didn't let go. Neither did she. "Go upstairs. There's a Harvard sweatshirt in the bottom drawer of my dresser. And for God's sake, put on a pair of my boxers."

She raised an eyebrow.

"Top drawer on the left. I have to go to work. I'll... I'll get you some clothes and—"

Realization slapped me across the face. How drunk she was the night before. Her stomach. I dropped my hands from her face and shoved one into my hair. God, I was the worst kind of asshole. "What did you eat yesterday?"

She lowered her eyes and hugged herself. "A bowl of noodles."

"Fuck, Siobhán, why didn't you tell me?"

She let out a hysterical laugh and looked at me like I was crazy.

"Never mind. We're going to the grocery store when I get back." I took quick strides toward the door and pointed at the stairs. "Go."

She rolled her eyes. "Yes, sir."

Hand on the doorknob, I waited for her to disappear upstairs. The thought of Dominic seeing an inch of her naked skin drove my eyes to the edge of fire. I squeezed them shut and pinched the bridge of my nose. My mind was a turbulent mess. It constricted my chest and made it hard to breathe.

My plan was shot to hell. Everything I thought I knew about Siobhán was complete bullshit. But I had to keep her here. I couldn't let her go.

I didn't give a fuck if she told her family. Let them come after me. Maybe then I'd finally get to put a bullet through a Shaughnessy head. But I didn't need her running to the cops. She didn't have any evidence, but I didn't need the extra heat, especially with the expanding Source racket.

More than the cops, I was worried about Marco. I was within my rights to take Siobhán. He agreed at the sit-down—any Shaughnessy was fair game outside of Ciarán. But he'd make it into a *thing* regardless, and I wasn't ready to deal with his shit. Not yet.

Siobhán was the only leverage I had, the only path I saw to vengeance. I'd hold onto her, extract every ounce of information I could. Locked inside that pretty little head were the answers I needed. I was sure of it. I'd gain her trust and get her talking until she revealed her family's weaknesses. Then I'd exact my revenge. For myself and for her.

Chapter Fourteen

Luca

The girls' dressing room at The Dollhouse was enough to send my already racing heart into overdrive. Clothes, shoes, makeup, hair supplies, stacks of magazines, empty coffee mugs—crap covered every surface, an explosion of clutter as jumbled and erratic as the thoughts and emotions swirling through my mind. The urge to start cleaning had me flexing my hands. I licked my lips, closed my eyes, and took deep breaths until the tightness in my chest and lightness in my head eased. All I needed were clothes for Siobhán. Maybe a brush. Then I could get the hell out of there. Come back later when my nerves could handle the mess.

But I couldn't let it go.

"How the hell do you know what's clean around here?" I shouted and kicked a pile of magazines out of my way. I stepped over an empty pizza box and stood between the two sofas in the middle of the room, my hands shaking with anxiety.

Laura and Trixie were dancing first shift, and we opened in a little over an hour. They sat on stools in front of the light-rimmed mirrors in street clothes putting on makeup. Mia and

Dani, two of our in-house Sources, had early appointments. They sat on opposite ends of the couch facing the door. Mia scrolled on her phone, and Dani flipped through a *People* magazine. A box of Kool-Aid hung from her mouth by its straw. She had three appointments tonight; high blood sugar would help.

Not one girl bothered to respond, much less look up. So much for being in charge.

"I want this shit cleaned up." I pointed at the floor. "When I come back tonight, this place better be spotless, capisce?"

That got their attention. At least, as much of their attention as I was ever able to garner. Mia lifted her eyes from her phone and smiled, and the girls doing their makeup lowered their brushes. "Yes, Mr. Moretti," Dani said, but her focus never left her magazine.

"Fucking Christ," I mumbled and shoved my hand into my hair. I needed to get the hell out of there before I had a full-on panic attack. "Dani. Stand up for me for a second."

"Why?" she asked around the straw and flipped another page.

"Because I fucking asked you to, and I'm the one who pays you."

She let out an over-exaggerated sigh, put the magazine and the juice box down, and pushed herself off the couch. She crossed her arms, stuck out a hip, and gave me a bored look.

Chestier than Siobhán, although that wasn't saying much. Same height too, give or take. Maybe two sizes thicker. Close enough.

"Get me some clothes—*clean* clothes—that would fit you." I waved a hand. "A couple pairs of leggings, shirts, whatever. Some of the new underwear that got delivered last week."

"Okay..." she said and gave me side-eye. But shockingly, she followed directions and moved around the room collecting items as though the disarray was organized into logical piles.

The Dollhouse had a sizable budget for its dancers and in-house Sources. Vinnie believed, and I agreed, that one way to turn a strip club into a viable front was to class the place up, make sure every girl was clean and well-dressed. Police had better things to do than investigate a joint on the up-and-up. Especially when the girls giving them free lap dances with their drinks were well-adjusted and healthy.

Dani slung a bunch of garments over her arm. I picked up the *People* magazine she'd been reading along with a few others and shoved them into my gym bag.

What the hell was I doing? Picking up supplies to make Siobhán feel at home while I kept her locked up and manipulated her for information? *Fuck.*

Dani flipped through the garments in the closet against the far wall, and pale blue caught my eye.

"Wait," I said. "What's that? The blue."

"This?" She pulled the hanger off the rack and held a sheer teddy in front of her. "That should work."

Images of Siobhán wearing nothing but that teddy filled my vision. Sheer fabric stretched around her lithe body. Thick, rosy nipples pert and visible beneath a blue the same color as her eyes. Red lips turned up in a wicked smirk made all the more impish by the slight crookedness of her front tooth. My fangs would descend, and I'd bite her breast through the thin blue fabric, feeding on her blood even as I tongued her nipple and made her groan.

My dick twitched. I licked my lips and shifted my weight. This was *not* how Stockholm Syndrome was supposed to work.

I gave Dani a terse nod, and she threw the teddy over her arm with the rest of the clothes. She rooted around in a big box with a Victoria's Secret label on it, picked out a few scraps of lace, and held out both arms. "Here."

I opened the gym bag. She dumped the clothes inside.

"Get this place cleaned up before we open," I ordered and zipped the bag shut. "I'll be back in a few hours, and I do *not* want to see a mess."

"Richie never used to make us clean," one of the girls grumbled.

My eyes sparked with frustration. "Do I look like fucking Richie?" I shouted. They stopped what they were doing and paid attention. "Get this shit. Cleaned. Up."

I slung the gym bag over my shoulder and made for the door but stopped short. "Dani, when Jenny gets in, tell her I need to see her tonight."

"You got it, boss," she said.

The sun in a clear sky was a welcome reprieve from the dim lighting of The Dollhouse. It helped calm my nerves. I needed air after all that mess, and the brisk late-morning breeze filled my lungs and allowed me to breathe. Feeding would take care of the other half of the mess—the one inside my head.

I wasn't the pinnacle of control when it came to women— far from it—and I almost crossed a dangerous line this morning with Siobhán. Hunger had fueled some of my lust, and the last thing I needed was to do something stupid because I hadn't fed in a week. I needed to keep my eye on the prize—putting my vendetta to rest—and I couldn't do that unless I had a clear head. Siobhán wasn't at my house to feed from or to fuck. She was there for information, information I could use against her family for revenge. That's all that mattered.

Chapter Fifteen

Siobhán

"I still can't believe you drive a 1985 308 GTS," I said.

Luca turned off the engine, and the roaring beast quieted. We climbed out, and the Ferrari-red paint blazed in the noontime sun. He parked diagonally across two spaces as far as possible from every other car in the lot, which meant we were tucked in a corner even though there were plenty of spaces up front.

"Granted, they were the most widely produced Ferraris, and the most accessible to mere mortals, but—" I ripped my eyes away from the sexiest car I'd ever seen to find Luca halfway across the parking lot. I hurried to catch up. "That car is almost forty years old, but it looks like you drove it off the lot yesterday. Not to mention the engine. Purrs like a kitten."

He snorted. "How do you know so much about cars?"

"I already told you. Da's a mechanic. Or was. I grew up around cars. And there's never a shortage of expensive ones at a chop shop. Plus, there were always car magazines lying around. I got bored. It was something to do." I grabbed his forearm. "Can I drive it?"

He looked at me in horror. "Absolutely not."

"Why not?"

He scoffed. "You'd probably strip the clutch."

I folded my arms and arched an eyebrow. "'Cause I'm a woman I don't know how to drive stick?"

He narrowed his eyes.

"I'm going to drive that car."

He got in my face. "No, you're not."

"We'll see about that," I said through an evil smile and crossed the last stretch of parking lot.

The automatic doors of Starmarket swooshed open. Someone must have set the air conditioning to Penguin Enclosure, and that grocery store refrigeration smell turned my empty hangover stomach, but I didn't care. I was just stoked to be out of the house.

Luca reached for a basket, and I snatched it from him and shoved it back on the stack. "We need a cart."

He groaned.

"What? You have no food in your house, and you've given me zero information as to how long you plan on holding me hostage. I need to eat. And as much as I love vodka and olives, I can't survive on martinis."

"Fine," he said and jerked a cart out of the corral.

I led us toward the bakery. "So where'd you get it? Auction?"

"No. It was my father's. He bought it new a year or so before he died. He was obsessed with that car. 'The pride of Italy, figlio mio. And Magnum drives one.'" He chuckled, and the rare display of genuine happiness when talking about his past made me smile. "After he died, Vito—you know who Vito is, right?"

I cocked an eyebrow. "Marco's consigliere?"

He frowned, and a hint of suspicion colored his displeasure.

"I'm not a rat, Luca. I'm just not stupid."

"Right," he said, but drew the word out. "Anyway, after he died, Vito locked everything up—the house, the car, the boat"—my head snapped up—"Yes, I own a boat, and no, we can't go out on it." I frowned. "Froze his assets. Set up a trust."

I picked up a loaf of Wonder Bread and put it in the cart, garnering a hefty amount of side-eye.

"Everything transferred into my name when I turned eighteen, but I didn't touch any of it till after college."

I picked up a package of chocolate chip cookies and held it up to him in question.

He shrugged.

"We're shopping for you too," I said. "There's nothing to eat in that house."

"I'm fine."

"What? You don't eat?"

"Of course, I eat."

"You can't cook?"

He gaped at me as if I'd blasphemed. "I'm Italian. Of course I can cook. I just choose not to. Easier to pick up some gabagool or a slice at Tarantino's."

I tossed the package in the cart. "Soup aisle."

He turned the cart, and I followed.

"Well, that car is in perfect condition," I said. "Amazing."

"It *was* in perfect condition," he said all surly and cocked an eyebrow.

I canted my head.

"It was in perfect condition until someone barfed on my passenger-side floor mat."

I scoffed. "That's your own damn fault. You kidnapped me and almost threw me off the Tobin Bridge, remember? I did nothing wrong."

He grabbed my arm, pulled me close, and stopped the cart. "You may not be a rat, but you're still a Shaughnessy. Don't forget that, because I won't."

"I'm not doing this here," I hissed. I yanked my arm free and marched down the soup aisle. I loaded two cans of chicken noodle into the cart and paused. "Any idea how long you're going to keep me prisoner?"

He folded his arms across his chest. "Until you help me even the score between our families."

"I'd love to hear how you think I'm going to do that." I put two more cans in the cart, then grabbed the handle and started driving it myself. "Care to clue me in on the grand plan?"

He eyed me sideways, his lips pressed into an irritated line.

"Ah. I see. There is no plan. Fantastic. Really fucking great, Luca." I turned for the dairy section. "Selfish asshole," I mumbled under my breath.

"Excuse me?"

I stopped, faced him, and moved my mouth slowly through each word. "Selfish. Asshole." I raised my eyebrows, and he scowled. I spun away and kept moving. "No better than Ciarán or Rory or any of the other selfish assholes in my life."

"Don't compare me to those lawless fucks. And what the hell's that supposed to mean anyway?"

"Lawless, huh?" I snorted. "Says the kidnapper. And it means exactly what you think it means. You're all the same. Selfish assholes."

"I got you clothes, didn't I? We're grocery shopping, aren't we?"

I glared at him and his smug face. "Oh, yeah. You're a real paragon of charity. I'll be sure to order you an engraved plaque." I looked down at the slightly-too-big leggings and my off-the-shoulder long sleeve—the only clothes appropriate for public. "Booty shorts, crop tops, scraps of fabric I can only assume are underwear. Not to mention that—that blue thing."

His nostrils flared at the mention of the sheer teddy I found buried in the gym bag. I'd thrown it across the room, pissed at his presumption and the flare of heat that had shot between my legs.

I poked him in the chest. "If you think I'm going to wear that for you, you've got another thing coming."

He stepped into my space and flashed his trademark sexy smirk. "Thought you might want to practice your lap dance skills. Wouldn't want you to get rusty."

My cheeks burned. "Ugh!" I stormed away with the cart and left him chuckling in my wake.

I stopped in front of the cold case and nearly jumped for joy—full rows of my favorite coconut milk chocolate pudding cups. I started stacking them in the cart.

"Presumptuous too. All you care about is yourself. It doesn't matter how what you want impacts me. Case in point —you have no reason to keep me. Your original plan is shot, and your new plan doesn't exist beyond *use Siobhán for revenge*, which"—I pointed at him with a pudding cup—"for the record, is not an actual plan"—and tossed it in the cart.

"*For the record*," he shot back, "I do have a plan."

"Oh yeah?" I folded my arms. "Lay it on me."

"I have questions. You're going to answer them."

I made a disgusted noise, something between a scoff and a snort. "Did you lose brain cells when you put on all that extra muscle? For the eight millionth time, I'm not a rat."

He stepped around the end of the cart and crowded me. "Your cousin is working with the feds," he said, low and scathing. My empty acid-stomach flipped, and I shook my head. "*He's* the rat, and you're going to help me prove it."

"I already told you. I stay out of my family's business." The words came out robotic, trying to hide that I suspected he was right about Ciarán. "Besides, I don't talk. Not to Marco. Not to Ciarán. Not to you."

"Oh, you will." He leaned in close enough that I smelled his cologne. "Give it enough time, and you will."

"So... You're keeping me prisoner until I talk?" My indignation resurfaced, stomping all over my worry.

He backed up with a smug turn to his lips.

I put my hands on my hips so I wouldn't grab his biceps and shake him. "It doesn't matter to you how this might impact me and my life, does it? Not even accounting for the *trauma* you caused. You know I'm leaving Terme, which means you know this vacation isn't a vacation. I have interviews lined up for the next two weeks, interviews that were extremely difficult to get. There isn't exactly an overabundance of five-star resorts within driving distance of my parents. Who, by the way, I have to take care of, because Rory and Ciarán are just as selfish as you."

My frustration and anger at the entire fucked-up situation would make my stomach start cramping if I didn't tamp it down, but I couldn't help myself. I jammed my finger into Luca's rocky chest—hard this time—and hoped my pointy fingernail hurt like hell. "And when I miss those interviews? When I don't even call to cancel? I lose those opportunities. Forever. You think those resorts will hire a GM who can't be bothered to cancel an appointment, much less show up?"

His jaw and lips twitched as if fighting a grimace, but otherwise, he remained a stony wall.

"I can't go back to Terme. Especially not after this debacle. And I can't go back to Ireland and leave my mother who is afraid to walk and my father who has dementia to the mercy of unreliable, egotistical men. Which means *you* are ruining my career. For no reason." The heat in my cheeks was as fiery as the burn in my stomach. "Selfish." I poked him again in his chest. "Asshole." And once more, with feeling. "Plain and simple." I grabbed the cart and pushed it forward.

Rory. Ciarán. My uncle Paddy. My own da. Every asshole I

dated who just wanted to fuck the tall skinny blonde. Luca. They were all the same. Self-absorbed, macho assholes who expected me to take care of them and any shit situation they created. The only exception? Marco. Despite his machismo, he gave me opportunity and support. A real chance at making a life in Boston. A home. And of course, because fuck my life, he turned out to be a don in the Italian Mafia.

Everywhere I turned, the life I never chose haunted me. Everywhere except Ireland.

I stopped and threw some bananas into the cart.

"What are you going to do with all that pudding?" he asked.

I looked at him, incredulous. "Were you listening?" His face revealed nothing. "Why am I even asking that? Of course you weren't." I resumed my quest with the cart. "What do you think I'm going to do with it? I'm going to eat it."

"No one can eat that much pudding."

"Wanna bet?" I cocked an eyebrow.

"Aside from the bananas, there's not a single healthy thing in that cart."

"Healthy is relative."

He scoffed.

"Judgy much?" I sighed. "All right, Susan Powter, crash course on my digestive system." I sped down the freezer aisle. "One of the bullets went through my stomach. They had to section off the damaged portion, so my stomach is about half the size it's supposed to be, which means I can't eat very much in one sitting. On top of that, they removed feet"—I met his eyes and stuck my head out—"*feet* of my small intestines and several inches of my large, which means, of the small amount I can eat in one sitting, only a fraction of the nutrients gets absorbed. I can't digest raw vegetables or any unprocessed grains without spending hours in the bathroom and wanting to end my life."

He grimaced.

"Sexy, right?" I reached into the freezer and grabbed a pack of cherry popsicles. "And, after all the surgeries, what's left of my stomach pumps out acid like nobody's business. I have a wicked case of reflux, which means no foods with too much acid or spice and a steady intake of extra-strength Tums." I tossed the popsicles into the cart. "Oh! And to add insult to injury, I was lactose intolerant before any of this happened, so..." I waved my hand over the contents of the cart like Vanna White presenting a dystopian smorgasbord. "These are my safe foods—high-calorie and processed as fuck. Stuff I can eat that won't make me miserable. Healthy *for me*. Any questions?"

He stared at me, eyes wide and jaw slack.

Despite my bravado, my impromptu rant made me highly uncomfortable. I never told anyone about my over-the-top dietary restrictions, much less their origins. I made up all kinds of stories over the years about my scars, too. Surprisingly easy since the average person had no idea what a bullet wound looked like, especially amid all the other incisions.

Luca was the first person to see my stomach and immediately know what happened. I'm not sure why I told him the details. Maybe because he'd already guessed the gist. Or maybe because I wanted him to know why I'd "lied." It had never been about pulling a fast one on him or Marco. It had been about escaping my past.

But this? Telling him the gory details of what I could and couldn't eat?

Maybe I wanted to stick it to him. Drive home the fact that all the bullshit he made up about me and my motivations was just that—bullshit. That his decisions based on his stories were impacting my life, and I didn't need one more man using me to make their life simpler. Maybe I wanted someone to care. Maybe I wanted *him* to care.

I'd exposed my truths and made myself vulnerable to the worst possible person. A man who had, in a way, cheated on me, then decided I was the root of all evil, kidnapped me, and tried to kill me. And I just explained to him that if I wasn't careful with what I ate, I'd end up on the toilet.

What the fuck, Siobhán?

Falling back into conversation with Luca was too easy. All the lunches and chats and small talk before The Incident. Not to mention the strange magnetism that drew us together no matter where we were or who was around or what was happening. Like the universe was shoving us together, forcing us into something neither of us wanted but were destined to face.

"Whatever," I said. "It doesn't matter." Because it didn't matter. All that mattered was that I was trapped, indefinitely, with no possibility of escape. "Let's just get this over with and go back to the house."

"Shoes!" Luca announced as soon as he walked through the door between the garage and the kitchen.

"Oh my god, you're obsessed!" I said and toed them off.

"That was quick," Dominic said from the living room. The TV was on. "Did you get me a calzone?"

I set the grocery bags on the island. Luca was already arranging items in the fridge like he was playing competitive Tetris. Labels out.

"Yes, I got your calzone," Luca said. "It's on the counter."

"Perfetto. Grazie. Hai finito di giocare a fare la famiglia per oggi?"

Luca's head snapped to where Dominic sat on the couch. Dominic had one of those boyish faces that made the upturn of his lips look especially mischievous. I had no idea what he just said, but I couldn't help chuckle at Luca's reaction. It was nice to see someone else needle him for a change.

"Vaffanculo!" Now *that* I understood. Luca pointed at Dominic. "Watch yourself. I'm still your capo."

Dominic raised his hands in surrender, and his smirk broke into a wide smile. "Mi dispiace, capo. You want me here babysitting instead of doing pickups, that's your call."

Luca slammed the door shut—"Corretto!"—and walked over to the entertainment center.

I leaned across the island and pulled the focaccia I'd ordered at the Italian deli out of the bag. We stopped there on the way back from Starmarket to pick up Dominic's calzone, and I wasn't about to miss an opportunity for fresh bread covered in olives and olive oil to cure my hangover stomach.

I sank my teeth into the doughy goodness and groaned. My eyes closed, and I slumped into the barstool, relaxing my head on its back. I hadn't eaten anything but those noodles in over a day, and the focaccia was the best bread ever in the history of all bread.

The silence was deafening. I rolled my head toward the living room and opened my eyes. Dominic and Luca stared at me, the former like he was waiting to see what indecent noise I'd make next, the latter like he wanted to haul me upstairs and lock me in my room.

"What?" I said through the mouthful.

Luca slammed the cabinet door, locked it, and walked back into the kitchen, glaring at Dominic along the way.

"All right." Dominic pushed himself up off the couch and walked to the front door. "I'm going outside." He bent over to put his shoes on. "Calzone, per favore?"

I reached for the paper bag, but Luca snatched it from my fingers, eyes dark and shooting daggers.

"What's your problem?" I mumbled and ripped off another mouthful.

The door opened and shut, and moments later, Luca hovered over me. He gripped the back of my barstool in one hand and held my cell phone out with the other.

"Give me the passcode to unlock it. Tell me who you need to call to reschedule your interviews."

My mouth hung open, the lump of bread stuck between my teeth.

"And don't get any ideas," he warned. "I'm putting it on speaker."

I swallowed and gaped at him. "Thank you."

"Yeah, well… I'm not about to be compared to Ciarán Shaughnessy."

I nodded, dumbstruck by the conflict plainly written in the twitch of his jaw and the way he shifted his weight.

"I need to get to work," he snapped. "Let's make this quick."

I got down from the barstool. "Excuse me."

He moved out of my way.

I went to the fridge and grabbed a bottle of water.

Nothing made sense. Not him keeping me here and certainly not this latest foray into benevolence, however reluctant or relative. But one thing was clear—I needed to get out of there. I needed to escape Luca Moretti's bizarre jail. And once I did? I needed to get out of Boston, away from Luca, and back to safety.

Chapter Sixteen

Luca

Sunday nights at The Dollhouse were slow, at least the front of the house. Trixie thrust her breasts forward and pressed her backside against the pole, gripping it over her head. She slinked down its length until she squatted at its base, knees spread wide. The handful of regulars around the stage chatted, drank, and smoked cigars, only half tuned in to the mostly naked woman writhing in front of them under the stage lights. A few patrons watched the Sox play Tampa—what a shitty game. The rest of the club was empty beneath the dim lights and thin layer of cigar smoke.

I walked past the bar and lifted my chin to Joe the bartender, a grizzled, tight-lipped blood demon as old as Boston itself. It was a common misconception that blood demons didn't age. We did, although not in the same way as humans and not at the same rate. Somewhere between forty-five and sixty, blood demons reached maturity, and with each passing year, the rate at which we aged decreased logarithmically until it appeared as though we weren't aging at all. That's why you had so many blood demons walking around looking like they were fifty, fifty-five years old.

But no amount of immortality could erase the signs of a hard life or hard living. Years wore you down, immortal or not. You could see it in their eyes, the way they drilled right through you. Or in the set of their faces. It took a lot to ruffle the feathers of an old bird. They'd lived too long and seen too much.

Vito was like that—the way he looked at you, the way he held himself, his patience. And he was only a hundred and forty, give or take. Not even middle-aged by blood demon standards.

Through the double doors, the back of the house was as big as the front and where we made our real money on Sunday nights. Written off as offices for the Valenzano Trading Company, the rooms off the main hallway provided spaces for private dances and appointments with Sources. They were locked now, but in an hour, blood demons would start arriving for their meals, and I'd have four revolving doors to monitor.

Down the hall and through another set of doors, my office and the girls' dressing room occupied the rest of the property. I poked my head into the dressing room, ready to take out my pent-up frustration on the girls if the place still looked like a shithole. Luckily for them and for my sanity, they'd created a semblance of order. The floor and countertops were visible, and I didn't spot a single empty pizza box.

Laura, Dani, Mia, and Jenny were dressed and ready for the night. They lounged on the couches and flipped through magazines. Dani and Mia sipped Kool-Aid.

"Jenny." She looked at me with doe eyes, and I groaned inwardly. I didn't want to deal with her tonight, but I needed to feed. Probably needed a blowjob too. Take the fucking edge off. "Room three. Twenty minutes."

She smiled like she'd won the lottery. "Okay, Luca."

I pointed a finger at her. "No blow before I feed, capisce?"

"Fine," she said, irritated.

I hated that shit. I could taste the coke in her blood. It was bitter and foul and made me even more neurotic. And twitchy. It was getting really fucking old.

Across the hall, the main office was as big if not bigger than the dressing room, complete with a fridge and small bar, lounge chairs, and a window, a nice feature when your boss has a cigar permanently wedged between his lips. Speaking of the demon, Vinnie Valenzano sat at the card table across from Gio playing poker. I walked around them to my desk.

"Nice of you to show up for work," Vinnie said, not bothering to look up from his cards or remove the cigar from between his teeth.

I took off my suit jacket, slung it over the back of the chair, and leaned against my desk. "I was here earlier. Made sure everything was in order."

He puffed on his cigar. "Everyone around here's on their own fucking schedule," he grumbled and tossed a couple of chips into the pot. "Taking their damn time."

Gio grunted. "Sì, sì."

"Top earners aren't kicking up what they used to," he continued. I opened my mouth, but before I could comment, Vinnie shot me a look. "I don't want to hear a single fucking word about the goddamned economy."

I clamped my mouth shut. He refocused on his hand and threw down a card.

"This business doesn't run on the economy. I want my capi to do their fucking jobs. I want *earners*." He slammed his fist on the table, and the chips rattled.

Gio threw down a card.

Vinnie eyed it, lips tight and nostrils flaring.

Gio leaned back in his chair and watched him.

"Eh, cazzo," Vinnie said and tossed his cards onto the table —"Porca puttana"—and grabbed his drink.

"I met with Richie and Matteo yesterday," I said. "The Source funnel to Terme is in place. We're ready for traffic, but we need to move slow. The feds have been coming around more than usual. Even Vito's twitchy. But we should see profits start to climb over the next couple months."

"Couple of months..." Vinnie swiped his hand down his face. "I want this shit turned around." He jammed a thick finger into the card table. "Now."

Gio leaned forward. "As your consigliere, I'd be remiss if I didn't point out—not all your capi are underperforming. Richie and Johnny Lam are doing fine." He turned to me and cocked an eyebrow. "You could be doing more."

I folded my arms. "In the month I've been in this crew, I learned this place, figured out how to run it more efficiently, and set up the bridge between us and the DeVitas." I showed Gio a thin smile. "In a month."

"Giusto," Gio said and nodded.

"But yeah. Now that's done, I can do more."

"See," Vinnie said and pointed a finger at me. "That's the attitude I need. From my capi *and* their earners." He focused his sharp attention on me and struck the card table again with that same finger. "I need you here on time, milking this place for every penny, and I need you running jobs. I need you earning." He drained the whiskey from his glass. "The Playground is next. I'm done with this shit."

He pushed his big frame out of the chair and buttoned his suit jacket. I was tall, but Vinnie had bulk. We were around the same height, but he had about fifty pounds on me, give or take, and I wasn't exactly a small guy.

He clasped my shoulder with his meaty paw. "Marco never used you to your full potential. I'm not making that mistake." He flashed his wolfish smile. "You've got that ruthless streak in you. Same as your father. Isn't that right, Gio?"

Gio leaned back and gave me a knowing smile. "I'd call that shit he pulled on Marco pretty ruthless."

My stomach lurched.

"Time to use it." Vinnie squeezed my shoulder. "I got a call from my guys down at the docks. There's a warehouse full of those—come si chiamano? Video games systems..." He waved a beefy hand through the air and glanced at Gio, who shrugged.

"The new Playstation?" I asked.

"Sì. Playstations. Five hundred units. Get a crew together and make the lift."

Anticipation flew through my body. A job. And not just any job, a half-million-dollar haul. Finally.

The jobs I ran under Marco were safe—shakedowns, fixing books. Easy stuff. One of the ways he held me back. But this? This was a chance to make a name for myself separate from Marco and separate from my father. A chance to be a top earner in my own right. I was hungry for it. Hungry to prove I deserved to be a capo in the Mafia. Hungry to make the Moretti name mean something again. Hungry for my turn.

"Ho capito," I said, determined and eager. "Quando?"

"Tomorrow night. The truck leaves the warehouse at the start of second shift—around eleven." He released my shoulder and headed for the door. "Do it on the turnpike outside the city. Pick your crew. Two, three men tops. All soldati demoni del sangue. I don't need anyone breaking omertà over stupid shit, capisce?"

"Capisce."

Vinnie grabbed his fedora off the coat rack and set it on his head. He pulled the brim low. "Don't fuck this up, Luca. I want that cargo, and I want you earning. You do this right, there's more where that came from."

"I'm a Moretti. It'll be done, and it'll be done right."

He opened the door and leveled me with a no-nonsense stare. "It better," he said and walked out the door.

———

THE PRIVATE ROOMS at the back of The Dollhouse were all laid out the same. Dimmable lamps lit the ten-by-ten-foot spaces and cast an amber glow across a single wooden end table and a couch. A dial mounted on the wall next to the door allowed occupants to set the volume of the music piped in from the main bar. Hardwood floors and leather upholstery made for easy cleanup of bodily fluids. Simple and utilitarian, the rooms got the job done.

Jenny had the lights lowered, and the sensual music was loud enough that I noticed. She lay on her side, head propped up in one hand. She wore the clear platform heels she preferred due to her height, or lack thereof, and a skin-tight black lace teddy. It barely covered her fake breasts and was so short that the clasps of the garter belt holding up her sheer stockings were visible. She parted her hot pink lips and ran her hand down her waist to where the teddy ended at the apex of her thighs. She tugged at the hem in a move meant to entice.

I squeezed my eyes shut and pinched the bridge of my nose. I didn't want to snap at her and her ridiculous seduction game. It made her pouty, and put me in a foul mood.

"What's wrong, Luca?" Her high, squeaky voice was nails on a chalkboard.

"Nothing." I rolled up my shirtsleeves. "Sit up."

She obeyed, always eager to appease me.

I stepped forward until I stood in front of her and unbuckled my belt. She'd be too drained after I fed to suck me off. I unzipped my pants, reached inside my boxers, and pulled out my dick. Not a single drop of blood rushed to where I needed it to go.

Goddammit.

I made a fist around my dick and started working myself. Jenny licked her lips. They were too full, and the hot pink was the wrong shade.

I squeezed harder and picked up the pace. The blonde was off too, her hair all large and unmoving.

I grabbed one of her tits with my free hand. It didn't feel right. Too big.

"Fuck this," I said and tucked my limp dick back into my shorts and zipped my pants. "Get up." I buckled my belt.

Her disappointed expression irritated the hell out of me. I spun her around so her back faced my front. I rested my forearm across her chest to hold her in place and shoved aside the big plume of stiff hair that smelled of chemicals. She tilted her head, presenting her neck.

My fangs descended, and my eyes glowed to match the dim lights. I bit her neck and started to feed.

Her body relaxed. I closed my eyes and cleared my head, trying to focus on nourishment instead of Jenny's mewls and squirming. My plan backfired.

Siobhán knelt between my legs at Vesuvio. Her red lips wrapped around my dick. Her blue eyes locked with mine. Her head bobbed along my hard, swollen length.

My dick twitched. I bit down and pulled in a mouthful of blood.

Jenny groaned from the surge of venom. She stuck her ass out and rubbed it against my jutting length. I shifted my hips back and took another deep drink, ready to be done with this entire unpleasant affair. She reached around my back, grabbed my ass, and pulled me into her. I released her from my bite and pushed her away.

She stumbled, unsteady from the venom and those ridiculous heels. But I was done. Done with my meal and done with her.

I licked a drop of blood from my lips and rolled down my shirtsleeves.

Jenny regained her footing and held her fingers to her neck, mouth agape. I grabbed her hair, swatted her hand away, and swiped my tongue across the wound. It quickly closed.

She stared at me in wide-eyed shock.

"Log your time for a feeding," I said and reached for the door. I paused and glanced over my shoulder. "I'll be using a different Source from now on."

She lifted her chin, defiant, but there was no mistaking the disappointment in her eyes or the anger in her taut mouth.

I closed the door behind me and buttoned my cuffs as I walked back down the hall to my office. I'd fed enough to get me through the next week if needed and, more importantly, avoid the temptation waiting for me at home. Besides, I had bigger problems than a feeding cut short by a gold-digging Source. I had a twenty-five-year-old crime to avenge and a hijacking to plan.

Vinnie's cybersecurity officer was as competent as Marco's, and within an hour of my request, an email popped into my inbox telling me everything I needed to know. I'd sent him a message outlining the information I needed after a few quick Google searches. Like most cyber guys, he preferred communicating via email, but unlike others, he never used phones. Ever. But for all his paranoia, Vinnie's guy was good, and two hours after receiving his email, Leo and I pulled to a stop a block past a two-family detached row house in one of Dorchester's Irish neighborhoods.

Leo parked the unmarked sedan but didn't turn off the engine.

"In and out," I said. "Ten minutes. Leave after fifteen."

He nodded, and I exited onto the dark city sidewalk.

Ronan O'Doyle lived on the bottom floor of one of the countless cookie-cutter homes lining the densely populated city streets. It hadn't been difficult to get an address once I found out he was still alive. Hell, it hadn't been difficult finding the name of the gang who attacked the Shaughnessys. Not when a teenage girl had been caught in the crossfire.

A TV backlit the curtains on the lower level and announced the highlights of the night's Sox game, loud enough to wake the upstairs neighbors. But no lights were on behind the upstairs windows. Good.

I walked up the wooden porch steps and knocked on the door.

A chair creaked, boots hit the floor, and my supernatural hearing picked up each footfall over the obnoxiously loud TV. The deadbolt clicked and the door swung open.

A middle-aged man of average build, average height, and average features, Ronan O'Doyle had thinning hair and bushy, unkempt eyebrows. He narrowed his hazy blue eyes, and the creases lining his forehead deepened. "What d'ye want?" His voice had an unmistakably Irish lilt, but the words sounded as if he'd dragged them through gravel.

"That's no way to welcome a guest, is it? Ronan O'Doyle?"

"What's it to ye?" he asked and lifted a Sam Adams to his lips with his left hand—a left hand missing its index, middle, and ring fingers. Irish mob handiwork at its best. The only confirmation I needed, and the confirmation that had just ended his life.

I pulled out my piece from the inside of my suit jacket and aimed it at his heart.

He looked at the gun, then looked at me. He swigged his beer.

"Inside," I said.

He backed into the living room, and I shut the door behind me.

Sparse. A bachelor pad free of decoration except for a framed poster of the 2004 World Series Champion Red Sox hanging above an empty fireplace, a big screen TV loud enough to deafen the hard of hearing, and a well-worn leather recliner. A side table topped with two empty beer bottles and a remote stood between the armrest and the fireplace. No evidence of a landline.

"Have a seat." I gestured to the recliner with my gun.

O'Doyle moved toward the recliner as if a stranger holding him at gunpoint wasn't out of the ordinary, and sank into his chair, making it creak.

I held out my hand. "Your phone."

He twisted in his seat and reached into his pocket. "This some kinda shakedown?" he rumbled. "'Cause I already told Johnny I don't got his money. I'm good for it next month." He pulled out a cell and handed it to me.

I dropped the phone in my pocket and lowered my gun. "How'd you lose those fingers, Ronan?"

He glanced down to where his thumb and pinky finger held the beer bottle on top of the recliner's armrest.

"Dog got 'em," he said to his missing fingers. "Real nasty mutt."

I snorted. "That's not the story I heard."

I hadn't expected anyone from the O'Doyle crew to have made it out of Southie alive, much less their ringleader. Leave it to the cyber guy to dig up an address and the dirty details.

He shrugged. "Don't really give a fig what you heard."

"You should."

"Why's that?"

"'Cause what I heard"—I stepped forward—"was that instead of putting you in the dirt for shooting his niece, Paddy

Shaughnessy cut them off." Another step. "One for each bullet you put in her stomach."

His face went flat. "Not sure where ye heard that tripe."

"What I want to know is how you're still alive. That's the mystery I can't figure out. Everyone in the O'Doyle crew is in the ground. Southie cops found them in a dumpster, each with a hole in his chest. Execution style at point-blank range. But not their leader. Not Ronan O'Doyle. Why's that, Ronan?"

"Ye seem to know a lot about it. Why don't ye tell me?"

"I can make this easy on you or hard. Your choice. You're going to die anyway. Might as well make it easy."

He shifted in his seat like he was settling into the idea, then lifted his beer, examined it, and drained the bottle.

"I knew an arms dealer from Dublin workin' for the IRA." He shrugged again. "Paddy decided I was more use to him alive than dead."

I ground my teeth, trying to tamp down my rising fury. Guns. I knew those Irish fucks had no code, but to trade Siobhán's honor—her worth—for fucking guns?

Heat clawed up my neck. There was no fucking way Ciarán didn't know about this, and the need to prove his connection to the feds and end his sorry ass took on new urgency.

"That's the difference," I spit the words out, disgusted, "between Cosa Nostra and a lawless mob. We live by a code. We have honor."

The words stung as they passed my lips; the guilt over what I did to Marco was a bitter poison I could still taste even if he had left my father's murder unavenged. It made me sick.

"We'd never sell out family for fucking guns. Especially one of our women." The heat climbing up my neck reached my eyes, and I let them burn as surely as Ronan O'Doyle would burn in hell. "It's time you paid for your sins. Blood for blood. And unlike your boss, the only gun I care about is the one you used to hurt her."

He paled and swallowed hard, making his throat bob, but he knew better than to fight. He'd meet his end, and at least he was facing it like a fucking man.

I lifted my gun. "This is for Siobhán Connelly."

Crack!

He grunted, and his hands went to his stomach just to the right of where his beer gut sat above his belt.

"One."

Crack!

His mouth hung open, and he stared down at his blood-covered hands over the new bullet hole in the center of his gut.

"Two."

He closed his eyes.

Crack!

His body jerked with the impact of the third bullet, and he slumped in the chair.

"Three."

He'd bleed out before anyone got to him, but I wasn't about to take the chance that this fucker might survive to live one more day after what he did to Siobhán. He shouldn't have lived this long.

"E questo è per me," I said and put a bullet between his eyes.

Chapter Seventeen

Luca

The entertainment center's cabinet doors unlocked with a rattle, and I swung them open to access the safe.

"You make a better door than a window," Siobhán snarked from the couch.

"What're you, twelve?" I glanced over my shoulder to glare at her and her smart mouth but was distracted by all the creamy skin.

Tiny green athletic shorts straight out of a '70s gym class put her long, slender legs on display. Her feet were propped up on my coffee table, knees rocking from side to side, and her red-painted toes wiggled atop the wood. Her hair was pulled back, and her lips were wrapped around the tip of a bright red popsicle. She sucked it in and out of her mouth, and fuck if my dick didn't jerk at the sight.

She raised her eyebrows like I was inconveniencing her by interrupting one of the old movies she had on every time I walked into the living room. Movies she'd probably seen a million times. I shook my head and turned back to the safe.

I ejected the magazine of my 9mm Glock to make sure it was full. It was. I locked it back in place and shoved the gun beneath the waistband of my track pants. I moved to shut the safe but thought better. I grabbed my compact pistol and ankle holster. Lifting my pant leg, I fastened the holster and gun to my ankle. I closed the safe, shut and locked the cabinet doors, and dropped the keys in my pocket.

The neon display on the microwave told me I had thirty minutes before I needed to be back at The Dollhouse.

Siobhán held the half-eaten popsicle in front of her parted lips. They were swollen from the cold and cherry-red with food coloring.

"Cosa?" I asked and walked into the kitchen. My shoulder holster and jacket were slung over the back of a barstool. "It's not like you've never seen a gun before."

"I've never seen *you* with a gun before."

I shrugged into my shoulder holster. "You know what I do for a living." I removed the 9mm from my waistband and tucked it into the scabbard.

"You don't usually carry a gun."

I frowned, tossed my track jacket back on the chair, and walked into the living room, folding my arms across my chest. "Not often. No."

She gaped at me, red popsicle melting. "You've had those the entire time."

I narrowed my eyes.

"You could've shot me. Before you realized I wasn't a rat." Bright red sugar water dripped onto her finger and slid down her hand toward her wrist. "Buried me in the forest." She swallowed. "Or thrown me in the pond."

"Yeah, well..." I mumbled and rubbed the back of my neck.

Truth was, I didn't throw her off the bridge. Truth was, no matter how much I'd wanted to end her, I didn't. And now? Now there were other ways to get my revenge that didn't require a bullet through Siobhán's head or her body floating in the Charles.

Ciarán was in bed with the feds no matter what Vito believed. And if I could prove it, no one would bat an eye when I put a bullet through his head. Not Roman. Not Vinnie. Not even Marco.

According to Siobhán, she and Ciarán were tight, which meant confidences had been shared and conversations over-heard. She might not think she knew anything, but she did, and I'd have her singing like a canary before I let her go.

An unhinged impulse to scoop her up off the couch and kiss the frown off her face nearly knocked me sideways. Anger replaced the ache in my chest. It burned away the unwelcome impulse, replacing it with ash.

"Careful with that fucking popsicle," I snapped and walked back into the kitchen. I grabbed my jacket off the chair. "I don't want red shit all over my couch."

"Asshole," she mumbled and pushed herself up. She joined me in the kitchen, dumped the half-melted mess into the sink, and washed the sticky red tracks from her hands. She leaned back against the counter and folded her arms across her chest.

I clenched my teeth. She was wearing my Harvard hoodie. It was so huge on her it ended past her shorts. Seeing her in my ratty old college sweatshirt did uncomfortable things to my insides.

"Stop wearing my clothes," I barked. "I brought you an entire bag of stuff."

"Yeah, from your hoes. No, thank you."

"My hoes? Seriously, Siobhán?" I smirked. "I told you before—jealousy is not a good look on you."

"You're so full of yourself."

"Am I?"

"Yeah. You are."

I scoffed and leaned my hip against the island, crossed my arms, and cocked an eyebrow.

"You blame our entire falling out on me lying. You take zero responsibility for your actions." I heard her blood surge; I was attuned to its rush. It pushed redness up her neck and into her cheeks. "I walk into Vesuvio the night before a first date we'd planned for weeks, and what do I find? You attached to the neck of some—some floozy! For an entire year, I had to watch you waltz through the lobby or come to events with whichever *goomar* you decided looked good on your arm. And, to top it all off, you blame *me* for what happened?" She thumped her chest with a fist wrapped in my sweatshirt sleeve, face splotchy and blue eyes flashing. "That's not jealousy, Luca. That's a normal reaction to being slapped in the face. Repeatedly."

I dropped my arms and closed the distance between us, my frustration heating my blood as surely as it heated hers. "You know, you talk a lot about trust for someone who isn't willing to give it herself." I stopped in front of her and grabbed the counter on either side of her hips. She rested a hand on her chest and tilted her head back to meet my eyes. "You wanted me to believe you didn't lie to hide things from me. You wanted me to trust you even though you're living a double life." I searched her eyes, making sure she was paying attention. "But when I told you what happened at Vesuvio wasn't what it looked like, when I told you over and over that you don't know what you saw..." I raised my eyebrows, and she pursed her lips. "Don't talk to me about trust when you refuse to return the favor."

I ground my teeth, waiting for some smart comment or reaction. Nothing. Instead, she fidgeted the hoodie string and held my gaze like we were playing some fucked-up game of chicken. Fine.

I pushed off the counter, stepped back, and sneered. "And yeah, that's jealousy, Shamrock. Plain and simple."

Her eyes and nostrils flared.

The doorbell rang.

I went to the door and answered it.

"Ciao, Luca," Dominic said and stepped inside.

"Ciao."

He held up a six-pack. "It's going to be a long night."

"But a good one." I slapped him on the shoulder and grabbed a beer. "Dom and I are working tonight," I said for Siobhán's sake. I fished the lighter out of my pocket and popped the top off the bottle. "I'm taking you to The Dollhouse. Rocco'll keep an eye on you till we get back." I looked at her to make sure she was listening and almost choked on my beer.

Siobhán unzipped my hoodie. Her eyes were lowered, her lips slightly parted and stained red from the popsicle. She shrugged, a coy and unsuspecting move that made the hoodie fall from her shoulders. It bunched around her waist where she held onto the zipper. The T-shirt underneath was so small it hugged even her tiny frame, and without a bra, the outline of her dark rose nipples was graphic, their tight peaks straining against the thin white fabric.

With a tug, the zipper came undone. She gathered the hoodie from around her wrists and tossed it onto the island. "Here's your sweatshirt."

I didn't miss the twitch of her lips or the glint of menace in her eyes. I set my beer on the island, holding it in a death grip.

"Hi, Dom," she cooed and met him on the opposite end of the island.

Dom's hand rested atop the six-pack he'd placed on the counter. His mouth hung open, eyes fixed on her chest.

I flexed my free hand.

"Let me get those for you," she said in that sultry voice she used when she fucked with me. She took the six-pack and spun around to face the fridge.

And that's when I noticed her shorts.

BAD ASS was printed across the back in bold white letters as if the length of the shorts and the visible crease between her ass and her thighs weren't obscene enough.

My free hand balled into a fist, and I strangled the beer bottle.

She opened the fridge and eyed the inside. "Where to put these…" She tossed a smile over her shoulder. "It's so full after grocery shopping yesterday!" She stuck the tip of her tongue between her teeth and winked at Dom.

I pressed my lips together trying to prevent myself from driving my fist into my friend's face until his eyes swelled shut.

"Oh! Perfect!" She bent over at the waist and carefully plucked one beer at a time out of the cardboard and placed it on the bottom shelf.

The gym shorts rode up, revealing the entire bottom half of her ass. Only a thin sliver of fabric covered the crease between her cheeks. She shifted her weight from one long leg to the other, her bare ass wiggling with each deliberate move.

Dom rested an elbow on the counter, making himself comfortable, and unabashedly watched the show, a wide appreciative grin on his smug face.

Rage rose from my chest, up my neck, and into my eyes. My breath came hot and fast, trying to maintain control and not leap across the island to slam Dom's face into the marble until he was incapable of looking at Siobhán ever again.

She popped back up and clapped her hands together. "There!" She faced Dom and stuck out a hip. "Unless… Did you want one now? Because I'd be more than happy to service you." She giggled and shook her head. "Oops! I meant serve you."

Crack!

Beer splashed and foamed. Shattered glass clinked on the marble, and the jagged edges of the bottle's neck spun in a slow circle. My fist clamped around the label and a few thick shards. Beer spilled through my fingers to join the puddle of debris on the counter.

Siobhán shot me a cool, knowing look—eyebrow raised, lips twisted in a self-satisfied sneer—then slammed the refrigerator door, walked out of the kitchen, and went up the stairs, taking them two at a time. "Just changing into leggings and grabbing a long sleeve!"

"Put a fucking bra on!" I shouted after her. I shook the label and glass from my palm onto the counter. "Goddamn mess," I grumbled.

A dish towel hit me in the face. I wiped my hands and looked up. Dom's shit-eating grin begged for my fist.

"Cosa?" I snapped. "You got something to say?"

He pressed his lips together, fighting a smile, and lifted his hands in surrender. "Niente, capo. Niente." He made for the front door, shaking his head. "I'll be in the car."

I pulled the garbage basket out of the drawer, held it beneath the lip of the counter, and wiped the evidence of my possessiveness into the trash. Siobhán may have proved her point, but I'd be damned before I let her fuck with my head like that again. I wasn't about to let a pair of long legs, hard nipples, and a smart mouth distract me from making a name for myself in Vinnie's organization or claiming my vengeance.

Chapter Eighteen

Siobhán

An endless stack of *People* magazines and a change of scenery turned my evening from just-another-night-in-the-clink to relatively acceptable. At least this version of jail had a mini fridge stocked with Kool-Aid, and I was allowed to wear shoes.

The Dollhouse wasn't bad for a strip club. Not that I'd been to many strip clubs or had seen the inside of a strip club dressing room. But the bar and decor gave off a classier vibe than I expected. Polished walnut crown molding. Soft amber lights. Gold accents to rich russet upholstery. It didn't reek of smoke, and my feet hadn't stuck to the floor when we walked through the main room of the club. Still, a far cry from Terme di Roma or Terme di Sicilia—not that I'd visited those properties either—but if they were anything like Terme di Boston, The Dollhouse must have been a big adjustment for Luca.

I huffed and flipped the page. Like I cared. *Jerk.*

A big smile grabbed hold of my face thinking about how badly I'd pissed him off earlier. He'd had it coming. He was so full of himself. It was about time he experienced a dose of his own medicine. And hoo boy he did *not* like the taste. At first, I thought he crushed the beer bottle with his bare hand, but that was ridiculous. He must have slammed it on the counter. Either way, he'd been furious with jealousy.

This whole kidnapping thing had gone from terrifying to confusing in a matter of days. Luca wasn't going to kill me, that much was clear. And the more I thought about it, the more I convinced myself he'd never been capable of killing me in the first place. He thought he was, but the way he held me on that bridge, the way his fingers tightened around my arms, the way he pulled me close as if protecting me from himself...

I drained the rest of my Kool-Aid and tossed the box in the trash.

And then there was my stomach. Set aside the fact he'd intended to go down on me in the middle of his kitchen—I shivered remembering his mouth on my skin—he'd been visibly upset by my scars. So much so, he left a bruise on my right hip from squeezing me so tightly. He even took me to get groceries and let me cancel my interviews.

I dropped my hands and the magazine into my lap. That was some sick Stockholm Syndrome shit right there. Worse, this wasn't the first time I'd made excuses for his bad behavior. Just last week I'd sat in a mineral bath next to Anna wearing my rose-colored glasses and dreaming of the future that might have been.

At every turn, I forgave Luca his sins—pretended he hadn't betrayed Marco, pretended he wasn't a playboy asshole, pretended he wasn't my enemy. And for what? The vain hope he'd miraculously realize he was wrong? That he'd call me his little shamrock again with love in his voice instead of hate?

I sighed and glanced at the clock. Ten thirty. Dominic said they'd be back to pick me up around closing time, but I refused to spend the next two and a half hours ruminating over Luca. I needed a drink.

The dressing room door opened, revealing a wall of thick

back muscles. I tapped the wall. "Excuse me." The wall's head turned a fraction to the left. "Can I get a drink? Like a dirty martini or something?"

"Mr. Moretti said you'd ask for drinks."

"Okay..."

"He said you're allowed two."

"Allowed?" I clenched my fists. "I'm going to fucking murder him," I muttered under my breath. "Tell the bartender I'd like a double dirty martini. Extra olives." The wall raised an eyebrow. "That's still one drink."

The corner of his mouth lifted, and he nodded toward the dressing room behind me. "Go have a seat."

"Thank you," I said and shut the door.

I paced the room, investigating the piles of clothes, shoes, makeup, and accessories strewn across surfaces and spilling out of the closet and boxes. There was just so much... stuff.

This must drive Luca crazy, I thought with satisfaction.

The door opened behind me.

"That was quick," I said, but instead of a muscled wall holding a drink, a petite woman with long raven-black hair and skin even lighter than mine stood in the doorway. She wore black leather hotpants and a lime green tank top that accentuated the deep green of her big round eyes. She was strikingly pretty, but in an unconventional way. The kind of pretty you don't see in magazines, but when you see it in real life, it makes you pause.

"Hello," she said with a genuine yet curious smile.

"Hello."

She closed the door behind her, walked over to the mini fridge, and pulled out a juice box and a Kit-Kat. "I'm Mia." She sat on one of the stools along the wall of mirrors and unwrapped her snack. "You must be Siobhán. Mr. Moretti's girl, right?"

I huffed and reclaimed my place on the couch. "I'm not sure I'd call myself his *girl*, but yeah."

She took a bite out of her Kit-Kat and smiled. "The way he lectured me and Rocco about keeping an eye on you and making sure you're comfortable..." She raised an eyebrow. "You're about as *girl* as it gets for Mr. Moretti."

My jaw dropped and I blinked, once again trying to make sense of Luca and his baffling behavior.

The door opened, and the wall—Rocco—stuck his head and my drink inside. "Here you go. Better make it last. You only get one more."

I rolled my eyes and pushed off the couch. "Thanks," I said dryly and snatched the glass out of his beefy hand.

The olive juice and vodka hit my lips, and I instantly started to relax. It was the familiarity more than the alcohol that calmed my nerves, and as I sank back down onto the couch, chatting with my new jailer Mia didn't seem so bad.

"You work here?" I asked.

"I do," she said and popped the last bit of chocolate into her mouth.

"Dancer?"

She shook her head. "I have no idea how they do it. I'm so uncoordinated. I work the back of the house."

I tilted my head, not sure what she was talking about.

She smiled. "The private rooms. Here in the back."

"Ah."

She gathered her hair, bound it in a high ponytail, and inspected her neck in the mirror beneath the lights.

Whoa. That's one epic hickey.

"How long have you worked here?" I asked.

"About five years," she said and grabbed a lip liner off the counter.

"You like it?"

"Yeah, it's all right. The work and pay are steady. The tips are even better." She shrugged and meticulously outlined the pale bow of her lips. "What about you? What do you do?"

"I'm the General Manager of Terme di Boston."

She met my gaze in the mirror, eyes wide and lip liner frozen midair. "You work for Marco DeVita?"

"Yes."

"What's that like?" she asked with awed interest and exchanged the liner for a lipstick.

I chuckled. "I imagine pretty similar to working for Mr. Moretti. He's Luca's uncle, you know."

She refocused on her lips, coloring them a deep maroon. "Terrible thing about his parents, isn't it?" She shook her head and tossed the lipstick into a bag on the counter. She fished a powder brush out of another makeup bag. "I mean, losing both of your parents at such a young age? I was in the foster system growing up, so I never knew my parents. But losing your family the way he did seems worse." She tapped loose powder across the bridge of her nose. "That's gotta mess with a person's head."

You have no idea.

"Especially what happened to his mother." She lowered the brush and regarded me through the mirror. "I heard it was a blood incompatibility."

I wrinkled my forehead. "Doesn't that usually affect the baby?"

"I have no idea." She returned to inspecting her makeup. "But I heard his father was inconsolable. Maybe it was a blessing he didn't live long after she passed." She stopped and turned on her stool with a grimace. "Sorry. That was totally morbid and inappropriate. I shouldn't have said that."

"It's okay," I said even though my stomach twisted into a knot. "Luca doesn't talk about what happened. It's nice to chat with someone else who knows him."

She gave me a warm smile. "Any time. He's pretty tight-lipped around here too, but he's always been kind to me. For what it's worth, he seems to have done all right for himself despite everything. Better than all right. He's only been here a month, and this place is already running more smoothly. And, more importantly"—she pointed at me with the end of her blusher—"I'm making more money. So whatever you need to do to keep your man happy..."

I laughed and shook my head. I wasn't about to argue with the woman.

The door opened and a head of bleach-blonde hair on top of artificially large breasts walked in. Her eyes landed on me like heat-seeking missiles, and she narrowed them like she could eliminate her target with a single hateful glare.

"Hey, Jenny," Mia said. "This is Siobhán."

Jenny lifted her chin and took short steps on ridiculously high platform heels past me to the makeup counter. "I know who she is," she said icily and sat to Mia's right.

My memory kicked in and connected the dots—Luca's date from the DeVita Foundation gala. I downed a big mouthful of martini.

The door opened again, and the two dancers who'd been on stage when I arrived filed into the room in nothing but thongs and heels. Time to shrink into the corner of the couch with another *People* magazine instead of ogling their perfectly lush curves, strong legs, and full breasts. *What I wouldn't give...*

They grabbed robes and plopped down on the couch opposite me.

"My feet are killing me tonight," the woman on the right said and rubbed her foot. "New shoes are torture. Are you new? Are you dancing tonight? I could use a break."

"No. She's with Luca," Jenny sniped and filled the air around her with a cloud of aerosol. She swiveled her head from side to side and must have decided her hair was sufficiently shellacked, because she set the spray down and picked up a tube of lipstick. "You know he came to see me yesterday."

"Jenny," Mia said in a chiding tone.

Jenny ran the bright pink across her lips. "It's true. She should know."

A pang of jealousy slammed into my chest. I was about to launch into a grandiose explanation of why I couldn't care less about who Luca saw but was interrupted by a disgusted scoff from the other couch. The woman on the left dropped her magazine into her lap and rolled her eyes.

"Nothing happened, Jenny, and you know it. You're just trying to cause trouble." She leveled me with an irritated look. "She's jealous. She's been trying to bag Mr. Moretti for the better part of six months"—she shot a hard look over her shoulder—"despite him making it very clear he's not interested." The woman picked up her magazine and leafed through the pages. "Not to mention, he barely even bit you before he stormed out."

My head rocked back in surprise.

"Trixie!" Mia's eyes darted between me and the woman on the couch.

"What?" She looked over her shoulder.

Mia widened her eyes in a non-verbal "shut up."

Trixie shrugged and returned to her magazine.

Bit her? I drained half my martini.

"Whatever," Jenny said and stood. "I need to get ready for my next appointment." She teetered across the room, sparing me a nasty glance when she reached the couches, and walked out the door.

How this random woman despised me so much when we'd never exchanged more than a handful of words was beyond me. Then again, my blood had boiled at the gala when I saw her hanging off Luca's arm. But I hadn't really been angry with her. I'd been angry with Luca.

"Ignore her," the woman on the right said, still massaging her foot. "She's bitter. She's been trying to bag one of the made guys for years. Before Mr. Moretti, it was Richie." She looked at Trixie. "Remember?" Trixie nodded. "Before Richie, it was..." She furrowed her brow. "What was his name?"

"Enzo," Mia said and got up from her stool. She smoothed her tank top in the mirror.

"Enzo. Right. Point is, Jenny's always been out for one thing—money." She raised her eyebrows. "She's just salty she's run into another dead end."

"Damn straight," Trixie said.

"I have an eleven o'clock," Mia said and glanced at me. "You going to be okay until I get back?"

"I'll be fine," I said and lifted my drink. "I've got one more of these to go, remember?"

She laughed. "Right. I'll end my session a couple minutes early. Make sure I'm back before Jenny." She exaggerated an eye roll, and I let out a nervous chuckle.

So Jenny was a gold digger. Fine. Whatever. Go get it, girl. My brain was stuck on the biting comment. Did Luca have some sort of biting fetish? Was that even a thing?

As much as I hated thinking about The Incident, he *had* been attached to that girl's neck. Rather aggressively. And just now, Mia had a massive hickey on her neck that looked suspiciously like a bite mark. I mean, I'd heard of kinks like choking or being dominated, but neck-biting?

Something about Mia's reaction didn't sit right either, like she was worried about keeping the biting thing a secret beyond protecting my feelings. The suspicion pushed at the back of my mind and wouldn't let up. It tried to force me into another part of my brain but couldn't quite make the connection.

I downed the last of my martini. Strange fetishes aside, I was relieved nothing had happened between Luca and his former blow-up doll Jenny. Maybe too relieved. In fact, I shouldn't have cared at all. Then again, Luca shouldn't have smashed a beer bottle on the counter earlier.

God, we were toxic together, and this close proximity thing wasn't doing either of us any favors.

I pushed off the couch. I needed to get away from him and this entire fucked-up situation. But since I couldn't, time for another drink.

By one a.m., the only people left in The Dollhouse were me, Rocco, Mia, and the bartender. Mia was finishing her last appointment, but the rest of the patrons had left about ten minutes prior. The dancers were done by twelve thirty, and lucky for me, Jenny's last appointment was at eleven.

Rocco let me out of my holding cell, and I sat at the bar while he helped clean. I found a deck of cards on one of the tables and laid out a game of solitaire.

Mia walked up, her client in tow. "Can you let him out, Rocco?"

"Sure thing," Rocco replied.

She stretched her arms overhead, and the big wall of bouncer led a short, wiry man with curly red hair to the front door.

"I'm beat," she said and yawned.

"Same." I flipped over a stack of three cards. "And I didn't even work tonight."

"You hungry? I'm starving."

I was, but I learned to answer "no" to that question a long time ago. Nine times out of ten, I couldn't eat whatever the person was offering and turning down food was awkward business. "I'm good. Thanks."

She scrunched her nose. "I think I have some protein bars in my car. And I need to get my sneakers. Rocco?"

"Yeah?" He relocked the front door.

"Walk me to my car? I need to get a few things before we lock up for the night."

"You got it. Keep an eye on her, Joe?" Rocco nodded in my direction.

"Yeah," the bartender said and continued to stack pint glasses.

I went back to my solitaire game and imagined all the pudding I'd eat when I got back to Luca's house.

The front door rattled like someone was trying to open it. When that didn't work, they pounded on the glass. The bartender jogged over, unlocked the door, and Vito Balistreri walked in.

"They here yet?" he asked, unmistakable urgency in his clipped question.

"Vito," the bartender said, surprised, and hurried to keep up with Mr. Balistreri's quick strides. "We're closed."

He stopped. "They're not here yet."

"Who?"

"Luca. Dominic."

"No. They left hours ago."

He glanced at his watch. "I need clean towels and a bottle of vodka." He pointed at the double doors that led to the back. "Where's the best light?"

"Prolly the girls' dressing room. What's doin'?"

"We got trouble."

"Well, Mr. Moretti said they'd be back before closing to pick up his lady." The bartender jerked his head in my direction.

Mr. Balistreri turned to where I sat at the bar and narrowed his eyes. "What the hell are you doing here?"

Chapter Nineteen

Luca

We parked a quarter mile apart on the long, straight stretch of Mass Pike. Sal had dropped off the fake U-Haul and the black cargo van at a gas station outside Needham about an hour before we arrived. He ran Vinnie's scrapyard in Revere and had a refurbished box truck he painted to look like a U-Haul. The van he stole out of state and filed off the VIN. Both had clean throw-away plates. Didn't need the job going south because someone spotted a stolen vehicle.

Thunder rumbled, a distant menace. It had been overcast all day, but by dusk, the clouds darkened. The air was thick with the static of an impending storm. It was only a matter of time.

I rubbed my knee, extended it, then bent it, trying to get some blood flow into the aching joint. I'd always thought people were full of shit when they said they could feel the cold and damp in their joints but tonight had me thinking maybe I was wrong.

The thing about superhuman healing is that it doesn't work like the movies. Blood demons couldn't be torn to shreds, twisted and broken, and then, magically, the pieces fell back into their rightful places. The laws of physics didn't take a break because we were a different species. Tissue self-healed, for the most part. It regenerated and knitted itself back together without leaving scars. But bones and joints? The more complicated pieces of hardware? Not so easy.

Vinnie's doctor realigned the joints and set my kneecaps in the warehouse, but the right one hadn't healed properly. Something was off. It weakened my knee and caused a hitch in my step. A little souvenir from Vinnie Valenzano's warehouse of horrors.

I glanced at my watch. Just past eleven thirty. Second shift started at eleven. Any minute now.

"You sure it was a good idea leaving your girl at The Doll-house?" Dominic asked, watching the darkness behind us through the rearview mirror.

"She's not my girl. And no, but I didn't have another option."

"I mean..." He eyed me sidelong. "You could let her go."

"And you could mind your own business."

He huffed. "You're my capo, Luca, but you were my friend first." He adjusted the mirror. "We've known each other since we were kids. I'm just lookin' out."

Dominic's mom and Gina were tight, always organizing shit at the Italian American Community Club when we were kids. Dom and I spent a lot of time getting into trouble while they planned their next fundraiser or potluck. Then I moved to Italy. But we never lost the easy camaraderie that came from growing up together.

"You don't hear me telling you what to do with Mia," I said.

He shot me a surprised look but quickly schooled his features and resumed monitoring the mirror. "I don't know what you're talking about," he said.

I snorted. "Right."

"Besides, I didn't kidnap Mia. Non lo so, fratello. Doesn't seem like holding a girl hostage is gonna end well for anyone."

Thunder clapped. Loud. Closer. I scanned the windshield. Nothing. But it was coming.

Living with Siobhán was like living inside a powder keg. The sexual tension and barely contained hostility created an incendiary situation that would explode in my face if I wasn't careful. Tomorrow I'd start in with the questions, maybe feed her a little bullshit first to prime the pump. And as long as I stuck to my plan, everything would work out. At least for me.

"Here we go," Dominic said and threw the car into gear.

Semi headlights appeared in the passenger mirror. I looked over my shoulder through the rear windshield. The cab was full-sized and red. "Wait for confirmation."

The truck rumbled toward us on the otherwise empty highway. The cab's logo—a fat white circle with yellow letters that read *FISHER*—sped past us in a blur.

"That's our guy," I said. "Let's move."

Dom flipped on the headlights and accelerated onto the turnpike.

We approached the van where Mikey and Leo waited. Dom flashed the headlights. They turned theirs on and pulled onto the Pike behind us, two miles out from the truck's planned exit. Mikey drifted into the passing lane and picked up speed. He crept past us and the semi before merging back into the driving lane.

Fat rain droplets blurred the bright green reflection off the exit sign a quarter mile ahead of the off-ramp. My blood pumped faster. Adrenaline drove my lungs and turned my eyes. I channeled the power to hone my focus.

A half-million dollars. A half-million dollars and the Moretti family reputation.

We escorted the unsuspecting semi off the ramp through the quickening rain and onto an empty industrial park thoroughfare. The stoplights flashed red. A single car passed in the opposite direction at the second intersection. We pulled forward, heading for the third set of lights.

Rain pelted the windshield. No cars in either direction.

I hit the call button on my phone. It connected after one ring. "Do it," I ordered and clicked off.

The van stopped at the blinking red lights. The semi followed suit. Dom stopped the U-Haul. I unbuckled my seat belt.

The semi's horn blared. I jumped out of the passenger seat, pulled out my Glock, and cut between the U-Haul and the semi. Mikey threw the van in reverse. It hit the front of the semi's cab, pinning it in place.

The truck driver opened his window. "Hey! What the fuck?" he shouted over the patter of rain.

Lightning flashed. I jumped onto the step, pulled myself up by the mirror, and pointed the gun in his face. "Hands where I can see them."

Thunder cracked. The semi driver showed me his hands.

I tried the door. It was locked. "Unlock the door."

He did, then shoved his hand back in the air.

I opened the door, unfastened his seat belt, and gestured to the passenger side with my gun. "Move."

The driver slid across the seat.

"Keep those hands up." I climbed into the cab, slammed the door, and wiped the water out of my eyes.

"Oh man," the truck driver said, voice shaking. "I wasn't even supposed to be on this route tonight."

"Face the window."

"Don't kill me, man. I got a kid."

"Face the fucking window," I said more slowly.

He did, and I pistol-whipped the back of his head. He slumped in his seat. He'd be fine when he woke up, but he'd have a wicked headache.

I honked the horn. Mikey pulled the van forward through the intersection. I gave him a half-block lead, then followed, checking my side mirror for Dom. The U-Haul was right behind me.

The caravan turned down the next side street, a narrow access road between two warehouses, each of which spanned the entire industrial park block. A chain-link fence topped with barbed wire surrounded the concrete loading docks. They were barely visible beneath the torrential rain blurring the flood lights. The ventilation windows at the top of the low cement-block buildings were dark.

Nausea washed over me. For weeks, the only natural light I saw in Vinnie's warehouse came from ventilation windows just like those. I swallowed the bile and blinked the memory away.

I pulled over and turned the semi and its headlights off. The street went dark outside the diluted glow of the loading docks, but with our heightened vision, we didn't need more. I bound the semi driver's wrists behind his back with a cable tie, then climbed out of the cab and jogged to the back of the truck.

Dom reversed the box truck, lining the back up with the semi trailer. Leo used a bolt cutter on the gate lock. Mikey stayed with the van as lookout.

Dom rolled up the rear door of the box truck, and Leo and I opened the trailer. Pallets topped with stacks of game consoles filled the space. Leo opened his switchblade with a *snick* and sliced through the plastic wrapped around the nearest pallet. Dom climbed into the back of the box truck. I stood on the ground between them. Rain hammered my head. Leo handed me a console, and I handed it to Dom.

Our supernatural speed fueled each movement, and once we fell into a rhythm, we transferred two, three consoles at a time. But five hundred boxes were nothing to shake a stick at, and the clock was ticking.

Three-quarters of the way through the cargo, sirens wailed in the distance, a faint echo beneath the pounding rain. A reminder that anyone could round the corner at any time.

"Hurry up," I shouted. "Move!"

We picked up the pace, loading four boxes at a time. My muscles burned with effort.

I handed Dom the last of the boxes, and the roar of an engine and glare of headlights rounded the corner. The flash of a police light bar blinded me for a fraction of a second. I blinked to adjust my vision. A car sped toward us.

Another engine sounded behind me. I glanced over my shoulder. A second black-and-white barreled into view from the opposite direction, and its siren let out a single punishing yelp.

"Cazzo! Go! Go! Go!" I waved at Dom and Leo to get in the box truck.

The first police car skidded to a stop.

Leo jumped from the semi trailer directly into the back of the box truck but struggled to lift the gate. It was stuck. Dom pulled out his piece and dashed behind the box truck toward the driver-side door.

The second squad car spun sideways to a stop, sandwiching the cargo van between itself and the semi-cab.

Two cops got out of the car on my left and pointed their guns. "On the ground!" one of them shouted. "Hands behind your heads!"

I pulled out my gun and darted forward, taking aim. The cops ducked behind the car. I fired four rounds and blew out their front tires. I took cover behind the semi-trailer's rear door just in time. The cops fired back, and the hail of bullets struck metal.

Another round of gunfire rang out through the night.

Dom. He stood at the front of the fake U-Haul behind the cab, taking shots and giving the cops another target.

I peeked around the door. The cops from the first car crouched behind the front and rear bumpers. At the other end of the semi, Mikey jumped out of the van and sprinted toward us. The cops in the second car flung open their doors.

I broke my cover and fired two rounds at the first car, letting them know I hadn't forgotten about them, then took four shots at the second car, trying to buy Mikey time.

Lightning flashed overhead. It illuminated the scene and a horrifying twist of fate. Mikey lost his footing on the slick pavement and careened forward. He landed flat on his stomach, his left arm bent at an unnatural angle.

A bullet whizzed past my head. I darted behind the trailer door, my blood pounding in my ears loud enough to drown out the rain.

They're taking head shots.

My chest heaved. I closed my eyes and slowed my breathing.

I'm not dying here. I can't leave—

"Got it!" Leo shouted. My eyes snapped open, and Leo raised the box truck's gate.

We needed to get the fuck out of there. "Dom! Cover me!"

The gunfire picked up from behind the front of the fake U-Haul. I dashed forward.

Guns cracked. Bullets flew. I raised my piece and got off another couple rounds before yanking the passenger door open and launching myself into the front seat. Dom stood at the corner of the cab, relying on the angle to protect him. But as I rolled down the window to give Mikey cover, one of the cops from the first car popped up from behind the rear bumper and fired.

The first bullet hit Dom in the stomach and went clear

through. It knocked him back, and as he reeled, a second bullet hit his left shoulder.

"Argh!" he screamed and stumbled behind the cab.

"Get in!" I shouted and fired back. The cop ducked behind the rear bumper.

The driver's side door opened. I aimed my gun at the second cop car, and my stomach bottomed out.

Mikey flailed on the ground beneath the assault of the two cops from the second car. One tried to pin him with a knee in his back. He failed, no match for Mikey's strength. Mikey pushed himself up, but the second cop brought up his gun and pointed it at Mikey's chest.

"Fuck!"

Mikey was done. He knew better than to take a bullet point blank. He'd survive, but our secret wouldn't, and no soldati demoni del sangue would ever betray our truth.

"Get us out of here, Dom. Now!"

The engine rumbled to life, and with one hand, Dom threw the truck into gear. He grabbed the steering wheel and slammed on the accelerator. I fired round after round as we sped away, making sure they didn't take out our tires. I stopped once we were out of range, rolled up the window, and watched Mikey grow smaller in the passenger-side mirror.

"Cazzo!"

Dom took a hard turn and groaned. He was covered in blood, the entire front of his shirt soaked through, made worse by the rain. His breath came in short pants, and his face was pale and drawn.

"Can you make it to the Pike?"

"Yeah," he ground out between gritted teeth.

"Do it. Then take the first exit. I'll drive."

He gave me a quick nod and let go of the wheel long enough to push the soaked hair off his forehead and out of his eyes.

I took out my cell phone. "Come on," I muttered under my breath. "Pick up."

"Yeah?" Vito's gruff voice came across the line after the fourth ring. *Thank fuck.*

"They sent Dom a Message," I said, using terms we understood but wouldn't get flagged in a transcript. "It didn't go through. He's leaking pretty good."

"Goddammit. Where?"

"Barbie's in an hour." Barbie's was code for The Dollhouse.

"Yeah," he said and hung up.

I sat back and watched the rain streak past the window. The rivulets shone like lightning under each passing streetlight. We secured the haul, and barring any further entanglements, we'd get away with it. Nothing could trace the lift back to me or Vinnie, but I felt like shit. Worry burned a hole in my gut as real as the hole in Dom's stomach.

Dom had been shot twice and was losing a lot of blood. Ben Levine, the Valenzano doc, was always on call, but Mikey'd been pinched, was about to spend the night in the slammer. Vito'd removed a lot of bullets over the years, and he'd have been my next call anyway; Marco's lawyers handled all blood demon arrests through the DeVita Foundation.

We still had to get the goods to the warehouse and those cops had no doubt called for backup. I'd take side streets instead of the Pike after I took over driving. Less conspicuous. Leo'd move on with the cargo once we got to The Dollhouse.

The feds would get involved after a lift this big. At the very least they'd hear about it, which meant more heat. But none of that caused the rancid burn traveling up from my stomach.

I placed my hand over my parents' names inked into the wet skin above my heart. I rubbed the space there, trying to ease the ache. That bullet had whizzed right past my temple, inches from ending my immortal life. And all I could think about was who would take care of Siobhán if I was gone.

Chapter Twenty

Luca

"Vito!" I held the front door to The Dollhouse open with one hand and kept Dominic upright with the other. He leaned on me, his good arm slung across my shoulders. I ushered him inside. The door slammed shut behind us, and I threw the deadbolt. "Vito!"

One of the double doors that led to the back swung open and Vito appeared. He looked us up and down and frowned. "Let's get him in the back."

He held the door open, and we limped through. "How you doin', Dom?" he asked.

"I've got a bullet in my shoulder," he growled. "Fucking great."

Vito moved past us down the hall. "The lighting's better in the dressing room. I'll need him up on the counter by the mirrors if I'm going to cut that bullet out."

Dom groaned. "Can we not talk about cutting shit out of me?"

"Sorry, kid." We hobbled through the second set of doors. "But we gotta get that thing out so your shoulder heals right."

Vito walked into the dressing room. "Get him over there by the mirrors. Up on the counter."

I maneuvered Dom sideways through the narrower opening, suddenly glad I gave the girls shit about keeping the dressing room clean. The floor was clear of obstacles all the way to the mirrors.

"Oh, God." Siobhán's voice startled me.

My head snapped to where she stood in the corner of the dressing room. Staring at Dom's stomach, her face went white, the little color usually highlighting her pale cheeks gone. She lifted her thin fingers to her mouth, and her hand started to shake.

"Fuck," I cursed and moved faster.

I arranged Dom with his back toward the mirrors and removed his arm from my shoulder. He shimmied himself onto the counter. Vito started assessing the damage.

"No. No, no." Siobhán's small voice wavered, pulling me to the other side of the room.

I went to her and placed my hands on her shoulders, but her wide eyes remained fixed on Dom.

"He's been shot," she whispered, lips trembling. "He's been shot. In the stomach. He needs to go to the hospital. His stomach..." Her lips kept moving, repeating the words without sound.

I followed her blank stare over my shoulder. Vito was cutting the bloody mess of Dom's shirt away. I blocked her view, but her eyes remained fixed on Dom's position as if she could see right through me.

"Siobhán. Look at me." I took her face between my hands, but her gaze remained downcast and unfocused. "Look at me, Siobhán," I said louder. "Come on, baby. Look at me. Look right here."

Her eyes crept toward my face. Her pupils were dilated, her breathing short and shallow. Sweat beaded her forehead. A full-blown trauma response. If I didn't get through to her, she was going to black out, and we didn't need another patient.

"Stay with me, okay? Dom's going to be fine. Vito's helping him."

Her eyes locked with mine, and instead of looking through me, recognition snapped into place. She laid her palms on my chest.

"There's so much blood. That's what they keep saying. There's too much blood." She squeezed her eyes shut, and tears poured down her cheeks. "She's losing too much blood. She's not going to make it." Her body convulsed.

"Dio." I wrapped my arms around her and squeezed. Her arms folded between us, and she rested her forehead on my chest.

"It's okay." I ran my hand up and down her back. Her body trembled beneath my touch. "You made it, remember? You're here. Right now. You're with me. And those assholes are gone. Finished. They can't hurt you. I made sure myself. You're safe with me."

She released a sob and clung to me. I glanced over my shoulder.

There was a lot of blood, and the rain made it look worse. As drenched as we were, the blood had spread across his shirt. But the dark splotch over his stomach was unmistakable; a bullet had entered there.

Siobhán started to cry, soft, quiet sobs.

I rested my chin on her head. "I know, baby. I know." I cradled her head in one hand and ran the other up and down her back. "Dom's going to be fine. I promise. Vito's going to get him all stitched up. He'll be okay." I kissed her hair and let her cry.

"When's the last time you fed?" Vito asked behind us.

"I dunno... Last week?" Dom's speech slurred.

"Stay with me, kid. Luca!"

I looked over my shoulder. Dom's shirt was gone. The wound in his stomach was almost closed, but blood poured down his arm from his shoulder.

"We got a bleeder," Vito said. "Musta hit an artery, and it's still in there. At least the one in his stomach went straight through."

"Oh, yeah," Dom grumbled. "Felt fucking great."

"You'll be fine, but you'll heal a helluva lot faster if you feed." Vito glanced at me. "He's lost a lot of blood."

I pursed my lips and nodded. I pulled back and held Siobhán by her shoulders. "Where's Mia?" I asked, gentling my voice.

She stared at her fingers tangled in my shirt.

"Siobhán." I tipped her chin up. Her eyes were glassy and haunted. "Hey, baby, come on now. I know you're stronger than that. Where's Mia?"

"Mia..." She swallowed. "She went to her car to—to get something. Rocco went with her. She didn't want to go alone. They should be back." Her eyes searched mine. "There's so much blood..." Her bottom lip trembled. "His stomach..."

I pulled her back into my arms. "I know, baby," I whispered into her hair and kissed the top of her head. "I know."

The door opened, and Mia walked in followed by Rocco.

"Dominic!" Mia shouted. Her eyes darted to me and Siobhán, then back to Dominic and Vito.

"Dom needs a Source, Mia," I said.

"Yes, of course," she said flatly and dropped her umbrella and her bag. She took off her jacket and tossed it on the couch.

"I'm going to need someone to hold him down while I remove the bullet," Vito said.

Siobhán whimpered, and her shaking turned violent.

"Rocco," I said and nodded toward Vito. "Help him. I gotta get her out of here."

"You sure do," Vito said with an edge he didn't want me to miss. "One hand on his shoulder, one across his legs, capisce?"

Rocco followed Vito's directions, and Dom rested his head against the mirror and closed his eyes.

"I'm not gonna ask why she's here," Vito said. "Don't wanna know. But get her out of here."

"They got Mikey," I said.

"Goddammit."

"He knows what to do." There was a protocol when a blood demon got pinched—call the DeVita Foundation.

"Did he get shot?"

"Not that I saw."

"Good. We can't do anything about it tonight. Call me in the morning."

"Va bene," I said and led Siobhán to the door. "Domani allora."

"You might wanna leave the room for this, tesoro," Vito grumbled to Mia, and the door clicked shut.

I hurried Siobhán out the back and locked up behind me. Rain came down in sheets, loud against the metal overhang. Siobhán shivered. I wrapped my arm around her shoulders, tucking her into me and away from the cold.

Leo drove on, taking the fake U-Haul to the drop-off location, and Dom's car was still at the gas station in Needham, which meant I had no wheels. I dialed one of my crew. He answered after a couple of rings. "Barbie's. In the back. Ora. Sbrigati." I shoved the phone back in my pocket and wrapped my other arm around Siobhán.

"You okay?" I asked.

She tilted her head up. "The fresh air helps." Her lips twitched, attempting a smile, but she couldn't quite make one happen. "All the blood on"—she swallowed and blinked hard —"all the blood on his stomach..."

"I know, baby. But Dominic wasn't shot in the stomach,"

I lied. "It just looked that way from all the rain and the blood from his shoulder. He's going to be fine."

Surviving a bullet to the shoulder, I could explain. A gunshot through the stomach?

"Thank God." She rested the side of her face against my chest and burrowed into it like she wanted to crawl inside.

"What's a Source?" she asked.

Fuck.

There were so many reasons I didn't want to answer that question. I hugged her closer. "Don't worry about it," I said and hoped like hell she'd forget that word and everything else she saw and heard that night.

A TRUCK RUMBLED down the street outside. The single lightbulb hanging from the warehouse ceiling swayed. A Bowie knife glinted beneath its movement.

Vinnie hovered over me, face devoid of emotion. He gripped my hair, jerked my head back, and lowered the blade to my right eye.

"Nooo!" I screamed and turned my head from side to side.

White hot pain exploded into existence, a flash of lightning that seared my eye and transported me from Vinnie's dingy warehouse to the upstairs of Vesuvio.

Marco stood before me, masked in darkness. The red glow of his eyes met mine from beneath the shadows of his downturned face.

"You're no longer a DeVita," he growled.

"No, Zio, per favore. Non capisci." I shook my head. I needed to explain. Then he'd understand.

"Now get out of my sight," he said with finality.

His image faded, replaced by a black casket in an empty field.

It was so big. Why was it so big?

I tugged at my collar. Too constricting. Why did Zio make me wear a tie?

I pulled and pulled, but the collar squeezed tighter and tighter. It cut off my air. Darkness clouded my vision. The casket started to fade.

I yanked on my collar. Hard. "No! Take me back! Papà!"

"It's time to go, Luca." Mamma Gina squeezed my hand as tightly as the collar around my neck.

"Nooo! Not yet!"

Vinnie's face materialized through the darkness, and the cold steel of the Bowie knife returned in a burst of agony. Blood covered its sharp edge and streamed down my face, a surging river of red. He released my hair, and I collapsed. He pulled a handkerchief from his breast pocket and wiped the blade clean.

I heaved and thrashed. Blood poured from my empty eye socket into a pool on the cold concrete.

Or was it a bed?

Blood covered a rumpled nightgown. My mother lay atop the sheets, hands folded across her unmoving chest, her beautiful face pale and lifeless.

A newborn wailed, cutting through the blood's silent swell. My father stepped into view, shirtsleeves rolled up, his forearms and the baby he held stained red with my mother's sacrifice.

"I named him Luca." My father's voice cracked, and the crimson pool consumed the bed. "I named him after you, my beautiful Lucia. Vivrà per te."

Blood crept up her body and surrounded her face.

"No," I said to my father. "No, I want to see her."

He looked at me, eyes as red as the rising tide. "She died for you, Luca."

Blood filled the room. It passed his waist.

"No!" I shouted.

He held the newborn baby out of its reach.

"She died because of you," he said.

Until it enveloped him too.

"Luca." My father's voice faded, distant and muffled.

"Nooo!" I screamed.

"Luca."

"Don't go!"

"Luca!"

My eyes snapped open, and my arm shot out. I clamped my fingers around the intruder's neck.

Thin fingers with pointed nails tapped the edges of my hand. "Luca."

The same voice had called out in my nightmare.

"It's me. It's Siobhán."

My eyes focused.

"Luca, you're hurting me."

"Siobhán?" I loosened my grip and searched the darkness.

Siobhán's glassy eyes regarded me with concern. She placed a hand on my forearm and peeled my fingers off her neck. "You were shouting," she croaked and massaged her throat. She pushed the sweaty strands of hair off my forehead. "But it was just a bad dream. You're okay."

My chest heaved. Sweat covered my forehead, neck, and chest, and my breath came in short, frantic bursts. I shoved a hand into my damp hair and grabbed Siobhán's with the other, trying to ground myself and calm the adrenaline rushing through my veins and making my heart race.

"Breathe." She squeezed my hand. "Just breathe." Her brow furrowed, and she searched my face. "What did they do to you?"

I shivered and looked away.

"Hey," she said and inched forward. She cupped my face

and turned it back to hers. "It's over. Whatever happened, it's over."

I anchored myself in her pale blue eyes, a light in my empty world, until my breathing slowed and exhaustion claimed me. The close call and the botched job and my haunted dreams were too much. I fought to keep my eyes open, not wanting to lose her, my anchor, to the darkness.

Siobhán let go of my hand and scooted off the bed. "Get some sleep—"

I rolled onto my side and grabbed her wrist, pulling her back onto the bed. I covered us with the comforter, wrapped my arm around her waist, and snuggled her until her tiny body was tucked into the curve of mine.

She stiffened.

I breathed in her scent. She'd bought a bottle of her shampoo when we went to the grocery store, and she smelled familiar and sweet. Like peaches. I shoved my nose into her hair and nuzzled her neck.

"What did you mean earlier?" she asked.

"Hm?"

"At The Dollhouse. You said they can't hurt me. That you made sure of it."

"Just that—I tracked down the men responsible for hurting you. Made sure they were all taking a long nap."

She lifted her head off the pillow.

"No more nightmares, Siobhán. You're safe."

She laid her head back down—"Thank you"—but her body remained rigid.

"I haven't forgotten you're a Shaughnessy," I said into the darkness.

"I know." She relaxed as if exchanging those words reclaimed our normal.

"I hate Shaughnessys," I whispered.

She slid her hand down my arm until she found mine

tucked beneath her. She interlaced our fingers and brought our arms to rest between the slight swell of her breasts. "I know," she whispered back. Her soft lips pressed against my fingers, once, twice.

I nudged my leg between hers, bringing her closer. Her breathing slowed to match the gentle, regular rise of her chest beneath my arm. And with the air cleared and my body wrapped around Siobhán, I drifted into a deep and peaceful sleep.

Chapter Twenty-One

Luca

"Have a seat, Mr. Moretti."

The cop's sharp tone startled me, and my attention snapped to the counter in the waiting room of the Framingham jail. I'd been pacing the length of the small space for what felt like hours. I glanced at the clock. It had been twenty minutes.

The electrical buzz of the soundless TV reverberated through the silence. The relic was perched high in the corner of the shitty waiting room surrounded by water-stained ceiling tiles. The news was on, but no one was watching, the orange-plastic bucket chairs lining the perimeter empty.

"I'm good," I snapped and resumed pacing. It was the only way to stem the tide of my rising anxiety, fueled by images and sound bites from the hijacking, the aftermath at The Dollhouse, and the nightmares that drove Siobhán into my bed and into my arms. They flashed in and out of my mind, feeding off my lack of sleep.

The door swung open, and Gina walked in. Her dark hair was arranged in soft waves around her face, not a strand out of place, and her white blouse and navy skirt were pressed with military precision, not a wrinkle in sight despite driving all the way from the North End. Her heels clicked against the scuffed linoleum, and her perfume wafted ahead of her as she approached. The familiar scent calmed my nerves.

"Che cosa è successo?" She glanced around the waiting room. "Dov'è Vito?"

The cop eyed us.

I tipped my head to the door beyond the front desk. "In with Mikey. Got here about twenty minutes before I did." I answered her other question in Italian. "He got tackled on the job." I doubted the idiot cop understood, but I kept my voice low regardless.

Gina's mouth flattened into a disapproving line, but the judgment in her penetrating stare was edged with worry. Always a backdrop of worry.

The inner door buzzed, then opened, and Vito walked through. You wouldn't know by the way he dressed or his deadpan features that he'd performed surgery only a few hours ago in the dressing room of a strip club. Then again, Marco's consigliere was anything but your run-of-the-mill lawyer.

Outside the gym, his classic three-piece suit screamed cutthroat attorney. He'd tamed his unruly curls, combing them back, and eliminated the usual stubble that usually covered his square jaw with a clean shave. But his stocky build, crooked nose, and undercurrent of menace guarded him like a pit bull and told you not to cross Vito Balistreri outside the courtroom.

He spotted Gina and held out a hand. "Gina. Bene." She took it, and he kissed her on both cheeks.

"Sta bene?" she asked.

"Andiamo fuori." He turned to the cop at the front desk. "Mr. Barbieri's second guest has arrived. Gina DeVita from the DeVita Foundation. We're going to step outside to discuss my client's case, then she'll be back for her visit." He didn't wait for an answer, gesturing toward the door.

We exited the waiting room into the damp morning. Shallow pools of rainwater dotted the parking lot, the expanse of pavement covered in a sheen of wet. The sky had cleared to a calm, pristine blue, and the crisp air was fresh and clean, as if the events of the previous night had been washed away. Except they hadn't. The evidence sat in a prison cell inside.

I had a meeting with Vinnie at one. I called him on my way over to assure him that the situation was under control and the half-million dollars' worth of electronics was safe in his Revere warehouse. It took the edge off his foul mood, but he wasn't exactly pleased.

"Armed robbery, grand theft, and resisting arrest," Vito said. "The arraignment is Wednesday, but given the charges, the bail won't be anything the DeVita Foundation can't afford."

Immigrants were drawn to areas where they knew someone or at least spoke the same language. But blood demons had another reason to stick to the Northeast—the DeVita Foundation. It provided not just community but representation, and no one wanted to travel too far from legal protection.

Blood demons as far south as Connecticut had the DeVita Foundation number either memorized or somewhere on their person. The average citizen rarely needed it, but in our line of work, that number was as important to survival as feeding. Marco's team of lawyers, led by Vito, and immigrant services, led by Gina, kept our secret safe from law enforcement. They took responsibility for all blood demon affairs except the Source racket. Jail time was a death sentence for a blood demon without a means to feed. Our people were committed to protecting our secret and to consent, but when you were starving, instinct threatened even the noblest convictions. The

DeVita Foundation made sure no one had to face that situation.

"Any injuries?" Gina asked.

"No," Vito said. "They roughed him up good, but not enough to cause questions."

"When's the last time he fed?"

"You'll have to ask him. He looked healthy. Should be fine till you post bail."

She nodded. "I'll talk to him, make sure he doesn't need a Source." She moved for the door and grabbed Vito's arm. He stiffened, and his eyes fixed on Gina's fingers wrapped around his elbow. "I'll stay with him until you come back," she said.

He gave her a terse nod.

She squeezed his arm and walked inside.

In less than a heartbeat, a lit cigarette materialized between Vito's lips. He sucked it down in long drags, and I doubted it was only because of Mikey. Vito cared for Gina. They'd known each other for longer than I'd been alive. He'd been as much a part of the DeVitas' lives as my father. But the reverence with which he regarded Gina always made me wonder if his sentiments went beyond brotherly love.

"Kid, you are one unlucky son of a bitch," Vito growled between puffs.

I snorted. "You don't need to tell me that."

"Talked to the cops before I talked to Mikey. One of the security guards at the warehouse forgot his fucking cell phone. Must've been inside when you started the lift. Saw the action when he came out and called the cops."

"Dannazione."

"Be glad that's all it was and not an FBI tail." He raised an eyebrow and placed the cigarette between his lips. "Or a setup."

I shoved a hand into my hair and stared at my shoes. I'd been careful, followed all the rules—scoped the route, exchanged cars, used multiple locations—but you couldn't account for shit like someone forgetting their goddamn cell phone.

He blew out a plume of smoke. "Doesn't mean they're not involved."

My head shot up.

"Mikey said a stiff in a suit showed up last night. Asked a lot of questions. Said one of the cops called him 'Agent.'"

"Cazzo," I said and paced away. "Did Mikey talk?"

"Not a word. Begs the question how'd the feds find out so quick?"

"They're becoming a real pain in the ass."

"They've always been a pain in the ass, and trust me when I say they can be a helluva lot worse." His words were dry through the smoke but no less of a serious warning. He tossed the cigarette butt on the ground and put it out with his toe.

"You think they have an alert out to local precincts? Cops saw Mikey and called it in?"

"Likely. Mikey and the size of the lift."

"Prejudiced fucks." I pointed my finger at the front door like Agent Johnson was inside. "That stronzo is out to make a name for himself, and he's creating a goddamn witch hunt to do it."

"He's persistent, I'll give him that." He pulled out another smoke and lit it. "Any witnesses can ID Mikey?"

"I doubt that security guard could ID any of us. He may have realized what was happening, but with the rain and the lights..." I shook my head. "There's no way he saw our faces. Not from that far away. And the truck driver only saw me."

Vito nodded and dragged on his cigarette.

"I'm sitting down with Vinnie and Gio this afternoon. We need to tell the capi—everyone needs to be on their best fucking behavior."

Vito nodded. "I'll tell Marco."

"Make sure he knows I didn't fuck up," I snapped. "That was bad luck. Nothing more."

"Easy, kid. No one's blaming you. Coulda happened to any of us."

I tugged on my hair. "Tell that to Vinnie."

He took a long drag. "What was Siobhán Connelly doing at The Dollhouse last night?"

I frowned. "I thought you didn't want to know."

His eyes narrowed through a trail of smoke. "I changed my mind."

I licked my lips. "Nothing. Waiting for me to get back."

"Marco considers her part of his crew. Like a niece."

"My relationship with Siobhán is none of Marco's business."

"It is when it affects his business."

"It doesn't," I snapped.

He glanced at his watch. "Relationship, huh?"

"No—I meant... You know what I meant."

"I do. I also know who her family is and how you don't always see straight when it comes to them. You want to salvage your relationship with Marco, best not dig that hole any deeper."

I scoffed. "Who said I wanted to salvage it?"

"Keep playing the tough guy, Luca, but I know this hurts you as much as it hurts him. You're both just too goddamn proud and stubborn to admit it."

"Tell him that."

"You think I haven't?" He dropped the cigarette and ground out the butt. "Not to mention what your feud is doing to Gina." He pursed his lips as if restraining a verbal assault to match the fury in his eyes.

I clenched my teeth, biting back my own retort. I hadn't gone there for a lecture.

"It's time you thought long and hard about what this

vendetta is costing you. Ask yourself if it's worth it." He cocked an eyebrow, turned on his heel, and took quick strides back into the building, buttoning his suit coat as he went.

I took the keys out of my pocket, spun them on my finger, and walked across the visitor lot to my car. Time to check on Dominic, grab some food, and head to Revere for a meeting with Vinnie.

As for Vito's question...

I unlocked the door, buckled in, and started the engine. It roared to life, an angry growl, loud and persistent.

What was the cost of avenging my father? I couldn't imagine a price I wouldn't pay to hurt the Shaughnessys the way they'd hurt the Morettis. To take something from them they could never take back. To free myself from the anger and pain that haunted me. To free myself from my nightmares.

I revved the engine, shifted into reverse, and backed out of the space.

A new ante had entered the pot. One I hadn't considered —Siobhán.

She was supposed to be my instrument of revenge, but was I okay with her being its victim as well? I'd told her she was safe. "No more nightmares," I said. But hurting her family would hurt her too. It would open old wounds, create new bad dreams.

I stomped on the clutch, threw the engine into gear, and slammed on the accelerator. The Ferrari's tires squealed as I peeled out of the parking lot.

Revenge was worth any cost. No exceptions. Especially if the Shaughnessys finally got the message that crossing the DeVitas, Valenzanos, or Morettis meant consequences. Consequences so dire, they'd never make that fatal mistake again.

Chapter Twenty-Two

Siobhán

Amazing how the pages of *People* blended together after you read enough of them, and I was pretty sure this was my millionth copy. I slammed the magazine shut and let my head fall back with an exasperated sigh. A person could only watch so much TV, and by noon, I'd already watched *Casablanca* and four episodes of that reality TV show about yacht crews. I took my time with lunch, even attempted a one-sided conversation with Rocco the Wall—he was filling in for Dominic after last night's incident—but that only got me as far as one o'clock.

I tried picking the entertainment center lock for thirty minutes. Turns out, I had no idea how to pick a lock and, without my phone, no way to Google how to pick a lock. After bending the tip of one of Luca's knives—and burying the evidence at the bottom of the utensil drawer—I gave up on my latest amateur escape attempt.

I glanced at the microwave. Three. *Ugh*. Not only was Luca holding me hostage, he was subjecting me to an obscene form of torture—boredom.

He should have been back. Rocco told him multiple times

he had to be at The Dollhouse by three. Whatever. Not my problem. My problem was what to do about Luca when he got home.

My family did a decent job keeping guns out of sight when we were kids, but that didn't mean we never saw them. Or heard them. Guns were a fact of life in Southie in the '80s. So were knives. General violence. I had a thick skin when it came to that stuff. I'd even kept calm, relatively speaking, during the hold-up at Vesuvio. But seeing a gunshot wound? Seeing the bloody mess of Dominic's shoulder and the stains on his stomach? It transported me right back to my teenage trauma.

Hours later, Luca fell prey to his own nightmares. He'd been thrashing and fighting his sheets when I followed the shouts into his room. I called his name over and over, desperate to wake him up and save him from whatever trauma he was reliving.

Last night was completely fucked up, and that included sleeping in Luca's bed wrapped in his arms. What a pair we made. Both severely fucked in the head and taking comfort from the one person we were supposed to hate.

We didn't talk about any of it that morning. He was out of the shower and dressed by the time I woke up. He hurried out the door and left The Wall in charge. But any minute he'd walk through that door, and we'd either pretend like nothing happened or admit that maybe we didn't hate each other as much as either of us wanted to believe. That maybe being wrapped up in each other felt right, because it was the missing piece keeping Luca and Siobhán so broken. Maybe our star-crossed relationship had an inevitable end, and no matter how hard we tried, fate was determined to have its way.

The doorbell rang.

My magazine flew into the air. "Jesus Christ," I gasped, my heart racing.

Where the hell was Rocco? He'd been camped out on the

porch all afternoon. He should've seen whoever was at the door.

I went into the kitchen and got a glass of water.

The doorbell rang again. Whoever it was, they weren't going away, and apparently, Rocco was nowhere to be found. Or maybe he locked himself out?

I crossed the kitchen, opened the door, and immediately regretted the decision.

"Agent Johnson," I said in a tone that contained every ounce of disdain I held for the man.

His head jerked back. "Ms. Connelly. What a pleasant surprise."

"Maybe for you."

"I can honestly say you're the last person I expected to open that door. And I pride myself on not being surprised when it comes to my job."

"We both know you haven't been very successful at your job now, don't we?"

The sinister bend to his narrow mouth belied his affected laughter. "Is Mr. Moretti home?"

"No."

Growing up in the mob, I knew how to deal with nosy outsiders—one-word answers. Uncle Paddy and Da had me well-trained. Don't offer any more information than the necessary minimum. Make them work for their dirt.

"Do you know when he'll be home?"

"No."

His ingratiating smile turned menacing. "Fine. I'll ask you my questions instead."

"You can try." I folded my arms across my chest.

Agent Johnson had been trying to dig up dirt on Marco for as long as I'd worked at Terme, always hanging around chatting up employees in the hopes of grooming a rat. But I hadn't been lying—I wasn't a rat no matter which side of Boston I was on.

"You live here?" he asked.

"No, but you already know that."

"Then, why are you here?"

"None of your business."

His eyes travelled down to the ridiculous top Luca brought back from The Dollhouse. *MILKSHAKE* was written in hot pink block letters across my chest. The neckline of the tank top was slit such that strip club breasts would have stretched the opening and displayed serious cleavage. On me, the fabric hung loose, revealing only a suggestion that breasts existed.

He gave me a smarmy grin. "Were you here last night?" he asked, the innuendo thick.

"Yes." True and noncontroversial. You had to pick your battles with these people. Know when to own up and when to pull back.

"Was Mr. Moretti here last night?"

And there it was. The real reason he was standing on Luca's front porch.

Regardless of what Luca had done—to me or last night—Agent Johnson was *not* on my side. He wasn't on anyone's side but Agent Johnson's. The wrong answer could cause a lot of trouble.

"Yes," I said.

"You sure about that?"

The best way to handle the bait of an open-ended question? Another open-ended question.

"Don't you think I'd know if the other half of the bed was empty?" I raised an eyebrow.

He narrowed his eyes. "Was Luca Davide Moretti with you here last night? All night?"

"Define all night."

The aggressive growl of a Ferrari wedged itself into our conversation.

"Don't play games with me, Ms. Connelly. You won't like the outcome."

"No one's playing games, *Agent*. I can't answer your question if you refuse to be specific. Are we talking about sundown to sunup? When I changed into my pajamas until the time my alarm went off? Define. All. Night."

"You're stalling."

The Ferrari rounded the corner, a lightning bolt of red streaking up the driveway.

"Call it what you want"—the engine went silent, and Luca jumped out of the front seat—"but I'm not going to answer an ambiguous question just so you can twist my words to satisfy whatever case you're trying to make."

Luca's face was all hard lines, the darkness of his eyes tinged rusty and focused on Agent Johnson. He marched up the walkway to where we stood on the front porch and wrapped his arm around my waist.

"Hey, baby," he said.

I looked up in surprise.

He grabbed my nape and pressed a short, fierce kiss below my ear. My body zinged with adrenaline, shock, and desire. I gaped at him for a heartbeat before my brain snapped into action and reminded me of what was happening.

"Hey, baby," I replied, trying to keep my cool despite how good those words tasted on my lips. And how good his lips felt on my neck. The heat that flared in Luca's eyes made me shiver. I placed my palm flat against his chest on top of his tattoo.

"Was this asshole harassing you?"

"No. He was fishing. Like usual." I glared at Agent Johnson. "Isn't that right?"

Agent Johnson's eyes snapped between us and landed on

Luca. "Where were you last night between the hours of midnight and three a.m.?"

"Between my legs," I said before Luca could answer. His pecs flexed beneath my hand. "And unless you need more details than that, I suggest you kindly fuck off."

Agent Johnson refocused his smug contempt on me. "You sure about that?" he asked for the second time that afternoon.

He had something on Luca, or he was bluffing. But I didn't think he was bluffing. No, Agent Johnson was the type of man so full of himself, he couldn't help baiting us with a card better kept to his chest. He wanted us to know he had something. Idiot.

Luca and I needed to get our stories straight, which meant I needed to throw Agent Ego off guard and get him the hell off Luca's porch.

"Three orgasms sure," I said through a sultry smile and winked. I launched onto my toes and placed an open mouth kiss on Luca's neck. "Isn't that right, baby?" I purred into his ear, then nipped the lobe between my teeth.

Luca's fingers dug into my hip, no doubt leaving another fingertip-shaped bruise, but he played along, hugging me close. "That's right. And more tonight if you're good." He swatted me on the ass, and I yelped.

Agent Johnson cleared his throat and shifted his weight.

I nuzzled Luca's neck and trailed my fingertips from his chest toward his waistband.

Agent Johnson looked everywhere but me and Luca.

"Get the fuck off my property," Luca said.

He backed up, hands in the air, but with a thin smile that meant trouble. He strode down the path toward the driveway. "Don't leave town, Mr. Moretti," he called over his shoulder. "It wouldn't be a good look going back to Italy now." He pivoted and walked backward toward his sedan. "Not good at all." His parting words were flat and matter-of-fact. He got into his car, as beige and ordinary as him, and drove out of the cul-de-sac.

"Come on," Luca said and pulled me into the house.

"I need a drink," I said and made a beeline for the kitchen.

He slammed and locked the door. "What did he ask? What did you say?"

"What the hell happened to Rocco?" For all my bravado, my hands shook when I reached for the upper cabinet.

"He had to get to The Dollhouse. I was almost home, so I told him to go."

I grabbed a martini glass, set it on the counter, and opened the freezer.

Luca slammed his hand into the stainless steel, forcing it shut. "What did you say?" he asked in a tone that told me now was not the time for snark.

"Nothing. I mean, nothing more than what you heard. Same shit." I narrowed my eyes and tugged on the door handle. He eased up, and I reached inside for the frosty bottle of vodka. "He used the usual tactics—open-ended questions, then super specific questions, but—"

"Did you tell him anything?"

"What do you think I am—*stunad?*" I rolled my eyes, opened the other side of the fridge with an exaggerated jerk, and retrieved my beloved olives.

He snorted and ran a hand through his hair. "Okay. Fine."

"I'm not a rat, and this isn't my first rodeo." I went about the business of preparing my dirty martini. "Not to mention, I would think, after that little show we put on, you'd trust me enough to know I was trying to cover for you, give you an alibi. Although, next time, a little heads-up, please?"

I paused pulling olives out of the jar, closed my eyes, and let out a tremendous sigh. "What the hell am I talking about?" I mumbled to myself. "Next time." I shook my head and plunked a final olive in my drink.

I swigged the martini. Liquid heat spread across my chest and soothed the ache in my stomach. "Anyway, we need to get our stories straight beyond fucking from midnight to three in the morning." I lifted the martini glass to my lips and my eyebrows to my hairline.

Eyes dark with feral avarice, he prowled forward and caged me against the island. He took the martini glass from my hand and set it on the counter. My heart leaped into my throat, and I stared at him wide-eyed as his hands wrapped around my waist and held me in place.

He brushed my neck with the tip of his nose and brought his lips to my ear. "Did you like our little act?" His warm breath tickled my skin, sending goosebumps down my arms and a jolt of desire straight to my sex. "Baby?"

I sucked in a breath and started to melt. He saved me, lifting me off my weak knees onto the island. My fingers tangled in the silky strands of his hair. He wedged my legs open with his hips and stepped between them. His hands cupped my ass, and his fingers dug into my cheeks, inching me closer, pulling us together.

"All that talk about making you come..." he whispered against my neck, and I shivered from the brush of lush lips against the skin beneath my ear. "Three times..." He nosed my earlobe. "After swearing you're not a liar." He bit my earlobe and tugged. My sex tingled with need. "I can't let you turn into one now, can I?"

Something between a groan and a sigh escaped me, and my eyes fluttered closed. His warm breath caressed my skin, an indecent promise, and electricity followed in its wake. He lowered his head to my collarbone and nudged my head to the side. Something sharp trailed up the length of my neck, the sensation so overwhelming, I squirmed beneath his unrelenting hold, craving sensation where I needed it most.

"You're wet for me, aren't you?" His voice was low and gravelly.

I nodded, dizzy with desire and hoping like hell this wouldn't end the same as our other encounters—heated to a frenzy and frustrated as hell.

He gripped my shorts and pulled hard, forcing me to wiggle where I sat so they'd come off and end my torture. He slipped them around my ass and dropped them on the floor. The marble was cold, but my sex was hot.

"Lean back, baby," he said and moved closer, forcing me to recline enough that my hips tilted.

He trailed his fingers from my hip to the scrap of white lace barely covering the swollen lips of my pussy. He pushed it out of the way and ran his middle finger from my entrance through my folds to my clit. A low rumble reverberated in his chest, and he lifted his head from my neck to look me in the eyes.

"You're fucking soaked," he said, desire flashing in the crimson flecks that dotted his dark irises.

He slid his finger back down and dipped it into my entrance.

I gasped, and my head fell back. He caught the nape of my neck, holding me in place, and watched each reaction that crossed my face with rapt attention as he worked his finger in and out of my pussy.

"So fucking wet," he growled and added another finger.

"Ahhh," I sighed loud and breathy. At the exquisite stretch. At the illicit pleasure. At Luca.

"I'm going to fuck you with my fingers until you're begging for my dick."

My pussy clenched. The thought of Luca inside me nearly pushed me over the edge. I squirmed, tilting my hips so he'd rub my clit, but fuck him if he ever thought I'd beg.

"Not yet." He chuckled. "Three orgasms, isn't that what you said?"

I rocked my hips, desperate for more friction.

"Answer me."

"Yes," I said. "Three."

"Good girl." He pushed his fingers deeper, and I moaned. "You play nice, you get what you want."

My upper body went limp under the sweet satisfaction of Luca's touch, and I twined my fingers tighter in his hair.

"First, I'm going to make you come all over my hand."

He dragged his teeth along my neck, nibbling and sucking as he went. He curled his fingers inside me each time he pumped them in and out. He wouldn't need to do much more to deliver on his first promise.

"Then, I'm going to take you from behind. Hold your hair while I give you the pounding you deserve for all your mouthing off."

He bit my neck, harder this time, and a strange pinch made me gasp. Liquid fire radiated out from a tiny pinprick, but it dissipated as quickly as it arrived. Whatever it was, I wanted more of that delicious sting.

"I swear to God, Luca, if you're talking shit right now, I'll find a way to push *you* off that bridge."

He chuckled, dark and sinful, and his thumb descended on my clit, rolling over it in slow circles. The shock raced through my body like lightning. I jerked, and he tightened his grip.

"And after your second orgasm..." He licked my neck where I'd felt the pinch and nipped at my ear, never stopping his thumb's torturous circles. "After I fuck you deep from behind, I'm going to flip you over and fuck you again, nice and slow." He picked up the pace of his thumb and his fingers, and I stilled, balanced on the edge of spectacular. "I'm going to make you feel every inch of my big dick owning your tight little pussy." And with a curl of his fingers, I came undone.

My muscles clenched. My shoulders shook. My world shattered into a million pieces. Everything destroyed by Luca Moretti.

"Hell yeah, baby. Come for me. Fuck my hand and come for me." He stilled his fingers inside but kept the pressure on my clit like he knew exactly what I needed to ride out the orgasm, to make it last as long as it could. I ground myself against him without shame and without restraint.

Panting and shaking through aftershocks, I slumped against him and rested my forehead on his. Our combined breath was frantic and hot.

He pulled his fingers out, lifted them to his mouth, and licked them clean. "I've dreamed of tasting you." His dark eyes locked with mine through each sinful taste. "You're even sweeter than I imagined."

He rubbed the pad of his thumb against my lips until they parted, and he dipped it into my mouth. I closed my mouth around his thumb and ran my tongue over it, tasting myself. His chest rumbled with satisfaction.

He pulled his thumb back but paused on my bottom lip. He stared at where his thumb held it, and his nostrils flared as if exercising immense control, as if the temptation of my mouth was a line he refused to cross. In one swift motion, he stepped back, lifted me off the island, and set me on my feet. I wobbled, shaken from my orgasm, but he held me up until I regained my balance.

He rubbed my nipple through my shirt, pressed it hard, and rolled it under his thumb. He slid his other hand around my hip to my ass, squeezed, and forced me against him. His rock-hard erection pressed into my stomach.

"Upstairs." He swatted my ass. "Now. On my bed."

Who was I to disobey?

Chapter Twenty-Three

Luca

The scotch was bracing, but after coming home to find Agent Asshole on my porch and finger-fucking Siobhán on my kitchen island, I needed bracing.

Watching Siobhán handle Agent Johnson killed any remaining suspicion that she was a rat. She could've spilled or used the opportunity to leave. Instead, she gave him the runaround. She played along, a little too well, and gave me a raging hard-on.

I shot the rest of the glass and poured another. I'd started down this path and there was no turning back. My dick wouldn't allow it. I kicked off my shoes and bounded up the stairs to my bedroom.

Siobhán was sprawled atop my comforter, one hand behind her head, elbow out to the side. The other traced the top edge of her thong. She bent one of her long legs and rocked her knee from side to side. The tiny scrap of white lace covering her perfect pussy was made even more sexy by that ridiculous tank top. It was just tight enough that her nipples poked through the thin fabric. I downed a mouthful of scotch.

She was ready, squirming on the bed and rubbing her thighs together. The way she devoured me with her eyes made my dick twitch and leak.

I set my drink on the nightstand and unbuckled my belt. "You ready to be thoroughly fucked?"

Her lips parted on an intake. "Yes," she answered, soft and breathy.

She watched me undress, not hiding her appreciation or desire. She'd looked at me like that before. Across the lobby, at the gala, the night upstairs at Vesuvio. Like she wanted to devour me. I had no doubt my eyes held as much heat if not more. They started to turn downstairs with my fingers inside her. My fangs descended too despite my best efforts at restraint, and I nicked her neck. The instinct to bite down almost bested me, but I'd never take her without permission, and permission required explanation. I had to remain in control.

I pulled off my undershirt and stood in my boxers. Her eyes traveled the length of my torso. She swallowed, licked her lips, and rolled onto her side, reaching for my waistband.

I dropped my boxers, and my erection sprang free. Her eyes widened, and she propped herself up, inching closer.

"You want this, baby?" I took my dick in my hand and rubbed the pre-cum dripping from the tip all over its swollen head. "Is this what you want?"

She reached for me again, and I stepped back. I stroked myself, agonizingly slow, but I wanted her to beg. "Uh-uh. I told you downstairs—you need to play nice. I asked you a question, and I want an answer. Now what do you want?"

"I want you," she said, low and husky.

"Which part of me?"

"Your cock."

"Where do you want it?"

She raised her eyes, and a wicked smile crossed her pale pink lips. "Fucking my pussy."

"Christ."

I wanted her. I'd wanted her from the first day I spied her across the lobby at Terme. And that desire, that need, had never ebbed. Even after I found out there was more to her story, after she pushed my buttons, after I took her to the bridge...

"On your knees," I growled.

She scrambled onto all fours, and I climbed onto the bed behind her. Misshapen scars from where the bullets exited marred her back's otherwise smooth skin, and I wanted to kill that fucker O'Doyle all over again. The instinct to protect her, to claim her and make her mine, had me grinding my teeth.

She looked back expectantly from behind the fall of her hair. I gathered it in my fist and pulled her to her knees. She pressed her back against my front, and her nails dug into the sides of my thighs, the same position as when she'd clung to me on the bridge.

I'd clung to her that night too, not wanting to let go. I'd have ended my torture and avenged my father, but not if it meant losing Siobhán.

The realization rocked me, but I couldn't ignore the truth. I wanted this woman in ways that defied reason, and I hated myself for what it was doing to me. She made me forget who I was and what I wanted. I was Luca Moretti, and I wanted revenge, revenge against her family. Instead, all I could think about was how good it would feel to finally sink into Siobhán Connelly.

I slid my free hand up her shirt and found her nipple. "Do you want this big dick inside you?" I snarled the words in her ear.

"Yes," she said, her breath coming in short gasps.

I tightened my grip on her hair, yanked her head back, and

squeezed her breast, pinching her nipple. "Tell me you want a fucking, Siobhán."

She blinked, and her throat at this angle bobbed through a swallow. I rocked my hips forward, pressing my erection into her ass. Her soft skin against my hard dick was heaven.

"I've wanted you to fuck me for two years, Luca." Her declaration was rich and sultry. "I've been waiting for you to fuck me since the day we met."

I released her breast and ran my fingers across her bottom lip. She sucked them into her mouth and tongued them, the same as when she'd blown me that night at Vesuvio.

"That mouth," I said and bit her shoulder, careful not to prick her with my fangs. They'd elongated, not fully, but enough that if I wasn't careful, I'd nick her again. I moved my nips and licks up her neck to her ear. "So wicked." I sucked her earlobe into my mouth and tugged on it with my teeth.

I pulled her hair, forcing her head onto my shoulder. "Are you ready to be punished for all that mouthing off?" I shoved my hand down the front of her thong, feeling my way through the moist strip of hair to her clit. I pinched it between my thumb and forefinger.

"Ah!" She sucked in a breath and scratched her fingernails up my thighs. "Yes!"

"Are we safe to fuck without a rubber?"

"Yes," she said between panting breaths.

"Thank fuck." I wanted to feel her. We'd stripped away all pretense, and I wanted nothing left between us.

I sucked on her neck one last time, wishing I could sink my fangs into her flesh, but released her instead, pushing away temptation. "On your hands," I ordered, and she obeyed.

I spread her legs with my knees, grabbed her ass, and squeezed. I tilted her hips up, opening her to me. The pale skin around her pussy was slick with desire, and the white string of lace against her pink, swollen flesh an indecent invitation.

"Fuck, I need to be inside you." I grabbed the thong at her waist and ripped the strip of fabric from her body. She yelped and her body jerked, but she thrust her hips back and tilted her ass up, welcoming me.

I ran the head of my dick through her folds, coating myself with her wetness and teasing her opening. She squirmed and wiggled with each swipe. I couldn't wait any longer. I lined myself up with her entrance and sank into her until I felt her pussy against my balls.

She cried out, a yelp of pain and a moan of pleasure.

I pressed my hips forward, bottoming out with a grunt. "Holy fuck, you're tight."

I inched my dick, slick with her cum, out of her tight heat, then plunged back into her warm depths. Her body stretched to accommodate me but squeezed me like a vise, a perfect sheath made for my pleasure and my pleasure alone.

Moving in and out of her tight little cunt, watching my thick cock stretch her pussy wide and take my length... It was the most erotic thing I'd ever seen. The visual alone was enough to make me come, never mind the lewd noises she made with each thrust.

Siobhán watched me over her shoulder, cheeks flushed, eyes dilated. Pleasure and pain played across her face, evident in the bend of her parted lips as she got used to my size.

"Such a tight little pussy. When's the last time you had a dick inside you?"

She shivered, and her eyes fluttered closed. I fisted her hair and slammed into her. She yelped.

"Answer me," I said.

She opened her eyes, and they flashed with challenge. "Two years ago."

I groaned, and my dick throbbed at the implication. I pulled until she lifted onto her knees. She tangled her fingers in my hair, elbows wide, pert breasts and thick nipples jutting. "No wonder you're so tight. You were waiting for this dick, weren't you?" I wrapped my other arm around her and fingered her clit. "This pussy is mine, isn't it?"

"Unh," she moaned, deep and throaty. Her fingers twisted in my hair, and she rocked her hips. "For now," she taunted, barely above a whisper in her temptress voice.

I tugged on her hair. "It's mine," I snarled and slapped her clit. She cried out. "And I won't let you forget it."

I coated my fingers with her wetness, running them over her clit to where the base of my dick stretched her tight entrance. I released her hair and pushed her down until she was back on all fours.

I squeezed her hip, holding her in place, and started to move. I picked up speed until I railed her hard, slamming my hips into her. "You gonna behave, baby?"

"Never!" she cried between gasps and the slap of skin on skin.

"If you want this dick again," I said and spread her wetness from my fingers across her other hole. She whimpered and pressed her hips back. "If you want me to make you come..." I licked my thumb, coating it, then circled her back entrance, adding just enough pressure to make her beg.

"Please! Luca! Please!"

"I told you I'd make you beg." I slid my thumb into her ass.

She moaned, an animal-like sound that almost pushed me over the edge. "Yeah," I said through a self-satisfied grin. "You'll behave."

Breathy sighs and grunts and the wet sounds of fucking filled the bedroom. I kept up the pace, pounding her pussy while dipping my thumb in and out of her ass. I was close, but I wanted to feel her come around me before I let go.

"Luca! I'm going to come!"

"That's right, baby. Come for me. Be a good girl and come for me." I pushed my thumb deeper, and she came apart.

She wailed, loud and unrestrained, and the walls of her pussy clenched. She squeezed my dick so tight, the sensation building in my spine erupted. I came hard—the orgasm of my life—my body shaking with each stream of cum I shot into her body. Claiming her. I never wanted to stop claiming her.

She rode out her orgasm, and I shivered through the last vestiges of mine until we stilled, spent and panting from a violent explosion years in the making.

I removed my thumb from her ass but didn't pull out. I didn't want to. Not yet. I didn't want the moment to end. I wanted more. I wanted to fuck her all night and all day. For weeks. For months.

For eternity.

My mind raced trying to process those foreign, unwelcome thoughts and the way my body tingled with an impulse to wrap her in my arms and never let go.

My dick softened as I tried to make sense of what happened. I pulled out, climbed off the bed, and wandered into the master bathroom, confused and reeling. I washed my hands, grabbed a cloth, and soaked it in warm water.

Siobhán sat on the bed, propped up by the headboard and still wearing that ridiculous tank top. A muss of blonde, her hair stuck out at odd ends. One knee out to the side revealed a tiny strip of blonde and swollen lips glistening with our shared pleasure.

"You've never looked more beautiful." The whispered words broke free before I could stop them.

She lowered her eyes, the pink of her already flushed cheeks deepening.

I sat on the edge of the bed and leaned back, propping myself up on my elbow. I cleaned between her legs, captivated by all the creamy skin and patches of tiny freckles. She watched me—I felt her following each of my near-reverent motions—and I finally caved. I looked up.

She smiled, playful and knowing, like we shared a secret neither of us wanted to admit. I searched her eyes, and in them, I finally saw the truth. She never meant to hurt me. Ever. How could she? She was in love.

The uncomfortable realization took root, twisting and winding through my insides. I struggled to swallow, the suffocating sensation clawing its way up my throat.

She stared at me, satisfied, eager, and trusting, waiting for what came next.

"Are you hungry?" I asked, and the question moved through the air like we were underwater, the words slow and surreal.

She wrinkled her brow and blinked. "Yes, actually."

I dropped the washcloth and ran my hand up her leg, from her knobby knee to her stomach. "I'll make us dinner." I traced my fingertips over the scars that crisscrossed her abdomen, wondering when we'd pull out of this underwater trance.

She watched my finger, mesmerized, until I stopped over one of the entry wounds. She sat up, scooted forward, and threaded her fingers into my hair, running her nails over my scalp. I shivered, and my eyes fluttered closed.

"What are we having?" she asked.

"What would you like?"

"I like Italian," she said.

I fought a smile. "Get dressed. I'll be downstairs." I leaned forward and kissed her neck just below her ear, wishing I could have another type of meal. "You're due a third orgasm. I haven't forgotten."

My lips lingered on her neck. It felt intimate and beautiful. And wrong. Because she loved me, and there was no space left in my heart for love. Revenge occupied every inch of its dark chambers. But when she dragged her fingernails across my scalp, I kissed her there again, needing her to feel the same fullness in her heart that I wanted to feel in mine.

I pulled away and swatted her on the hip. "Let's go."

Siobhán walked across the hall to her bedroom. I tugged on a pair of joggers and made my way downstairs, dazed and confused. We'd crossed a line, and whatever happened next, there was no turning back.

Chapter Twenty-Four

Siobhán

The rustle of plastic and the clank of pots and pans traveled up the stairs. I padded down them dressed in leggings, a sweatshirt, and post-sex euphoria. My cheeks were warm, the flush Luca put there likely brightening my pale complexion. I fanned my face; I needed to play it cool.

I combed my hair with my fingers, taming the rat's nest into a ponytail, and took the tie from between my teeth to fix it in place. But my insides remained a tangled mess. More than usual.

Half of me wanted to flit across the kitchen with the corners of my mouth pinned to my ears in a blissful grin. The other half wanted to smack the first half upside the head and remind her that she'd been kidnapped and nearly killed. By a player. And not just any player. A player in the Mafia who'd broken her heart and had a vendetta against her family. Not exactly a situation where a rational person should be glowing.

I stepped off the stairs and into the kitchen. The soft light of the early evening sun and the fresh breeze through the French doors set the stage, but Luca stole the show. His role? Domestic god.

Half his hair was tied back the way he'd worn it the morning I found him playing the violin. His fitted joggers sat low on his hips, and the naked expanse of his muscled back flexed with each item he placed on the counter. Goosebumps prickled my skin. Pleasant, happy, hopeful goosebumps.

"What's all this?" I stopped behind him and peeked around his shoulder at the array of ingredients and bowls. Behind me, two plastic Starmarket bags sat on the island. "And when did you get groceries?"

"I told you I could cook." He bent down and retrieved the colander from the lower cabinet. "The groceries I got on my way home. That's why I was late. But I left them in the car when I saw Agent Asshole."

"Agent Asshole." I snickered. "Perfect."

"Right?" He lifted his chin toward the island. "Make yourself useful and open the wine."

All that was left in the plastic bags was a package of fresh pasta and a bottle of red. I placed the items on the island. "Bags?"

"Inside the door to the garage. On your right."

I took the bags to the garage, shoved them in the bag hanging on the inside of the door, and walked back into the kitchen to the cabinets next to the fridge where Luca kept his wine glasses. He diced a slab of pancetta on the other side of the sink. I watched him for a moment, holding a glass in each hand, struck by the novelty of the scene unfolding. So domestic. So normal. So not us.

"What?" he asked.

"Nothing. Just admiring your technique."

He snorted. "The corkscrew is in the drawer with the utensils."

"Got it." I snapped out of frozen disbelief and went to work on the bottle of Merlot. "What are we having?"

"Lobster carbonara," he said in his delicious Italian accent, never taking his eyes off his work.

My stomach clenched, and I winced. This is why I avoided eating with others unless I was in a restaurant where I could order my own meal. Having to explain that I couldn't eat whatever it was the person had so thoughtfully prepared went beyond embarrassing and straight to mortifying.

"How fancy," I mumbled, dreading the awkward moment when I'd have to tell him I couldn't eat cream sauce.

He huffed and set the pancetta aside. "We live in Boston, Siobhán. Lobster costs the same as chicken." He grabbed the shallots and started peeling. "And it's more flavorful. Gina used to make this a lot before we moved to Italy."

"I—uh..." God, this was torture. "So, um... I can't eat—"

"Do you trust me?" He stopped his knife and looked over his shoulder.

I raised an eyebrow. "Are you serious?"

He chuckled. "Fair."

He set the knife down, wiped his hands on a towel, and plucked two containers off the counter. He stepped to where I stood poised with the wine and held them out, showing me their labels.

"Cashew Cream," I read in awe. "Vegan Parmesan Cheese." A bright warm light spread out from my heart and the bliss-filled grin I'd been holding back finally broke free. I looked up from the containers into one of Luca's rare smiles that showed his teeth and reached his eyes. "How did you..."

He went back to the counter and resumed dicing. "After last night, I figured we could both use some comfort food. Lobster carbonara tastes like home to me. Takes me right back to the North End, sitting in the kitchen watching Mamma Gina make dinner. I googled your"—he waved his knife through the air—"conditions over lunch. Figured out what I needed to make this happen. Et voilà!"

Tears pricked my eyes. He had his back to me, but I faced the island anyway to dab them with the back of my sleeve. "Thank you," I said hurriedly and poured the wine. "That was really thoughtful." My voice caught, and I cleared my throat.

"No worries. It was easy."

"No," I said with more vehemence than I'd intended. "No, it's not." I handed him a glass, and he must have noticed the steel in my voice, because he set his knife down and studied me, eyebrows drawn together. "It's a burden. On everyone, and they never forget to remind me." I held up my glass. "Sláinte."

"Salute."

Light. Fruity. "Delicious. Thank you."

"Like I said—easy. Hand me that pasta, will you?"

I grabbed the spaghetti off the island and handed it to him.

He set it on the counter, placed a big pot in the sink, and turned on the faucet. He leaned back and folded his arms. "And, for the record, it's not a burden. Not in the slightest."

I huffed. "I should revise that statement. It's only a burden when they actually remember I have dietary restrictions. Most of the time it's, 'Oh, right, Vahnie, you can't eat that, can you? Sorry. Here's some bread.'"

I sipped my wine, but the bitterness lingered. "Do you know what it's like preparing food you can't eat? Especially when the people you're preparing it for regularly and conveniently forgot about your lactose intolerance as a kid? The number of times I ate a mouthful of mashed potatoes only to spit it back out because it was filled with butter and sour cream... And that was before my stomach got ripped to shreds."

Luca's face darkened into a scowl. He turned off the water, took the pot out of the sink, and set it on the stove.

I closed my eyes and took a deep breath. "Sorry. I didn't

mean to get all riled up. I don't usually talk about this, and it's kind of a hot button issue for me."

"You don't need to apologize. Your mother is the one who needs to apologize."

"No, it's fine." I walked around the island and hopped up on a barstool. "She did the best she could with what she had. Da and Rory were the priority. It's how she was raised. And —" I caught myself.

"And what?" He eyed me over the rim of his wine glass.

The trees beyond the deck were budding. Some of them had even sprouted leaves. They rustled in the early evening breeze off the pond. There was a freshness there, so many new beginnings. Maybe that's what was happening between me and Luca. Maybe we were turning over a new leaf. Maybe if I trusted him, he might learn to trust me.

But trusting men went against every lesson I'd learned. Don't be vulnerable, you'll only get hurt. Protect yourself, because no one else is looking out for Siobhán but Siobhán.

Then again, no man had ever taken me grocery shopping or researched my conditions or attempted to make me dinner. The same man had also crushed my heart. Multiple times.

The cashew cream and vegan parmesan cheese stared back at me from the counter. Maybe things were different this time.

"It's not just my mam. Or the food. It's—" I waved a hand through the air. "It's all the stuff underneath that gets me riled up."

"I get that," he said dryly.

The corner of my mouth lifted. If anyone understood layers of trauma, it was Luca. I tilted my glass and traced the rim of its base on the marble, swirling the wine inside as though the words I needed might materialize in its legs.

I knew why I stayed in Ireland so long, why I wanted to quit Terme and run away. Why I put on a strong front and made sure everyone knew I had my shit together and could take care of myself. But speaking that truth, sharing that part of myself with another person made it real, made me vulnerable. It's why I never said it out loud before.

"I don't feel safe," I said quietly into my glass and raised my eyes.

Luca's pouty lips pressed into a tight line of displeasure.

The water reached its boiling point. The ripples stole his attention, and he resumed dinner prep. Without those devastating eyes focused on me, my truth bubbled over. Apparently, I'd reached my boiling point as well.

"I haven't felt safe since the shooting. But the men who shot me weren't the only ones responsible. My family and the men in my life did the rest of the damage."

He shot a glance over his shoulder, hostile and protective, then tossed the diced shallots into the saucepan. They sizzled in the hot oil.

"Life went on. No one thought to treat my trauma. Mam wanted to pretend like nothing happened. Talking about it meant admitting her family was the cause. So she went about her business as if nothing had changed. Kept cooking the meals she'd always cooked, refusing to acknowledge I couldn't eat half the things she prepared. Eating was a nightmare, but the actual nightmares were worse."

Luca's penetrating stare drew my eyes up from my wine. His burned with understanding, an empathy that only came from shared experience. I didn't know his demons, but I knew what it was like for them to keep you up at night.

"I lost all sense of safety, inside my house and out. If I ate the wrong thing, I was miserable for hours, sometimes days. I became scared of food. If I left my house, who knew what might happen. Southie felt like a warzone. Walking to school meant risking my life. I was terrified to leave my house. And no one cared. The only person I trusted after that was myself. So I left."

"You might as well not have had a family," he said with a bitter edge and took the pot off the stove.

He poured the boiling water and noodles into the colander. A mushroom cloud of steam erupted from the sink. On the stove, the sauce simmered and grew fragrant. My defective stomach rumbled with hunger.

"Why did you come back?" he asked. "After all that time."

I shrugged. "Mam's hip surgery. Da's dementia. Someone had to take care of them."

His forehead scrunched, and with a disapproving shake of his head, he added the pasta to the pan.

A wry smile captured my lips. "Italians don't have the corner on macho, alpha-male attitudes, you know."

He snorted and turned the noodles over in the sauce.

"Rory—my brother—he wasn't about to take responsibility. God forbid anyone ask the prince to help out around the house. And Ciarán..." I sighed. "In all the years I lived in Ireland, Ciarán was the only person who visited. But he wasn't going to take care of my parents. He's the boss, and a boss shouldn't have to worry about things like that. He offered to hire someone, but..." I shook my head. "I couldn't do that to them."

"So you came back."

"So I came back. And unknowingly landed a job with an Italian Mafia don."

He snorted and placed steaming plates of lobster carbonara on the island. "He wasn't a don when you started working for him."

I shoved my nose into the steam, closed my eyes, and breathed in the savory aroma. "This smells amazing."

"I know," he said atop the rattle of the utensil drawer.

I huffed. "I mean, I didn't know he was connected at all,

not until you took me upstairs at Vesuvio. It took me a few days to piece together your names with what I heard growing up. The next week, Marco called me into his office and told me that whatever conclusions I'd drawn, I should forget them. That he wasn't involved, and he kept his distance."

He placed cloth napkins and utensils next to our plates.

"He also reminded me of the NDA I signed when I started," I added dryly.

Luca chuckled. "Him and those NDAs..." He sat next to me and lifted his glass. "Buon appetito."

I clinked my glass against his. We drank and dove into our meals.

"Oh my god," I groaned with the first mouthful, and my eyes rolled back. "You really can cook."

"Told ya." He took a bite, and his eyebrows drew together in concentration as he chewed. "I was skeptical about the substitutions."

"Most people are, but it's not bad, right?"

He stabbed a piece of lobster and twirled spaghetti onto his fork. "Not bad at all. It's different, but I'd eat it again." He shoveled the tremendous bite into his mouth.

"Thank you." I sipped my wine, needing to hide the emotion clogging my throat.

"It was nothing," he said through the mouthful. "I don't get to cook very often. It was a great excuse to dust off the old pots and pans."

"No, I mean, for taking the time to..." I frowned, looking for words in my plate. "To accommodate my..." I waved my fork through the air. "My whole deal."

"Accommodate?" He set his napkin on the counter. "I already told you—it's not a burden."

"It feels like a burden. Even to me sometimes. You're the first person who's taken the time to do something like this, so, thank you."

He examined me a moment longer.

"Shouldn't we get our story straight about what happened last night?" I asked, desperate to change the subject.

"I thought that's what we were doing." He waggled his eyebrows.

I laughed and swatted him on the arm despite the heat creeping up my neck and pooling between my thighs. "You know what I mean. When you got home. When you left in the morning. That kind of thing."

He narrowed his eyes, finished chewing, and pointed at me with his fork. "Ten p.m. You were here the entire time—I'll let the girls know—and I left to meet Vito in Framingham at the jail at eight-thirty."

I frowned. "Why did you go to the jail? What happened last night? Is Dominic okay?"

"Uh-uh." He shook his head. "You grew up in this world. You know better than to ask those kinds of questions. You want to be an accessory after the fact?" He brought his wine to his lips and raised his eyebrows.

"No," I said sullenly and stabbed a piece of lobster. "Sorry. You're right. It's been a long time since I've been around this stuff on a day-to-day basis." I twirled my fork in the creamy spaghetti. "I'm just worried about Dominic."

"Dom's fine. I stopped by to see him before my meetings this afternoon. He's a little grumpy," he said with a comforting smile, "but I promise—he's fine."

I believed him, but an uneasiness nagged at my nerves. A quiet warning that said, get out! Stay away from this man and run far, far away!

Dominic might be okay, but he'd been shot, someone was in jail, and the FBI had shown up at Luca's door. Each of those events in and of themselves should have been enough to make me redouble my efforts at escape or at the very least resolve to buy the first ticket out of Boston as soon as he let me go. But the moment Luca crossed that final line, the moment he touched me, every instinct telling me to run vanished.

I had no idea what any of this meant—probably nothing —but this thing between us, this force driving us together despite everything working against us, wouldn't allow me to pull back. Never mind our enemy families. Never mind his macho, playboy antics. Never mind his dark vendetta. I wanted Luca Moretti even if he seemed determined to destroy us both.

"Don't you ever get sick of those old movies?" he asked.

"Hm?"

"Those old movies you watch. Seems like every time I walk past the living room, you're watching a movie from before either of us was born."

"Way older than that, actually," I said and took a bite of pasta.

"Don't you get tired of watching the same things over and over again?"

I shrugged a shoulder. "Don't you get tired of eating pasta?"

He glared at me, and I stuck the tip of my tongue between my teeth. His eyes lingered on my mouth, and damn if that one look didn't send heat straight to my core.

I cleared my throat. "In all seriousness, no. They're a comfort. Like old friends. I started watching them as a kid. Da brought home a VHS player—probably lifted." I shot Luca a knowing look. He let out a snort and nodded, no doubt familiar with new electronics magically appearing in his home growing up. "Mam was watching *Double Indemnity* one night. Rented it from the local Blockbuster. Remember those?"

"Not really. I mean, I know what they are, but we'd moved to Italy by then."

"Ah, yeah. Well, that movie blew my mind. Barbara Stanwyck was a force—fierce and independent. Vicious. And the plot? Whew! That movie still holds water, and it came out eighty years ago. Can you believe that?"

"Never seen it."

I slow-turned to face him. "Excuse me?"

"Cosa?"

"We need to remedy this situation immediately."

He chuckled.

"Seriously. This is an egregious oversight."

He held up a hand. "All right, all right. I'll watch it."

"Okay." I turned back to my plate. "Just wanted to make sure."

He chuckled again and shook his head. "You really love that movie, huh?"

"It's what introduced me to Old Hollywood, and I've been hooked ever since. The movies, the aesthetic, the fashion."

"I'd always wondered how you settled on your style."

"Now you know."

"It suits you," he said, and his shy smile surprised me.

"Thank you."

I twirled more pasta onto my fork and thought back to high school and how I'd taught myself pin curls. I'd even kept a notebook filled with ideas for my dream house once I finally got out of Southie.

"I think it was a way for me to escape, especially after the shooting. A way to create a world around me that was so different and far away from everything I knew and saw in the real world. Like I said, a comfort."

"Like my violin."

I met his eyes. "Like your violin."

He nodded.

Halfway through my plate, I reached my stomach's limits

and had to stop. Anything more and I'd cross the line into problem territory.

I tossed my napkin on the counter, and Luca shoveled another huge bite into his mouth. He turned his fork through his dish, and his forearm flexed, biceps bulging from the bend in his elbow. I tore my eyes away from his muscles. The wolf had wrapped himself in sheep's clothing, and like a fool, I'd ignored my better judgment and embraced his softer side.

"That was delicious," I said. "I don't get to eat dishes like this unless I go to a vegan restaurant, and with my schedule, I rarely have the time."

He pointed at my plate with his fork. "You going to eat that?"

I laughed. "No, I'm stuffed. Go for it."

He pushed his empty plate aside and slid mine in front of him. "You know," he said and twirled pasta onto his fork, "you don't have to quit. Marco keeps his business ventures separate. You're safe there."

I stood on the footrest and reached across the island to grab the wine. I poured a splash into my glass, swirled it, and drank.

"Trust me, I don't want to quit. I love my job, and in terms of my career, I'm at the top of my game. Did you know out of the handful of Michelin Three Key hotels in the US, Terme di Boston is the only one that has a woman for a General Manager?"

His head snapped up, and he stopped chewing. "No, I didn't," he said through his mouthful.

"Surprising in 2024, but true. The next closest Three Key is in New York City, and that's too far from my parents, so..." I tossed back the rest of my wine, maudlin and resentful about what I'd given up because of my family. "Anyway, I do need to quit. I'm not safe there, Luca, and you know it."

"I don't know that."

"You don't get it, do you? I'm sitting here because of who I am. The secret's out. I'm a Shaughnessy. It's only a matter of time before someone takes advantage of that and I'm thrust into another situation like the one at Vesuvio or last night or"—I craned my neck and gave him an accusatory look—"at the Tobin Bridge."

He winced.

"I can't handle the stress. My stomach can't handle the stress. I don't want to live my life constantly looking over my shoulder. It nearly killed me before I moved to Ireland. I can't live like that again. I won't."

"The only people who know are Marco and Vinnie. Well, and Vito. And probably Gio too, but they're consiglieri. It's their job to keep their mouths shut. And me. Your secret is safe. Omertà isn't just a word. It's an oath. It has teeth."

"And Anna. And Gina." I shook my head. "Look, I'm not saying any of those people are trying to cause trouble on purpose, but this is how it starts. It's already spread too far. Not to mention, you don't have to be involved to be hurt by this life. I didn't get shot when I was sixteen because I was involved. I got shot because I was *there*. I don't ever want to be *there* again."

He wiped his mouth and tossed his napkin onto his empty plate. "I don't know." He stared into his wine, swirling it, then drained the glass and leaned back. "Seems to me you've been forced to accommodate everyone else—where you live, what you eat, where you work. Dio, even your accent." His words were soft and distant. "Doesn't seem fair."

Didn't I know it.

I stacked the empty plates and utensils and walked them over to the sink. "You of all people should know—life is nothing if not unfair. We've both had our share of shitty circumstances, Luca. You can't stew in the past. I mean, you can, but that's no way to live. All you can do is move forward and make choices to give yourself the best possible chance at happiness."

"That's not good enough. Not for me. And it shouldn't be for you either."

I shrugged. "It is what it is. I accepted my lot in life a long time ago."

He got up, stretched his arms overhead, and yawned.

I surveyed the mess and Luca's sleepy eyes. "Let me clean up, okay? You cooked. I'll clean. That's fair."

He quirked a wry grin. "Using my words against me?"

"Damn straight. Seriously though, you had a long day. I, on the other hand, sat on the couch watching TV and reading *People*. I got this."

His eyes darted around the kitchen. "Okay..." He licked his lips, and his face twisted with worry. "There's paper towel under the sink. And disinfectant. And rags. Don't be stingy with the disinfectant." His breath quickened. "All the dirty rags need to go on top of the washing machine in the laundry room when you're done. And make sure you get all the food chunks off the plates before you put them in the dishwasher. There's no disposal unit in there, you know? The detergent is under the sink. Don't forget to run it."

He grabbed the back of his neck and surveyed the counters.

"Hey." I took his hand and gave it a squeeze. "I know how to clean a kitchen, okay?"

"Sorry." He closed his eyes through a deep breath. "I'm... particular when it comes to cleaning."

I widened my eyes. "You don't say!"

He let out a nervous chuckle.

I squeezed his hand again. "I got this. Trust me."

He smiled, still wary but less so, and made for the stairs.

I got to work.

Three nights ago, Luca Moretti held me perched on the

ledge of the Tobin Bridge, ready to sacrifice my life to exact his revenge. Now I was cleaning his kitchen. After he cooked dinner for me. After fucking me senseless. Talk about whiplash.

The entire fucked-up chain of events was par for the course with me and Luca. Our relationship had never been anything but incendiary. The only question was how long before it blew up in our faces.

Chapter Twenty-Five

Siobhán

The pale blue teddy was in a rumpled ball behind the gym bag Luca brought back from The Dollhouse. I'd thrown it there when I unpacked the bag, disgusted by his presumption. It didn't disgust me now.

I shook it out and held it in front of me. He'd picked it out because he'd wanted me to wear it for him. Even then.

That man didn't know what he wanted. One big ball of conflict, he just felt and acted on whatever emotion was winning the race at the time. He wanted me physically—I'd known that from day one—but was it something more? Did his feelings run as deeply as mine?

I ripped the tags off, pulled the sheer, stretchy material over my head, and barely recognized the woman who stared back at me in the standing mirror. I ran my fingers across lips usually painted ruby red but instead were pale pink. They matched my fair Irish complexion and the freckles that dusted my nose. A few stragglers dotted my cheekbones and met the wrinkles at the corners of my eyes. Without makeup, my blonde eyebrows were barely visible beneath the lines that creased my forehead.

I fingered the ends of my hair. I let it grow out for the first time in years, but without my curlers or pins, it fell stick-straight to my shoulders. I tucked it behind my ears, and my eyes drifted down my body.

It looked the same as it had for as long as I could remember—too thin with too many sharp angles. The teddy should have been tight, should have hugged curves I'd longed for my entire life. Instead, it bunched at my waist, and my hip bones jutted prominently through the sheer fabric. At least my scars weren't visible, and my small breasts were perky. My full, pert nipples drew attention away from my stomach to my chest. A small victory.

I tilted my head and tried to see myself the way Luca saw me—through hungry eyes filled with appreciation and lust—instead of how I saw myself—wrinkled with middle-age and scrawny, a body ravaged from growing up in the mob. I ran my hands over my hair, smoothing it and soothing my insecurities.

Heartache was real, and it was painful. It's what happened when that muscle was overused but not given what it needed to recover. Mine ached for Luca, in part because I couldn't imagine a future tied to someone who lived this life, in part because I wasn't sure he wanted a future with me at all. How could I put myself and my heart in jeopardy again? I shouldn't, and once I got out of there, I knew I wouldn't. I'd walk away.

But not tonight. Tonight, all I wanted was Luca. I'd deal with my heart later.

Across the hall in the master bedroom, the full moon cast an ethereal glow through the open window, illuminating the ridges and angles of Luca's magnificent body. The comforter was bunched at the end of the bed, and the sheet draped sideways across his hips but just barely. The full breadth of his abs and the trim hair beneath were as sinful a temptation as his powerful legs, trunks of muscle dusted with dark brown atop white linen. One knee was cocked, mirroring the bend in his right elbow. His forearm covered his eyes, and his chest rose and fell with the slow cadence of his breath.

I crawled onto the bed. His body heat and a hint of his cologne made me instantly wet. I ran my hand over his chest and kissed his neck.

"You owe me a third orgasm," I whispered into his ear.

A low rumble emanated from his chest.

I straddled his hips. He stirred, his arms and legs shifting, and his eyes cracked open. I trailed my fingernails down the ridges of his muscled torso. His eyes trailed down my body, and his hands followed. He ran them back up the sheer teddy from my hips to my breasts, hardening beneath me, growing to meet the demands of the desire burning in his eyes. My sex ached in anticipation of feeling him inside me again.

He thumbed my nipples through the fabric, and I gasped. My fingers went to my sex, needy for the same pressure there. I dipped them between my legs, coating them with my wetness, and circled my clit.

Another sleepy rumble vibrated his torso. He sat up, and I rested my hands on his shoulders. He splayed his across my back, and with only inches separating us, he stared into my eyes.

I combed the hair off his face and ran my fingers through it, dragging my nails across his scalp. His gaze hooded and dipped to my mouth. He licked his lips—those full, sinful lips —then returned his attention to my eyes, holding them, asking permission. But he wasn't asking permission from me. He was asking permission from himself.

My heart hammered against my chest, filled to bursting with affection for the man who looked at me like my lips were the only answer to his questions. I cupped the side of his face and ran my thumb along his cheekbone, wanting to memorize every detail, every ridge and wrinkle, every crimson fleck in his coffee-brown eyes. Stash them away, safe in the vault of my mind so that when this all came to an end, I could pull each treasure out and return to this perfect moment.

His lids fluttered closed under my touch, and I lowered my lips to our first kiss.

I brushed them against his, tentatively, knowing that everything would change after this moment—the moment we finally gave in to what we really wanted and how we really felt. His warm breath tangled with mine, and the space between us came alive with anticipation, years of longing on the verge of satisfaction. My lips tingled with it, sending shivers down my spine. But I didn't want to rush; I balanced on the precipice, knowing we'd never get to fall over the edge again.

The mouth I hungered after for years rose to meet mine with the gentlest touch, and electricity streaked through my body. He kissed my top lip, then the bottom. I darted my tongue out to taste him, wishing I could freeze time and forever occupy that place of unparalleled pleasure and rightness but knowing this might be my only chance.

He did the same, touching the tip of his tongue to my lips. And when our tongues finally met, I melted, and we kissed. We let go, moving in sensual harmony and revealing the full extent of the passion we'd held at bay for so long.

He wrapped his arms around me, holding me close and cradling my head. He slanted his lips across mine, sweeping his tongue into my mouth, each stroke languid and tender. I shoved my hands into his silky, thick hair, and he tightened his hold, pulling me deeper. But there was no objective, no destination. Just the kiss and everything we wanted to tell each other poured out through each caress.

He let the kiss fade until only our lips touched and we shared each other's breath. His hands slid to my hips, and he pulled back enough to watch himself run them up and down my sides. He stopped where the blue teddy pooled at my waist and slipped his fingers beneath the thin material, pressing them against my skin. He dragged his hands up my torso, pushing the teddy along with them, and when he reached my arms, pulled the fabric up over my head and tossed it aside.

I placed my hands on his shoulders; he rested his on my hips. We stared into each other's eyes, held in place by the emotion swimming between us with staggering intensity.

"I waited too long to kiss you," he said in an awed whisper and brushed his thumb across my cheek. "I could have been kissing you this entire time."

He lowered his hand to my upper back and, shifting his weight, rolled us. He laid me down, untangling us from the sheet, and hovered over me on his side. The fall of his hair framed his dark eyes. They were filled with a yearning that went beyond desire, and when he lowered his mouth to mine, he made love to it with a kiss that held their same promise.

The floodgate holding back my feelings for Luca came crashing down. The misgivings, the worry, the heartbreak— gone, and I surrendered everything to him. Not the playboy. Not the made man. Not my family's sworn enemy. But Luca. The man I'd loved from afar. The man who smiled just for me. My Romeo.

He climbed on top of me and spread my knees, wedging himself between my legs. I reached between us and found the weight of his balls. I cradled them and gently squeezed before running my nails over the sensitive skin. He shivered and broke the kiss, pulling back just enough to look into my eyes. He brushed the loose strands of hair from my face. I wrapped my fingers around the base of his cock and led him to my entrance, swirling the tip through my wetness.

He pressed his thick head into me, and his short, warm

breaths danced with mine. I threaded my hands into his hair and pushed it away from his face. The crimson flecks dotting the obsidian field of his eyes seemed to flare as he pressed himself forward.

He filled and stretched me, joining with me and granting my soul the piece of itself that had always been missing. He shivered, and the awe in his eyes matched the awe in my heart, a reverence for our perfect moment and the beauty created when two souls finally admitted how deeply they treasured each other.

He held himself up on one elbow, wrapped his fingers around the nape of my neck, and kissed me, easing himself out and pressing himself in as slowly and gently as he moved his mouth over mine. Tender kisses, one, two at a time, pulling away to look into my eyes, then dipping back down to reclaim my lips. His hips moved in a slow, sensual rhythm, and my hips lifted and shifted to match. We held onto each other as tightly as we held onto the moment, never wanting it to end.

He thrusted, and I squirmed with more urgency, the pleasure rising and demanding we fulfill our growing need. He released me from his kiss and propped himself up on both elbows. His forehead hovered above mine, and he started to pump in and out of me. I wrapped my legs around his hips, pressing him into my core, sensation building with each stroke of his cock and each grind against my clit.

"Baby," he breathed. "Baby, tell me when. Tell me when you're going to come." The pleading in his voice nearly sent me over the edge. He was close and so was I, and he wanted us to come together, wanted us to share that final intimacy.

"Now. Luca!" I barely breathed his name before my body plummeted into the abyss.

He shivered at my exclamation, thrusting faster, and I moaned, loud chords of bliss ripped from my body with each pulse of my orgasm. He thrust one last time and stilled, his body jerking as he came. We shook through our orgasms as one, sharing our breath and sharing our pleasure, clinging to each other and clinging to the moment.

We stilled, save our heaving chests.

He brought his fingertips to my lips and touched them like they weren't real. I wrapped his fingers in mine and kissed their tips. He licked his lips and swallowed. I smiled at his nervous tic.

He rolled onto his back, pulling me with him until I lay on my side, my head propped up in my hand.

Pouty lips, swollen from kisses. Smoldering eyes with flecks of crimson. Long dark hair framing an angular jaw covered in salt and pepper. I was a goner from the first moment I saw his face.

He tucked his forearm behind his head, and I traced my fingers down his chest to where the gold chain he wore ended in a small circular medallion.

"St. Anthony," I whispered. He raised an eyebrow, and I smiled. "You're not the only one who was raised Catholic."

He smirked. "Gina made me go to church every Sunday."

"So did my parents." I ran my fingertips over his broad chest. It seemed to soothe him, and his face softened into an expression bordering on peaceful. "Do you still?"

"Cosa?"

"Go to Church."

"No." His eyebrows drew together. "That's not true. I go when Nonna e Nonno—Gina and Marco's parents—are around. It makes them happy, but it's not for me."

"Same. I only go when it's my turn to visit Mam on Sundays." I picked up the pendant and turned it over. It was worn and tarnished. "Why do you wear this then?"

He lowered his eyes to my fingers. "It was my father's."

An irrational twinge of guilt hit me in the chest. "I'm sorry."

He removed his arm from behind his head, placed his forefinger beneath my chin, and tipped my head up. "Don't be. You didn't kill him." Steel backed his words, spoken as a decision. A decision he'd made for himself as much as for me.

I nodded, and he put his arm back behind his head.

"His name was Antonio—Anthony in Italian, right?"

"Yes, but that's not why he wore it."

The final sliver of the moon dipped below the tree line and left us in near darkness.

"Sant'Antonio is the patron saint of recovering lost items," he said. "The priests at Sacred Heart gave it to him."

He frowned, and his body tensed. I dropped the pendant and resumed trailing my fingers across his chest. He blew out a breath and relaxed.

"My father was an orphan. He emigrated from Italy with his parents. But back then, the North End wasn't like it is now. Back then, it was an overcrowded slum. His parents died soon after they arrived. Some sickness they picked up and had no means to treat. He ended up living on the streets but knew enough to go to Sacred Heart for meals."

He lifted the pendant and held it between his fingers. "The priests gave this to him, told him Sant'Antonio would protect him so he'd never get lost and would always find his way home." He looked at me, eyes wide and glassy. "Then he met Marco, and the DeVitas gave him a home. Marco gave this to me after the funeral. Told me to never take it off, because —" His voice cracked, and he swallowed. "Because no matter what, I was part of his family, and he never wanted to lose me."

Tears spilled down my face. What Luca did to Marco in a desperate attempt to kill the pain in his heart over losing his father... I couldn't fathom the sacrifice.

It made sense now. I'd been the one to tell Marco the hit hadn't come from the Shaughnessys, and with that one act, Luca lost his only family. Yes, he'd made a string of horrifyingly bad decisions, but I saw the trail of pain and loss that led him to blame me. None of it was logical, but after everything Luca had been through, could I expect him to be logical? After everything I had been through, was I?

I rested my head on the pillow, and he rolled onto his side to face me. He trailed his fingers down my torso and followed them with his eyes.

"Luca." I tucked his hair behind his ear.

"Hm?"

"Luca, look at me."

He flattened his palm over the scars on my belly and lifted his gaze.

"I know you're going to hurt me," I said without accusation and ran my fingers over his hair. Resisting my feelings for Luca was as impossible as resisting the instinct to breathe. I couldn't force them away even knowing his troubled soul might never love me the way I loved him.

He clenched his teeth, and the muscles in his jaw twitched. He ran his thumb back and forth over my belly.

"And I can live with that as long as you promise not to break me," I said with sincerity.

He wanted to reassure me that would never happen. I saw it in his eyes and the way his expression tightened. But he fought the urge; his nostrils flared with the effort of holding back a promise he couldn't keep. "I can't promise you that," he said, and his gravelly voice cracked under the weight of his honesty.

I stroked his hair and kissed his forehead even as a tear slid down my cheek. I closed my eyes, relishing the feel of his hair beneath my fingers and his forehead beneath my lips.

He wrapped his arm around me and pulled me into the

cocoon of his body until my cheek rested against his chest. He draped a leg over mine and nuzzled his face into my hair. His big body shook around mine, and he clung to me as if I might disappear from his arms.

I snuggled closer and planted soft kisses on his chest. "It's okay," I whispered, unsure if I meant the words for Luca or myself. "We're going to be okay."

Chapter Twenty-Six

Siobhán

"Wait," Dominic said, his eyebrows pinched in confusion. "I thought she was sleeping with that other guy."

"No," I said. "They were just flirting in the hot tub, remember?"

"Flirting?" He scoffed. "If that was my girl, she'd never be in a hot tub with another dude. No way."

I rolled my eyes. "The double standards with you made men are unreal."

He glared at me. "What's that s'posed to mean?"

"You have your goomars and that's perfectly acceptable, but God forbid *your woman* enter a three-foot radius of another man."

"Alls I'm sayin' is if she knew what was good for that other dude's health"—he raised his eyebrows and gave me a serious look—"she wouldn't get in a hot tub with him."

I chuckled and shook my head.

It was Friday afternoon, and Dominic and I sat on the couch watching reality TV. Luca and I had spent the past three days in bed making up for two years of pent-up frustration and not discussing the fact that Sex Fest 2024 would have a final performance. But today he had meetings, and he couldn't get out of Friday night at The Dollhouse. So our sexcapades were on pause, and he'd asked Dominic to come over and keep me company.

Luca wasn't worried I'd leave, which was good, because I didn't want to. I was on vacation after all, my interviews rescheduled or cancelled, and I hadn't had a break from Terme or caring for my parents in... Well, way too long given that I couldn't remember the last time I'd taken a day for myself.

He played the violin in the mornings while I drank my coffee. I made him watch *Double Indemnity* in bed one afternoon, and as I suspected, it blew his mind. We took long walks through Lynn Woods, and he showed me where he docked his fishing boat on Birch Pond. He even took me to Walden. We ate turkey sandwiches on a blanket under a tree overlooking the water and pretended the quiet picnic was our normal and not a fantasy that might never happen again.

And now I was binge-watching reality TV with one of his friends while he worked. A welcome yet surreal change of pace, even if the scene had no place in my long-term reality.

I was surprised he'd asked Dominic of all people to come over. The man had been shot at least once only five nights ago. I couldn't imagine him wanting to do anything but stay home and recover. But when he showed up at the house, he seemed fine, like nothing had happened. I asked him how he recovered so quickly. He shrugged and said the bullet had only grazed him and it wasn't a big deal. Not exactly how I remembered things going down Monday night.

The strange feeling I'd missed something important resurfaced and gnawed at my thoughts. It chewed on them in quiet moments, any bit of down time. It was the same uncanny feeling that had buzzed my brain that night at The Dollhouse.

And even though it thrummed louder and with more persistence, I still couldn't put a finger on the source.

A key rattled in the front door.

"Luca! È Gina!" a woman's voice called, and the door swung open. "Ho portato le lasagne!"

Gina DeVita appeared inside the front entrance carrying a foil-covered baking dish in one hand and her keys in the other. She wore big sunglasses that hid half her face, and with her pressed dress shirt and slacks, she looked like an Italian Jackie O.

Her gaze landed on the living room—"Oh!"—and she shut the door behind her. "Hello."

I scrambled up from the couch, silently thanking God I put a bra and my own clothes on that morning. I smoothed my hair out of my face.

"Signora DeVita." Dominic walked over to her and held out his hands. "Let me get that for you."

She swatted him away. "Nonsense, Dominic. I know where everything is. Just dropping this off. I wasn't sure he'd be home, but..." She jangled her keys.

She set the lasagna on the island along with her keys and sunglasses and fixed her big brown eyes on me. "Ms. Connelly. What a surprise."

"Ms. DeVita. It's nice to see you again." My GM persona snapped into place despite my lack of makeup, professional attire, or even shoes.

She regarded me strangely with a slight tilt of her head. After a heartbeat, she blinked and opened the fridge. "Oh!"

Each "Oh!" from Gina DeVita made me increasingly self-conscious. I racked my brain for something to say and, more importantly, how to make this not awkward. For all intents and purposes, this woman was Luca's mother, and I was... I didn't know what the hell I was. Regardless, no ending to that sentence was anything but awkward.

"I've never seen more than condiments and leftovers in this fridge," she mumbled and moved a few items around. She took the tray of lasagna off the island and slid it into the fridge. She closed the door and clasped her hands in front of her. "Bene. Luca knows what to do." She glanced between me and Dominic like she didn't know where to address her explanation. "I'm glad he'll have some friends to share it with when he gets home."

Dominic shot me an uneasy look, clearly as thrown off by Gina's unexpected arrival as I was.

"Dominic, how's your mamma?" Gina asked.

"She's good."

"Still working at the Italian American Community Club?"

"Yup. I don't think she'll ever retire."

Gina chuckled. "No, I don't think she will. Tell her I said hello."

"Naturalmente, signora."

"Bene."

Silence gripped the kitchen and living room, holding us hostage. I shifted my weight and smiled, shocked by my inability to make small talk. Small talk was part of my job, practically a requirement in the hospitality industry, but I couldn't get past the sinking feeling in my gut. Luca and I had been living in a bubble for the past three days, completely cut off from the real world and consequences, and Gina DeVita's presence popped my half of our bubble, an abrupt reminder that whatever it was Luca and I were doing had an expiration date.

"Ms. Connelly," Gina said with a smile. "We never get a chance to chat. Every time we see each other we're so busy with work. I was going to stop for caffè before heading back to the city. Would you care to join me?"

I glanced at Dominic, hoping for an assist. He stared at me with an expression that said, "I have no idea what to do here."

"That sounds lovely, Ms. DeVita. And please, call me Siobhán."

"Siobhán. Such a beautiful name. Call me Gina. Signora DeVita is my mother." She laughed, and I let out a nervous chuckle. "Dominic, you don't mind if I steal Siobhán for an hour or so, do you?" She grabbed her glasses and keys off the island.

"Of course not. I was about to leave anyway. Just stopped by to say hi."

"Eccellente!" She turned to me. "Ready?"

"I'll put on my shoes!"

———

THERE WAS no shortage of Italian bakeries in Boston, and Saugus was no different. A lot of Italians had moved out of the city to the northern suburbs just like the Irish had moved farther South into Dorchester. Over the past few decades, Saugus and Revere had turned into the new Little Italys of Boston.

Gina's Mercedes was a quiet comfort compared to Luca's aggressive Ferrari. The budding greenery and suburban sprawl went by in calm silence with only soft classical music in the background. A short time later, Gina pulled into a strip mall parking lot.

"I'll be honest," she said, "you're probably the last person I expected to see at Luca's house this afternoon." Her words were teasing, but her smile was warm and kind. It held no judgment, just curiosity and perhaps a little hope.

I'd only spoken to Gina at charity events or when she stopped by Terme to have lunch with Marco. We hadn't exchanged more than pleasantries and small talk, but the calm drive and her motherly mien settled my nerves.

"I'm sure," I said with an apologetic smile. "Sorry for throwing you off guard."

"Don't be silly. It was a wonderful surprise."

The bell on the glass door of the bakery dinged when Gina pulled it open, and we walked into the inviting smells of fresh bread, sugar, coffee, and the lively din of conversations in English and Italian.

"I don't know if you're hungry, but they have a wonderful ricotta pie." She laid her fingers on my arm and leaned in. "And today is my treat."

"Thank you," I said, considering my purse was locked in Luca's entertainment center. "That's kind of you."

We waited in line, and the bustle of the bakery was a welcome change of pace from Luca's living room. I eyed the menu and pastry case, searching for something I could eat. Gina ordered in Italian, then scooted me forward so I could place my order.

"I'd like an oat milk latte and—" I pointed at one of the tarts in the case. "Does that say olive oil crust?"

"Yes! I didn't know you spoke Italian."

I chuckled. "I don't. The words just look familiar."

"E una crostata all'olio d'oliva, per favore," she said to the cashier.

"Thank you. I would have slaughtered that."

She laughed, and the cashier handed us a number. We took it to a table close to the windows.

"You're on vacation this week, is that right?" she asked.

"Yes," I said. "How did you know?"

"Anna. She was—" She gave me a knowing smile. "Well. You know Anna. Bundle of nerves."

"Understatement."

"She's worried about you. And Marco, of course. She wanted my advice about your leaving Terme di Boston."

My mouth dropped open.

"Don't be upset. Anna wants what's best for you. She also knows my brother," she added dryly and raised an eyebrow. "He can be a touch dramatic."

I laughed.

"Have you been enjoying your time off?"

I snorted despite myself. She may have known about my job hunt, but there was no way she knew her foster son had kidnapped me, tried to throw me off the Tobin Bridge, decided against murder, and instead had been fucking me like a lion in heat for the past three days.

She canted her head and gave me a curious look.

"Sorry," I said. "That's a loaded question."

I looked out the window. Images from that morning played back, a string of moments that made me smile and had butterflies dancing in my stomach.

He'd scooped me up out of bed while I was still asleep and naked from the night before and walked us into a steaming hot shower in the master bath. He washed my hair with the shampoo I'd bought when we went grocery shopping and massaged my scalp and shoulders with it. Holding me close, breathing me in. "I love this scent," he'd said and ran his soapy hands up and down my body, each brush of his fingers and squeeze of his palms making me melt with longing and affection. He picked me up, wrapped my legs around his waist, and pressed my back into the cold tile. Under the hot spray, he made love to me, his kisses and thrusts slow and worshipful. I thought I must be dreaming, because I couldn't imagine a happier time or being more in love.

"Siobhán?" Gina asked.

"Hm?" I turned back to face her, and a wide smile crinkled the laugh lines around her knowing eyes. My cheeks heated, no doubt flushing my freckled skin. "Sorry." I tried to hide my embarrassment by examining my nails.

She chuckled and reached across the table to squeeze my hand. "It's okay. I know that look," she said with a wink. "But your secret is safe with me. The Lord knows my head is filled with things I'm not supposed to know. My lips are sealed."

A server appeared at the table with our order, and I was grateful for the momentary reprieve.

"Perfetto," Gina said. "Grazie."

I wrapped my fingers around the hot mug and inhaled the latte's nutty aroma. I missed my oat milk lattes.

Gina's expression changed to something bordering worry. "I have to ask—I know my Luca too well not to ask—he knows about your family, right?"

I sipped the creamy goodness, letting it soothe me, and nodded. "He does. And so do you, apparently." I was disappointed by the confirmation but not surprised.

Like I'd told Luca, word would spread no matter how tight-lipped he thought everyone was. And he wouldn't be the only one thinking of ways to use me for my connections. My own cousin had done that exactly the night before Luca kidnapped me, trying to play on family sentiment to get dirt on Marco and the Italians. There'd be no end to how people would use me as a pawn in their fucked-up chess game.

"Hey. Ragazza. Va bene. I'd be a terrible mother if I didn't make sure everyone was on the same page. I love my boy more than life itself, but I know the pain he carries. The anger. He's suffered so much loss. Lucia, then Tony. Marco."

Emotion flooded her dark eyes, turning them glassy. She looked out the window and blinked rapidly.

She waved a hand, picked up her fork, and drove it into her slice of ricotta pie. She took a healthy bite, shocking for such a petite, well-mannered lady.

"No matter," she continued after a sip of coffee. "I'm

thrilled for you both. Luca has never dated anyone seriously. He's a lot like my brother in that way. Everything else was always more important." She pointed at me with her fork. "Until he met the right woman."

I dug into my tart, not sure how to respond. I didn't want to burst her bubble, but I also didn't want her to think we were anything more than a hot mess.

"Listen, Gina, I don't want you to get the wrong idea. Luca and I..." I searched her eager face, trying to find words to finish the sentence. I sighed—"It's complicated"—and shoved a forkful of tart into my mouth.

Her warm smile returned. "If there's one thing I've learned over the years, it's that nothing is easy when it comes to men. Doesn't matter if they're related to you or not, they always make things more complicated than they need to be."

I huffed. Wasn't that the truth.

"What was Luca like growing up?" I asked.

"He was such a sweet boy," she said, and her face lit up, bright with affection. "Always concerned about his nonna e nonno. Followed me around the house wanting to know what I was doing every second of the day. I guess that came from losing Lucia and Tony so young. I think he was scared that if I was out of his sight for too long, he'd lose me too."

She sat back in her chair, dropped her hands into her lap, and stared out the window. "It was awful when Marco left for Italy. Just terrible. Luca screamed and cried. We had to pull him off Marco's legs so he could leave." Her voice grew soft and distant. "Vito and I stayed in Boston to finalize the estate, but Marco had to get back. We thought it was better for Luca to stay here with me, but he started acting out." She shook her head, the nostalgia in her eyes replaced with sadness. "Parenting is hard, especially when it's dropped in your lap and you're trying to deal with your own loss."

She took another bite and chewed thoughtfully. I drank

my latte, wondering how a little boy, so young and innocent, could handle so much loss at such a young age.

"He was still so sweet," she said into her coffee, her affection for Luca evident in the bend of her mouth and the sadness in her eyes. "Still so concerned about everyone else, so charming and helpful. But after Marco left something changed. A—a switch flipped. Fights at school. Stealing. Rage-fueled fits." She looked up. "All the emotions someone so young shouldn't have, they all started coming out. Violently.

"As soon as the estate was settled, we moved to Italy. I couldn't handle him myself. But by then, the damage was done. The cork was out of the bottle," she said with an ironic smile. "He calmed for a bit with Marco's help, but once he got to high school?" She raised her eyebrows, puffed out her cheeks, and blew the air out long and slow.

The corner of my mouth tipped up. "I can only imagine."

"He and Marco, they were like oil and vinegar."

"I bet. Especially since they're so similar in many ways."

"They are, even though neither of them will admit it."

"I hope this doesn't come off as rude, but the two of you look way too young to have raised Luca. I always assumed Marco was five, maybe ten years older than me." The timelines had never added up, but I didn't want to pass judgment or make assumptions.

"Italian genes," she said and winked. "We're older than we look, and Tony was older than us. He and Lucia had Luca when we were all so young. Seems like a lifetime ago."

"Still, that must have been difficult. I know what it's like to have to be an adult before you're ready. I wouldn't wish that on anyone no matter the circumstances."

"Oh?" she asked and lifted the final bite of ricotta pie to her lips.

I picked at my tart. "The amount of growing up I did between the ages of sixteen and nineteen was…" I set my fork down and twisted my hands in my lap. "A lot. Too much, really. I missed out on being a teenager, even if I didn't know it at the time. I thought life meant surviving. I knew I didn't want to live like that though—scared of my shadow, scared of my family. So I left. Made my own way in another country at the ripe old age of eighteen." I shook my head. "It wasn't right. I see that now. But at the time, it was what I had to do to survive." I raised my gaze to meet hers. "And it looks like it's time to do it again."

She nodded solemnly and swirled the remnants of her coffee. "You can try and control your life, but life has a way of reminding you, you're not in control." She cocked an eyebrow —"Just ask my brother"—and drained the rest of her coffee.

"I didn't choose this life, but I can choose to stay as far away from it as possible. I'm not sure that's control as much as self-preservation."

"Yes, of course. But at what cost? You have family here too, no?"

"Yes."

"And Marco thinks of you as family. So does Anna."

"I know." I dropped my gaze. I couldn't hold her penetrating stare; it reminded me too much of Marco.

"There's a price we pay for living in their world, regardless of whether or not it was our choice to live in it. I wasn't given a choice. Marco made it for me, made it for our entire family. And because of his sacrifices, I live the privileged life I lead. But make no mistake, it's come at a cost, and some of the prices I've paid are very personal and very painful." Her voice hitched, caught on words that held deep sorrow. "But I don't begrudge Marco." She shook her head vehemently. "I love my brother, and that kind of resentment eats at your soul. I'd much rather accept the consequences of his world than face a life without my family."

Had all those years in Ireland been worth the price? What

would life have been like had I accepted the cost of being a Shaughnessy? What if, instead of running, I'd come back before Da's mind started to go? Rebuilt a relationship with my parents? Would I feel so alone? Regret punched me in the chest.

"You're a wise woman, Gina," I said.

She gave me a wry smile. "Remind my brother of that the next time you see him."

I chuckled. "Would you mind not mentioning this to Marco and Anna?"

She raised an eyebrow. "Fidati di me, I know when to keep a secret. Luca is a difficult subject, and Marco loves you like a favorite niece. This stays between you and me."

"Thank you."

"Prego. Ora, I'm going to get a box of biscotti for Marco." She picked up her purse. "He doesn't get up here often, and he loves their biscotti regina." She squeezed my shoulder and left for the counter.

The parking lot outside the bakery window bustled with activity. A man and woman got out of their car and walked quickly toward the hardware store next door. He said something with a goofy grin on his face, and she punched him in the arm. They laughed and were lost from view.

Buddies. Like me and Ciarán, once upon a time. Grabbing sodas from the convenience store. Going to movies. Joking. Laughing. We didn't spend nearly as much time together now as we did when we were kids, but I'd seen him more in the past two years than in the previous twenty. What had I missed by being away for so long? How many memories had I sacrificed so I could feel safe? Was it worth it?

Rory drove me crazy, but I still loved him. He was my brother. I wanted to see him do well and maybe one day pull his head out of his ass. Could I have helped guide him had I been around?

As much as I struggled with how my parents handled the shooting, they loved me. They'd done the best they could given their upbringing and their abilities. I'd accepted them for who they were years ago, and with that acceptance, I'd found peace with those relationships. Thank God for therapy.

And my found family. I left Da's sister behind when I moved back to Boston. All the friends I'd made in Cork over the years. Did I really want to uproot myself again? Walk away from Marco and Anna and my crew at Terme di Boston?

My entire life I'd kept everyone at a distance. No matter how close I grew to someone, there was always a separation because I didn't trust them. No one else would take care of me or keep me safe. The only person I could rely on was Siobhán. At least, that's what I'd told myself for the past twenty-five years.

Marco's actions flew in the face of those beliefs. He had never let me down, even if working for him came at a cost. Ciarán had stepped up to help with Mam and Da to the extent he could. I had my family back even if it meant proximity to danger.

And then there was Luca, the man I seemed tethered to by fate. I had no idea what we were doing or where this was going, and there were enough red flags to scare off any sane person. Send them right back to Ireland or, at the very least, away from Boston. But I wasn't sure I could walk away. When it came to Luca Moretti, rational decision-making took a back seat to my heart, and my heart wasn't ready to leave.

Chapter Twenty-Seven

Luca

Vito climbed out of his pickup truck just as I turned into the Lake's Edge Casino in Worcester. I jogged from the far end of the parking lot to where he leaned against his tailgate sucking down a cigarette.

"Vito," I said.

"Luca."

"How'd it go Wednesday?"

"Fine," he said through an exhale of smoke. "Mikey's out on bail. Judge didn't set a court date though. The prosecution requested additional time for investigation." He raised an eyebrow.

"The feds?"

"I'd put money on it." He tossed the cigarette butt on the ground and slapped me on the shoulder. "Andiamo."

Marco, Vito, and Vinnie had been coming to this high-stakes poker game for years. Run by wealthy French financier and information broker Assane Durand, the game hosted some of the most powerful and deadly men in the Northeast. And the occasional celebrity. Durand had either cut a deal with the owner or had dirt on him, because once a month, the penthouse gaming suite transformed into his personal battlefield where cutthroats tested their mettle over green felt on neutral territory.

I hadn't attended a game in years. Vito never missed, but Marco had an engagement with Anna's family, so I was Vito's plus one.

As much as I wanted to spend another night buried between Siobhán's legs, I wasn't about to miss an opportunity to ingratiate myself with Assane Durand. Information was the most precious form of currency, and Durand held the equivalent of the gold in the Fort Knox vaults. Unfortunately, he was as guarded with his information as the US was with its reserves.

I also needed to blow off steam. It had been a rough week with Vinnie breathing down my neck about moving those game consoles, Matteo's constant messages about booking Sources, and the usual fuckery that went down at The Dollhouse. Nothing like dropping a stack of Gs to distract my racing mind.

Slot machines buzzed and clinked, laughter and applause broke out from the craps tables, and beneath the raucous melody, the conversations of a packed casino provided a bassline. We strode quickly to the elevators at the back of the main hall.

"How are things at Pompeii?" I'd been intrigued by the acquisition since Marco first toyed with the idea of claiming a foothold in the financial district. The location had potential, and if things had gone differently, I'd have thrown my hat into the ring to manage the new club.

"Mired in paperwork," he said. "That historical classification is a real pain in the ass."

I snorted, and we stepped into the elevator.

"But we're pushing it through." He eyed me. "With the help of a few city officials who can't stop betting on the Pats."

I cocked a knowing grin. "Hey, whatever works. The sooner that place opens, the better. I'm getting real twitchy about the Irish. More than usual." He raised an eyebrow. "That thing with Mikey, the feds showing up all the way out in Framingham. Cops aren't that motivated without being clued in, and we all know whose take they're on in this city."

"Here's where I say your vendetta is making you paranoid."

"But you're not going to say that, are you?"

He stared back at me, lips pursed.

"I didn't think so."

We stepped off the elevator into the lobby outside the penthouse. The guard at the double doors recognized Vito with a nod, keyed in the passcode, and opened the door. We walked into the luxury suite turned private gaming hall, and another guard waited next to a strongbox the size of a small cabinet. He held out a metal detector and waved us forward.

"Weapons," he said and unlocked the cabinet.

I pulled the gun out of my shoulder holster and handed it to him. Vito did the same. He placed them in the strongbox, locked it, and ran the metal detector over both of us, focusing on our ankles and torsos.

"Go ahead," he said and waved us through.

I rebuttoned my jacket, and we moved toward the back of the entryway and through another set of doors.

Thick damask drapes with gold brocade, gilded Louis XIV mirrors, tables, and chaise longues, and a sparkling crystal chandelier made the opulent space look as though we'd walked into a ballroom at Versailles instead of a casino penthouse in Worcester, Massachusetts.

Beneath the bright lights, a full-sized poker table took center stage complete with one of the casino's dealers. Vinnie sat at the table, huffing down a cigar. A cocktail waitress sat across his lap, and I was surprised the antique chair didn't give out under their combined weight. He whispered something in her ear. She laughed, swatted his arm, and launched herself out of his lap toward the bar at the back. He turned to the two men sitting on his right.

To Vinnie's left, Assane Durand quietly stirred his drink, his ebony skin stark against his high-collared white dress shirt and fat tie. Thick horn-rimmed glasses perched atop a broad nose that, given his long, thin face, made for a distinctive profile. The glasses amplified the unique color of his calculating eyes—light brown, almost gold. Such a stark contrast to his dark complexion, you couldn't help but stare.

"Welcome," he said, and his velvety French accent added to the palatial ambiance. "Have a seat, s'il vous plaît. We're about to begin."

We moved toward the two empty chairs on Durand's right, and that's when I saw him.

"What the *fuck* is he doing here?" The vitriol escaped before I could contain it.

The room fell deathly silent, and the eyes of every man descended on me. I felt their focus even though mine was locked on the source of my outburst.

Ciarán Shaughnessy lifted his gaze from his drink, curiosity alive in bright blue eyes that matched those I'd left only hours before.

The tips of my fangs pressed into my bottom lip, and I started, ready to end my vendetta right then and there. But Vito squeezed my shoulder and held me back.

"Cool it, boss," he mumbled and brushed past me to take the seat next to my enemy.

If it were possible to murder someone with my eyes, Ciarán Shaughnessy would already be dead. I closed them, not wanting the humans to see me turn, and breathed steadily through my nose, fighting the power in my blood and willing my fangs to retreat.

"This is neutral territory, messieurs." Durand's cool, conversational tone only made his pronouncement more imperious. "All are welcome."

"Who the *fahck ah* you, pretty boy?" Ciarán snapped in a Southie accent as thick as Siobhán's when she let it fly.

Vito glared across the table to where Vinnie watched the scene unfold with amused interest. "A heads up might've been good, Vinnie," he growled.

"He knows better than to start something here. Don't you, Luca?"

I narrowed my eyes. This was a setup. A fucking test. I ground my teeth and took the seat to Vito's left.

Ciarán Shaughnessy eyed me. "Luca? Luca Moretti?"

The man sitting on Vito's right could have been Siobhán's twin, and the resemblance made my stomach turn. He folded thick freckled arms across his chest, and his lips cocked in an irritating smirk that made me want to punch him in his smug face.

"*Fahck.* I'd've brought more muscle if I knew this hothead was showin' up."

"Messieurs," Durand said, terse and abrupt. His golden eyes captured mine then Ciarán's. "This is a civilized game. If you are unable to conduct yourselves in a polite manner, my associates"—he lifted his chin to where two men the size of small giants stood on either side of the door—"will escort you to the lobby, and you will no longer be welcome. Comprenez-vous?" He leveled us with his uncanny stare.

I replied with a terse nod.

"Bien. Let us begin."

The dealer stepped up to the table. Vinnie leaned into his conversation with the men on his right. Durand gestured over his shoulder to the waitress. Vito stacked his cash. I did the same, then took the cigar case out of my breast pocket and got to work. There was no way I'd make it through the night without taking the edge off. Fucking Vinnie and his fucking tests.

"I hear you have quite the vendetta against me, Moretti." Ciarán's accented voice crossed the corner of the poker table.

I picked up my cards and gestured to the waitress. "Glenfiddich. Neat. Single malt. The older the better." She nodded and left to get my drink.

Cigar between my teeth, I fanned the cards and examined my hand.

"Not just you," I said through a cloud of smoke. I placed my cards face down and avoided meeting Ciarán's gaze. I couldn't. He looked too much like Siobhán, and it was pissing me off. I locked eyes with Vinnie instead and wrapped my thumb and forefinger around the cigar, removing it from between my teeth. Smoke trailed out from between my lips, a slow serpent slinking toward the ceiling. "Your family."

Vinnie nodded, almost imperceptible, but he was pleased I was holding it together.

Ciarán snorted. "You Italians and your blood feuds..."

The man next to Vinnie tossed a wad of cash onto the table. "Five thousand," he announced in a heavy Russian accent.

Everyone else threw in, and the game began.

The waitress returned with my drink. I inhaled the oak notes and let the woody sweetness dance on my tongue.

"An eye for an eye, isn't that it?" Ciarán asked.

"Oh, I don't know." I folded. My pair of fours wasn't doing me any favors. Not in this crowd. "There are other ways to even a score."

I picked up my drink, sat back in my chair, and the mouthful of scotch burned a trail down my throat into the hollow pit of my stomach. My plan to pump the leverage living in my house for information had been sidelined by the fallout from the hijacking, but there was another way I could use Siobhán to exact my revenge. One that hadn't occurred to me until that moment.

Ciarán Shaughnessy studied his cards, only a hint of a smirk on his thin lips. He'd aged more than she had, his blond hair a motley of close-cut golds and grays, the lines on his face etched deep into weathered skin. But her nose was there, dusted with freckles that spread across the pale skin of his high cheekbones.

He had her eyes. The motherfucker had her eyes, and I hated him for it. Because in those eyes I saw another answer, another way to cause the Shaughnessys pain, and it was disgusting and wrong and I was going to do it anyway.

He flipped his cards over and threw a stack of cash into the pot. "Seems to me my da is the one who evened the score. Payback for coming around Charlestown and operating on Irish territory. You know the rules."

"I do." I glanced at Vinnie and brought my glass to my lips. "More than most."

Vinnie held my gaze, face unreadable.

"Territories…" I mumbled, disgusted. "Stronzo. My father was taken from me by a bunch of Micks little better than common thugs. No code. No honor. The score is far from settled."

"Watch your language, Monsieur Moretti," Durand interjected. "Civilized."

I tilted my head in deference, but the rage boiling my insides wasn't about to back off this verbal joust. Or my chance to initiate an endgame.

Ciarán folded, ending the round, and glared at me. "You gonna settle it then, or are you all talk?"

I smiled, smug and mocking, knowing the ace in my pocket, and drained the rest of my scotch.

He shook his head. "Whatever, Moretti. I don't give a fig what you do."

The dealer collected the cards and dealt the next hand. I finished my cigar and ordered another drink. Vito and I talked about the community boxing tournament planned for the following month. Vinnie chatted with the Russians, Ciarán with the man between him and Durand.

Another hour passed, and so did the second round. The scotch did its work; my rage cooled to a simmer. Suit jackets were discarded, sleeves rolled up. Vinnie even shared one of his precious cigars with the Russian next to him. Durand remained as buttoned up and proper as ever.

Cards landed in front of me. The final hand. Durand kept the monthly sessions to no more than three hours.

I reached into my left pocket and brought one of the two cell phones there into my lap. I made sure it was the right one and clicked the volume all the way up. I put it back in my pocket and picked up my cards.

"Have you talked to your cousin lately, Shaughnessy?" I asked and examined my hand.

In my periphery, Ciarán froze. He must've realized the tell and tried to play it off with a roll of his shoulders he wanted to look like a shrug.

"I'm Irish Catholic. I have a lot of cousins," he said with feigned indifference. "You'll have to be more specific."

I kept my eyes on my cards. "Oh, I think you know which cousin I'm talking about."

Vito cleared his throat. The other players' heads were down studying their cards. Vinnie ordered another drink.

"No, I haven't," he said through his teeth. "She's on vacation. But you already knew that. She works for your uncle."

I tipped my head in acknowledgment.

Vinnie eyed me from across the table, brows drawn together, probably wondering where this was going.

I waited for the inevitable. The question Ciarán Shaughnessy didn't want to put out there but couldn't resist asking.

Antes were tossed into the pot. The dealer placed the turn on the table, and I studied reactions, a great excuse to watch Ciarán squirm.

He chewed on the question. The muscles of his jaw worked around his distaste for it, and he spat it out. "Why?"

A pair of aces. I upped the ante and shrugged a shoulder. "Curious if she's mentioned whether she's enjoying her time off." I sipped my scotch.

Ciarán's eyes narrowed. "Not sure what you're implying, Moretti, but you'll have to do better than that to throw me off my game."

He met the ante. So did the rest of the table, oblivious to the verbal antes Ciarán and I exchanged. Except for Vito. He reached for a fresh pour of Jack Daniels and drained the glass.

"No one's trying to throw you off your game." I gave him my best shit-eating grin. "No need." Good thing murder-by-glare wasn't a thing, or my immortal ass would've been dead. "You're the one who asked if I was going to settle the score."

"Is that a threat?" He sat forward. "I swear to God if you go anywhere near her—"

"Monsieur Shaughnessy," Durand warned.

"Considering why she left Boston, I'm not sure anyone in your family should be taking the moral high ground on Siobhán's safety."

"What's that supposed to mean?"

"Tell me"—I cocked an eyebrow—"does she know O'Doyle's been alive all these years?" I raised my eyes and captured his, wanting to witness every second of his reaction. "And that you knew?" Color climbed his neck, and his eyes flashed with hatred. "I've seen the scars, and they run a lot deeper than her skin."

"You have no idea what you're talking about," he ground out through a tightly clenched jaw.

"Whatever makes you sleep at night." I kept my eyes

locked with his and sipped my scotch. "But she's safer in my bed than she's ever been with your family."

Ciarán launched to his feet, upending his chair, face red with rage. "Lies!" He pointed at me across the table, his other hand balled into a fist at his side. "Keep my cousin's name out of your filthy fucking mouth, or I'll rip your goddamn tongue out!"

"Monsieur Shaughnessy!" Durand barked. "This is your final warning. If you cannot control yourself, I will have my men see you to the door."

Ciarán seethed but dropped his pointed finger. He was having a hard time keeping himself under control, but my guess was he didn't want to fuck up his invite to a seat at Durand's table. No one wanted to lose access to a man who not only dealt in cards but information. His jaw worked, and he bent to right his overturned chair.

"Monsieur Moretti." Durand's voice returned to its normal timbre. "I appreciate the decorum you've maintained, but please refrain from provoking Monsieur Shaughnessy." His gold eyes glinted with what looked a lot like amusement.

I plastered an innocent expression on my face and raised my hand in deference despite having zero intent to fold. The rising tide of my anger at Ciarán Shaughnessy's self-righteous bullshit drove my hunger for vengeance to new heights. The son would pay for the sins of the father.

Ciarán stood behind his righted chair, but as he rolled his shoulders and cracked his neck, he mumbled something under his breath.

"What was that?" I bit out.

"I called you a *fucking liar*." He reached into his pocket and took out his cell.

I kept my face unmoving, a mask of indifference even as my insides jumped.

He stepped away from the table, showed us his back, and

raised the phone to his ear with one hand, shoving the other in his pocket.

A shrill ringtone cut through the silence like shots fired.

Ciarán spun around, searching for the source.

I looked down, surprised and confused, and reached into my pocket where Siobhán's phone screamed to be answered.

It rang again, and I held it up. "How'd that get in there?"

"Figlio di puttana," Vito swore under his breath.

Ciarán's eyes widened, and the color drained from his face. He held the phone to his ear as if desperate for someone to answer it. So I did.

"Must've picked up the wrong phone when I left the house," I said into Siobhán's phone while holding his horrified gaze.

Color returned to Ciarán's face, and it flamed red with outrage. He dropped his phone and stormed across the room, coming at me with balled fists. "Where is she?" he shouted.

I launched from my chair and stepped back. I glanced at my watch. "Probably in bed by now." I smirked. "Waiting for me to come home and—"

Ciarán hauled off to punch me. I had half a mind to let him connect. It would give me an excuse to beat the ever-loving shit out of him. But this was a test, and I didn't need Vinnie riding my ass. I needed revenge.

My guard went up in record time thanks to my work in Vito's ring, and I blocked the punch.

"I swear to fucking God, Moretti, if you touch her, I'll fucking kill you. Do you hear me? I'll fucking kill you!"

A high-pitched whistle flew across the room. Durand's bodyguards didn't waste any time. Within seconds they materialized on either side of us. Ciarán dropped his arms to his sides, seething, but the low simmer of my hatred had sped to a rolling boil.

"How does it feel, Shaughnessy?" I asked, slow and menacing, my voice thick with spite. "How does it feel to have someone you love taken from you?" The pain I wanted Ciarán Shaughnessy to feel clawed its way out of my lungs with each venomous word. "How does it feel knowing I had more than her name in my *filthy fucking mouth?*" I stepped forward, fighting the rage that threatened to turn my eyes. I glared down at him and lowered my voice. "That she belongs to me? That she's mine?"

He swung at me. With my supernatural reflexes, I caught his right fist in my hand and squeezed, hard enough that he froze.

"And I'm going to remind you of that. Every. Fucking. Day. *That's* how I'm going to even the score. By torturing you with the knowledge that I took her from you. I took her from your family. And you will *never* get her back. Blood for blood."

He roared like an animal and swung a left cross. I threw up a block. He yanked his arm back and his right fist out of my grip, coming at me with feverish attempts to land a punch. "You fucking asshole! I'll fucking kill you!"

Durand's men grabbed Ciarán's swinging arms. Which was a good thing, because my fangs descended, and I was a heartbeat away from fully turning and unleashing my rage.

They pulled him off me, and I stepped back, hands raised, breath heavy in my nostrils as I focused every ounce of control on keeping my lips sealed around my fangs and my eyes from lighting up like a goddamn Christmas tree.

"Get him out of here," Durand ordered.

They tugged at Ciarán's arms and moved for the door, but after a few steps, he shook them off and marched toward it himself.

"Fuck this," he said and stopped with his hand on the knob. "I want my gun. And my phone."

Durand gestured to the waitress behind him. She lowered

her ear, nodded, and retrieved the dropped phone, returning it to its owner.

"You may pick up your gun tomorrow after you've collected yourself, Monsieur Shaughnessy," Durand said coolly.

Ciarán landed a death glare on me. The hate in his eyes matched the hate in my heart. No one stood between us except Durand's guard, and his attention was focused on Ciarán.

I let my power fly, and my eyes flared. I cocked my lip, baring my left fang. I tongued the tip and winked. His eyes went wide, and his jaw dropped, but then his features hardened, and he flung the door open and stormed out, slamming it behind him.

I had him, and this revenge would be sweeter than I imagined, because I would drag it out, a long, slow punishment while I collected evidence of his involvement with the feds. I'd prolong his pain with every picture and every video I sent him of me owning Siobhán. And once I found proof? I'd put a bullet between his eyes.

The adrenaline rush from driving the stake into his heart tonight combined with the anticipation of twisting it over and over again made me eager to get out of there and begin his torture.

I closed my lips over my fangs, rolled my shoulders, and took a couple deep breaths to get my eyes under control.

"Messieurs," Assane Durand said, "it seems our game has come to an unexpected end. S'il vous plaît, collect what is yours."

The other players stood, polished off their drinks, and gathered their cash. I walked back to my seat at the poker table under the assault of Durand's unwavering golden stare.

"Monsieur Moretti. Consider tonight a warning. Next time, I won't be as patient."

Durand never broke eye contact, and I swear he never

blinked. It was unnerving. I gave him a deferential nod, and finally, he released me. He stood, buttoned his suit jacket, and left the table, making his way to the doors at the back of the suite without further ado.

"Fucking hotheads," Vito grumbled.

I picked up my cash and tucked it into my jacket, too focused on the satisfaction of fucking with Ciarán Shaughnessy to register Vito's words.

"Luca," Vinnie said.

He stood at the table where Durand's men opened the safe with our guns. His tight expression gave nothing away and left me wondering if I'd passed his test or if I was about to get reamed.

I met him at the table, and the guard handed me my piece. I tucked it into my holster, buttoned my suit coat, and followed Vinnie out of the suite.

He clasped my shoulder and squeezed. "Well played. See what happens when you follow the rules?"

We stopped at the elevators. Not many people were taller than me, but Vinnie had me by an inch. He arched a dark eyebrow beneath his slick salted hair. "Don't let Marco find out," he said in a warning tone. "You might be playing by the rules, but that doesn't mean you won't piss him off. And he's the last person you want to piss off."

The elevator dinged.

We rode to the ground floor in silence, my mind's singular focus on my next move. Vengeance was within reach, and I wasn't about to let it slip through my fingers just to appease Marco. Fuck him.

***

"Siobhán!"

I stormed into the kitchen from the garage, my insides

heated from stewing for the hour and a half it took me to drive from Worcester to Saugus. I tossed my jacket over a chairback.

"Siobhán!" I shouted up the stairs and went back into the kitchen for a glass of scotch.

My body vibrated with anticipation and my mind raced, but I needed a drink to settle my stomach as much as my nerves. Nausea cut through my excitement every time I thought about the video I was about to record and send to that prick from Siobhán's phone.

"Siobhán!" I shouted again.

The French doors slid open, and Siobhán stepped into the kitchen, yawning and rubbing her eyes. "Luca?"

A knot formed in my chest centered around my heart. She had on my old college hoodie again, the one that was too big on her and ended below her shorts. One of the sleeves fell past her hand. The other one she held scrunched up in her fist. She shuffled toward me with sleepy eyes and a guilty smile.

"Sorry. I know you don't want me wearing your clothes, but..." She stopped in front of me and wrapped her arms around her middle. "It's warm, and it smells like you, and I wanted to sit outside on the deck." Her smile turned sheepish. "I must've fallen asleep. It was so cozy out there with the big blanket and your sweatshirt."

The ends of the knot around my heart pulled tight. I slammed the scotch.

She placed her hands on my chest and tilted her head. "I'm glad you're back." Her lips twitched with a hint of a smile.

The knot strangled my aching heart, and for a moment, I couldn't breathe. Nausea swelled, and a wave of dizziness washed over me. I willed myself to push her away and tell her to get on her knees. To drop my pants, pull out my dick, and pull out her phone. But I didn't. Instead, I stared into eyes that looked up at me with so much love, I thought I might be sick.

I stepped back, and her hands fell from my chest. I shoved mine into my hair and tugged, hoping the pain might force air back into my lungs. My eyes darted, looking anywhere but Siobhán's adoring face, but the knot around my heart continued to suffocate me from within.

"I can't do this," I mumbled and stumbled into the living room.

"Do what?" Siobhán's voice was soft and concerned. "What's wrong? What happened?"

I crouched in front of the entertainment center, unlocked it, and grabbed her purse. I quickly shut and locked the doors.

"Luca?"

I couldn't look at her. I set her purse on the island, took her cell out of my pocket, and dropped it in. I braced myself with both hands on the counter and let my chin fall to my chest, staring at nothing. "Go get your stuff," I said in a low rumble. "I'm taking you home."

The blood rushing in my ears sounded like a torrent amid the silence.

"Right now? It's—it's three in the morning." Her hand landed on my back. It moved up and down along my spine and with each touch meant to soothe, the knot tightened, and stars danced before my eyes. "Why don't you come to bed. We can talk about this tomorrow."

"There's nothing to talk about," I said to the counter. "I told you I'd keep you here until I figured out what to do with you, and—" I swallowed. "I'm taking you home."

She dropped her hand. "So that's it? You're done with me?" she asked, her voice shaky and confused.

I didn't answer.

"I see. Couldn't figure out how to use me, so you fucked me instead and now you're done?"

I ground my teeth. What was I supposed to say? That I was going to hurt her family by hurting her. That I wanted to use her and her feelings for me to create as much pain for them as I'd endured for the last thirty-five years. That I needed her out of my life, because I couldn't do it, and every day she stayed was one more day my father remained unavenged.

I pushed off the counter. Her blue eyes flashed with hurt and contempt.

"You asked me not to break you. I'm trying—" The words caught in my throat, and I swallowed.

She nodded to herself. Her lips twisted and trembled as she fought tears, but worse than that was the look in her eyes. They weren't bright with rage or downcast with sadness. No. They brimmed with disappointment. Disappointment for herself. Disappointment for us. Disappointment in me.

"Coward." She spat the word out, showed me her back, and marched up the stairs, leaving me alone with my vendetta.

Chapter Twenty-Eight

Siobhán

Thump! Thump! Thump!

I folded the pillow around my head and burrowed deeper under the covers. The last thing I wanted to do was get up, much less talk to anyone.

Thump! Thump! Thump!

My front door rattled with the pounding. It was louder this time, even muffled through my pillow.

"Go away!" I shouted.

Thump! Thump! Thump!

"Siobhán!" Ciarán's deep voice boomed through the door. "If you're in there, you better open up, or I'm calling the cops!"

Fuck. He would too. Goddammit. He was the last person I wanted to talk to. Well, second to last. My tank for dealing with alpha-male bullshit was empty, but I didn't need him calling the cops and making things worse.

I climbed out of bed. "Gimme a sec, will ya? Jesus Christ, Ciarán, you're going to wake my neighbors."

"Oh, thank God." The relief in his voice was palpable even through the door.

What the hell is going on?

The clock on the bathroom counter read eight a.m. I looked in the mirror and immediately regretted the decision. My eyes were puffy, bloodshot, and cradled by dark circles, stark against my pale cheeks. My hair was askew, matted on one side from shoving my face into the pillow and sticking out at odd angles on the other. Hot mess was an understatement.

Not that I should have expected anything better. Luca had driven me back to Somerville without a word. He dropped me in front of my house, and as soon as I shut the door, he sped away, the roar of the Ferrari's engine his only goodbye. I started ugly crying the moment I walked into my empty house, hurt and anger alternating as fuel for my dramatic bouts of sobbing. They didn't stop until I cried myself to sleep, only to be woken up by Ciarán pounding at my door.

I grabbed my toothbrush. Something had happened at Luca's poker game. I was sure of it. But Luca had so many demons, who knew if I'd ever find out the truth. And did it matter? I knew our bubble would eventually burst. I just hadn't expected its end to be so abrupt.

I rinsed my mouth, tied my rat's nest into a ponytail, and made my way to the front door. I twisted the dead bolt and walked into the kitchen to make coffee.

Ciarán barged into the foyer like a bull in a china shop, slamming the door behind him. He stormed over to where I stood in front of the coffee maker, took me by my shoulders, and examined me like he was looking for signs of damage.

"Vahnie," he breathed. He drew me into his arms and squeezed so hard he cracked my back.

"Ow! Ciarán! What's wrong with you? I haven't even had coffee yet."

He pulled back. "Thank God you're okay. You are okay, aren't you?"

"Aside from a bruised rib," I said dryly.

"Did he hurt you? Tell me the truth. What did he do to you? What did that fucking psycho do to you?"

"What are you talking about?"

"That piece-of-shit Jersey Shore motherfucker, Luca Moretti. What did he do to you?"

I stiffened and pressed my lips together. I swatted at his hands and focused on the coffee maker, willing it to drip faster. "It's too early for this shit. I need coffee. But to answer your question—none of your goddamn business."

He stepped closer, looming over my shoulder. "Like hell it's none of my business. I'm the head of this family, and you're a part of it whether you want to admit it or not. I'm responsible for your safety."

Blood rushed up my neck, making my ears ring and my face hot. I placed my palms flat on the cold countertop to steady myself and angled my face toward his. "Excuse me?"

He shifted his weight, and his eyes darted to the coffee maker which gurgled and gasped as it finished brewing. He shoved his hands into his jeans pockets and stepped back into the dining area. "Luca Moretti is a fucking lunatic with a vendetta. I want to know what happened. How can I protect you if I don't know what happened?"

I closed my eyes and let my head fall back. I was so tired and emotionally drained; I wanted to pick up the pot of coffee and chuck it at Ciarán's head. Instead, I retrieved my favorite mug from the upper cabinet, poured myself a cup of coffee, and leaned my hip against the counter. The scalding brew burned my tongue and throat, but the sting grounded me enough to combat Ciarán's bullshit without sending him to the hospital with third-degree burns.

"You've got a lotta fucking nerve," I said and blew on my coffee. I sipped more of the only thing keeping me from losing my shit. "You know that, right?"

His eyebrows drew together as if he didn't know, but the

way he kept his hands in his pockets and shifted his weight—the same way he'd done since we were kids—told me he knew he'd stepped onto thin ice even if he didn't know how or why.

For the most part, I kept my anger and resentment toward my family safely locked away, but Ciarán's willful ignorance blasted the vault door right off its hinges. "You've got some balls coming over here after all this time pretending like you give a shit about me."

His face softened. "Vahnie, I—"

"Nope." I held up a hand. "Don't give me those puppy dog eyes and Vahnie bullshit. Where were you after I moved to Cork and had emergency surgery because my spleen finally ruptured? Huh? Where were you every birthday and holiday I spent alone? Where were you when I needed someone to take care of Da so I could keep my job in Ireland? Huh, Ciarán? Where the fuck were you?"

The muscles in his jaw twitched, and his fists balled inside his pockets.

"That's what I thought," I snapped.

"I'm here now, aren't I? Making sure you're safe?"

"Too little, too late. And I don't know what's making you think I'm any less safe now than before."

"He's using you to get to me. You know what he did last night? He baited me, made me call your cell phone just to make a show of pulling the damn thing out of his pocket."

And there it was. Mystery solved. Two mysteries solved, actually—Luca's odd behavior the night before and Ciarán standing in my living room at eight a.m. on a Sunday morning.

Luca's comment—he was trying not to break me—finally made sense. He couldn't bring himself to use me against Ciarán, and the only way he knew how to prevent that was to take me home. But as I pieced together the scenario that might have unfolded, my simmering anger toward my family heated to a raging boil.

"This isn't about me at all, is it?"

His head jerked back, and he scrunched his face. "What? Of course it is. He's using you."

"Finish the sentence, Ciarán," I said, taunting and bitter. "Finish the fucking sentence!"

He gaped at me, confused. He didn't get it, and wasn't that the story of my life?

"You said, 'He's using you *to get to me.' That's* the end of the sentence. This isn't about me at all. It's about you. It's about being a Shaughnessy. It's about protecting your reputation. You don't give a flying fuck how this affects me. Well, guess what, Ciarán? I'm done. I'm done being dismissed. I'm done taking care of everyone else when no one gives a shit about me. I'm done being taken for granted.

"I came back to Southie because I'm a responsible fucking adult and my elderly parents need me. But I should've known nothing else would have changed. I'm still a second-class citizen in my own goddamn family. So excuse me if I don't believe you when you say it's your responsibility to protect me. If that was true, if the Shaughnessys gave a shit about keeping me safe, I wouldn't have a stomach full of bullet holes and surgery scars."

My chest heaved as years of resentment and hurt were finally given air.

"Now wait just a damn minute, Siobhán. How is that my fault? I was a kid, just like you. I took care of you. I went to the hospital. I sat with you. I tried to get you out of the house after they released you. Don't put that ugly shit on me!"

"Oh, I'm sorry. Was I not being fair? Calling you out on your bullshit? You may not be to blame for what happened when we were kids—that honor falls solely on your da and my parents—but the apple didn't fall far from the tree, Ciarán, and you're doing the same shit as your da. You say you want to protect me, but just last week you asked me for dirt on Marco DeVita. If you were so concerned about my safety, you wouldn't be trying to get me involved.

"You don't get to have your cake and eat it to. Involving me is not protecting me. Protecting our family name and your reputation is also not protecting me. So you can kindly fuck off with all your fake concern. I'm done."

Ciarán's mouth hung open, and he stared at me like I'd slapped him across the face. Multiple times. While wearing a gauntlet. Good. Fuck him.

A weight lifted from my shoulders at finally saying my piece. For all intents and purposes, Ciarán was my twin brother, and I didn't give a rat's ass that he was the boss. I needed to speak my truth, and he needed to hear it.

"I—" He cleared his throat. "I didn't know you felt that way," he mumbled, stunned and shaken.

I snorted. "No surprise there. You never bothered to ask. No one has ever bothered to ask."

He pulled his hands out of his pockets and rubbed his forehead. "You deserve better from me." His shoulders slumped on an exhale. "Fuck. I'm sorry. I should have known."

I waved a hand, suddenly very tired, and sipped my coffee. "What's done is done."

"You deserve better than Luca Moretti though."

"Yeah, well, that's not up to you, is it?" I raised a judgy eyebrow. "And it doesn't matter anyway, because we're not together. Never have been."

"I knew it!" He pointed at me and stepped forward. "I knew he took advantage of you. Did he rape you? So help me God—"

"No, he didn't rape me! Jesus Christ, Ciarán!"

"Then what the hell happened? 'Cause from the shit he

was saying last night—that he took you from us, that you were his—it sure as hell sounded like he was using you."

Oh, Luca.

I sighed and pinched the bridge of my nose. I could only imagine the idiotic, caveman pissing contest that had gone on between the two of them. A headache formed at my temples fueled by lack of sleep and alpha-male stupidity.

"I can't let this shit go, Vahnie. You know I can't."

I pinned him in place with a scowl. "Oh, yes you can. You can, and you will. Don't you dare go after him and pretend like you're doing it for my sake, because I am telling you right now, that is not what I want. If you want to show me that you've changed and actually give a shit about what I want, about what is good for me, you will leave Luca Moretti alone. Do you hear me? You will end this insane blood feud before someone I care about gets hurt. *That* is what I want."

His jaw worked, a study in conflict. I had him cornered, and he didn't like it. But I was done with everyone pretending like they gave a shit about me and showing me they didn't. Actions spoke louder than words, and it was time I held my family accountable.

He crossed his arms. "Fine," he barked, and his blue eyes flashed. "But if he ever crosses the line with you, if he ever comes at me or our family..." His words rumbled with a heaviness I couldn't ignore. "Don't put me in a position where I have to choose, Siobhán, because you know I won't have a choice."

I stared into my coffee. I couldn't imagine Luca letting go of his vendetta, and that knowledge roiled, a rotting pit in my already sour stomach. "I know."

"One last thing, then I'll let it go. What you do in your private life is your business, but I need you to listen to me on this." His voice took on an urgent quality and drew my gaze up to the grave expression on his face. "There's something different about the Italians. I know the stories sound like old-world superstition, but..."

He examined me, lips tight and assessing. I knew my cousin. He wasn't sure he could trust me but couldn't chance the outcome if he didn't.

"I have deals in the works to protect us, to protect our family. And that means finishing the job my father started and ridding Boston of the Italian Mafia once and for all. But I need you to be honest with me."

I scoffed. "I hope you don't mean getting in bed with the feds like Uncle Paddy. That's as bad as being a rat. And honest about what? I've never lied to you."

"There's evidence—evidence that those old stories aren't just stories. That there's something unnatural about that crew. If I help them find more, they've assured me leeway with my businesses. Certain... protections."

"You can't be that stupid, Ciarán. Trusting the feds? Are you kidding? At least the Mafia has honor, a code of ethics they refuse to break. The only thing the feds care about is themselves. As soon as they finish with the Mafia, they'll turn on you."

He shook his head. "I don't think so. This is bigger than organized crime, Vahnie. Much bigger."

I stared back at him, dumbfounded by his blind eye.

"Did you ever notice anything different about Moretti?"

I narrowed my eyes. "Different how?"

"His eyes. His teeth. Did he ever try to bite you?"

Adrenaline shot into my system. "What?" I shook my head like it needed a reset to hear him properly. "What are you talking about?"

He examined me again, searching my face for a sign. "Nothing," he said, apparently satisfied when all he saw was shock. "It's nothing. Forget it."

But it wasn't nothing. That feeling returned, the one

where I knew a connection existed, nagging to be discovered, but my brain couldn't quite make the leap.

Ciarán glanced at his watch. "I gotta go. I just wanted to make sure you were safe. Be careful, okay? Promise me you'll watch your back?"

"Promise," I said, barely registering the question with the scenes and sensations flooding my mind.

He nodded, kissed me on the cheek, and walked out the door.

I moved on autopilot—topping off my coffee, opening the living room drapes, curling my feet under me on the corner of the couch. Instead of the trees and powerlines outside my window, crimson flecks in eyes as black as night filled my vision. They glinted under the lights of an otherwise dark room, glowing a rich crimson.

Luca flashed an angry sneer in his kitchen, revealing an eyetooth longer and sharper than I'd remembered. The next time he showed his teeth, the pointed tip was gone.

Dominic sat on the counter in The Dollhouse's dressing room covered in blood. It spread across his stomach and shoulder. Luca said he hadn't been shot in the stomach. Dominic said the bullet had only grazed his shoulder. Neither matched what I'd seen. Dom had been shot twice, one of the bullets lodged in his shoulder, and the other went straight through his stomach. He was fine less than a week later.

Luca's mouth pressed against a woman's neck at Vesuvio. Mia's neck turned toward the mirror revealing an angry hickey. *He barely even bit you.* The dancer's chiding words directed at Jenny.

My fingers brushed the spot on my neck where I'd felt a sharp pinch the night Luca and I first made love. I hadn't given it a second thought, too caught up in the other sensations dominating my pleasure. But now? Something had pierced my skin, and when he ran his tongue over the same spot, it tingled.

The devil in 'em. Da's accented rant had me crawling off the couch and fishing Tums out of my purse.

The stories were just that—stories. Weren't they? And it's not like Ciarán had given me any proof that the feds had evidence. They probably hadn't given him any either. He was too blinded by the idea that he could eliminate his competition by playing nice with the real enemy. But what if they weren't stories? What if something unnatural was the connection I'd missed all along?

I popped a Tums into my mouth, climbed back into the corner of the couch, and let out a long, tired breath. The past week had felt like a month, but I still had another week of vacation, and I was going to use it to find a new job. My plan to distance myself from the DeVitas hadn't changed. And I wasn't involved with Luca. Not anymore.

I set my coffee on the windowsill and hugged one of the throw pillows to my chest. It didn't soothe the heartache, but then again, I wasn't sure anything would. How I still had feelings for that chaotic, troubled, and potentially demonic man frustrated the hell out of me. Maybe because I knew the fallout could have been much worse, and he'd spared me the pain.

Nothing about us had ever been simple. Or rational. This latest development was par for the course. Vampire? Sure! Why not! The only way to guarantee some other catastrophe wouldn't materialize was to remove myself from any situation where we might run into each other. Should be easy once I broke ties with Terme di Boston.

Time heals all wounds—wasn't that the saying? In time, the heartache and my feelings for Luca would fade.

There was another saying—out of sight, out of mind.

That was the tough part. Time would only work its magic if I could stay away.

Chapter Twenty-Nine

Siobhán

"Thank you for making the first week of the summer season a success." I met the eyes of every department head at the conference table. "Keep up the good work." I clasped my hands and fought like hell to maintain a smile as a fresh wave of nausea crashed into me like a tsunami. "Dismissed." I choked out the word, lucky my guts didn't follow behind it.

The team rose from their seats, but only a few made their way to the door. The rest took their time, chatting and checking their phones.

Sweat beaded my forehead. I dabbed the moisture with a tissue I had balled in my pocket. *Pull it together, Siobhán.* I'd dealt with stomach and digestive issues my entire life. Just another day on the job.

"Josh. Tammy," I said, pushing through my discomfort. I rounded the conference table to meet them at the door. "I went over your proposal for the Fourth of July event on the terraces. I have a few questions about expected volume and the catering you have planned."

My stomach turned over, and it took every ounce of

willpower I had not to heave into Josh's coffee mug. Maybe now was not the time to talk about the Fourth.

I walked around them and through the door; they dutifully followed me into the hallway. "Let's get together Monday and go through the plans, yeah?"

"No problem, Ms. Connelly," Tammy said.

"Fabulous. Ten a.m. My office."

"See you then," Josh replied.

They walked down the hall toward the lobby, and as soon as they rounded the corner, I dashed into the bathroom, flung open the door to the accessible stall, and fell to my knees over the toilet, throwing up water and bile and the small amount of oatmeal I'd choked down that morning. Over and over, I heaved until there was nothing left. I slumped against the tile wall, my hand pressed to my stomach and my breath coming in shallow pants.

I'd had more than my fair share of stomach issues over the years, including bad bouts of nausea when I was stressed and my stomach pumped out too much acid, but this was ridiculous. After almost a week, I'd be lucky if I could make it through the rest of the day without falling asleep at my desk. Maybe I had the flu. I pressed the back of my hand to my forehead, but I wasn't warm, just clammy.

My stomach finally settled, and I pushed myself off the bathroom floor. I splashed cold water on my face and rinsed my mouth. I dabbed at the water, careful not to smudge my makeup, then leaned against the counter.

I was pale. Paler than usual. And my eyes were glassy. But aside from the lack of color and nausea...

Annoyed, I left the bathroom and walked down the hall and across the lobby to where the department offices occupied the east wing of the first floor. I sat behind my desk and grabbed my water bottle. The ice water coated my mouth and soothed my throat. It had to be stress. Probably from internalizing so much bullshit over the past few months. My stomach finally decided it had enough. Vesuvio, the whole ordeal with Luca, and now Da.

He took a turn for the worse the Monday after Luca dropped me off at my house. I don't think any of us wanted to admit how far the dementia had advanced until that week. Mam called in a panic at five in the morning—Da was missing. He'd gotten up in the middle of the night, dressed himself in coveralls he hadn't worn in years, and "gone to work." The cameras at the shop told us he unlocked the doors around three a.m. Rory found him at six, standing over his old work bench staring at a set of tools and muttering something about a 1980 Ford Mustang.

We couldn't put it off any longer. No matter how much Mam protested, Da needed around-the-clock care. For the past month, I'd spent all my free time moving Da into an assisted-living facility and comforting Mam. She struggled getting used to a new normal that didn't include caring for her husband in the home they'd lived in for forty-five years.

All that on top of managing Boston's most exclusive resort and spa. After having my heart ripped out of my chest. Again.

I closed my eyes and let out a long sigh. Definitely too much stress. My insides had always been the gift from hell that kept on giving, but if the nausea continued one more day, I needed to visit my gastroenterologist.

I opened my calendar to check my schedule for the rest of the day. No more meetings. Just a blissfully open afternoon to close out a long work week. Thank God. Although, I would have gladly rescheduled that big department meeting to the afternoon when my stomach settled.

Wait.

I sat back in my chair and drummed my nails against the armrest, thinking back over the past few days. Mornings had been miserable, each day worse than the last, but as soon as lunchtime approached and I managed to choke down some food, I felt mostly fine.

Every time I'd thrown up over the past week, it had been in the morning. In fact, late last night, I wolfed down a huge— for me—peanut butter and jelly sandwich on Wonder Bread, my go to snack anytime I needed to pack in serious calories. No problems.

My stomach flipped but not from the nausea.

I opened the health app on my cell phone.

Current Cycle (48 Days)

"Oh, no. No, no, no."

The cell phone slipped from my hand and landed on my desk. I grabbed my water bottle and drank, trying not to panic. I forgot to record it, that's all. I did that sometimes. It must have slipped my mind with all the kidnapping and heartbreak and parental care. Besides, I was on the shot. I'd been on the shot for ten years. Every three months for—

Oh, God.

My hand shook on top of my mouse. I scrolled back week after week until I reached the second week of March. And a doctor's appointment. The Monday after Vesuvio was held up and Anna was hit by a car. A doctor's appointment I'd forgotten and missed.

My stomach bottomed out. I bent over the wastebasket and threw up the water I'd just drank.

This was *not* happening. This *couldn't* be happening. I was forty-four years old. I missed one—*one*—shot. In ten years! Yes, we fucked like rabbits on Viagra for almost a week but at my age the probability alone...

No. The nausea had to be coming from something else.

I picked up my desk phone and punched zero.

"Front desk. How can I help you?"

"Brian, this is Siobhán. I'm leaving for the day. If anything comes up, I'll deal with it Monday."

"Understood, Ms. Connelly."

I shut down my computer, grabbed my purse, and ran out of my office for the parking garage.

ACROSS THE LIVING ROOM, five plastic sticks of different colors and sizes were lined up on my dining room table. I bought one of every brand at the drug store.

I paced my living room, one arm wrapped around my middle, and clicked my nail against my front teeth, trying like hell to find the courage to go over there even though I already knew what those sticks would say.

I did the math on the way to Somerville from downtown. Three times. The timing was too perfect. Or too horrible, depending on your perspective. And that was just it. I didn't know my perspective.

It was mid-June, and I hadn't seen or spoken to Luca in over a month and a half. He hadn't reached out to try and resolve things, but then again, neither had I. I thought about it, several times in fact, but didn't have the spoons to deal with his drama on top of everything else.

My job search was on indefinite hold and so were my unresolved feelings for Luca. Everything had to wait while I took care of my family.

I stopped pacing and laid a hand on my stomach. My family.

I never considered having a family of my own. Getting married. Buying a house with a white picket fence. Having two-point-five kids and a dog. None of that was on my radar screen. I wasn't one of those people who planned out their life to check off the arbitrary boxes that someone decided made up the American Dream. My American Dream involved two things—a self-made career and safety.

I also wasn't one of those people who had strong feelings about kids. I never dreamed about having them, but I also never felt sad when it seemed like I'd missed my window. I'd never thought about it either way. But now?

I eyed the dining room table and the sticks that divined my future like so many crystal balls. If they were positive, would I be excited? Scared? Would I cry tears of joy or despair? If they were negative, would I be relieved or disappointed? And after I had my answer, what would I do?

My stomach flipped. There was only one way to find out.

Chapter Thirty

Luca

The last thing I expected while sitting in my office Friday afternoon eating spuckies with Gio and Vinnie was a text message from Siobhán. She wanted to talk. At her place. My insides twisted into a complicated sequence of knots I couldn't untangle. There was curiosity for sure, suspicion definitely, but also relief. One of us had ended the stalemate. No surprise she was the one to do it; she was the strong one.

I exited Route 1 into Charlestown and headed west toward Somerville, my unease growing with each city block. Which said a lot given how the past month and a half had gone since ending things with Siobhán.

Restless nights bled into routine days. The few days reprieve from my nightmares vanished without her in my arms. All I could do to force myself to sleep at night was spend more time at Vito's gym. I drove myself hard for hours on end until exhaustion won the battle against anxiety.

I threw myself into work. The Dollhouse hadn't turned out that much profit in years, and the Source funnel to Terme di Boston was finally picking up steam. I worked every job

Vinnie gave me—another big lift, thankfully free of cops, and the occasional shakedown.

I also threw myself into my endgame, determined to find evidence that Ciarán Shaughnessy was in bed with the feds. I had Leo tailing him almost every day. Unless I needed a distraction to fill my time. Then, I tailed him myself. Anything to keep my mind off Siobhán.

The most troubling change? I stopped feeding for pleasure. In fact, I went almost three weeks without feeding at all. Outside of my time in Vinnie's warehouse, that was the longest dry spell of my life.

My fangs started aching after ten days, leaking venom and throbbing with need. By the end of the second week, my strength waned, and dizzy spells plagued my workouts. But I pushed through, driving myself even harder and relishing the pain and vertigo dulling my focus. With each passing day, the hollow pit in my stomach expanded until my survival instincts kicked in and I almost lost control of my inner predator. I turned one night after work in the parking lot at Starmarket, poised to attack an innocent woman walking out with a bag of groceries. It scared the hell out of me. I got in my car and drove straight home.

Mia came into my office the next night and offered her neck. She was worried about me and promised to keep things professional. I hesitated, some sick part of me wanting to prolong my punishment, like I somehow deserved to be blood-starved for letting Siobhán go, but my fangs' persistent ache and the constant stomach pains were too much to bear. If I didn't take Mia up on her offer, I wouldn't last much longer before losing control.

Feeding from Mia did the job, and I'd be okay for one more week before I needed to visit her again, but there was only one person whose blood I craved.

I parked in the cul-de-sac, turned off the car, and sat for a moment, as nervous as a teenager at his date's front door before prom. Which was ridiculous. I was a capo in the Italian Mafia. I had more money than I could spend in a lifetime. I'd fucked more supermodels than I had fingers. Yet there I sat, anxious as hell and wondering what I'd say when I finally saw her again.

What future did we have together anyway? She was a Shaughnessy. I was a Moretti. I couldn't let my father's murder go unavenged. My vendetta would always stand in our way no matter how much we tried to convince ourselves otherwise. I shook my head and got out of the car.

And then there was the matter of my not being human. Not everyone accepted the existence of blood demons as easily as Anna had with Marco. My mother hadn't.

Where did that leave me and Siobhán? Nowhere. But I was too selfish not to take any opportunity to see her again. I took a deep breath, let out a long exhale, and knocked on her door.

She opened it, and nostalgia punched me in the chest. The Siobhán I'd known for years—the one transported right off the set of an early Hollywood movie—stood before me. Her white cap-sleeved blouse showed off her long delicate arms and neck. Her maroon pencil skirt was cinched tight around her tiny waist with a wide black belt. It accentuated her subtle curves and long legs and reminded me of the lithe body hidden underneath. She'd kept the length in her hair but tamed it into its familiar style, each curl perfectly set, each wave artfully placed to frame her beautiful face.

"Siobhán." Her name passed my lips like a prayer.

Her ruby red smile, inviting as ever, was tentative, almost hopeful. "Thanks for coming," she said and ushered me in. "Sorry for the cryptic message, but I wanted to talk in person."

Her home looked different now than when I'd broken in and waited for her in the dark. Style and personality came through in every detail, from the vintage stained glass floor lamps to the art deco pieces hanging on the walls. A stack of magazines sat on a coffee table in front of the couch, and her body's indent was still visible on the cushion.

"How are you, Siobhán?" I asked, a stilted attempt to fill the awkward silence.

She walked past me into the living room, wringing her hands. She wouldn't meet my eyes, and the creases across her forehead deepened.

I frowned and moved closer. "What's wrong?"

The delicate muscles of her neck bobbed through a swallow, and her lips parted as if struggling to voice what was stuck in her throat.

"I'm pregnant."

The words slammed into my chest like two bullets at point-blank range. I blinked and shook my head. I hadn't heard her properly. I couldn't have heard her properly.

"Wha—" I cleared my throat, trying to force air back into my lungs after the impact. I shifted my weight and tilted my head. "What?"

"I'm pregnant," she said, and the words ricocheted off the walls, echoing in my ears.

"Are—are you sure?"

She tore her eyes away from mine and focused them on her dining room table. I followed her gaze to five white and pink and purple sticks. I stepped up to the table, limbs heavy like I was dragging them through quicksand.

Pregnancy tests. All lined up in a neat row. Plastic arbiters of justice sealing my fate.

"They're all positive," she whispered.

Sealing Siobhán's fate.

My mouth went dry. "How..." I couldn't form thoughts much less words. I stared at the tests in disbelief.

"I missed my doctor's appointment in March when every-thing—when everything happened at Vesuvio. I forgot."

"You forgot," I repeated, and dread pooled in my gut.

"Anna was in the hospital. I was living my worst nightmare. You were gone..." Her voice trembled. "God, Luca, I thought they were going to kill you. That doctor's appointment was the last thing on my mind. Until today. I—I've been sick for a week."

My head snapped up. Sick? Already?

A rising pool of blood stained the edges of my vision. Dread clawed its way up from my gut and wound gnarled fingers around my chest. I slammed my eyes shut. "You forgot." The words came out sharp and edged with panic.

"Luca," she pleaded. "Please, look at me."

I opened my eyes, and Siobhán's face was etched with worry. She twisted her fingers in front of her.

The pool of blood that haunted my dreams closed in around her, and dread transformed into fear. It tightened around my chest, and the panic that ensued snapped my brain out of idle and into overdrive. It raced through time and space, landing on our first night together.

"I asked if we were safe. I asked if we should use protection."

She blinked and shook her head. "I—I thought you were talking about STDs. I've been on the shot for so long, I didn't—"

I cried out, the pained noise squeezed from my lungs by the cruel twist of fate.

She reached for me.

I backed away before the firmness of her fingers convinced me this was reality and not another one of my fucked-up dreams. "This isn't happening," I shouted, and my hands flew to my hair.

Siobhán's eyes glistened bright blue, and tears spilled onto her pale cheeks. Her image faded into a familiar, horrifying scene straight out of my nightmares.

Pale and starved, my mother lay on a bed, screaming through my bloody birth. My father stood over her with his sleeves rolled up, holding her hand as the doctor tried to save her. The ever-present pool of blood surrounded her. It crept toward her face, and the doctor and my father dissolved into red.

I blinked rapidly, desperate to clear the images from my mind. "This isn't happening," I said again and tore my eyes away from the hurt in her face and her quivering lip. But the images that replaced her made me stagger.

It wasn't my mother lying on that bed anymore. It was Siobhán, her belly swollen with our baby, her scars stretched and jagged across her stomach. Her too-thin arms and legs had grown skeletal, her body trying to give our baby what it needed to survive. And failing.

She looked at me from her deathbed with the same haunted expression my mother wore the day I came into this world and she left it—scared but resigned. I took her hand. She smiled, the adoring smile she saved for me. Then the light left her eyes, and the smile faded. Her body went still. Pale, cold, lifeless. History repeating itself, and it was all my fault.

My hands fell from my hair and landed on my heart, the stabbing pain there so powerful it threw me off balance. I stumbled back and grabbed hold of the dining room chair. It skidded across the floor as I tried to steady myself.

A black hole expanded in my chest at the thought of losing Siobhán. It trapped all the air. I couldn't breathe.

I killed her. I killed them both.

"Mio Dio," I whispered. "Cosa ho fatto?"

"Luca," Siobhán said through pained sobs. "Luca, I'm so sorry."

Tears poured down her face. But she was already dead, and I killed her.

"Siobhán—" My voice cracked around her name. I gasped for air. I couldn't breathe. I had to get out.

She reached for me. I waved her away and stumbled toward the door.

"Luca, please. Talk to me," she sobbed, hysterical.

"I can't." I braced myself on the doorjamb. "I…"

She grabbed my arm, trying to pull me back from the brink, but I had to escape the nightmare.

"Please," she cried.

"I can't." I flung the door open, yanked my arm out of her grasping fingers, and hurried down the stairs.

"Luca!" Siobhán's pained sobs followed in my wake. "*Luca!*"

Blood rushed in my ears. My chest burned from lack of oxygen, and stars danced across my vision. I doubled over, propping myself upright with my hands on my knees until air finally made its way back into my lungs and I could breathe again.

I climbed into my car and gripped the steering wheel, clinging to it like a tether to reality. I rested my forehead between my white knuckles and tried to regain control, but my eyes turned, fear driving my primal instincts to survive.

Siobhán's lifeless body remained fixed in my vision. I stood over her, begging her not to leave me. Like Marco left me. Like my father. Like my mother. But with each desperate plea, her body faded, consumed by the red void until I stood alone in the darkness. Utterly alone.

Chapter Thirty-One

Luca

Rage coursed through my veins as surely as the blood that kept me alive. Heat shone through my eyes, and my fangs descended. Fully turned and ready to fight.

Matteo pounded the heavy bag. Civilians sparred in the ring. More lifted in the weight room. Vito tracked my entrance from behind his desk.

"Where's Marco?" I unzipped my hoodie and tossed it on a bench.

The two men in the ring paused long enough to spare me a glance. Matteo backed off the heavy bag. Vito got up and made his way across the gym.

"You better cool down, boss," he said.

The calm in Vito's gruff voice sent heat straight to my eyes, making them flare with vengeful fury. "Dove! È! Marco!"

"Qui!" My uncle's voice rang through the gym.

I spun around.

Marco walked out of the locker room in gym shoes and boxing shorts, taping his knuckles. "Cosa vuoi, Luca?"

"You know what I want. I want what you owe me. I want what you owe my father."

He turned his attention to the ring and lifted his chin at the two men gaping at us. They scrambled out.

He finished his wrap with fluid, automatic motions. "You sure you want to do this?" he asked, nonchalant.

I took off my shirt, tossed it on the bench, and grabbed a roll of tape. "I wouldn't be here if I didn't."

Vito grabbed my biceps. "Don't do this, Luca. This isn't what you want. Think of Gina."

I jerked my arm out of his grip and glared. "I'm thinking of my father." I bit the edge of the tape, ripped it, and started wrapping my other hand.

He shook his head and backed off, disappointment evident in the downturn of his mouth.

Marco watched me from the corner of the ring. I finished taping, tossed the roll onto the bench, and didn't waste any time. I climbed between the ropes and threw up my guard, dancing on the balls of my feet. Rage fueled each hasty movement.

He stepped forward, arms at his sides, stoic and impenetrable. "I'm going to give you one for free. One punch to get it out of your system. But I won't hold back after that, capisce?"

"Arrogant prick." The words flew as quickly as my right cross and hit Marco with an audible crack. Blood sprayed and splattered the mat. It dripped down his face, and his eyes flared to life.

"Fucking idiot," Vito grumbled from the ropes and tossed Marco a towel.

Marco's eyes blazed an angry red as deep in color as the blood he wiped from his broken nose. "Feel better?" he asked.

"A little," I said, still bouncing on my feet. I bared my fangs, and with a surge of power, they sharpened to their full length. "But I'll feel a hell of a lot better after I break the rest of your face."

Marco snorted and shook his head. "Fucking hothead," he

grumbled. "I thought Vinnie beat it out of you." He brought up his guard. "Sounds like you need another lesson."

I threw up my fists in just enough time to block Marco's wicked left hook. The punch struck my forearm like a battering ram. Christ, he was fast. But so was I. And bigger after all the hours I'd spent in Vito's gym. I went after him in a fury, a series of jabs ending in an uppercut that Vito once told me was as powerful as Marco's. He blocked every punch.

My power flowed freely, something I hadn't allowed since my twenties. It surged with each beat of my heart, pumping strength and speed into my muscles, and every impact between my fists and my uncle's skin tore down walls I held in place with unwavering control.

He handed me over to Vinnie, left me to be tortured like some common thug.

I went at him from a different angle. Jab. Jab. Marco blocked the punches, and I danced away.

And for what? For trying to avenge my father? For trying to avenge his best friend? His brother?

I lunged, threw a quick left cross and a right hook. Block. Block. His red stare never wavered, but he wasn't striking back.

I bared my fangs and screamed. "Fight me! Fight me, goddammit! Why won't you fucking fight me?"

I wanted him to pound me into the mats. I wanted him to hurt me. I wanted him to punish me for what I'd done.

"Fucking hit me!" I let my right hook fly; he blocked it. "I stole from you!" Jab. Jab. "I trashed your club!" Cross. Uppercut. "Anna almost died!"

Punch after punch, I swung at him like a rabid animal. He took everything I threw, his guard up, waiting for the next barrage. Sweat poured down his face and mingled with blood. It dripped down his neck in red trails that matched his eyes.

I'd clung to his legs, screaming, crying, my little fingers

wrapped in the fabric of his pants. I'd held on with every ounce of my six-year-old strength, pleading with him to stay. I begged him not to leave me like my father had left me. Like my mother.

The remaining power in my blood surged like a tidal wave and the final wall crumbled.

"I hate you!" The ugly truth flew from my lips as fast and furious as my fists drove into his stomach. "You left me, and I hated you!"

He doubled over from the impact of the punches and my words.

Sweat stung my eyes. My arms burned with strain. The last vestiges of my power flared to life, and I swung at his temple with everything I had left. His head snapped to the side.

"You! Weren't! Fucking! There!" I jabbed at Marco's face with each heated word.

He took it all, absorbing my anger and hate until my arms gave out and my swings didn't reach his face.

"You weren't there." My voice cracked, and my body convulsed.

Tears joined the sweat on my face, but I kept swinging, empty, feeble punches that Marco brushed aside.

He grabbed the back of my neck and pulled me into him, wrapping his arm around my shoulders.

"You should have been there," I cried, my body shaking through each pained sob. "Why weren't you there?" I struggled to break free, pounding my fists against his arms and shoulders. "You could have saved him. You could have protected him." The side of my fist thudded against Marco's tattooed shoulder. "He needed you, and you weren't there." I lifted my fist to land one final blow. "*I* needed you, and you weren't there."

My knees gave out. I sagged into Marco, unable to hold myself upright. He sank with me to the mats and wrapped his arms around me, holding me like a child. The pit of sorrow in my heart cracked open, and the loss and despair that lived there finally broke free. Uncontrolled sobs wracked my exhausted body.

"Nipote. Ragazzo mio." Marco's voice wavered with strain. He kissed the top of my head. "Mi dispiace tanto. I'm so sorry. The Lord knows how sorry I am. I'd give anything to bring Tony back. Anything."

I shuddered and cried.

He pulled back and took my shoulders in his hands, holding me at arm's length. "Luca." His deep voice cracked over my name.

I sat back on my heels, shaking, and my arms fell to my sides. I stared at my palms, open and empty. There should have been something in them, something to hold onto, but there was nothing. I had nothing.

"Everything I loved that wasn't taken from me, I destroyed." I raised my eyes. Marco's face was a mask of pain and guilt, and I couldn't bear it. "I'm being punished for my sins."

Marco's eyebrows pinched together. "Luca. What happened?"

"I killed her," I whispered.

"Who?"

"My mother."

Marco's face twisted in horror. "Mio Dio," he whispered. He squeezed my shoulders and shook me. "Mio Dio, no. Luca, no. Lucia was in shock. She wouldn't drink. It wasn't your fault."

"Papá loved her, and I killed her." Fresh tears spilled down my cheeks. "And now the only good thing that's ever happened to me, my one chance at happiness..." I swallowed the lump in my throat. "She's the only light in my godforsaken life, and I killed her too."

"Chi?"

"Siobhán. She's going to die, and it's all my fault."

"What are you talking about, Luca? What happened to Siobhán?"

"She's pregnant," I croaked.

Marco's confused expression transformed into one of shock and just as quickly pity. But I didn't deserve his mercy.

I hung my head, defeated and shaking and unable to face a future without Siobhán, especially when that empty existence was one of my own making.

SMOKE SWIRLED through the air and stung the back of my throat. I washed it down with the rest of my scotch, and the harsh bite soothed me. Mamma Gina grabbed the bottle and poured another splash into the crystal.

Marco leaned forward, grabbed my shoulder, and squeezed. "Bene, nipote. Bene," he said around his cigar. "Calm those nerves."

I exhaled a shuddering breath. He patted my shoulder, then sat back, holding an icepack to his swollen nose.

Vito had set it for him before we left the gym, and Gina refused to give him any whiskey without ice. Vito also gave me an emergency blood bag. I could barely walk after emptying myself in the ring, especially with how little I'd fed over the past month. The bag hadn't been enough to refill the well, but it would get me through until I could visit a Source.

The unseasonably warm June air was moist with humidity. Gina'd thrown the kitchen window open to let Marco and I smoke inside, a rare occurrence that I hadn't witnessed since I was a kid. I puffed on my cigar and blew the smoke into the cobbled alley. Night had fallen, and the smoke swirled beneath the amber glow of the porch light.

One winter night, almost forty years ago, that same porch light made the snow falling outside appear to glow. My father and Marco sat in the same spots we sat in now. The window had been cracked enough to let the smoke out but keep the warmth in. They chatted in Italian. Drank. Laughed. The scene was forever etched in my memory.

I swigged my scotch, a bracing mouthful, and set the glass on the sill where Nonna—now Gina—kept potted herbs. Tonight, it held an ashtray and our drinks. The smoke and the scotch and the open window brought a sense of rightness to the space we occupied, a sense of home.

"She's strong," Gina said from the kitchen table. "Tough as nails, that one."

I huffed. "You have no idea."

"Lucia wasn't nearly as strong."

Marco shot Gina a look, and I followed his gaze to my foster mother.

She dipped her chin and raised her eyebrows at her brother. I knew better than to challenge Mamma Gina when she looked at you like that. So did Marco.

"I'm being honest," she said in a tone that garnered no argument. "It's about time we all started being honest."

Marco shifted in his seat and placed his cigar between his teeth.

Gina's expression softened. "Your mother was a gentle soul, Luca. It was one of the things Tony loved about her. She was innocent, naïve at times. Her feelings ran so deep... I always thought that's why she was so talented at music. She had a beautiful heart." Gina's eyes and voice overflowed with fondness and nostalgia. "But it was a fragile heart. So very fragile."

A lump formed in my throat, and I turned away, unable to handle the sadness woven between her words. I needed Zio's strength.

Marco's eyes fixed out the window. The muscle in his jaw that twitched when he got emotional jumped, but aside from that, he remained still. A rock. I'd always seen him as cold and distant, but now I recognized it as strength. He'd protected his family the only way he knew how.

"Siobhán's different," Gina continued. "She's a fighter. She'll survive the truth, and she'll survive this pregnancy. You need to trust her, trust in her strength. Trust how much she loves you."

I glanced at Gina out of the corner of my eye.

"She loves you, Luca. It's clear as day. And I know you love her too."

"I can't lose her," I said, fear strangling my words.

"You won't. Not if you fight for her."

The oven beeped.

Gina's chair scraped the floor. I brought my cigar to my lips and puffed, comforted by the burn of the smoke and the clank of dishes and utensils.

"I know you resent me," Marco said, low and gruff. His eyes remained fixed out the window. "But—Dio, Luca—I didn't know what the hell I was doing. It's not like you came with an instruction manual." He tossed the ice pack on the table and lifted his whiskey. He took a long drink and winced when he lowered the glass. "All I knew was I had to do right by Tony."

He placed his cigar between his lips. The cherry flared red with each pull. It turned the tobacco into smoldering ash, remnants of the past.

"He had so many hopes for you. He wanted you to have the opportunities his parents wanted for him. An education. A home and a family. A sense of security. He wanted to give you the life he never had." Marco's dark eyes burned with the love I knew he felt for his best friend, my father. "But more than that, he wanted you to be happy."

Marco searched my eyes. "That's all Tony ever wanted for you, and when he died—"

His voice caught. He snapped his mouth shut, and his jaw worked as he forced his emotions to obey. He brought his cigar up, took a long drag, and blew a slow, steady stream of smoke out the window.

"And when he died, all I knew was I had to give my brother what he wanted—a better life for his son." Marco's nostrils flared, his impenetrable control wavering under the intensity of the promise he made all those years ago. "I could never replace your father, Luca, and the Lord knows I did a shit job trying."

The guilt I felt over what I'd done to the man who'd tried to protect me, who'd tried to do right by his best friend, over-whelmed me. "Zio, I—I'm—"

"Fammi finire," he said and held up a staying hand. "Killing a Shaughnessy won't bring him back, and living in misery is the last thing Tony wanted for you." He leaned forward. "You want to even the score? You want to honor your name and your father's legacy?"

The burn in my throat was too strong for words. I nodded.

"Live, Luca. Live your life. With happiness and love in your heart. Live the life your father wanted for you, the life he never got to live." Marco's voice broke, and his eyes were rimmed with tears. He looked back out the window. "If you can do that, justice is served."

He picked up his glass, drained the rest of his whiskey, and placed his cigar between his teeth.

"Mi dispiace, zio. Per tutto."

"I know, nipote mio. So am I."

The air changed, and the heaviness that weighed on my relationship with Marco lifted. Forgiveness replaced animosity, understanding replaced resentment, and peace settled over our family for the first time in decades.

The pop of a cork broke the silence. Wine trickled into crystal.

"Mangiamo," Gina said.

We snubbed out our cigars and carried our glasses with us to the kitchen table. Marco sat at the head where he'd sat my entire life, his rightful place. Gina sat to his right, and he took her hand. I sat to his left, my father's seat at the DeVita table. Marco held out his hand. I glanced up, and he nodded. I placed my hand in his and reached for Mamma Gina. She smiled and took my hand, running her thumb across the backs of my fingers.

Time brought us full circle. Our family was whole again, thirty-five years of struggle put to rest. We'd face our futures together, stronger for our scars, and hope filled the space in my heart where only revenge had lived.

I had a family, and with their support, that family would grow to include the woman I adored beyond all reason and another Moretti, born from our love.

Chapter Thirty-Two

Siobhán

"Yes!" Marco's voice boomed through the door.

I opened it and walked into his office.

He scrawled something across the papers stacked on his desk. "Siobhán," he said, still focused on his work.

"Mr. DeVita."

That caught his attention. He stopped his pen, looked up from his desk, and arched an eyebrow.

"Marco," I amended through an awkward smile.

He tossed the pen on the blotter, picked up a half-smoked cigar from the ashtray, and puffed it back to life. Cigar between his teeth, he walked around the desk and leaned back against its edge. "You have something you want to tell me?" He wrapped a finger and thumb around the cigar and blew the smoke up to the vents in the ceiling.

He knew. My shoulders slumped. I'd wanted to be the one to tell him. He deserved that respect.

"I'm resigning my position at Terme di Boston," I said quickly.

He bowed his head a fraction. "And?"

"And..." I scrunched my forehead. What else was there?

"And The Dubliner is going to hire me back as their General Manager. I'm moving back to Ireland."

The muscle in his jaw twitched. "What problem is that going to solve?"

I swallowed, second guessing my decision in the face of the man who'd given me so many opportunities and loved me like his own. But no matter how much he cared about me, no matter how much he wanted to protect me, I wasn't safe in Boston, and I had more than one person to think about now. I had to protect my baby as fiercely as I protected myself.

"The risk of being around my family and yours. I never asked to be a part of this world, and I'm doing the only thing I know will keep me safe."

He pressed the heels of his hands into the desk. "I told you once—it's never over for people like us. Do you remember?"

"I do."

"I spent a long time, longer than you can imagine, running from this world before I realized I was running from life." His dark stare, so honest and raw, penetrated my defenses as much as the truth of his words. "Everything comes at a price, Siobhán, but not just in our world. You're chasing an illusion of safety, and the price you're going to pay for that is your family. And I'm not talking about the Shaughnessys. You walk away now, you'll lose the people who will do everything in their power to protect you because they love you and they want to keep you"—his eyes dropped to my stomach—"and your baby safe."

His eyes travelled back to where my mouth hung open in shock.

Luca was the only one who knew, but after his reaction, I couldn't have imagined him telling anyone, least of all Marco.

I laid a hand on my stomach and the tiny fleck of life growing inside. "Then you know it's not just about me anymore. I don't want my baby to grow up scared of their family, always looking over their shoulder, wondering if they'll make it through the day. I lived that hell, and I wouldn't wish that on anyone, much less my own child."

His eyes darkened. He snubbed the cigar out, pushed off the desk, and stood before me, an intimidating wall of power and challenge. "You going to take care of that baby yourself? Work full-time and be a full-time mother with no family around to support you? What happens when you get sick? Hm? Or the baby?"

I lifted my chin, defiant. "I've taken care of myself my entire adult life with no help from anyone. I protected myself when no one else would. I'll figure it out. I always do."

"Alone, thousands of miles away from your baby's father and everyone who loves you."

"Yes, alone," I snapped, my throat tight. "I've always been alone. I've done everything by myself. I moved to another country by myself. I survived there by myself. I built a career by myself. And I'll do this by myself too."

"Why? You don't have to do this alone."

"Why? *Why?* Because I can't survive having my heart broken one more time. The pieces are barely holding themselves together as it is. Everyone who's supposed to love me has let me down one too many times. They've put me in danger and done nothing to make sure it doesn't happen again.

"You want to know why I'm moving back to Ireland? Why I want to take care of this baby alone? Because I don't trust my own family to help me. Because I don't believe anyone will have our backs. Because I don't trust Luca to love me the way I deserve to be loved."

A pained sob escaped me with that final admission, and a tear fell down my face. I lifted the back of my hand to cover my mouth as another sob ripped free of my lungs. Marco reached for me, but I waved him off, taking deep breaths to regain control. I swiped the tear away and straightened my spine.

"I've done everything in my life by myself. This will be no different."

Despite my assertion, exhaustion that went far beyond physical weighed on my confidence. My soul was so deeply tired—tired of constantly having to take care of everyone and everything, tired of solving problems, tired of being disappointed. For once in my life, I wanted someone to take care of me, to shoulder the burden of responsibility without my asking. I wanted someone to give me the break from life I so desperately needed.

Like Luca had done, even if it was fleeting. He'd researched my condition and made a special meal for me without any motivation or making it into a big deal. He wanted to do it to make me happy. Maybe that's why I thought things would be different and that the universe was right to thrust us together. That Siobhán Connelly would finally get her happily ever after.

But reality wasn't the same as the movies, and I learned long ago not to expect that kind of happy ending.

Marco's jaw twitched, and his lips pressed into a flat line. I knew that look; he had it any time he was about to blow up at someone.

"You're scared," he growled, trying to restrain the frustration in his voice and failing. "So you're running. From one set of problems into another. That's not my definition of safe, and you're smart enough to know it shouldn't be yours either."

I hugged an arm around myself and looked away.

"Have you told Luca you're leaving?"

"No. Not that he'd care. He made it crystal clear he wants nothing to do with me or his child." The truth hurt worse saying it out loud, if that was even possible, and my lips trembled despite the bitter edge in my voice.

Marco dragged a hand down his face. "Maledetto Luca," he muttered.

I had no idea what that meant, but the exasperation in his voice and the tired expression on his face gave me a clue.

"Did he actually say he wanted nothing to do with you?" he asked.

People talk about blood draining from a person's face. I knew what they meant, but I'd never seen it firsthand. Not until I told Luca I was pregnant. He went white. Literally. Even his lips paled to an eerie shade of pink. He'd been terrified and ran out in a panic, but he hadn't said why, and he'd never said he wanted nothing to do with us.

"No," I said. "He didn't."

Marco held out his hands. He still wore the fat ring on his right pinky, but now a thick gold band wrapped around the ring finger of his left hand. Sadness amplified my bitterness seeing that symbol of love and commitment and knowing I had to do this alone.

I placed my trembling hands in his, and he wrapped thick, steady fingers around mine and squeezed.

"Promise me something," he said.

I nodded.

"Promise me you'll hear him out." I opened my mouth to protest, but he thrust his chin and regarded me with that fatherly look of his, so I snapped it shut. "It's not my place to make excuses for Luca or explain what happened. That's his story to tell. All I ask is that when he reaches out—and he will reach out—you listen. If you still want to leave after that, if you still can't imagine a future here, I'll support you and do everything in my power to make sure you and my futuro nipote are safe and happy." He granted me a rare half-smile filled with understanding, tenderness, and hope.

Fresh tears pricked my eyes. Marco's love and concern for me never wavered. And apparently, it hadn't wavered for Luca either. Despite what Luca had done, Marco was asking me to give him a chance. He must have forgiven his nephew, and it made me trust Marco even more.

Maybe they weren't all the same, these made men. Maybe I just had really bad luck. Forty-four years of bad luck. But if Marco could hear Luca out after what he'd done, the least I could do was listen to my baby's father.

"I promise," I said.

"Bene." He squeezed my fingers and kissed my forehead. "Now I need to get back to these construction contracts." He dropped my hands, walked around his desk, and sat in his throne-like executive chair. "Pompeii isn't going to renovate itself. Unfortunately," he added dryly and picked up his pen.

I huffed, moved for the door, and paused. "Thank you, Marco," I said over my shoulder. "For everything."

He tipped his head. "Non c'è di che, piccola."

I smiled, walked out, and closed the door.

I rode the elevator to the first floor and imagined what life would be like if I closed the door on this chapter in my life, if I closed the door on Terme and Boston and the DeVitas and my family. Was I ready to start over again? Was the illusion of safety worth the price?

Chapter Thirty-Three

Siobhán

The mid-June sun and humidity left the streets unseasonably empty. Granted, at two in the afternoon on a Wednesday, most people were still at work—I should have been at work—but even the tourists were hiding from the oppressive heat. Luckily, my morning bout of nausea subsided after lunch because walking through that soup over the North End's uneven cobblestones in my condition was not my idea of a good time.

My stomach was tied in knots. It had been working overtime since I found out I was pregnant and had doubled down on its efforts to make me miserable after Marco's lecture. The final straw? Luca texting me and wanting to talk. Stomach three, Siobhán zero.

I couldn't stop ruminating over my decision to move back to Ireland. Did I really want to leave my family, found or otherwise, when I needed them the most?

Part of me said yes, absolutely. It didn't take me long to decide that I wanted to keep the baby, which surprised the hell out of me considering Luca's reaction. But the idea of having my own family brought such warmth and joy to my heart, I couldn't deny that's exactly what I wanted—a life and a loved one separate from the Shaughnessys' dark world. If I moved to Ireland and raised the child myself, I'd finally have the happy, well-adjusted family I always wanted.

And it's not like any of my relatives would help anyway, not with Luca being the father. I hadn't told Ciarán or Rory yet, and I was not looking forward to those conversations. I planned to put them off as long as possible.

On the other hand, Marco and Gina were right. My family had grown beyond the Shaughnessys, and I had no doubt the DeVitas would support me. But fear for my safety and now my baby's safety was never far from my mind.

And then there was Luca. His text message arrived late Monday night.

> I don't deserve it, not after the way I acted, but please give me a chance to explain. I need to make this right. I need to make us right.

I'd stared at the message for hours before responding.

> We've tried us. Us doesn't work.

> You know that's not true.

> Do I? I can't do this again, Luca. It hurts too much.

> I'm so sorry, Siobhán. Please. Just let me explain.

> Fine, but I'm not doing it for me. I'm doing it for the baby.

Luca was my baby's father. Even if we weren't together, he had a right to be in our child's life if that's what he wanted. I had to at least grant him a moment to say his piece.

Red cursive letters painted on a white plastic sign announced my destination—"Paganini's Since 1942." The deli's glass façade revealed an empty house. Empty except for Luca. He shot to his feet when he spotted me, and my stomach flipped. I wasn't ready for this conversation, but I opened the door anyway.

A bell chimed as if heralding the start of act three in our drama.

The restaurant was decorated like the spaghetti scene from *Lady and the Tramp*, complete with red-checkered tablecloths, Chianti-bottle candleholders, and pictures of the Italian countryside. An older gentleman with a substantial stomach and an equally substantial mustache cleared dirty dishes off one of the tables and shouted in Italian over Frank Sinatra's familiar voice.

"Va bene," Luca shouted back. He stepped past me and flipped the sign on the door so that "Closed" faced the street. He gave me a sheepish smile, thrust a hand into his hair, and licked his lips. "Hi, Siobhán. Thank you. For coming."

I swear the man had a sixth sense when it came to getting under my skin. His apologetic tone. His nervous tics. His cologne. The fitted black slacks hugging his thighs. The gold chain peeking out from beneath the collar of his equally fitted black button-down. His scruff. He'd kept it. It was trimmed close, and I fought the urge to run my thumb along his jawline and kiss his pillowy lips. But I wasn't there for me. I wasn't even there for us. I was there for our child's future.

"Hello, Luca," I said.

He rested his hand on the back of his neck and with a labored swallow lifted his gaze. Time stopped the way it always did when our eyes locked, and the same pull I'd felt since the day we met tugged at my heart. He blinked as if also trapped in our undertow and pulled out a chair at the table in front of the window. "Please," he said.

I smiled at his attempt at chivalry, set my bag down, and took a seat.

He sat across from me and looked everywhere but my face. I folded my hands atop the table.

He opened his mouth, then slammed it shut, and his eyebrows drew together. "I'm sorry." The corners of his mouth turned down, and his head tilted, imparting weight to his words.

I nodded, because what he said was true. He was sorry. But... "What—" I cleared my throat. "What, exactly, are you sorry for?"

His eyes widened on a full breath, and he leaned back in his chair. He puffed out his cheeks on the exhale and glanced out the window. "I don't even know where to start," he said quietly.

"Well, you could start with how you left me sobbing hysterically after telling you I'm pregnant with your baby."

He winced. "Yeah. I should probably start there."

"I needed you." I promised myself I'd stay cool, but my pain at what felt a lot like betrayal was too powerful. "I was shocked and scared and instead of talking to me, you left. Without a word."

"I panicked."

"And I wasn't panicking? I'm pregnant!"

"I know, I know. I should have stayed. A better man would have stayed. But I'm not a good man, Siobhán. Never have been."

I shook my head. "That wasn't the first time you walked away from me, and now you expect me to pretend like that's okay? Like you haven't broken my heart multiple times?"

And I had pretended. I'd worn my rose-colored glasses hoping things would go back to the way they were before The Incident. I'd wanted him to make me feel special again, to fill my heart to near bursting. I'd wanted to feel like I mattered to him, like we belonged together. I'd pretended, because I desperately wanted to get that feeling back.

"No more," I said. "I'm done. I'm done having my heart stomped on only to come back and let you do it again."

"Don't say that. Please. I shouldn't have pushed you away, but I'm not as strong as you, and I'm sorry for that too. Letting you go that night was a huge mistake, and I've regretted it every day since." He shoved a hand into his hair. "Fuck, Siobhán, I didn't know what I was doing. You have to give me another chance."

"Have to?" I cocked an eyebrow. "I want to trust you, Luca. I really do. But I have no reason to believe this time will be any different."

"It is different, because I'm done walking away. I'm done running from this, from us. That's why I asked you here. Because I need to explain why."

He leaned across the table and wrapped his big hands around mine. I pulled back, not wanting him to touch me—every time he touched me, he broke another piece of my heart—but he wouldn't let go.

"My reaction had nothing to do with not wanting you or the baby. God, Siobhán, I can't imagine a life without you. But I—" His lips slammed shut.

"What?" I prompted, eager against my better judgment. That spark of hope just would not die.

"Do you remember the night you came into my bedroom? The night I had those bad dreams?"

"Yes."

"You told me you had nightmares too. About the shooting."

I nodded.

He stared at our joined hands and ran his thumb across the backs of my fingers. "I relive the weeks after Vesuvio. The night Marco disowned me. My father's funeral. The images fade in and out of my mind. They string themselves together like scenes from some fucked-up movie."

He stopped and pressed his lips together, and his grip on my hands tightened.

"But the one that always wakes me up..." His eyebrows drew together. "The one that makes me scream..." He shook his head. "It's not even a real memory. At least, not one of mine. My mother—" His voice cracked, and his lips twisted into a frown. "She's lying on a bed covered in blood, and she's dying. And I know"—his voice wavered—"I know it's my fault."

"Oh, God. Luca—"

"My father is holding me. I'd just been born. He's crying. He loved her so much. And I—I killed her."

"No. Luca, no." I shook my head and squeezed his hands. "You didn't kill her. Mia told me what happened. It was a—a blood incompatibility. I've heard of that. You can't blame yourself."

"It's not that simple. You need to know the truth."

"Then tell me. Because I don't understand, and I want to understand."

Luca's thumb moved back and forth at a frantic pace.

The restaurant door opened with a chime and a swoosh. I glanced over my shoulder, rattled by the interruption.

Marco stepped inside. Vito, Vinnie Valenzano, and an older gentleman I'd never seen before filed in after him, sparing us surprised glances as they moved toward the back.

"Goddammit," Luca growled.

Marco released the door and rested his hand on my shoulder. "Ciao, Luca. Siobhán. Didn't expect to find you here."

"I wanted a safe and *private* place to talk," Luca shot back.

Marco's lips quirked. "Same, nipote, same. Mikey's trial is next week, non ricordi? We have business to discuss." He quirked an apologetic smile. "And Vinnie was hungry."

Luca shoved a hand in his hair.

"È tutto a posto, no?" Marco said. "Plenty of space."

Luca waved him off and looked out the window.

Marco looked down at me and winked. "Listen to what he has to say, capisce?"

The warmth in Marco's eyes put me at ease. "Capisce."

"Bene." He patted me on the shoulder and walked to the back of the restaurant. He sat across from Vinnie, already deep in conversation with the other two men.

"This is not how I wanted to have this conversation," Luca grumbled.

His fists were balled on the table, his jaw tight and angry.

"It's fine." I wiggled my fingers into his fists, forcing them to relax. "Ignore them."

"Right. Okay." He nodded and leaned in, pulling me toward him. "It's not that simple. We didn't have a blood incompatibility. I mean, we did, but—" He shook his head. "It's why I freaked out when you told me we"—he swallowed—"we're going to have a baby. I kept seeing you covered in blood just like my mother. I—I freaked out."

"Oh, Luca, I—"

"I'm sorry this is what it took for me to realize what I had and how I feel about you, but I'm here now. I get it. Nothing else matters if you're not in my life. Not the past, not the future, not this vendetta. Nothing. Losing you is a nightmare I never want to face, and I regret every day I wasted not making you mine." His voice shook, the intensity of his words reflected in the crimson specks of fire shining in his eyes.

"I—I don't know what to say." My mind raced trying to process his heartfelt admission and whether it changed anything. "I've given you so many chances. Every time I think things have changed and I let you back in, it hurts that much more when you break my heart." My voice cracked. I didn't want to go down this road; I didn't know if I could survive losing him again.

"You called me a coward that night I took you home, and you were right. I was a coward. I was a coward that night you caught me feeding at Vesuvio. I was a coward hiding behind my anger toward your family. I've held on to this vendetta for so long, the thought of letting it go scared the hell out of me. But the only thing that scares me now is living one more day without you."

Each word of Luca's confession landed hard, his regret and realizations sincere and profound. They transformed that spark of hope into a flame and forced my heart to beat for him once more.

But my brain hitched on one word. "Feeding?"

The bell above the door chimed.

Luca lifted his gaze and gritted his teeth. "Dannazione. Seriously?"

"Luca! Siobhán!" Gina DeVita's voice echoed through the small space. "What are you two doing here?"

I lowered my head and pinched the bridge of my nose, needing a minute to collect myself before facing Gina.

"Oh," she said and understanding replaced her bright tone. "Well. I'm here to pick up Vito. We need to get to the courthouse before it closes. Mikey's trial is next week. I'll be out of your hair in un attimo.

"Vito, sei pronto?" Gina tossed the words over her shoulder.

I lifted my head, not wanting to be rude. "Hello, Gina," I said and managed a smile.

"Ciao, bella. How are you feeling?"

"Okay. Thankfully, the morning sickness sticks to the mornings." I gave her a wry smile.

"You've been sick?" Luca interjected.

Gina glared at him, and I rolled my eyes.

Vito stepped up to our table. "Luca. Ms. Connelly. Gina."

"I'll talk to *you* later," she said to Luca through a disapproving frown. She shifted her attention to me and gentled her expression. "How about I come over this weekend and show you how to prepare my mamma's recipe for ginger tea? Generations of DeVitas swear by its power to cure morning sickness."

"That sounds wonderful, Gina. Thank you."

"Naturalmente, mia cara." She turned to Vito. "Andiamo."

Gina and Vito walked out of the deli, and the little bell above the door chimed again in their wake. I squeezed my eyes shut and took a deep breath.

"This was a terrible idea doing this here," Luca said.

I sighed the breath out. "It's fine, Luca. Really."

"I thought you'd be more comfortable in public." He waved a hand through the air, sat back in his chair, and stared out the window. "And it's not like there are a lot of public places where it's safe to talk about this stuff."

"We can go somewhere else if it's bothering you." Maybe he couldn't think of somewhere else to go?

His gaze remained locked out the window.

"I mean, I don't know why we couldn't talk about this at some other restaurant. Or a coffee shop. There are plenty in the square."

He narrowed his eyes but kept them fixed out the window. "Luca?"

I followed his gaze to where Gina and Vito stood chatting in the street. A car rumbled across the cobblestones, slow and plodding. It reached the deli, and its tinted windows rolled down.

Luca sprang to his feet, knocking the table onto its side. "Get down!"

I jumped out of my chair, and he lunged in front of me amid the crack of gunfire and shattering glass.

Chapter Thirty-Four

Vito

"I'm parked right up the street," Gina said and rifled through her purse.

I pulled a pack of smokes out of my back pocket. "You sure you want to lose your spot?" Parking in Boston was a pain in the ass, but parking in the North End was its own circle of hell.

She chuckled. "I'm willing to make the sacrifice. It's way too hot for the T." She extracted her keys as if she'd struck gold, and the smile on her face shone as bright as the summer sun.

I lit a cigarette.

A silver Hyundai Elantra rounded the corner and crept up the street. Too slow. Even for cobblestones. I squinted through the glare coming off the bumper. No plates.

I took a drag off my cigarette and placed a hand on the small of Gina's back. "Let's go."

I urged her forward, keeping an eye on the unmarked car. We hadn't taken more than a few steps before the driver's side front and rear windows rolled down.

"Fuck." I tossed the cigarette, but before I could get my

body between the car and Gina, gunfire rang out through the square.

Glass shattered and sprayed behind me. Gina screamed.

I grabbed her, pulled her into me, and threw us to the ground, covering her body with mine. Blood splattered the sidewalk. It came from Gina's arm.

"Vito," she cried. "What's happening?"

"Don't move, tesoro. Stay down."

I pulled out my gun, but at this close range and no cover, the last thing I wanted to do was draw attention. I had to protect Gina.

Shots came from both directions, a relentless barrage —*Crack! Crack! Crack!*—interrupted by shouting.

Soles clapped the pavement. Another burst of rapid fire.

A hand clamped around my biceps and hauled me to my feet. Gina cried out, an agonized sound that ripped through my chest.

I swung at the head attached to the hand around my arm. My right hook connected with a thick skull and strength seeped out of the man's hold. He wobbled on his feet for no more than a heartbeat before falling to the ground unconscious.

I pivoted to find Gina and froze. A man with dark hair, blue eyes, and a spray of freckles across his face held her pressed against his chest, his left arm wrapped around her neck. She clung to his forearm and biceps, her face leeched of color and her dark eyes speckled in crimson, wide and terrified. Blood soaked through the sleeve of her blouse.

He lifted a gun and pointed it at my head. I raised my hands. I was fast, but not point-blank-range fast, and that bullet, where it was aimed, was a blood demon killer.

"Stay away from my sister," he shouted, and my stomach dropped. I saw the resemblance in his eyes. "You hear that, you Italian fucks? You leave my sister the fuck alone!"

"You idiot," I shouted. "She's in there! Siobhán is in there right now!"

He paled, his bravado wavering. His eyes darted from me to the shattered glass, giving me the opening I needed.

I lunged and batted the gun out of his hand. Gina squirmed and kicked, and I twisted his arm off her chest.

Splitting pain shot through the back of my skull and sent a flash across my vision. It took me to my knees, and dizziness blurred the world around me.

Siobhán's brother regained his hold on Gina, but this time pointed the gun at her temple. She stilled, the fear in her eyes clear even through my wavering vision. He glared at me and backed away. The crack of gunfire continued, but it sounded distant like I was in a tunnel. I swayed on my knees.

"Grab him," he said. "Put him in the trunk. He said they need two."

He? Two of what?

Someone hauled me up by my armpits. I bucked my head back, landing a blow to the hard skull behind me. My captor yelped and dropped me.

"For fuck's sake, knock him out!"

I stumbled forward. I had to get to Gina.

Siobhán's brother pushed Gina into the backseat of the car.

Another blow to the back of my head. A flash of light. The street blurred out of focus, and I pitched forward into darkness.

Chapter Thirty-Five

Luca

Bullets tore into my back and ripped tunnels of pain through my chest. We dropped below the two-foot brick wall beneath the shattered window and hit the ground. My back and chest were on fire. I had no idea how many times I'd been hit. It didn't matter. All that mattered was Siobhán.

I cradled her head in one hand, my other arm wrapped around her back. I dragged my arm out from under her through broken glass and pushed myself up enough to make sure she hadn't been hit. My shirt was plastered to my chest, wet and sticky with blood. Red smears sullied her white blouse, but there were no holes, no growing stains. It wasn't her blood; it was mine.

"Grazie a Dio." I rested my lips on her forehead.

Siobhán squeezed her eyes shut, gripped my shirt, and pulled me closer. I lowered myself back down, covering her with my body.

"I'm here, baby," I said amid the rain of fire and shouting. "I won't let anything happen to you."

She nodded against my shoulder.

I lifted my head up and surveyed the scene.

The skeletal remains of the deli's glass exterior offered little protection from the chaos. Gio and Vinnie were sprawled flat on their stomachs, guns out, taking furtive glances over the low wall and between the metal frames. Marco pressed his back against the wall to the left of the door behind one foot of brick, the only other cover between us and the shooters. His eyes shone as bright as road flares, and he inched forward like the devil himself, fangs bared in an angry snarl, gun cocked and ready.

Vinnie's eyes burned bright and caught sight of my unhinged uncle. He army-crawled around the booth through shattered glass. "Marco! Take the left!"

Marco waited for a break in the fire, then stepped out from behind the brick and released multiple rounds at different targets, adjusting his aim after each pair of shots fired. Vinnie popped up with surprising speed given his size and joined him, focusing on targets to the right. Another volley ripped through the restaurant, and they flung themselves back against the wall.

Siobhán started crying.

"Shh." I placed my hands on either side of her face, covering her ears, and kissed her hair. "Hang on for me, baby. It's almost over. Hang on."

I sure as hell hoped it was. My chest screamed for attention. I fought my power, not wanting my eyes to turn and add to Siobhán's trauma.

Another set of rounds from Marco and Vinnie.

Car doors opened and slammed shut.

Vinnie darted forward, determined and brazen, his crimson gaze focused on whatever was happening outside. He didn't stop until another round flew into the restaurant. He stepped behind Marco, ejected the magazine, and snapped it back into place. "I'm almost out."

Another car door.

Marco craned his neck around the corner only to snap his head back as more gunfire cracked through the otherwise quiet space.

A heartbeat of silence, then the squeal of tires.

"Cazzo!" Marco screamed and launched through the broken door. Vinnie followed, and their guns released like the Fourth of July had come two weeks early.

Siobhán shook and curled herself into me.

I kissed her head. "It's over, baby." My vision swam before me. "It's over."

I shifted my weight off her before I passed out and slumped into the brick. I needed to release my power, but she wasn't supposed to find out like this. I closed my eyes.

"No," Siobhán said, quiet and horrified. "Oh, God. Please, no."

I cracked my eyes enough to see her. She knelt next to me, tears streaming down her face, and her hands hovered over my chest as though she wanted to touch me but wasn't sure she should.

"Help!" she cried. "Somebody, please help!"

I grabbed one of her hands and squeezed. "It's okay, baby. I'm fine."

"You're not fine. You—you've been shot. Oh, God. Luca." She started crying in earnest and placed her other hand on my shoulder. "I'll get help. I'll find help."

She looked around, frantic, and moved to stand. I pulled her back down.

"Siobhán. Please. Look at me." Her eyes were bloodshot and watery, but she did as I said. "I promise you—I'm fine."

"How many you take, kid?" Gio appeared and squatted next to us.

Siobhán gaped at him like he was crazy.

I winced. "At least two. Not really sure."

"Let's have a look," he said and lifted his chin.

I propped myself up and saw stars. Gio grabbed my shoulder and held me in place.

"What the hell are you doing?" Siobhán shrieked. "We need an ambulance." She looked around. "Where's my purse? I need to call an ambulance."

Gio's eyebrows drew together. Now it was his turn to look at Siobhán like *she* was crazy. He shook his head and frowned. "She doesn't know?" He jerked his thumb in her direction.

"Know what?" she shrieked.

"No," I said. "She doesn't know."

Gio shifted me forward so he could look at my back. I sucked a breath in through my teeth.

"Three," he said. "Sit back." I leaned against the wall below the window. "But only two up front." He took out his cell phone, hit the screen, and held it to his ear.

Siobhán's forehead creased in confusion, and her eyes snapped between Gio and the holes in my chest. They pumped out blood like fountains, my natural healing slowed from holding back my power.

"Hey, Doc. We got a situation. Yeah. They sent three Messages. One didn't make it through. Yeah. We'll move him to The Mountain. See you in twenty. Grazie." Gio turned his attention back to me. "Dr. Levine's on his way, but you're mighty pale, kid, and we gotta move. Time to turn the lights on."

I glanced at Siobhán, then back at Gio.

He raised an eyebrow. "It's not like she wasn't going to find out eventually."

"What are you talking about?" Siobhán asked, her voice shrill. "Find what out? What the hell is going on? We need to get him to a hospital!"

I sighed, closed my eyes, and let go.

My power surged, flying through my veins with each pump of my heart, energizing me, healing me. My torso itched as the tunnels from my back to my front slowly stitched themselves together, cell by cell.

"I didn't want you to find out this way," I said. "I wanted to explain. That's why I brought you here."

"Explain what? Tell me!"

I opened my eyes, revealing their fire, and I curled back my lips, revealing my fangs.

Siobhán gasped. Her hand flew to her chest, and she fell back. She studied my face, her eyes wide and pupils dilated. "Oh my God."

Chapter Thirty-Six

Siobhán

"I wanted to tell you," he said and winced. His face was white. It made his glowing red eyes all the more terrifying. "I brought you here to tell you."

"This can't be real," I mumbled. "This can't..." I shook my head.

He held up his cut and bloody forearms. "It's real." He pulled a shard of glass from one of the longer gashes. Blood flowed in its wake but stopped almost immediately, Luca's skin closing around the wound.

I stared in shock, unable to move. That couldn't have happened. Maybe it was blood loss. Had I been cut somewhere? Or a gas leak. Maybe one of the bullets hit a pipe. But even as my mind raced through every possible excuse, the truth stared me in the face with red eyes and pointed fangs. The pieces had been there all along, scratching at the back of my mind for months, nagging me to fit them together and acknowledge their connection.

But knowing and seeing were two different things, and I'd had enough surprises for one day. My body heaved—once, twice—and I vomited on the vinyl floor and broken glass.

The rush of blood from emptying my guts made me light-headed. I sat up slowly and dabbed the corner of my mouth with the back of my hand. "Aren't you lucky," I said, the surreal situation and my dizziness making me numb. "Other women faint or scream when they go into shock. Yours throws up."

Vinnie Valenzano's giant body appeared where the glass door used to be, surrounded by shattered remnants clinging to an empty frame. He stepped through, and the sign that signaled "Closed" crunched under the weight of his fancy leather shoe.

He scanned the mess, and his gaze landed on Luca, slumped against the wall, his red eyes hooded and tips of his fangs visible between parted lips. Vinnie's unhappy expression drifted to me, then Gio. "Couldn't get a read on the plates—unmarked. They got Vito and Gina."

Luca let out a primal scream. His eyes flared, and his fangs elongated, sharp and deadly. "Who's they? They're fucking dead!"

"Save it. Don't know." His gaze slid to me, then back to Luca. "But I have a good fucking idea."

My stomach clenched and seized. I dry-heaved, my body trying to expel the acid.

"Marco's headed to Vesuvio," Vinnie said to Gio, his voice clipped and efficient. "I'll get word to the capi. We're looking for a silver Hyundai. Stay here and deal with the cops."

I shut my eyes and slowed my breath.

My ears rang from the gunfire, but loud Italian punctured my muffled hearing and made me jump. The man in the apron who'd been clearing dishes when I first arrived gestured at the shattered glass, broken chairs, and bullet holes. Vinnie raised his hands in a placating gesture. When the man didn't calm down, Vinnie barked a few words in Italian and pointed toward the back. The man wrung his apron, spun on his heel, and marched away.

Vinnie ran a hand down his face and lifted his chin toward Luca. "I gotta get him out of here."

"Took three in the back," Gio said. "One's still in there. Dr. Levine's on his way to Vesuvio."

"Get this blood cleaned up before the cops get here," he said to Gio.

Gio nodded and headed for the back.

"You got enough juice to walk?" Vinnie hunched over Luca and held out a hand.

"Yeah."

He put his other hand under Luca's armpit.

"Fuck! Not there!" Luca snapped. "That's where the bullet is."

"Let me help," I said and scrambled to my feet. Blood rushed to my head, and my knees buckled. I caught myself, took a deep breath, and pressed on.

My eyebrows knit together trying to figure out how my scrawny ass was going to help a man who weighed twice what I did to his feet. I squatted, grabbed Luca's hand, and put one arm around his shoulders.

Vinnie and I pulled.

Luca winced. "Argh!"

"Sorry!" I said, but at least Vinnie and I had Luca on his feet.

He sagged into me, but Vinnie held him upright with an arm around his waist. "Come on, Luca. Man up. You've been through worse."

Luca glared at Vinnie but straightened.

"Out the back," Vinnie said. "We can take the alleys, but we gotta move."

"Yeah," Luca said with a grunt, his breath heavy and strained.

We hobbled through broken glass toward the exit, my focus darting between Luca's pale face and the ground, making sure I didn't trip over anything. Crimson speckled his eyes, swirling pools of browns and reds, but it was still Luca. The Luca I'd always known. The Luca whose eyes held those same red flecks when I'd told him about my scars. The Luca who brought me to the deli to share his secret. The Luca who just told me he couldn't live without me. The same man.

He eyed me sideways. "You're not freaked out?"

I shot him an incredulous look. "Are you kidding? I'm wicked freaked out, but we need to get out of here."

We moved quickly once we fell into a rhythm. For once, I was thankful for the heat; the streets were empty. Luca's shirt was black. That helped. But my white blouse was covered in blood. The faster we reached Vesuvio, the better.

Fifteen long minutes later, Vinnie pounded his fist against the back door.

Enzo answered, and as soon as Vinnie pivoted to get Luca through the door, I got out of the way and let Enzo bear the other half of Luca's weight. Sweat poured down my face, and my arms shook from the strain.

"Let's get him to the couches," Enzo said and lifted his chin to the leather seats behind the stripper pole.

Luca slumped onto the bench, resting against its back with his uninjured shoulder. His long hair was matted to his forehead, his face leeched of color. His eyes returned to their normal color, only a few red specks dotting his coffee brown irises.

Marco paced the length of the bar, shouting into his cell. He must not have liked what he heard on the other end, because he let out an angry roar, picked up a barstool, and threw it clear across the room. It hit the far wall and clattered to a stop on the floor. He shouted into the phone, and his eyes burned like hot coals.

I wavered on my feet.

Vinnie grabbed my arm and steadied me. "Gonna need you to pull it together, sweetheart. Now's not the time, capisce?"

I nodded. "Capisce."

"Get some towels," he barked at Enzo. "Let's get him cleaned up before the doc gets here." Vinnie took out his phone, walked behind the bar, and grabbed a bottle of whiskey and a glass.

Marco pointed his phone and gaze at Luca. "Stai bene?"

"Yeah," Luca croaked. "I'll live."

Marco aimed his attention and phone at me.

I nodded.

He brought the phone back to his ear, and the string of loud Italian continued.

I sat on the couch next to Luca. His mouth turned into a sheepish half-smile that accentuated the tip of his eyetooth. It wasn't as long or sharp as it had been at the deli, but there was no denying it wasn't human.

"Nothing's ever easy with us, is it?"

I huffed. "No. Never."

Enzo dropped a stack of towels on the bench and handed one to me.

"Thanks," I said.

I combed the damp hair off Luca's face with my fingers and wiped the sweat away with the towel.

He grabbed my wrist and ran his thumb against the back of my hand. "I'm sorry. I should have trusted you. I should have known you were strong enough to handle the truth. You're the strongest person I know." He winced, and the red sparks in his eyes flared. "My mother died, because she couldn't handle what my father was, and the thought of losing you the same way..." He shuddered and closed his eyes.

I dragged my fingernails along his scalp the way he liked. He took a couple of breaths, calmed, and opened his eyes.

"What happened to her?" I asked.

"She never recovered from the shock. My father, Gina, the doctors—they forced her to eat, but they couldn't convince her to drink my father's blood, and she refused to let him feed from her. That's how my species bonds, and a human carrying a demone del sangue needs both blood and venom to survive."

"Demone del sangue," I repeated.

He nodded. "A blood demon."

Loud pounding made me jump. Enzo disappeared around the corner and, moments later, reappeared with a man in khaki pants, a collared short-sleeve polo, and a full head of curly black hair.

"Luca," the man said. "Didn't realize you were the patient."

"Hey, Ben," Luca said and winced.

He eyed Luca's blood-stained shirt. "You've looked better."

Luca snorted. "You're just jealous I still look as good as I did in college."

"And cocky as ever I see. All right, let's have a look."

Luca shifted and hunched forward. He unbuttoned his shirt and winced as he pulled his arms out of the sleeves. He grabbed at the back of his undershirt. "Cazzo," he swore, and his arms fell to his sides.

"Here," I said. "Let me." I pulled the undershirt over his head.

Smeared blood covered his upper back, and red-tinted rivulets of sweat trailed down the trough of his spine. Three angry welts as red as his eyes stared back at me. On his left side, the bullet had gone in and out through the meaty part of his muscle just above the clavicle, a perfect hole in his back and an explosive mess out the front. Not even an hour had passed since the shooting, yet the jagged edges of the exit wound were healed as if it had been days. Blood wasn't pumping out of the hole, and only a thin dribble leaked from the entry wound. To the right of his spine but lower, a pair of wounds—an entry in his back and an exit on his chest—matched those on the left.

The third and final hole in his back didn't have a partner on his chest. Centered on his right shoulder blade, the bullet hole leaked, slow and steady. The stream of blood mingled with sweat and trailed down his right side.

"There's a bullet in your right shoulder," Dr. Levine said.

"No shit."

"I don't know how deep it is, but since the other two came out the front, my guess is your shoulder blade stopped it."

"Perfetto."

"This isn't the best place to be poking around in your shoulder."

Luca glared at Dr. Levine. "You don't say," he said in a strained whisper.

"I need to cut you open to get that bullet out, but I'm concerned it's still bleeding. It should be partially healed." Dr. Levine narrowed his eyes. "When's the last time you fed?"

"Two weeks ago, give or take." Luca lifted a couple fingers dismissively. "There was a blood bag in there somewhere."

Dr. Levine scowled. "Why'd you go so long?"

Luca's eyes drifted to me and back to the doctor. "Long story."

"Well, you're running on empty, and after digging around in your shoulder"—Luca winced—"I'll need you healing at full capacity."

The doctor's gaze drifted from Luca's face to his lap. I hadn't realized it, but my hands were wrapped around one of Luca's, and his other rested on my thigh.

"Can you feed from her when I'm done?" he asked.

Luca looked at me, his eyes filled with apprehension. And

hope. The moment of truth—would history repeat itself? Or could I accept Luca for who and what he was?

"Of course," I said with a smile and tucked his sweaty hair behind his ear. "Whatever he needs."

Luca squeezed my hand, and his eyes fluttered closed. "Thank you."

"Enzo!" Dr. Levine called across the bar. "Help me get him onto the pool table. I need the light."

I got out of the way, and the men moved and arranged Luca.

Marco continued to pace, cell phone held to his ear, but he monitored their progress with more than passing interest.

I massaged my forehead. "I need a drink," I mumbled.

"You and me both," Vinnie said and ushered me to the bar. Luca lay on the pool table on his stomach, and Enzo helped Dr. Levine with the lights. "Lucky for us..."

I huffed and sat on one of the stools. He grabbed the bottle of whiskey sitting on the bar next to a glass beaded with condensation and poured a splash over the half-melted ice. He lifted the bottle in my direction and cocked an eyebrow.

I placed a hand on my belly. "I can't."

He glanced down at my hand, snorted, and shook his head. "Fucking Luca." He shot back his drink and poured another.

"Argh!" A strangled scream tore through the bar. I jumped, horrified by the sound, and looked over my shoulder.

Marco blocked my view of the pool table, cell phone still held to his ear. He shook his head.

"Better keep your eyes over here, sweetheart," Vinnie said. "You don't want to see that."

I nodded even as Luca let out another tortured scream. I rifled through my purse and found my Tums. I popped two in my mouth and tried to focus on chewing and not the impromptu surgery happening behind me.

My hand went back to my belly and rubbed it in slow circles. I wasn't safe. My baby wasn't safe. The day's events reinforced what I'd already decided—I needed to leave Boston.

The truth about Luca's reaction to my pregnancy and the revelations about his true nature changed nothing. They didn't change how much I wanted to have a family, and they didn't change my decision to raise this baby in Ireland on my own. If I needed to feed or be fed upon or both, I'd do it, but I'd do it where we wouldn't be shot at in the middle of a Wednesday afternoon.

I loved Luca. Always had. Always would. And after today, I knew he loved me too. But that changed nothing. Love wouldn't keep me and my baby safe.

A hand landed on my shoulder and squeezed. Marco. "It's done," he said. "He's in the break room down the hall." He tipped his head in the direction of the short corridor on the other end of the bar. "After he's done feeding, Paulie will drive you to Terme. You'll spend the night there with Anna."

"But—"

"This is not open for discussion, Siobhán," Marco said, his voice raised. "I need to know you're safe, and Terme is the best place for that until we can figure out what the fuck is going on."

I clamped my mouth shut. Now was not the time to argue, and it wouldn't be the worst thing in the world to spend the night with Anna. I hopped off the barstool.

"Go," he said and kissed the top of my head. "He needs you."

Luca sat in the middle of a couch, his back to the door, left shoulder and head resting against the cushion. His skin was clean, and a square piece of medical gauze covered the wound on his right shoulder. He was pale—paler than before—and his chest rose and fell with slow, regulated breaths.

Dr. Levine stood behind the couch, furiously typing on his cell phone.

I sat on the couch facing him and ran my fingernails through his hair. "Hey."

He swallowed and lifted his eyes to meet mine. "Hey."

"How are you?"

"I've been better."

"He needs to feed," Dr. Levine said and shoved the phone in his pocket. He walked around the end of the couch and raised an eyebrow. "I'll leave you to it, but don't wait so long next time."

"Yeah, yeah," Luca said.

Dr. Levine snorted. "Nice meeting you…"

"Siobhán," I said.

"Siobhán." He reached into his back pocket, retrieved his wallet, and pulled out a card. "Call or text me if anything seems off, but he should be fine once he isn't *starving*." He aimed the last word at Luca.

Luca chuckled and winced.

"Later, buddy," Dr. Levine said and made for the door.

"Later."

The door clicked shut.

Luca searched my face. "You sure you want to do this?"

I ran my fingernails through his hair again. "Absolutely."

Faint red specks appeared in the coffee-brown field of his eyes. "Come here." He tapped my leg. "Put them across my lap."

I did as he said and scooted closer. I draped my arm along the back of the couch and rested my head on top of my arm.

"Stay just like that," he whispered.

"Will it hurt?"

The corner of his mouth lifted in a mischievous smirk. "No. The venom feels good." He brushed his lips across mine. "Very good."

My lips parted on an intake, my body tingling from being so close to Luca again, like it came alive in the presence of its missing piece. He placed soft kisses along my jaw and nuzzled the space below my ear the way he'd done so many times before.

"I've dreamed about this," he said, and the words tickled my neck. I tilted my head on instinct, craving more. He placed a kiss there and lingered. "Dreamed of pressing my fangs into you and tasting you."

I shivered, his dark declaration as sinful a pleasure as his lips. He ran his tongue along the hollow of my neck where my pulse pounded for him. He closed his lips over the soft space in an open mouth kiss.

"Thank you," he whispered against my skin.

A sharp pinch made me gasp. My eyes went wide, and my hand flew to Luca's shoulder. He groaned, and the pinch transformed into a burning pressure. The sensation crept up my neck, following the path of my artery to my head before shooting back down. And with my heart's next beat, pleasure spread through my veins like wildfire.

Each heartbeat heightened my sense of touch, and desire pooled in my core. Every press of his body against mine, every brush of skin on skin, created a surge of carnal bliss.

Luca's tongue caressed my skin beneath his fangs as he drank, directing my blood into his mouth. With each pull on my neck, his fangs delivered more of his delicious venom, and animalistic sounds wrought from satisfaction rumbled through his chest.

His hand traveled up my leg to my back, and he pressed me closer, taking more of what he needed and I wanted to give. I clung to his shoulder, and my nails dug into his skin. High, flighty sighs and breathy gasps of pleasure escaped me as the heat in my veins continued to build. My body was on fire, alive with Luca's venom, and my heart was full, bursting with intimacy. No more secrets, just our true selves connected like never before.

His mouth slowed, and he relaxed his grip. He pulled his fangs out of my neck, swept his tongue across the wounds, and kissed me there. I shivered.

He looked into my eyes. "You're perfect," he whispered.

Color had returned to his face, and his eyes flared a bright and brilliant crimson. His lips were swollen and pink, and the sharp tips of his fangs extended beyond a smile filled with adoration. Luca the blood demon was as beautiful as Luca the man.

He cupped my face and ran his thumb along my jaw. "How do you feel?"

Relaxed. Consumed with pleasure and hope. Utterly in love. I leaned into his touch. "Better now that I know you'll be okay."

He wrapped his fingers around my nape and pulled me into him, pressing his lips to my forehead. "Yeah," he said. "I'm going to be okay."

My heart squeezed. For me and for him. For the love we shared and the inevitable end to this brief moment of happiness. Because he wouldn't be okay after I told him I was leaving. And still, it changed nothing.

Chapter Thirty-Seven

Siobhán

"Thanks, Paulie," I said.

Marco's tight-lipped driver gave me a terse nod. "I'll be in the foyer if you or Signora DeVita need anything."

I gave him a wan smile. "I'm sure that's not necessary."

"Signor DeVita's orders are always necessary," he said and clasped his hands in front of him.

I sighed and knocked on the door.

"Coming!" Anna's muffled voice and frantic footsteps echoed through the thick mahogany. Moments later, locks clicked, and the door swung open. "Siobhan!" Anna said, breathless and flustered.

She ushered me into the austere penthouse and hurriedly shut the door. Sophie appeared as if on cue. Her purrs and headbutts to my calves made my throat burn and tears well, this time with relief. But I refused to let go. If I let go, I'd devolve into a complete mess, and I wasn't about to let that happen. I was the strong one. I was *always* the strong one.

I took a deep breath, swallowed the burn, and blinked away the tears. "Hi, Anna."

She laid a hand on my arm and looked me up and down. "Oh, honey."

I could only imagine what I looked like. Rumpled. Covered in Luca's blood. Makeup smudged from crying. Hair askew. "Yeah, it's..." I took another deep breath. "It's been a day."

"You—you need Sophie snuggles." She reached for my purse, and I absently handed it to her. "But let's get you cleaned up first."

"Yes, please. I feel like every inch of me that isn't covered in dried blood is covered in dried sweat."

She grimaced. "Come on."

I followed Anna to the back of the penthouse, behind the partition that separated the open living space from the dressing area and kitchen.

"Everything I own is going to be too big and too short on you." She stopped in front of a walk-in closet the size of my bedroom and rifled through a dresser. "Here's a pair of shorts and my comfiest sweater."

That's what did it—the little goose's sweater. The floodgates opened, and I doubled over sobbing.

"Oh, honey." Anna rubbed my back in circles between my shoulders. "Let it out. Just let it out."

Did I ever. The pent-up shock and fear and worry poured out in tears, a runny nose, and high-pitched wails. And through it all, Anna stood by my side, hand on my back in quiet, unwavering support. Like a friend. Like family.

Eventually, my uncontrolled crying slowed. I allowed myself two final, stilted sobs, then straightened myself out. Anna darted into the bathroom and came back with a handful of tissues.

"I—I can't imagine how you're feeling right now."

I blew my nose and waved a hand through the air. "It's

fine. I'm fine. I just needed to get that out. I feel better now, honestly. I'll feel even better once I get cleaned up."

She led me into a spacious marble bathroom complete with a jacuzzi tub. She filled it with steaming water and bubbles scented with a hint of rose. I sank into the bath and soaked away the remaining tension and stress. I washed off the blood, sweat, tears, and emotions until all that was left were the memories of the day's events and the conclusion that I had to deal with a new reality. A reality in which Luca and my baby were blood demons.

I emerged from the bathroom a new woman, one who had to accept that another world existed, one she knew very little about. A world that belonged to the man she loved, and a world that belonged to her unborn child. I wanted to learn everything I could about blood demons, so I could be the kind of mother my baby deserved. Luckily, I was about to spend the night with the best possible teacher.

Anna sat on top of her and Marco's bed propped up against the headboard. Glasses covered nearly half her face. She dropped the paperback she'd been reading into her lap and patted the bed next to her. Sophie lifted her furry head and glared at the source of her disruption.

"You're in here with me and Sophie tonight," she said.

"What about Marco?"

"He'll be out all night given"—she swallowed—"given everything."

I climbed onto the bed. It was soft and the sheets were cool, like being cradled by a luxuriant cloud. Anna put her book and glasses on the nightstand and scooted down to rest her head on a pillow facing me. I did the same.

She stroked Sophie's fur, and the little gray-and-white attention whore started purring like nobody's business.

"Is Luca really forty-two?" I asked.

"Yes, he's really forty-two."

"And Marco?"

Anna's lips twitched. "Marco's... a little older."

"And by a little you mean..."

"He's, uh, ninety-four."

My head jerked up off the pillow. "Ninety-four?"

She smiled an uncomfortable smile and nodded into her pillow. I laid my head back down and started petting Sophie along with her. I'd worked out that Marco had to be older, but to hear it out loud, so plainly...

"Honestly," I said, "that explains a lot."

"I know, right? The timelines never added up for me either."

I sighed. "Is it messed up I think that's hot?"

She chuckled. "No. It's incredibly hot. And, for the record, you're handling this a lot better than I did."

I raised an eyebrow.

"Remember when I passed out after the charity gala dinner? That wasn't from too much champagne. Marco showed me he was a blood demon, and I fainted."

I huffed. "At least you didn't throw up."

She laughed. "Either way, it's not exactly the type of news you can brush off and say, 'Good to know! Thanks for sharing!'"

I laughed along with her. "No, it's not." I stopped petting Sophie and laid my hand on my belly. "Especially when you're about to have a baby with one."

Anna's expression turned empathetic.

"I'm sorry I didn't tell you," I said.

"You don't need to apologize. I know it was a surprise."

"It was." Sophie stood up, stretched, turned in circle, and lay back down. "And Luca's reaction didn't help."

"I'm sure it didn't. But you understand why he reacted the way he did, right?"

"I do."

"And look, the news was a lot for me to wrap my brain around, and I wasn't even pregnant. Give yourself some grace. It's been what, a few hours? And you were sh—shot at too." She blinked slowly and swallowed.

I put my hand atop hers, and we squeezed each other's fingers. "Thank you. I think I needed the permission."

"I get that. We all need permission sometimes. That's what friends are for. I'm here for you. Whatever you need. Right now, and after you have the baby."

"Thank you. I mean it. I've never had that kind of support from my family."

"Well, you do now. You're part of our family, Siobhán. You're not alone."

The knot in my stomach returned, the one Gina had tied in the bakery and the one that twisted and tightened any time I thought about moving to Ireland. But after what happened today, how could I not? Once again, I'd been caught in the crossfire. Gina was missing—taken. To what end? Only time would tell. How could I continue to put myself and my baby at risk?

We stroked Sophie's fur in comfortable silence. Some of the remaining tension in my shoulders eased, my stomach settled, and my racing thoughts calmed enough that I could finally ask the litany of questions begging for answers.

"Were you scared?" I asked. "When you found out?"

Her eyes widened. "Terrified. I ran from him right before I fainted. I tried running from him again after I woke up, but..." She scrunched her face.

"But what?"

"I'm not sure I was running from him, really. I think—I think I was running from the unknown. I'd been living in a safe little bubble, and Marco's world was so different from anything I'd ever known. Then to find out blood demons existed on top of all the Mafia stuff?" She raised her eyebrows and made an *O* out of her lips like she was whistling. I chuckled. "But looking back, I wasn't scared of him. Not really. I've never felt safer than with Marco. Or more loved."

"Really?" My face and voice twisted with skepticism. "I find it hard to believe you feel safer married to a Mafia don, Anna."

"But I do. I have a future filled with adventure and love, and for me, that's safety. I didn't want to lose my life by not living it. Marco gave me the security of knowing my life wouldn't be wasted, that I'd get to live to my full potential."

"You're so brave."

She snorted. "Am I? Or am I just more scared of losing Marco than I am of anything else?"

"Fair."

"I wasn't about to give Marco up just because his job puts him in physical danger. A lot of jobs do that. And I wasn't about to give him up because he's different than me. Being a blood demon is part of what makes Marco, Marco. I love that part of him. It's exciting."

I smiled. "Every time I learn something new about Luca, it makes me love him even more."

"He loves you too, you know, based on what Gina's told me."

Butterflies attacked my stomach. "I know."

"You're lucky. *I'm* lucky. Not everyone gets that in life. Before I met Marco, I thought I'd never experience being in love. It's like a new world opened up. And"—Anna's face turned bright red—"and the sex is out of this world amazing." She covered her eyes, and I couldn't help but laugh. Little goose.

"You bonded—I think that's what Luca called it—with Marco?"

"Yes," she said with red cheeks and a wide smile.

"Which means you drank"—I winced—"his blood?"

"I did. I mean, I do. I drink from him, and he drinks from me. As humans, we have to drink their blood if we want to be with them for life. They're immortal."

"Luca said the baby needs his blood. He said that's how his mother died—she wouldn't drink."

Anna's smile turned sad. "It's true. Lucia died, because she refused to drink. Marco said that happens with some humans. They can't handle the truth."

"But you did."

"I did. And I'm glad I did. I love drinking from Marco. Sharing each other in that way... It's so intimate. It makes me feel alive. Not to mention the taste." I scrunched my nose. "You're making that face, but that's not the face you'll make after you try it." She raised her eyebrows and fake fanned herself. I chuckled.

"But more than the sex, it's those quiet moments at night, sitting on the couch with him and Sophie, looking out at the Commons..." Anna's expression grew wistful. "I wouldn't give those moments up for anything."

"Hm."

She yawned, and it made me yawn too. We continued stroking Sophie's fur, and soon, Anna's eyes fluttered closed, and her hand stopped moving.

That day at the bakery, Gina said that she'd rather live in Marco's world than lose her family. But would she still feel that way after today?

Anna certainly did. Then again, I always told her Marco was a unicorn. He was devoted to her. He'd never betray her or leave her side. Luca loved me, but he'd broken my heart before. Could I count on him to be there for me and our baby? I closed my eyes.

Images from the afternoon flashed across my mind like movie stills. Shattered glass. The "Closed" sign, dented and lying on the floor. Luca diving in front of me.

What if he hadn't been there? What if I'd been hit? Worse, what if our baby had been hit? I placed my hand on my stomach.

Stills from a much older movie replaced the ones from that afternoon. A car slowly driving by. A hand extended out a window holding a gun. The bloody mess of my stomach spilling onto the chop shop floor.

I was the strong one. Always. But I wasn't sure I was strong enough to risk my safety or our baby for a chance at love.

Chapter Thirty-Eight

Luca

"What do we know?" Gio asked.

Marco dragged on his cigar. He'd been sucking them down like they were his only source of oxygen for hours. I couldn't blame him. They had Mamma Gina, whoever they were.

It was sometime after dinner, maybe seven or eight. Marco had closed the upstairs of Vesuvio for the night so we could strategize about what came next. Vito and Gina had been kidnapped, and we didn't know why. No ransom message had been sent, and there was no trace of the unmarked silver Elantra. While I was getting the bullet extracted from my shoulder, Marco and Vinnie made calls to their capi and contacts all over the city. Hours later, we sat around one of the poker tables with cigars and drinks.

"I counted four men," Vinnie said. "An unmarked Hyundai. At one point someone shouted, 'Italian fucks,' but I couldn't make out the rest."

Marco removed the cigar from between his teeth. "Stay away from my sister," Marco said, slow and grim. Smoke trailed from his lips with each word. "You hear that, you Italian fucks."

My heart slammed into my ribs. "Rory," I said. "Siobhán only has one brother."

Marco tipped his head.

What happened at the deli was traumatic enough, but when she found out her brother orchestrated the hit? I shoved a hand into my hair and pulled. "Dio. This is going to kill her."

Her family had put her in danger. Again. And not just her, but our baby. I might be able to protect her from bullets, but I couldn't protect her from her family no matter how much I wanted to spare her that pain.

"Do they know she's pregnant?" Vinnie asked.

"No, not yet."

Vinnie looked at Marco, and they exchanged an unspoken message.

"Does she know anything? Where they might've taken them?" Gio asked.

"No," I said and shook my head. "She stays out of her family's business, and I'm not going to ask her to get involved." I met Marco's eyes. "I won't put her in that position."

Marco held my gaze. "Luca's right. Siobhán doesn't know, and she's one of us. I don't want my grandchild in danger."

Grandchild... I was going to be a father. I was still trying to wrap my brain around the idea, but it created such warmth in my chest. And for the moment, Siobhán was safe. Our baby was safe. I'd go to her as soon as I could. Comfort her. Make sure she knew I wouldn't let anything happen to either of them.

"We need information," I said. "And I promise you, Siobhán doesn't have any, but I bet I know who does."

Gio lifted an eyebrow.

"Durand," Vinnie said.

I nodded. "Assane Durand. He's hosting a game Saturday night."

"We can't wait that long." Marco gritted the words out, and his eyes sparked.

"No, we can't." Without knowing the endgame, every hour could be the difference between life and death for Vito and Gina. "But we can reach out, see if he'll bite."

"He stays out of shit like this," Vinnie said.

"True, but it's worth a shot," I said.

"I'll send the message," Marco said.

"What about Providence?" I asked.

"What about 'em?" Gio asked. "Patrizi's not going to know shit about what's going on up here, not any more than we do."

"I already called him," Vinnie said. "Told him to keep an eye out."

I rolled my shoulder and sipped my scotch. The joint was stiff from the swollen muscle, and the exit wound still pinched, but I was almost fully healed thanks to Siobhán.

Feeding took on an entirely new meaning after drinking from her. It was intimate, special, and she'd shared her blood not just to provide me with sustenance but so I could survive. But I needed *her* to survive. A future without Siobhán was no future at all, and I would do anything to make sure I'd never face that possibility.

"Mikey's trial starts Monday," Vinnie said with an edge of suspicion and frustration. "Can't help wonder if Vito and Gina suddenly going missing isn't a coincidence."

"Maybe," Gio said and rocked his head. "Regardless, someone's gotta take care of the case."

"One of my lawyers will handle it," Marco said. "Anna can step in for Gina at the Foundation, but she's going to need help with anything related to Sources." He glanced at me, and I nodded.

"So," Vinnie said. "Aspettiamo." He leaned back in his chair, and it creaked.

Gio pulled out his phone. I lifted my chin at Marco and dropped my eyes to his cigar case. He slid it across the table. I took one—a Cuban, no less—and lit it.

"I want Luca back in my crew," Marco said flatly.

My head snapped up.

"No. Assolutamente no." Vinnie's voice boomed across the table. "He's part of my crew. That was the deal. Business at The Dollhouse has never been better." He pointed at me. "Because of him."

"Come on, Vinnie. You know the importance of family."

"I do, which is why I took him in when you disowned him."

Marco shifted his gaze to me. "People make mistakes," he said solemnly. "Besides, you've got more kids than you know what to do with. Or probably even know about," he added dryly.

Vinnie folded his arms across his chest and scowled.

"I have one son, and I want him close, especially now that he's going to be a father. I want him in my crew. Il mio sottocapo."

My stomach flipped. His son. And his underboss. The DeVita family heir.

"You're asking a lot," Vinnie grumbled.

Marco tipped his head in acknowledgement.

"Luca?" Vinnie fixed his scowl on me.

"I have a family to think about now," I said. "My own family. I have to consider what's best for them, what's best for Siobhán."

"What about The Dollhouse?"

"Dominic can run The Dollhouse. He knows what he's

doing and how I run things. He won't let any of that slip. He wants to make captain."

Vinnie's eyes darkened, and he glared at Marco. "You're not getting him back without giving me something in return." It wasn't an argument, and it wasn't a threat. It was a statement of fact. Vinnie pointed at Marco. "I'm taxing you five points for this."

"Three."

"And there'll be a transition period. I want Luca to oversee Dominic for the next month. Longer if needed. And if it doesn't work out—if he fucks up—you're paying for it."

"If he fucks it up, we'll work something out," Marco said.

"He won't fuck up," I said.

"You got that?" Vinnie said to Gio.

Gio nodded.

Vinnie shot back the rest of his whiskey and pushed out of his chair. "Are we done here? It's one of my countless kids' birthdays"—he sneered at Marco, and Marco snorted—"and I need to make an appearance before bedtime." He buttoned his suit jacket.

"We're done," Marco said.

"Text if you hear anything." Vinnie's expression subdued to one of mutual understanding and empathy.

"Naturalmente. A presto."

"A presto," Vinnie said and left Vesuvio, Gio in tow.

With nothing else to mask the noise, my sensitive hearing caught the din of mid-week revelers that punched through the soundproofing in the floor. Beyond that, Marco and I smoked our cigars in silence, and for the first time in years, the lack of distraction didn't bother me. We needed a minute to sit with everything in solidarity, in our new normal, untarnished by the past and focused on the future.

Marco snubbed out his cigar, threw his ankle across his knee, and folded his hands in his lap. "Siobhán is family. Her brother is not." His expression remained implacable, his words cold as ice.

"I understand," I said. "So will Siobhán. She might not like our world, but she understands it."

"How did she take it?" He wasn't talking about the attack.

"Better than I hoped."

"She's strong."

"She is."

"Strong enough for what comes next?" He cocked an eyebrow.

"Stronger," I said with confidence.

Marco picked up his whiskey and swirled it in his glass. I finished my scotch.

The muscle in his jaw ticked. "We'll find her," he said, his voice rough but resolute. "We'll get her back."

"We will," I said, unable to contemplate any other truth. I couldn't lose another parent. "Vito too."

He nodded and drained the rest of his drink. "It's good to have you back, Luca."

Emotion clogged my throat. I cleared it and swallowed. "It's good to be back, Zio. I won't let you down."

Marco stood, and I followed. He clasped my shoulders and that muscle in his jaw worked to keep up the strong front he put on for all of us. He patted me on the cheek. "So che non lo farai, figliolo. I know you won't."

Chapter Thirty-Nine

Siobhán

The heat wave broke overnight, and a warm breeze wafted through the trees surrounding Birch Pond. I closed my eyes and turned my face up. I needed its gentle touch, something to calm my nerves while I waited at Luca's front door.

I barely slept the night before, even with Anna and Sophie curled up next to me, rattled from the attack and Vinnie's off-hand comment about who he suspected kidnapped Vito and Gina. My knotted stomach forced me to graduate from Tums to Maalox, and the morning sickness didn't help. I was exhausted and queasy, but I needed to know that Luca was okay. And break the news that I was leaving. Better to tell him now. Delaying the inevitable would only make our separation more painful.

The deadbolt clicked, and the door opened. Luca stood in the foyer wearing basketball shorts, a sleeveless undershirt, and a surprised smile.

"Siobhán," he said, breathless. "I wasn't expecting you."

He looked past me, and I glanced over my shoulder to

where Paulie leaned against the hood of Marco's Range Rover. Marco still had me under lockdown, but I wasn't complaining. My nerves were shot. Luca lifted his chin, and Paulie did the same.

"I was going to call," he said, "but I thought I should let you rest. You mentioned morning sickness." His smile turned sheepish, almost nervous.

"I know. Sorry for the pop in. I wanted to make sure you were okay."

His shoulders relaxed, and he ushered me inside. "Fully healed. Thanks to you."

I kicked off my sandals and looked at him with an impish smile. "No shoes."

He wrapped an arm around my waist. "Come here," he said and pulled me into him. He kissed me passionately, furiously, love and relief pouring out through each caress of his lips and swipe of his tongue. I wrapped my arms around his neck and kissed him back with equal fervor.

He broke the kiss and rested his forehead against mine. "I'm so glad you're here." The hope and love radiating from his smile warmed and broke my heart.

His hair was half pulled up, and loose strands framed his handsome face. I pushed them aside with my fingernails and brushed my thumb across a creamy yellow smudge at the top of his cheekbone near his left temple. "What's this?"

He glanced over his shoulder, hesitating. "I wanted to surprise you when it was finished, but since you're here..." He took my hand and led me upstairs.

Halfway up, I registered the smell of wet paint. It got stronger as we walked down the hall. The door to the room across from the master had always been closed, but now classical violin emanated through the half-opened door.

An old boom box was perched on top of a metal ladder.

Plastic sheeting covered the floor and was meticulously secured in place with blue painter's tape. The windows were thrown open, their frames taped like wrapped presents, and natural light shone in without any curtains or blinds to stop it. The soft yellow paint gleamed as fresh and bright as rays of sunshine in what had always felt like such a dark world.

"Do you like the color?" he asked, eager and hopeful. "I know we don't know if it's a boy or a girl, but I looked online, and every baby website said yellow and green work for both."

My throat constricted, and tears welled. He was building a nursery. For our baby.

"Kinda perfect timing," he said. "I just finished the second coat."

I couldn't tell if the ache in my chest was my heart exploding with love or shattering because I was about to break his. A tear escaped, and I swallowed back the sob attempting to break free.

"Hey, don't cry." He brushed the backs of his fingers across my cheek. "We can always change the color," he said with a crooked smile. "I know it's premature, but I wanted to show you how much having a family means to me and that if you decide to keep the baby, I'll make a home for us."

"No, it's—" I shook my head. "I love the color." I couldn't bring myself to say what needed to be said.

"Good." He took my hand—"I want to show you something"—and led me to the closet where a glass of water and a picture frame sat on a small utility table. He picked up the frame. "These are my parents." Luca said the words with purposeful strength. As though he'd uncovered something deeply buried and wanted to share it with the world.

The Polaroid inside the frame was old and discolored, but the grainy image couldn't hide the joy in the faces of the two people it captured. An older version of Luca looked down at the woman who smiled into the camera. The love in his eyes reached across the years and grabbed my heart. Luca was there in the woman's face as well—lips as full as his, the same pouty shape and rosy color, and matching chocolate-brown hair.

"This is my mother Lucia and my father Antonio—Tony. They didn't get to live here together, but that's what they wanted for a time. To be a family. To build a family in this house." He looked at me. "This room was supposed to be a surprise."

I traced my finger over the glass, over the parents he'd lost, the family he so desperately wanted but had been taken from him when he was a child. And there I was, about to take that from him again. Take myself and our child away from him, because I was too scared to stay and fight for my safety. Because I was too scared to admit that I wasn't really safe anywhere.

Worse, I was about to create the same situation Luca and I had endured as children. If I took our child away from Luca so I could have my false sense of security, I'd be no better than my own parents. I'd just be creating a different brand of our fucked-up childhoods. Was I strong enough to break the cycle?

Luca set the picture on the table and rubbed the back of his neck. "Kinda doing things all backward, huh?"

I let out a nervous chuckle. "That's kind of our MO."

He took my hands. "Do you like it?"

"It's lovely, Luca."

He examined my face, and the smile left his lips. "But..."

"But I'm scared," I said. He pressed his lips together and worry replaced the hope in his eyes. "Not of you. Not of the whole blood demon thing." I shook my head. "I can't believe I just said that, but it's true. Anna explained a lot last night, and even though I have questions, I understand, and I'm not scared. But what happened yesterday... That's what I was talking about when I said I'm not safe in this world. And it's not just about me anymore. I have to think of our baby. I want to move back to Ireland."

He stiffened and squeezed my hands. "I'll protect us. I'll do whatever I need to do to keep us safe."

"You say that now, but who knows what could happen? Someone has Gina right now."

"And we're going to get her back," he said with steely resolve, eyes sparking. "Not to mention, you need me, Siobhán. You need my blood and my venom."

"I know. Dr. Levine explained that part to me. Paulie took me to see him this morning before I came here."

"What? Why didn't you call me? I would have gone with you. What did he say? Is the baby okay? Are you okay?"

"Luca." I placed a hand on his chest and smiled. "I'm fine. We're both healthy. He said the baby's heartbeat is strong and everything looks totally normal."

His shoulders relaxed, and he shuttered his eyes. "Grazie a Dio."

"But he also said I could use a—a Source for blood and venom if I needed to. He said he'd connect me with a doctor in London who works with blood demons and—and that's a quick flight from Cork. He'll help me find a Source to get me through this pregnancy."

Luca's eyes flared red. He curled his top lip, and his fangs elongated to vicious points. "Absolutely not!"

"You don't run my life, Luca Moretti," I snapped, my temper kicking in. "If I want to move back to Ireland, you better believe that's what I'm going to do."

"I'm not talking about moving to Ireland," he growled. "I'm talking about you drinking from another blood demon. I'm talking about letting another man feed from you. Absolutely. Fucking. Not." He grabbed my shoulders. "You are mine, Siobhán Connelly. Do you hear me? If you want to move to Ireland, I'll buy a fucking Celtics hat and move with you, but after all the shit we've been through, there's no fucking way I'm letting you go."

My breath caught, and if I hadn't known it was impossible, I'd have sworn my heart stopped beating. "You'd leave Boston?"

"Are you kidding?" His lips pinched, and his eyebrows drew together. "Gimme a sec." He darted out of the room.

Was this really happening? When was the other shoe going to drop? When was Luca going to crush my heart again? It was coming. It had to be coming.

He marched back into the room, determination etched in the lines of his face. "This is not how any of this was supposed to go," he said and licked his lips. "Our first time together, the pregnancy, the nursery, this…"

He lifted his hand, and between his thumb and index finger, a delicate gold band embedded with a row of rubies as deep a crimson as the specks of fire in his eyes glinted in the sunlight. And Luca Moretti—consummate playboy, breaker of hearts, Romeo to my Juliet—got down on one knee and looked up at me with expectation, hope, and so much love, the world around us faded into background and fate finally had its way.

"Something shifted the day I saw you in the lobby at Terme. I don't believe in all that fate stuff, but something about that moment…" He shook his head. "It sent a boulder hurtling down a mountain, and it didn't matter how many times I tried to change its course, nothing was going to stop that boulder. Nothing could stop our destiny, Siobhán. We were meant to be.

"I wasted so much time trying to purge my heart of pain with revenge, when all I needed was to let myself love you. And as soon as I did, the pain stopped. I'm finally free, and it's because of you. Nothing will ever be more important to me than loving you."

Tears spilled down my cheeks. I ran my fingernails along the edge of his hair, tucking it behind his ear, unable to imagine how we finally arrived at a destination that had evaded us for so long.

"We've both been searching for family our entire lives. That's all either of us has ever wanted. And we finally have it, Siobhán. Right here. This is our family. You, me, and our little miracle. I don't ever want to let that go. I will fight every day to make sure we don't lose this, and if that means I need to move to Ireland, I'll move to Ireland. I own a house in Roma. If you think you can grow your career there, we'll go there. We'll go wherever you want to go, because wherever you are, that's where I want to be. Because you're my family." He lifted the ring. "If you'll have me."

I stared down at the man I'd loved for so long, the man I'd lost more times than I could count, the man who held up a ring and whose voice trembled with hope and no small amount of fear, his entire future waiting on my answer.

Despite everything, Luca Moretti was the only man who'd seen the real me, and he'd done things for me not for his own gain, but because they meant something to me. He'd learned who I was, what I needed, and what I wanted, without help or prodding, just to make me happy. He was ready to uproot his life, move away from his job, his foster parents, and his community so I'd feel safe and could pursue my career. There was no qualification to the sincerity in his eyes. No hesitation. Just an earnest desire to give us what we'd longed for our entire lives—family. Luca and Siobhán's happy ever after.

The ring glinted between his thick fingers, fine and delicate and perfectly me. "It's beautiful," I said, dazed and breathless.

"It was my mother's." His voice shook through the declaration. "Or it was supposed to be. It's a bond ring. My father bought it for her, but they never bonded in blood. When I moved back to Boston and we unpacked the house, Gina recognized it." His lips bent in a crooked smile. "She helped him pick it out. She asked what I wanted to do with it, if I wanted to sell it. And I remember..." His eyebrows knit together. "I remember thinking I needed to hold on to it. That, for some reason, it was important for me to hold on to it. I never understood why. I do now. This ring was meant for you, Siobhán. It was always meant for you."

He took my left hand and widened his eyes, asking permission, not only for us to bond but for us to put the pain and loneliness behind us and create a new future. Together.

He wanted to be my family. Someone who'd take care of me and who'd always think of me first. Someone who I could lean on to help shoulder life's burdens. Someone who loved me as much as I loved him.

"Yes," I said, nodding like a fool. "Yes. To everything. To you. To our family. To this house."

His eyes widened.

"Yes, to this house!" Something between a laugh and a sob sprang from my lungs. Something that sounded a lot like a declaration of freedom. "I want more for our child than what we had. I don't want to raise them without the support of the people who love us, and those people are here. In Boston. I'm done running, Luca. I want to build a life here. I want this to be our family home."

He smiled, the genuine smile he reserved just for me, and slid the band onto my ring finger. And like everything else in our fate-filled story, it fit perfectly, as though it really had been made for me.

He brought my finger to his lips and kissed it, then rose and swept me off my feet, cradling me in his arms as he walked across the hall. I wrapped my arms around his neck, and he placed sweet, loving kisses across my cheeks and on the tip of my nose with a lightness I'd never experienced with him before. He'd let love into his heart, and it vanquished the heaviness put there by his quest for revenge.

He set me on my feet next to the bed and traced the outline of my face with his finger, the hint of a happy smile still blessing his full lips. He trailed his finger down my neck to the buttons of my blouse and started to undress me, slowly and reverently taking care of each button, my belt, my slacks, until I stood in my underwear. His eyes flared to match my lingerie—crimson lace.

He ran his finger along the top edge of my bra and lifted his eyes for no more than a heartbeat before tucking his finger under the lace and pulling it down to reveal my nipple. He craned his head, flicked the peak with his tongue, and placed a kiss there. He let go of the fabric, and it fell back into place.

His hands cradled my face, and he lowered his mouth to mine. His kiss was sweet yet sensual, content yet urgent, a combination of the past and present but wholly Luca. I moved my lips and tongue with his, matching every stroke, and knew I'd made the right decision.

Luca was right. *We* were right. We may have taken a long and winding path to find our happy ending, but we'd finally arrived. We were home.

He pulled back until his lips hovered over mine. "Do you understand what it means to bond? Did Anna explain it to you?"

"Yes." I nuzzled his cheek. "She did."

"We'll have to move every few decades. You'll outlive your friends, your family."

"You're my family."

He smiled. "Will you bond with me, Siobhán? Will you drink my blood and be mine for eternity?"

I nodded, emotion clogging my throat. "One lifetime with you would never be enough."

Fire erupted in his dark eyes. The color swirled in a mesmerizing display as captivating as his handsome face. He pulled off his undershirt and dropped his shorts, his desire visible through his boxers. He picked me up, climbed onto the bed, and settled me across his lap, his back against the headboard.

His lips parted, and his eyeteeth elongated and sharpened into points. The color in his eyes solidified into a steady glow. He'd shared his demons, and now he shared himself, open and bared, and he was beautiful.

He dragged a fang across his wrist, and a slash of blood appeared. I shifted my gaze from the crimson in his expectant eyes to the crimson trailing down his arm. I held his hand and lowered my head.

I ran my tongue over the thick trail of blood, and my body's reaction surprised me as much as the sweet taste. A force deep within me came alive, urging me to lap up every bit of blood from his arm and drink. My eyes widened and locked with Luca's. I laid a hand on my belly and searched his face for confirmation. He gave me a knowing smile and nodded. My heart soared, and I fell even more in love with him and our family.

I licked his forearm clean, and every drop of him danced across my tastebuds, rich, metallic, and delicious. My senses climbed, and that force inside me—our baby—grew in contentment, eager for more. I closed my lips over the slash at his wrist and pulled blood into my mouth. He sighed, a satisfied sound, and hardened beneath me. I drank eagerly and thoroughly, each mouthful more fulfilling than the last and each swallow strengthening our bond.

He eased me off his wrist, and I panted from the sensory overload. The caress of wind from the ceiling fan on my exposed skin, the satiny sheets beneath my feet, the brush of his fingertips along my spine. The rich browns in his long hair, the deep red of his eyes, the bright yellow sunlight dappling the verdant foliage outside the window. The rustle of leaves, his breath and mine, the beat of our hearts. Everything was fresh and new, like I was experiencing the world for the first time.

He licked the wound at his wrist, and the red slash faded to a pink line. He brushed his fingertips across my lips and rested his hand on the nape of my neck. "How do you feel?"

"In love. Completely in love."

"My little Shamrock." He squeezed my neck—"I'm the luckiest man alive"—and pulled me into a kiss.

I ran my fingers over his shoulder and up his neck and pushed them into his hair. I tugged, shifting my weight to the side, and pulled him on top of me. I stretched my arms overhead, and he broke the kiss with a sinful smile that was utterly Luca.

"I still owe you," he said.

"Hm?"

"I never did return the favor from that night at Vesuvio." His devilish grin was made all the more wicked by his pointed fangs.

My eyes widened. "I'm not going to argue."

He chuckled and slid down my body. He hooked his fingers around the top of my panties and pulled the lace down my legs. He tossed them aside, spread my knees wide, and licked his lips like he was preparing to feast. He captured my eyes, and his swirled with red eddies of lust. "Can I feed?" he asked, his voice laced with the same hunger that shone through his eyes.

"Yes," I said, breathy and excited. My heart beat faster in anticipation of experiencing his fangs inside me again.

"Get ready for the best orgasm of your life," he said through his signature cocky smirk.

I laughed and propped myself up on my elbows so I could watch the sexiest man alive pleasure me.

He lowered his mouth between my legs, swept his tongue over my folds, then pressed it between them, licking my crease. I whimpered and squirmed, impatient and ready for more.

A rumbling sound filled the silence, something close to a growl. It grew louder when he circled the tip of his tongue around my entrance, teasing and taunting me before thrusting it into my channel. He squeezed my thighs, forcing me to still, and licked me slowly from my entrance to my clit. He circled it with his tongue, then pulled the bundle of nerves between his lips and sucked.

"Ahh," I whined, relishing the feel of his mouth on my sex. My legs twitched from the targeted sensation, and I bucked my hips, desperate for more friction, desperate for more Luca.

He lifted his head, and his lips curled back to reveal his fangs. He captured my gaze and without breaking eye contact, followed the same path he traveled with his tongue with one of his fangs, dragging it through my folds from my entrance to my clit. Venom leaked onto sensitive flesh, and the delicious toxin tingled, a warm thrill on top of his heated touch. And when his fang reached my clit, he circled and flicked it with the pointed tip until the sensitive nub was covered with venom and pulsing with desire.

"Unh." The moan was deep, throaty, and unrestrained. My elbows collapsed beneath me, and my head fell to the bed, the stimulation from Luca's fang a shock to my unprepared body.

He swirled his tongue over my sex, spreading venom through my folds before performing the same sinful act with his other fang. My pussy clenched, and my muscles seized.

Pleasure climbed up my spine, then back down to my fingertips and toes, every nerve ending activated and aroused.

He pushed my knee higher, revealing more of my inner thigh, and trailed his tongue to the top of my leg, only inches from my opening. I lifted my head off the mattress, wanting to see him, wanting to watch what he'd do next.

Luca raised his eyes. His lips curled back, revealing the full extent of his long sharp eyeteeth, and his eyes' crimson glow flared into a blazing inferno. I gasped, and he plunged his fangs into my flesh.

"Ahh!" I cried out at the shock of pain, but molten pleasure quickly replaced the momentary sting as his venom spread through my bloodstream. He fed his hunger, pulling hard on my artery, and the bite, so close to my core, made my pussy throb with each beat of my heart.

He groaned, and the vibrations sent a shiver skittering across my skin. He ran his fingers up my other leg and pressed his thumb into my entrance, coating it with my wetness and dragging it through my folds. He drank from my thigh, exchanging his venom for my blood, and rubbed my clit. Fireworks burst across my body with every swipe of his thumb.

"Luca," I breathed. My head rocked from side to side. "Luca!"

My pussy spasmed, the sensations too much too handle, but the venom took away my ability to control, any capacity to hold back. With my heightened senses after drinking his blood, my orgasm consumed me, my body transformed into a conduit of pleasure.

Luca's thumb never stopped. He sucked harder on my leg, and the continued pressure and venom took my orgasm to new heights. Time froze at the apex of sensation, trapping me in perpetual bliss.

Finally, his thumb slowed. He removed his fangs from my leg and swept his tongue across the bite. I shivered and convulsed. Down and down, I traveled a slow descent, my body shaking and clenching and vibrating until I lay still, satisfied and thrumming in the aftermath of the most powerful orgasm of my life.

Heat from Luca's body crept up mine until he hovered over me. He kissed me gently, then buried his face in my neck, nuzzling the space he loved below my ear. "Thank you," he whispered.

I wrapped my arms around him and hugged him close. "Shouldn't I be the one thanking you?"

His chest rumbled with a low chuckle, and he pressed himself up, a smug grin across his swollen, pouty lips.

"That was amazing," I said.

"Told you."

I barked out a laugh and swatted his chest.

"So..." He moved a piece of hair off my forehead. "Am I forgiven for, you know"—he grimaced—"the whole bridge thing?"

I chuckled and shook my head. "Hmm." I tapped the tip of my fingernail against my teeth. "There is one more thing you could do. If you *really* wanted to even the score." I smiled wickedly.

"Oh yeah?"

I STOMPED on the clutch and threw the 308 into fifth gear. The engine roared, and the Ferrari leaped forward, pressing me back into the driver's seat but without so much as a jerk. Smooth as cashew butter.

I shot a smug look to my right.

Luca stared at me in awe. "You really are perfect," he said.

I stuck the tip of my tongue between my teeth and scrunched my nose.

"I love you so much," he said, shaking his head like he couldn't believe this wasn't a dream. To be fair, I couldn't either.

"I love you too." I took my hand off the shifter, grabbed his thigh, and squeezed.

We barreled down the open expanse of Highway 1, nothing but open skies and our future awaiting us. It wouldn't be easy, and it wouldn't be safe, but we'd face it together. As a family.

Epilogue

Vito

The Previous Afternoon

The sweltering heat struck me first. Followed by a splitting headache. The burn of something tight around my wrists. They were tied together behind my back.

Sweat dripped into my eyes. It stung almost as bad as my wrists every time we hit a bump. Light leaked into the trunk through the door seams and where the rear lights fixed into the body. But with my vision, even blurred as it was from the crack on my head, I could make out that the trunk was empty.

My head throbbed in time with my heart. My natural healing lifted the grogginess without effort, but I held onto my power. Didn't know what I'd need later, and only a fool used what they didn't need. Didn't know what shape Gina was in either. They took her too. The man with the gun—Siobhán's brother—had pulled her into the car.

Option one—break the bindings on my wrists. Wouldn't be difficult, but what about Gina? She'd been shot. He'd held a gun to her temple, and that hadn't felt like an idle threat. My gut told me he did that on purpose, that he knew to hold it there and not somewhere else. Even with my speed, I couldn't outmaneuver a bullet at point-blank range.

Option two—bide my time. Yeah, I was angry as hell, but I wasn't a hothead. Couldn't be an enforcer for as long as I'd been and be a hothead. Gina needed me. Best way to protect her was to keep cool. I could be angry once I found us a way out of this mess.

The car made a slow turn, and metal on metal, like a commercial garage door, clanked over the rumble of the engine.

The car lurched to a stop. Car doors opened. Muffled voices and shuffling. More metal on metal, likely that same garage door closing. Car doors slammed, and the trunk popped. I squinted, adjusting my vision to the bright lights. A man grabbed my biceps, hauled me out, and aimed a gun at my head.

The un-air-conditioned garage was large enough to house four cars across. It was bright with fluorescent lights and the sharp, metallic smell of tools and oil. The two spaces to the right of the Hyundai were empty, and oil stained the concrete. A car stripped of doors occupied the fourth spot up on a lift. On my left, two men in coveralls leaned against the counter smoking cigarettes. They eyed me and my escort. No sign of Gina.

"Move." The man who'd popped the trunk nudged me in the back of my head with his gun.

I moved in the direction he pushed, toward the single door in the corner. I took inventory of the garage, an accounting of anything that might clue me into location, potential weapons, or an escape. It was a run-of-the-mill chop shop, and based on the accents and who took us, my guess was Charlestown or Southie.

He opened the door. It was heavy. Reinforced. He kept the gun trained on my head and shoved me inside.

An office. Sparsely furnished—a desk, chair, and TV straight out of the last century, knobs and everything. Shelves of parts, paint, and oil covered all but one of the walls. No windows, but at least a portable air conditioner kept the space at a reasonable temp.

Gina sat slumped against the wall cradling her left arm. Her head rested against the exposed brick, eyes closed. Blood seeped through the rag wrapped around her biceps and stained her fingers. The pained expression on her face stoked my anger as much as the smear of blood across her left cheek. I clenched my fists.

The door clicked shut, and the rattle of keys in the lock sealed our fate.

She lifted her lids enough for me to see why she'd kept them closed; they glowed a faint red.

I sat to her right and leaned against the brick. "Is it bad?"

"I don't know," she said, her voice raspy. "I've never been shot before."

"Lemme see."

I peeled the rag-bandage away to reveal Gina's bloody left biceps. Most of the mess was dried blood, but a ragged wound leaked, a steady drip down her arm. I lifted it. She winced. The entry hole on the inside of the muscle was dark red but a perfect circle.

"It went through," I said. "Good." The exit had done more damage, but at least the bullet hadn't hit bone. "Would be a real pain on both of us if I had to dig it out."

Her lips flattened, and she side-eyed me.

"Small favors," I said with a shrug. "We should clean it up though. The less mess, the fewer the questions when it heals up quick." I pushed myself to my feet and glanced around the office.

"It won't heal as quickly as I'd like," she mumbled.

I frowned over my shoulder.

"I had an appointment with my Source tonight. It was supposed to be Sunday, but I rescheduled after everything with Luca."

I found a case of bottled water in the cabinet behind the desk. "Here," I said and sat back down. I took the rag, wet it, and cleaned the blood from her arm. "You'll be fine. It isn't that bad."

I'd tended to too many bullet holes lately. Yeah, I had experience doing it, but playing doctor wasn't exactly something I enjoyed. Done enough of it in the War, then again under Big Frankie. Being Marco's consigliere suited me just fine.

I removed most of the dried blood, leaving the area around the wounds alone. Didn't want to disrupt her body's natural healing. "Hold out your hands." I poured water into them, and she rinsed the blood off.

"You've got..." I wiggled my finger at my left cheek. She lifted her fingers to her right. "No. Here." I dabbed her face with the rag, cleaning off the smear of blood.

"Thank you." She laid her hand across mine and leaned into the touch. Tears brimmed her eyes beneath her long lashes. "Thank you for protecting me."

I cleared my throat and put distance between us. I wrapped the rag around her arm with as few blood stains showing as possible and secured it with a knot. I sat back against the wall and handed Gina the water. She took it and drank.

"What are we doing here?" she asked and handed me the bottle.

I drained it. The water was room temp, but after the sweltering heat and being locked in a trunk, I'd take it. Didn't know the next time we'd get fresh water.

"No idea," I said.

Keys rattled in the door.

"But I have a feeling we're about to find out."

THE END

Thank you for reading!

To find out what happened after Siobhán's lap dance turned into more than Luca bargained for, sign up for my newsletter to receive the exclusive—and spicy—deleted scene.

Luca and Siobhán finally found their happy ending, but Boston's blood demons have more stories to tell.

Find out what happens to Vito, Gina, and the rest of the crew in Her Dark Protector, coming 2026.

Acknowledgments

A special thanks to Erin Cashier, RN, Erin Sandene, BSN, RN, and Annemarie Weiss, MS, RD, CD, CEDS, for lending me their emergency medical and nutrition expertise. Accurately depicting how Siobhán could have possibly survived such a horrific attack along with the lifelong aftermath she experienced with her digestive system was extremely important to the story I wanted to tell. I couldn't have written this without you.

Thank you to my native Italian speakers, Giulia and Sara, for once again allowing me to slaughter your language, only to help me clean up the mess.

And to my editors, Nico Rosso and Margaret Curelas, who never cease to amaze me with their knowledge and insight. Thank you.

About the Author

Katelyn Brehm is a second-generation German-American and native of Milwaukee, Wisconsin. She grew up watching far too much Star Trek, so much so, she decided to dedicate her education and career to space exploration. When she's not reading and writing fantasy and romance, Kat works as an aerospace engineer at NASA's Jet Propulsion Laboratory. She lives in Pasadena, California with her husband and two cats, Mini Wheat and Pepper.

Visit Kat
www.katelynbrehm.com

Also by Katelyn Brehm

Demons Among Us

The Art Collector

The Siren's Song

Bonded in Blood

Her Dark Salvation

His Dark Vendetta

Her Dark Protector (Coming 2026)

9 798990 946132